The
Blood of a King

Book One
of The Rahmirion Chronicles

Wells & Bruzzi

The Blood of a King
Book One of The Rahmirion Chronicles
Copyright 2022 by Wells and Bruzzi

ISBN: 979-8-9867712-0-5

Published by
New Upper Books
Basking Ridge, NJ

Cover design by Mert Genccinar
www.artstation.com/mertgenccinar

To all those we carry with us in our hearts and memories.
"I'll be seeing you"

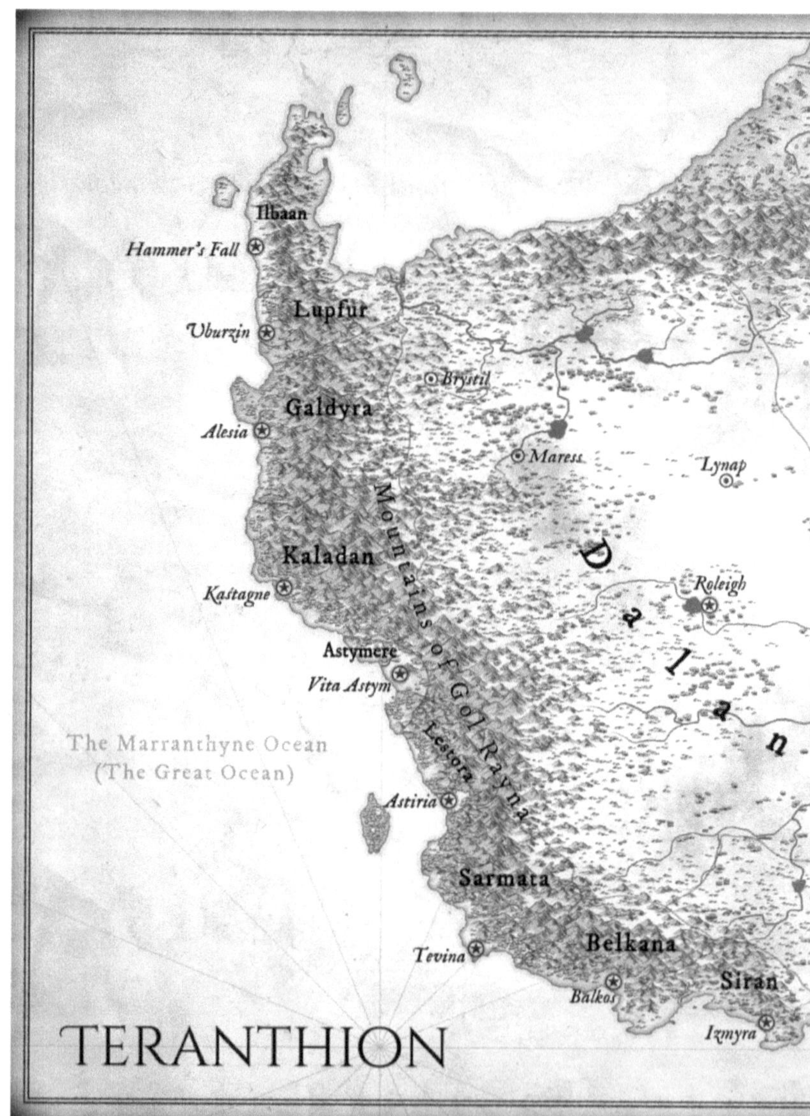

Ilbaan
Hammer's Fall
Uburzin
Lupfur
Brystil
Galdyra
Alesia
Maress
Lynap
Kaladan
Roleigh
Kastagne
Astymere
Vita Astym
Mountains of Gol-Rayna
The Marranthyne Ocean
(The Great Ocean)
Lestora
Astiria
Dalan
Sarmata
Belkana
Tevina
Siran
Balkos
Izmyra
TERANTHION

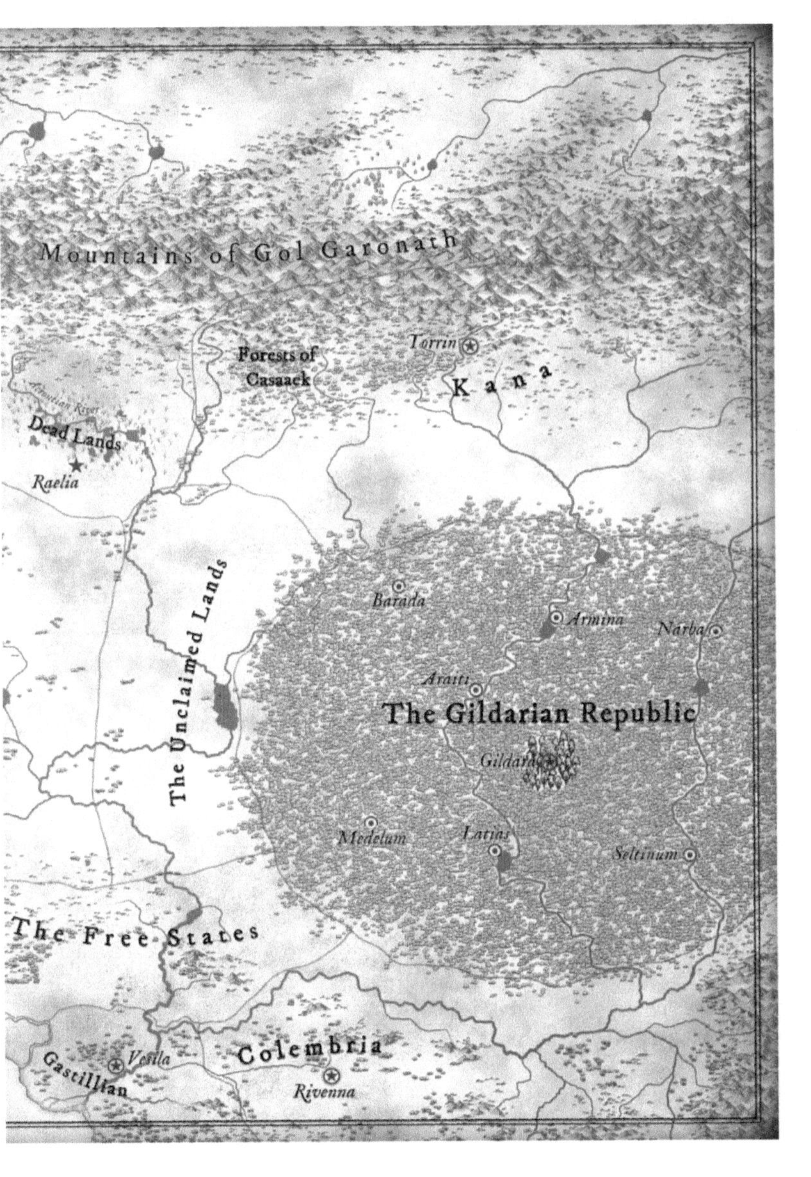

Mountains of Gol Garonath
Forests of Casaack
Torrin
Kana
Atraxian River
Dead Lands
Raelia
The Unclaimed Lands
Barada
Armina
Narba
Araiti
The Gildarian Republic
Gildara
Medelum
Latias
Seltinum
The Free States
Colembria
Gastillian
Vesila
Rivenna

Prologue

The Great Plains: The Raelian Empire
20th Day of the Third Month
Year: 5000 After Sovereignty

High Lord Raymund Wallis flew from his tent as the camp sprang to life in the dead of night. Large iron hearths lined the paths between hundreds of white tents, making the air itself dance with flame. Men in black armor scurried from their bunks to man the wooden ramparts of the hastily constructed camp walls. Horns blared and men shouted orders all around him. Raymund's eyes did not miss a single detail, yet they saw nothing. His mind was clouded by the message he had read only minutes before, though it already seemed like hours.

He made no effort to avoid the camp garrison as they charged along the central path running east to west, dividing the camp in two. He moved straight and true, as though there weren't a soul in sight. Each man leapt clear of him as though their lives depended upon it.

Despite the commotion, the scene was far from chaotic. The seven hundred warriors of the Black Army moved with urgency, but not panic. Sure of direction and purpose, they rushed to their posts with an efficiency and speed that was second nature after their long years of service to the crown.

Raymund proceeded against the masses, striding west along the camp divide, toward the heart of the fortification. There loomed the medical pavilion, a great ruby rising amidst a small sea of white fabric. The enormous red tent seemed to be three colors at once: orange from the countless torches bathing its lower reaches in an intense glow, scarlet halfway unto its pointed peak, and a top turned black in the light of the twin moons.

Shadows danced within the flaps of the pavilion's wide entrance. Two sentries, dressed in the full, black plate armor of the King's army, with spears in hand, stood guard on either side. With a deep bow followed by a quick shuffling of feet, they swept clear the heavy drapes from Raymund's path.

Six men in white tunics worked swiftly to clean the room of all unnecessary objects. Cots, litters, and basins of water had been arranged in a baker's dozen to Raymund's right, with one large, linen-draped operating table to his left. Smaller tables surrounded it, carrying vials, tubes, bandages, cloth, rolls of gut, and stitching needles, all arranged for bloody business. Ten large basins of water waited at the heart of the immense tent.

"Are we ready?" Raymund barked, louder than may have been necessary, but time was too precious to be wasted in repeating himself. Lord Galen, Great Healer of the Kingdom of Astymere, jumped in surprise, nearly knocking his carefully arranged instruments to the ground. The fury in his eyes quickly subsided when his gaze met Raymund's. The burly man bent his knee and bowed his head, revealing a small bald spot among the short brown hairs on the back of his skull. His six subordinates immediately followed suit. They did not dwell on ceremony, for no sooner had the gesture been given than the surgeons began to take up their tasks once more.

"My Lord," Galen said, his voice still weighted by weariness from being torn from his deep sleep. He turned back to his instruments with all the haste his sleep-deprived body would allow, which would have been impressive even for a man well-rested. His hands flew with a mindless steadiness learned from decades of experience. "I can't imagine there is anything we will be lacking, but I would be more assured if I knew exactly what kind of procedure I will be performing here."

"I cannot tell you that, my friend, for I do not know. King Henry's message was vague. You can read it for yourself." Raymund offered the crumpled message to the Great Healer. Red stains blotted the parchment, darker than the crimson cloak clasped to Lord Raymund's shoulders. Galen studied it intently, his brow growing more furrowed by the moment, until Raymund thought his eyebrows would come together as one.

"The Emperor?" Galen stuttered. "But why? *How*?" His eyes darted between his High Lord and the message.

Raymund rubbed his forehead where beads of burdened sweat had gathered. "I cannot say if Tiberian is responsible," he replied in his deep, steady tone, "but those are King Henry's own words, in his own hand. Treachery, he says. King Roland and Prince Lorynas of Dalan are dead. Our queen gravely wounded. If the gods are with us, she will not be beyond your aid."

"Why do we not ride out to the king? Why do we not send word home, or better yet, take our men and strike Tiberian while the city sleeps?"

Galen's bewilderment quickly turned to anger and his tone became combative, though Raymund thought nothing of it. That fiery spirit would be needed tonight.

"I admire your courage, Lord Galen. You know as well as any man that I would dive headfirst into the frozen pits of hell to deliver Henry from harm. But you would have us storm the walls of the White City with seven hundred men? Such action would be folly and you know it. We would be of no help to him, and our deaths would be in vain. As for sending word home, it is already done. I have sent our fastest wind swallow bearing word. High Lord Rahmos should have my letter in his hands before dawn."

"We could all be dead before Lord Rahmos reaches us." Lord Galen shook his head in disbelief. "I told him. I told Henry that we needed no less than two thousand men to properly defend this position, but he bent to every one of the emperor's demands, as though peace with Raelia had suddenly become so important to him. Of all the hare-brained…"

"Lord Galen!" Raymund barked, preventing the Great Healer from spewing one more insubordinate word. "Seven hundred was the number agreed upon by the Royal Council. You were outvoted, and your King felt our fellow council members were wise and sound in our decision. We can advise him on matters of defense in a hostile environment once we get him home. For now, we must make do with what we have. Is that clear?"

"Very well, my Lord," Galen replied. He returned to arranging his instruments, laying the bloodstained letter on the table. Raymund turned to leave. "My Lord," Galen called after him as he stood between the tent flaps. "He went out there to bring us peace. What could have happened?"

"Perhaps peace was never what Emperor Tiberian had in mind," Raymund said. He walked out into the brisk night. He moved east now, and unopposed, for all the men within the walls had taken position either upon the ramparts or before the four gates of the royal camp.

The stone of the road was painfully hard beneath his boots, and as the wind died down, his steps were the only sound bouncing off the white tents. His sworn bodyguards came into view; their black armor shone like mirrors in the moonlight, their crimson cloaks a shadowy auburn in the firelight surrounding Raymund's quarters. At a nod and a gesture from their lord, they fell in formation with him, creating a chorus of wordless footsteps.

The king's message had filled Raymund with rage, and confusion as to where to direct it. As he approached the eastern gate, he was reminded of an old Astymerian proverb that had been repeated through thousands of years of war with the White City:

> *Trust not the venomous adder*
> *Nor the Imperial Royal, he.*
> *For their nature is one, and when all is done,*
> *They shall bring death to thee.*

Raymund climbed the wooden steps and stood motionless atop the makeshift gatehouse. Peering over the tops of the sharpened stakes, he shuddered. *All ten kings of the Western Kingdoms traveled to the White City for the peace talks. How many of them have fallen under the sword?* His heart nearly stopped in his chest. *What if Henry never made it out of the White City?* Raymund quickly shook the thought out of his head and scanned the empty countryside for any sign of life.

The Great Plains stretched out into a dark eternity, the plenteous rolling hills in the distance blending with the dark horizon. A sea of countless blinking stars watched silently from above, not a single cloud blocking their vision. The gray stones of the Flat Way, the largest highway ever built by the Raelian Empire, smooth and practically polished, shone intensely wherever the moonlight hit them. The camp had been erected right on top of it, and from where Raymund stood, the road illuminated the dark grass for miles, stretching on like a great silver serpent.

The stout soldiers of Astymere stood at attention, waiting. Raymund was not entirely sure what they were waiting for. An attack? Another message? He hoped to see the king's carriage come flying out of the distance, carrying both him and the queen. He did not care if they were pursued. It had been nearly twenty years since he had had a proper fight against the Empire, and his sword arm began to itch. He would personally cut down a hundred of those star worshippers and die where he stood, hundreds of miles from home, if it meant his King would avoid the same fate.

The banners flying above Raymund's head vigorously

flapped as the wind blew once again out of the east. At the heart of each white flag, the black shape of Rahmirion, the spear of Rahm, so deep and absolute, stood unflinching.

The pounding of Raymund's heart became unbearable. He had only been able to count the number of times the wind died and rose again, eleven, before he decided he could wait no longer. *Henry and Beatrice could be tied to a sacrificial pyre and roasted to appease the gods of the White City while we sit here waiting for a signal that won't come.* He turned on the spot and charged back down the steps, his cloak billowing like a sail behind him.

He addressed the formation of seventy men standing at attention before the gates. "We shall ride out to the king and escort him safely back here. I want each of you to go to the stables and prepare a horse; we ride in ten minutes. Not a moment more. Understood?"

"Aye, my Lord!" a choir of hard voices replied.

He raised his hand, ready to excuse and set them about their tasks, when an archer shouted from the ramparts above. Raymund stayed his hand and nearly strained his neck turning to hear clearly.

"The hooves of thunder stallions, my Lord! I can hear them clear as bells! Riders on the Way! Riders on the Way! The king approaches!"

The air grew silent again, and now Raymund, too, could hear the unmistakable crashes of thunder rumbling over the hills to the northeast. The sky in that direction was clear and still as a millpond, but though they could not be seen, the thunder stallions charged with transporting the king made their presence known, even miles off as they were.

"Open the gate!" Raymund ordered. Ten men scurried to carry out the instructions. Four removed the log bracing and pulled the double gates open with relative ease while the others formed a shield wall, their spears ready. The remaining men of the unit fell in behind, shields before them, curved sabers at attention.

"Archers! Nock and draw!" came an order from the battlements.

Dim light made silver outlines against black armor as one hundred men moved above. The strained groans of a hundred bows and bowstrings could barely be heard over the approaching king's beasts. Raymund could now see the faintest glow of lantern lamps through the open gate, with a large swarm of dark figures charging across the Way. Dozens of riders surrounded the carriage, but from this distance, it was impossible to make out if they were friend or foe. For all Raymund knew, Raelians could be using the king's transport as cover to advance on the camp.

Acting on instinct, Raymund moved his right hand to the sheath at his left hip. The unmistakable shape of the king's carriage came barreling out of the darkness, pulled by six of his mightiest thunder stallions, horses nearly twice the size and three times as fast as a typical thoroughbred. Raymund tightened his grip, then drew his sword, Gods' Justice, with such speed that the thin, straight, black blade whistled as it cut through the air.

The company drew nearer, their forms black as pitch, consuming all light that hit them. Their identities were now unmistakable to a man of Astymere; the king was in good hands.

"Archers, stand down!" Raymund ordered the men above. The carriage charged onward, the hooves of the thunder stallions causing such tremors in the ground that Raymund feared they would pulverize the stones of the Way to powder beneath them. The bobbing lanterns and drivers' faces could now be seen as the oncoming party stood poised to run the stationary garrison down.

"Make way!" Raymund cried as the king's carriage and accompanying riders blasted through. They made it to the heart of camp before finally grinding to a halt. Raymund placed Gods' Justice back within her sheath as the gate closed behind him and followed as fast as his legs would take him.

By the time Raymund and his cohort reached them, one hundred horses sat unattended in the open square around the medical pavilion. The riders stood motionless in a tight formation outside the ruby tent, silently staring in. Raymund touched the carriage as he passed it on his way to the great tent. Arrows protruded from the walls on all sides, the singular odor of fresh blood sprayed across the outer walls was heavy, and he saw the unmistakable shine of a small pool of it soaked into the floor.

On he ran until he was on top of the black figures standing outside the entrance to the medical pavilion. Despite having spent his entire life in their company, the Knights of Rahm still unnerved him. The sworn defenders of the royal family wore black armor and cloaks that were nothing unusual to a man of the sword, but their helms showed not even the slightest trace of humanity. The face of each man was completely encased in black steel, the only openings two pitch-black holes where eyes were meant to be, and atop each head sat a curved crest more like a blade than anything else. Their double-handed long sabers were held at attention and blood, black in the dim light, dripped down their bright steel blades, falling to the ground, creating a chorus of repeated, random patters upon the gravel.

Lord Raymund tore through the tent flaps to find mayhem within. Galen's attendants struggled to keep three wounded men still as they lay upon the cots set for them. The closest to Raymund had an arrow sticking out from his shoulder blade, while the man next to him had one protruding from his belly. The third had a gaping gash traveling down from the center of his forehead, over the neck, and onto his right shoulder. Each man struggled with the healers in an attempt to get out of their cots, outstretching their arms with pleas that they could continue to help.

Raymund turned to see where they pointed and found a horrifying sight upon Lord Galen's operating table. Queen Beatrice lay there writhing, choking back silent tears pouring from her green eyes, bright and brilliant as emeralds. Her bronze skin was stained with blood that had soaked through her black, silk nightgown, and her dark brown locks were matted and clumped. Half buried in her swollen belly stood a black and gold dagger hilt.

Captain William Otter, a large, gruff, bald man with a graying brown beard, held her hands down. Another man, sobbing, used the right side of the table as a crutch for his own weak body. His skin was whiter than snow, and his hair was as black as the linen nightclothes he wore.

Raymund's eyes fluttered to the far end of the room, where the two men standing guard now sat upon stools, their armor above the waist removed. Each had a needle and tube running from their arm into a large, glass jar. *They give their blood for their Queen.*

"Is there anything I can do?" Raymund asked of Lord Galen.

"You can take these two and leave my tent," Galen ordered. "You will all contaminate my instruments if we continue this way."

"I won't leave her," the black-haired man grunted in reply. A fine spray of red dots crossed his cheek and neck. He raised his eyes to glare at Lord Galen. They were a blue that no painter in the world could recreate, a perfect balance between the deep darkness of sapphires and the light color of the sky on a clear day. Flecked sparkles filled that blue and burned with star-fire as his gaze went unbroken.

"My King," Lord Galen replied, respectfully but firmly, "I can do nothing with you standing in my way." He rapidly scanned his array of medical tools. "Leave now, and I may yet be able to save her. But you must be quick about it. Time is precious!"

"What of the child?" the king demanded. The anger in his eyes had turned to desperation.

"I can't say, my King," Lord Galen replied after a moment's pause. "I won't know the extent of the injuries until the blade and the child are removed. The longer we tarry, the less I will be able to do."

"Go, Henry," she said. Queen Beatrice attempted to swallow her agony as she negotiated with her husband. "Don't waste any more energy worrying for me, don't you dare... Pray for our child." The last of her strength faded as she slipped out of consciousness.

Whatever scruples Lord Galen had left, he forgot them immediately. "Out! Now! All of you!" he shouted.

Raymund pulled at his King with the aid of Captain William Otter. King Henry went willingly but fought once they reached the threshold.

"Deliver her to me, Galen!" he cried over his shoulder as Raymund and William ushered him on. "By Rahm's eyes, I charge you!"

A crowd of soldiers had gathered in the short time Raymund had been in the tent. Hundreds swarmed alongside the Knights of Rahm to lay eyes on their King, to prove to themselves that he was truly there among them, alive and unharmed.

King Henry of the House Karrok attempted to compose himself, but he faltered under the weight of the bloody night. It took many moments before he was able to stand upright without floundering. It came as no surprise that all who stood before the trio lowered their eyes to the ground and solemnly bent the knee. Henry nodded his approval and absentmindedly tried to take a step toward the carriage. He stumbled into Captain Otter's iron arms.

"The king is unwell," Raymund addressed the assembly. "He requires rest after fighting his way out of the White City. Leave him and return to your posts. You will remain there until you receive new orders. Get to it!"

With the same organization as before, hundreds of souls covered in black armor withdrew from the heart of camp and returned to their posts. All but the Knights of Rahm. Their place was with the king. No order Raymund gave could send them away. They followed as Raymund and William helped Henry to walk.

The trio got as far as the carriage out in the assembly square before Henry collapsed. The great Karrok-Ahl, one of many names passed down through the royal lineage of the Avaari tribe, had never been defeated in battle, an unstoppable force of nature for as long as Raymund had known him, and now here he was, crumpled on the ground, mentally and physically broken. Through the crackling torches and roaring hearths warming the night air, he heard the hushed sounds of Henry's weeping.

Lord Raymund Wallis knelt beside his King and cradled his head like an ill child, allowing him to let loose all his pain and frustration.

"I've failed her," Henry muttered to himself over and over. "I've failed her…"

"Rahm's eyes, William," Raymund said, attempting to maintain his own composure, "what in the frozen hell happened out there? You were summoned to the White City to broker peace!"

"That is what we were meant to believe, my Lord," Captain Otter replied in a hoarse, broken voice. "It seems this was Tiberian's plan from the start."

"How can you know this?"

"We…" Captain Otter choked on the words. "We interrogated the man who put the dagger in the queen's belly before Henry rent his head in two. The emperor wished to weaken the Western Kingdoms by destroying the royal families. He feared he did not have the strength to withstand us now that Dalan has joined us."

"But how?" Raymund asked. "How did they get an assassin past you and your men? Where were your knights?"

"No one got by us, my Lord," Captain Otter replied with a

hint of disdain. "They had to have slipped into the king's bedchamber when we attended supper this evening, the same as the rest of the kings. As for the Shadow Knights…" He looked over his shoulder to the group of one hundred motionless suits of armor standing not five yards off. "They weren't allowed inside the city. Emperor Tiberian claimed bringing them through the gates would be seen as an act of aggression and would not be tolerated. In the end, King Henry agreed."

"And King Roland, Prince Lorynas, is it true?" Raymund asked.

"Aye, my Lord," William replied. "The queen's father and brother are dead. After her attack, we rushed to warn them, but it was too late. Roland's brother Robert shall be crowned King of Dalan when he returns to Roleigh… if he makes it there."

"So he escaped… And what of the other kings?"

"Most live, though I cannot say if they met any trouble on the road when we parted ways. My Lord, we cannot remain here long. We had to fight our way out of the city and fight harder still on the road to get here alive. The imperial legions will be on us before midday tomorrow, and it will take more than a week for the armies of the West to mobilize for a counterstrike or even for our defense."

"As soon as Lord Galen finishes his work we will break camp and ride hard for the coast," Raymund said. "Even the imperial legions cannot move as fast as we can, as few as we are." He stared down at the sobbing king. "Help me get him up. He is beside himself."

King Henry was well over six feet and two hundred pounds of solid muscle. By the time they got him into his tent and onto the featherbed, they were breathing heavily and wiping sweat from their brows. Gravel crunched outside the tent as the Shadow Knights took up their position guarding the king, fanatically loyal and devoted to his bloodline. This night would forever be a smudge on their honor if the queen and her baby were lost.

"Must… get her out. Must… Must…" Henry was falling into a delirium under the stress.

"If she dies," William said softly, almost to himself, "we are doomed. The king will take his own life if she does not make it. You know this to be true. He is bound to her even more so than he was with…"

"Only Galen and Rahm can stop that now," Raymund said, cutting William off, for he could not bear to hear the name he was sure to speak. "All we can do is wait, and hope she lives. If Rahm sees fit to take her from us, we shall hope the child lives."

"Without Henry, that child will be our only hope," William said.

Raymund nodded. "Let us hope the blood of a king is worth more to the gods than just a crown."

Chapter 1

Vita Astym: Astymere
30th Day of the Tenth Month
5013 A.S.

Mayson rubbed the weariness from his eyes as he leaned his elbows against the stone balcony outside his room, looking east toward the rising sun. The crisp predawn wind slapped at his shirtless body, helping to brush lingering fatigue away like a pile of dead leaves. As his impending move to the Royal Marshal Academy crept ever closer, sleep proved to be more and more elusive.

After the hellish rains that raged through the night, the morning was silent and peaceful. He ran his fingers through his long, curly black hair and looked out over his future kingdom. The sun was beginning to crack above the Mountains of Gol Rayna on Astymere's eastern border, with beams of light streaking across the capital and its surrounding countryside.

Vita Astym was home to half the citizens of Astymere. It had slowly, over the generations, been carved out of the rock of Mount Karrok until finally it found its way down to the ground and expanded for several miles in all directions around its heart. The king and queen's palace in the center of the city seemed comfortably disconnected from the teeming streets around it. Hundred-foot walls surrounding Vita Astym would make any invader think twice before laying siege, but the palace was a fortress in itself. The prince's balcony looked down to the stretching palace grounds, guarded by a quadruple-layered wall, manned by the steadfast Knights of Rahm. Each layer possessed its own high steel portcullis and ebony gate.

This city had raised him. The streets had been his classroom, and bustling crowds had been his teachers. He loved the capital, from the fresh mountain air down to the last cobblestone.

Soon he and his brother would lose the palace, lose the stone streets, and the familiar people. They were off to the Royal Marshal Academy in a few days, and even though Mayson had waited his entire life to train there, a piece of him wished to stay in the place he proudly called home. He wished to be the child running the echoing halls, and to delay the inevitable, ponderous weight of a crown on his head.

Blinking the light out of his blue eyes, he turned to go inside and prepare for his morning training.

He stopped at the tall mirror mounted to the wall beside his canopied bed and began to examine himself. The image was crystal clear with the exception of frosted glass around the mirror's oval edge. Mayson always wondered how glassmakers could achieve such a thing.

The image before him was a familiar one: a young boy absently running his fingers along the scar that ran from the center of his sternum up to his left shoulder. He had heard whispers of how he got it for as long as he could remember. The Night of Knives, he would hear people mutter, before they noticed he was in the room. *So much blood spilt. So many killed. Why did the gods see fit to spare me?* He snapped himself from his musings and pulled his white linen training tunic from his wardrobe, running his thumb against the black form of Rahmirion sewn into the breast. His shirt was still over his head when the door flew open.

"Rahm's balls, why do we have to train so damned early?" Diero's voice was still froggy from nightly disuse. He gave Mayson a light, playful shove as he stepped in front of the mirror to check himself. Diero Carovensa was a slight boy with thin, lean muscles and sun-kissed, tan skin. His looks could only be described as beautiful, with a slim face and a smirk that exuded an unrealistic confidence. He tussled his golden brown hair, trying to rub the sleepy mess away.

"I wouldn't make a habit out of these complaints, brother," Mayson said, pushing Diero from his spot in the mirror and straightening his tunic. "We'll be waking up this early almost every day once we get to school. Father is trying to get us used to it."

Diero flopped down on the bed with a groan, looking up at the ceiling. "Well, from the looks of him, your father could do well with some extra sleep himself."

"It baffles me that after living here for eight years, you still call him *my* father." Mayson looked at Diero's reflection behind him as he brushed his hair back and bound it in a short tail atop his head.

"Well, he is *your* father, isn't he?" Diero asked as he sat up. Mayson heard him crack his neck as he sat waiting for an answer.

Mayson suddenly remembered himself.

High Lord Darian Carovensa had been dead for eight years, and Mayson hardly had any memory of him. The dark, vague fragments from his earliest recollection portrayed a man that was larger than life and impossibly strong, tossing Mayson in the air and catching him as though he weighed no more than an apple. His clearer memories painted a different picture. There were scenes of the great lord needing aid walking, and coughing fits that left his white kerchief spotted red. One of the last was a visit Mayson and his father had paid to Lord Darian shortly before he died. The great giant of a man had been bedridden, withered away to a shell of himself, and his rich, tan skin had grown sallow.

Mayson's father, King Henry, had taken Diero in as his own as Lord Darian requested. He and Mayson grew up like brothers, and at times Mayson had trouble remembering it wasn't by blood.

"I'm sorry, Diero. I forget myself." Diero shrugged it off and turned to face him.

"Not as sorry as you're going to be once we get started. Your mother is finally going to let us spar against each other, and I have been dying to take you down a peg or two." Diero began shadow boxing, throwing playful jabs and light kicks at Mayson's head and legs. Mayson deflected them all.

"Don't you mean my *father* is going to let us spar?" he asked as the onslaught kept coming.

"Oh, please. We both know who really doesn't want us fighting each other. If it were up to the king, we would have squared up years ago." Diero let a jab fly too lazily, and Mayson pounced. Knocking it away and grabbing it with his right hand, Mayson shot his left to within an inch of Diero's face before he could blink. With a nervous chuckle, Diero relinquished the game.

"Then lucky for you it hasn't been up to the king," Mayson said with a sly smile. He released Diero and returned to the balcony to await their summons. As per his father's countless instructions, he crossed his legs beneath him as the rising sun struck his face, closed his eyes and shut out the world. Whenever Diero was in the room, however, the world always had a habit of crashing back in.

"You're the lucky one," he said as he dropped down beside Mayson. "I was only goofing. Had I been taking it seriously I could have easily blocked that punch, taken your legs out, and gained the upper hand."

"You very well could have," Mayson replied, keeping his eyes closed and breathing deep. "But you didn't take it seriously, and that sloppiness is a symptom of a far more dangerous disease: arrogance. You've never met anyone who can beat you, but you will find plenty at the Academy. If you play these games with them, they *will* make you pay for it."

Mayson heard a disparaging chuckle as Diero got up. His voice sounded like it was coming from the railing as he spoke. "Those little lordlings don't know what's coming for them. We've been trained at the hands of the greatest killer Astymere has seen in three hundred years. I highly doubt there is a soul on that island that can put so much as a scratch on us."

"That attitude *is* going to get you scratched, Diero," Mayson sighed. "One good shot from any one of them and…"

"Up and moving, you lazy dogs," called a gruff, jovial voice from the door. Mayson snapped to attention, with Diero only half a moment behind him. King Henry was dressed in his own black silk fighting tunic embroidered with gold and silver Avaari runes across his chest and shoulders. The growing light of day illuminated countless scars against his snow-white arms, thick as tree branches. The deep black of his hair and beard were beginning to pepper with gray, and even a few white hairs were visible, but his eyes were just as brilliant in their middle age as Mayson's were. It was like looking into a mirror, or a portal in time, for the two were nearly identical in every way.

"Well, isn't this a surprise?" Mayson's father asked as Hammund, the Royal Palace's Head of House, came scurrying in behind him, his usual calm, serene face spotted with sweat and his breaths heavy. "Would you look at this, Hammund, my sons up and about and the sun hasn't even fully crested over Gol Rayna. Something must surely be amiss." He cracked a smile baring teeth nearly as white as his skin.

"A most unusual occurrence, my King, I'm sure," Hammund said through huffs and puffs, dabbing his forehead with a kerchief. "One would make the mistake of thinking they were future men of power who took their responsibilities seriously."

"Hammund, you aren't half as amusing as my father,"

Mayson quipped, "and he isn't one-tenth as amusing as he thinks he is. I'm up at this time every morning. I'm just a bit slow in starting my routine. I'd say that hardly warrants a reputation for laziness."

"And what about you, Diero?" Henry asked. "What do you have to say in your defense?"

"Absolutely nothing," Diero replied with a wide grin. "I'm every bit as lazy as your poor joke seems to claim. But I still get twice as much done in a day as any of you unfortunate souls. Speaking of unfortunate, what in Golron's Hammer is wrong with you, Hammund?"

"I've just run from the yards, my Lord," Hammund puffed as he folded his kerchief and placed it within the folds of his white robe. "High Lord Wallis has begun today's sparring a bit…early. He and Lord Addam await, most impatiently."

Henry cast a weary smile to the boys and patted Hammund on the shoulder, shaking his head. "And here I thought we were going to finally break our habits. Come gentlemen, time to sharpen our swords and dull our minds."

They exited out of the eastern doors of the palace into the bright, breezy morning. The courtyard was a field of manicured grass, veined with shrub-lined walkways, the center of which was flanked by two rows of evergreen trees that had been planted three hundred years prior. The grounds were divided into four sections: the garden, the open field, the meditation courtyard, and the walkway leading to the perimeter walls.

Raymund Wallis, Lord Paramount of the Northern Tip, and his eldest son, Addam, had been passing the time awaiting the king's arrival by sparring in the open courtyard. They jostled back and forth, and their steel clanged in the peaceful morning. Raymund spun, taking out Addam's legs from behind and knocking him to the grass. A pained grunt burst from the young man as he hit the ground. Raymund smiled down on his defeated foe as he pointed his blade toward Addam's nose.

"One of these days you'll learn, I hope, how to defend a move that has bested you no less than a hundred times," he joked. He held out his hand to help his son to his feet.

"One of these days you'll break your hip doing that spin, old man," Addam fired back.

Raymund arched back in a hard laugh at the notion. Raymund of House Wallis was one of Henry's three High Lords, who helped him govern Astymere. The High Lords of the Crescent had nearly universal power and were answerable only to the king himself. Raymund and Henry had been raised together, as had High Lords Urnest of House Rahmos and Darian of House Carovensa. Being raised as one family helped keep the establishment close and united to prevent infighting.

Raymund was two years past fifty, his light brown hair and short beard showing signs of graying. Though he was nearly as old as Henry, he had married and begun having children at the tender age of sixteen. Therefore, his sons, Addam and Droyan, were already men grown. Attached to Raymund's left hip was the ancestral sword of House Wallis.

Gods' Justice was a thin, straight blade made of black steel. The blade and the hilt were all of one piece, making it impossible for the two to become disconnected. The hilt was carved and fashioned into a figure of the Low God, Rahm, with his arms outstretched over his head, meeting and grasping the blade. Fitted into the face of the figure were two small rubies serving as eyes. Of the four Eternal Weapons that were bound to the great families of Astymere, God's Justice was the smallest and the fastest.

As Raymund moved to sheathe his sparring blade, Addam kicked out his leg from below, knocking his father to the ground. He pointed his sword at Raymund's nose with a sinister grin. "Either your age has made you terribly arrogant, or terribly slow," Addam said. "Either way, I'd say you're doomed."

"Boys," Henry said as they entered the courtyard. "Observe and take note the effects hubris can have on any fight."

"I have to agree, Father," Mayson said with a smile. "Had Lord Raymund been properly on his guard, a move that sloppy would have gotten Addam killed." The group laughed and embraced their guests. In candid moments like these, there was no need for bent knees, for they were all family here.

Addam had earned a name for himself in recent years as a master of single saddle riding upon a thunder stallion, which few besides the king and Dalani tribesmen were capable of. The part he had played during the fall of Raelia had cemented his reputation not only in Astymere, but throughout all of the Western

Kingdoms.

"Lord Wallis and I will get things started. I'm starting to feel a bit rusty lately," Henry stated, turning to Mayson and Diero. "Go and practice your meditations. We shouldn't be long."

"I've already done my morning centering, Father," Mayson replied. Admission to the Academy was inching closer by the minute, and now that he was awake and ready to work, it seemed finding inner quiet would be nearly impossible.

"So, go do it again!" Henry barked matter-of-factly. "There's no harm that can come from being *too* clear before a fight. And I would bet my crown that Diero hasn't meditated in over a week. Both of you go, and if you dick around instead of meditating, I will know. Then there will be hell to pay."

"Yes, sir!" Mayson and Diero replied as they tore off towards the meditation courtyard.

HENRY SPENT HIS TIME WAITING for Mayson and Diero sparring with Raymund as Addam watched. Raymund's skill with a sword was well known throughout the West, but Henry's was the stuff of legend. As light and fast as Raymund was, he was no match for Henry's lightning reflexes. Since the days before his coronation, it had been said among Astymere's generals that Henry was the finest swordsman to be found anywhere along the western coast, and perhaps even beyond. Sweat dripped from both men's heads as the drill came to a close.

"Something the matter, my Lord?" Henry gloated to his old friend. "You're looking a bit weary. I daresay even a bit *aged.* Should I have some water fetched for you?"

"Who are you calling aged? You have no less than four years on me," Raymund replied through winded breaths.

"And yet I still just managed to make you look like a broken old man," the king said with a warm chuckle.

Addam approached as he and Raymund caught their breath. "My King, Father, I'm sorry but I must take my leave. I must return to the Academy and ensure my lessons are all in order before the start of the new term."

"Are you sure you can't stay one more day?" Raymund asked. "Surely you don't need a week to prepare."

"You would be surprised, Father," Addam replied. "Most of

these lordlings and merchants' sons aren't as bright as Mayson and Diero. I've seen plenty of students get cracked by a skittish hoof because a new horse wasn't socialized well enough before start of term."

"I understand," Henry said. "Take a stallion if you need to make up time." He nodded to Addam, who knelt before his King, then stood up straight and gave both Henry and Raymund a hug before exiting the field toward the stables.

Mayson and Diero returned just as Addam disappeared. Upon making eye contact with Henry, they broke into a quick jog so as not to keep him waiting.

"Today we will become more fluent in your striking technique," Henry ordered, watching his sons catch their breath. Kataar, a martial art developed by Astymere's founders and used as the official fighting style of the Black Army for a millennium, was a brutal, fast-paced method of fighting based around multiple opponents. Designed for close quarters, it used elbow strikes and physical instincts to determine each move. Although their age and inexperience left a great deal to be desired, the boys were well ahead of others their age using this style.

"Feel my movements, and use your opponents' mistakes to your advantage," Henry said as he squared up with Mayson. "Keep your muscles loose, but don't get sloppy, and when you see the opening, you take it." The prince nodded at his father, doing his best to mirror him. They unlatched their sword straps and threw them to the side.

Henry approached Mayson with speed and ferocity. The prince stepped back once and then stood his ground. He was patient and careful, knocking away every attack he saw coming. The king went to hit Mayson's midsection, but his son slipped away, taking advantage of the size difference. When his father missed and slipped up, Mayson headed inside, letting out a grunt with each blow that landed to Henry's solid midsection, as he had been taught.

The sparring had gone on for several rounds of five minutes, with Mayson simply finding holes Henry allowed in his defense. He would never admit it out loud, at least not yet, but Henry grew sore from the increasing strength of his son's strikes.

He then sparred with Diero, who showed great skill and

understanding of the moves and how each strike blended in with the one before and after. Unlike Mayson, it was painfully clear that he was not as adept at making or even *finding* openings in an opponent's defense.

The chill of the early morning had gone, and the four of them were covered in sweat by the time the hand-to-hand combat had finished. Mayson and Diero stretched and rubbed their forearms, which had taken the brunt of the damage done during the lesson. Henry then threw two training swords between them, causing an awkward silence.

"So you really are going to let us draw swords on each other?" Diero asked with satisfied surprise.

"I am a man of my word, son. When the king says something shall be done, then it shall be done. Come on then, pick them up and let's get to work. You both move your arms well enough, but your footwork still needs improvement. It's fine enough for a couple of Agadi holding the front line in battle, but not for the future king and a future high lord. You sacrifice balance for a powerful stroke. Mistakes like that have destroyed many fine officers. You will not allow such a thing to happen. Is that understood?"

"Yes, sir," the boys replied.

"Good," Henry said. "Now, let's get going." The two reached for the curved sparring sabers, getting a feel for the leather grips of their hilts. Diero took the Stance of the Viper, holding his saber straight out in his right hand and bending his knees. Mayson took the Stance of the Dragon, lunging forward slightly on his right leg, and holding his saber out to his side in his left hand, aiming the tip at Diero's eyes.

"Wait, absolutely not, this is unfair," Diero barked, breaking his stance and turning to Henry.

"I beg your pardon, young man?" he asked.

"If I am going to spar, I am going to spar with a real opponent, not with Prince Wrong Hand the Backwards. Hardly anyone on all of Teranthion fights with their left hand; it would be a waste of energy for me and an unfair advantage for him. I'll spend the whole time tripping over my feet trying to match him."

"So, are you saying, young Lord Carovensa, that you are incapable of defeating this opponent unless he handicaps himself by fighting with his non-dominant hand?" Raymund asked. Henry remained silent, keeping an unbroken gaze on Diero.

"I'm saying he should fight with his right, because everyone else does! It's only natural! Am I the only one who thinks this? I feel like I'm losing my mind! I will never have to train or fight against another wrong-handed swordsman as long as I live, but *he* will fight plenty of right-handers. It's only natural that he switch."

"Diero! He should not have to limit himself just because *you* don't have the coordination to mirror your skills from one side to the other," Raymund began.

"My lord," Mayson said. Henry was almost unnerved by how calm and authoritative it was, almost as though it were a command. The idea was cemented when Raymund relented and gave him a chance to speak. "If Lord Carovensa feels he is at a loss if I fight with my left hand, then I am more than willing to oblige him, and switch."

"Is this some kind of trick?" Diero asked, resuming a more guarded stance.

"Not at all, brother," Mayson said, resuming his Dragon stance, this time with his left leg forward and his sword in his right hand. "It is only natural that I should be just as good with my right as I am with my left. Rahm knows that few I come across will have the same skill set, so by all means, let us do it your way."

"Very well then," Diero said, regaining his Viper stance with his usual wicked grin.

"I warn you, brother. If I beat you with my weak hand, your humiliation will be doubled. Let's begin."

Chapter 2

Vita Astym: Astymere
30th Day of the Tenth Month
5013 A.S.

THEIR BLADES MET FOR THE LAST TIME as the sun crept over the palace walls. The open grass field was now bathed in light and the usual mountain winds were calm, offering little relief from the rising heat. Mayson wiped the sweat from his face and flipped his damp hair back with a snap of his neck. Diero coughed heavily, clearing his throat of phlegm and spitting into the bushes.

"Well done, boys! Well done, indeed!" Raymund shouted. "I think it's safe to guess they've made it off the line. Wouldn't you agree, my King?"

"You've both been working on your footwork," Henry replied. "That much is clear. But your wrists are too stiff. Both of you."

"Do I not get some kind of reprieve for fighting *backwards* with my weaker arm?" Mayson asked through gasps.

"No, you don't," Henry said curtly. "I expect the same dexterity from your right arm as I do from your left. They must be interchangeable; only then will I be satisfied. Is that clear?"

Mayson's arm was throbbing. He hadn't held a sword in his right hand for that long in his entire life, and the thought made it seem even more unpleasant. He shook away the pain in his forearm as his father approached.

"Yes, sir," he replied.

Henry gave Mayson's face a light, jovial smack, with that same warm smile he wore whenever the time for hard lessons had passed and he was able to simply be *father*.

"Very good. That being said, I think you two will fare beautifully at school. Your wrists may be stiff by my standards, but you'll find theirs to be a bit more relaxed. I imagine you will be very dangerous men one day, but there was never any doubt of that." The king's attention turned to Raymund. "Please wash yourself before the Royal Council convenes today," he said. "What would they say if High Lord Raymund Wallis attended council smelling like a pig?"

Raymund laughed and bowed, then took his leave.

Henry looked to the sky and rubbed his belly, making Mayson

realize just how badly his own had been rumbling.

"Let's get a quick meal in before we get to work," Henry stated. "You two must be famished."

Mayson took no more than two minutes to wash himself. A quick dive into the heated copper tub in his bath chamber, a once over his body with the rough bar of soap, and he was out, drying and dressing himself in a white linen shirt and a black doublet with breeches to match as fast as his sore hands would go. He reached the dining hall first, just a few steps ahead of Diero, who had clearly attempted to beat him there.

The southern wall of the dining hall of the Royal Palace was one large glassless opening that offered a grand view of Southslope, the affluent southern quarter of the capital. Five large windows on the eastern wall let in morning light. The table, carved from lesser ebony, was inlaid with spiraling patterns of marble around the edges and could easily seat thirty people.

The royal family took their places at the end of the table once Henry and Beatrice joined the boys, who had stopped carousing just in time to avoid being caught. The kitchen hands placed bowls of oat porridge mixed with fresh blueberries before them. The cooks had sprinkled brown sugar atop the dishes, which filled the room with a lingering sweet scent.

Four plates piled high with roasted potatoes, boiled eggs, and thinly shaved pork loin followed. The tender meat was drizzled in a sauce made from the witch's finger pepper, a blended balance of biting spice and pleasant sweetness.

"Father," Mayson said in between mouthfuls. "I think I know how I can even out my arms. At least in terms of dexterity."

"Switch them up when yanking it?" Diero muttered under his breath. Only Mayson heard, and he managed a subtle shot into Diero's thigh with Beatrice and Henry being none the wiser. Diero choked down a groan and rubbed his leg delicately.

Henry swallowed a large bite. "The crown is all ears, young man."

"I know there is little time to affect these changes now, but perhaps when we return from the Academy, I could start training against multiple attackers at once, and use both hands to engage."

"You would sacrifice your shield arm for another sword?" Henry asked, resting his head on interlaced fingers. Mayson searched for a convincing argument as he twisted under his father's quizzical gaze.

He knew what he asked wasn't a small request, though it had been something he thought of every time his opposite hand was brought into question.

"A well-practiced sword would work just as well as a shield, wouldn't you agree?" Mayson asked.

"I suppose it could, boy," Henry said with a chuckle. "I suppose it could. That is, if you managed to work that sword as well as any shield."

"No fair!" Diero shouted. "If he's going to step into more advanced training, then I am too! There is no way in frozen hell I'm going to let Mayson's skills with a blade surpass me in leaps and bounds."

"Diero, mind your tongue," Beatrice warned.

"My apologies, my Queen. But my sentiment stands. If Mayson is going to learn how to fight double-handed, then I wish to as well."

"We will discuss this when you both return from school, once you have both learned a little more personal discipline. There will be no more words on this matter, not at my table. Is that understood?" Henry asked.

"Yes, sir," the boys replied. They both shot sidelong smiles at each other at the thought of being taught double-handed sword fighting. It was a rare skill, and if anyone on all of Teranthion could teach them, it was Henry.

Once the four had eaten their fill they made their way through the wide halls of the palace, encountering countless bowing servants dressed in black and white as they passed, crossing the green yards and filing through the four walls and their gates. A contingent of one hundred Shadow Knights, led by Captain William Otter, were never more than a few feet away, clearing a path for the king and his family in the crowded streets.

Henry, Beatrice, and Mayson often chose to walk amongst the people, while Diero grumbled that he would rather travel by carriage or litter. Henry would typically assist his subjects in their labors, helping innkeepers sweep their stoops, setting up stands for grocers and fruit mongers, and even making personal donations straight from his hand to theirs. He always told Mayson that a king must prove his worth, not only by fighting, but also by being a part of his people's lives. He did not just rule the people; he was one of them.

For as long as he could remember, Mayson felt the irresistible need to imitate Henry in most things he did. Henry was the example by which Mayson held himself, and if he could get a head start on doing things like his father, it would make his own reign all the easier someday. *That is a true king. Rahm as my witness, I will be a true king.*

It was early afternoon by the time the group crossed into Eastslope, the administrative center of the city. To their left, tall marble steps led to the first wall and gate of the Mouth of the Mountain—the seat of the throne of Astymere and the symbol of power for the Karrok family in the city. The massive cathedral had been built on a grand stone plateau to allow it to stand flat without falling victim to the slope of the mountain. The Mouth, like the palace, was protected by four-layered walls, each higher than the last and each with its own high steel portcullis and sealed oak gates.

The day was particularly warm but the shadow under each gatehouse was remarkably cool. The black fabrics of most Astymerian clothing soaked in the sun's warmth, and all appreciated the dip in temperature within the shade. As they passed under the third gate, Henry reached out and let his hand graze the large oak door. It felt as smooth as marble and surprisingly warm to the touch. Ages of long days in the sun and constant resealing had left it feeling like stone.

The entrance of the Mouth came into view as they made their way through the fourth and final gate. Once inside the walls, the building seemed more like a place of worship than one of governance. On either edge of the roof, a tall, thin tower came to a fine point at its summit. At the far end of the Mouth, against the mountain slope, a great steeple soared one hundred feet above the roof, with a balcony wrapping around its slender peak and large square windows marking the smooth façade. In the center of the building rose a great dome crowned with a golden spire, surrounded by a ring of smaller, silver spires.

At the top of the stairs, a row of ten large, concrete columns supported the overhang above them, leaving the entrance in shadow. The columns had all been inlaid with murals depicting the simple tribal life of the Avaari in three phases: before the Empire came to the Crescent, the initial war between the Avaari and the Empire, and the Avaari's five hundred-year subjugation under Raelian rule. As old as they were, they never seemed to fade or chip away, largely due to their painstaking maintenance by order of the royal family.

Henry and the rest entered the shade and came upon two ebony doors, each standing no less than ten feet high and six feet wide. Six steel hinges bolted into the stone held each monstrous door, and on each dark slab was carved scenes from the War of Independence fought five millennia past. At the top of the doors, split in the center where they met, a carved relief showed Rahm, Low God and Patron of Astymere, with his arms outstretched, bestowing his favor to the rebel slaves over their masters.

The doors slowly began to open from the inside, the steel hinges creaking and groaning as they moved. Each door came to a thunderous thud that echoed throughout the cavernous throne room when they would move no farther. The light flooded in through wide windows along both walls, illuminating the dark stone within. On either side, three columns of dark granite held the high ceiling in place. The floor was made up of marble that gave way to tiles at the center of the room, forming flowers with white petals, red centers, and black stems on a field of jade.

Before the throne, bolted into the floor, stood the table of the Royal Council. The wooden table was fitted with steel legs and had been inlaid with gold, and each chair was decorated with paint of the same color.

Henry walked past the council table, pointing Mayson and Diero to their chairs. He looked up and marveled the vivid mural painted on the inside of the dome as he passed beneath. It depicted the final battle of the War of Independence, fought on the slopes of Mount Karrok itself, featuring Astymir, the father of the kingdom, holding Rahmirion high as the broken Raelians fled before him.

Henry and Beatrice climbed two stairs to the shallow platform that held the four chairs of the High Lords, which faced out toward the council table. The pair climbed another three steps and approached their thrones upon a platform that sat high above the rest. Henry sat upon the Heart of the Mountain, a great throne of stone that had been carved in days long gone. Legend had it that the boulder had been harvested from deep within Mount Karrok itself to serve as the first king's throne. It had been mortared to the floor, making it appear as if the throne grew from the ground.

The queen's throne, on the other hand, was only twenty-three years of age. Henry had it made and positioned at his right side one year after their marriage, after she had proven to be quite the valuable advisor. Its finely sanded ash wood had been sealed with a light finish and cushioned with the emerald-green fabric of the banner of Dalan, to honor both her father and her people.

Before long, the council began to shuffle into the chamber at a leisurely pace. First of the High Lords was Urnest of House Rahmos, Lord Paramount of the Crescent Coast. Urnest Rahmos was a man of black skin and gray hair that had long since receded from the top of his head. A scar ran from the center of his forehead, down over his left eye, and onto his cheek, the result of an injury he had suffered during the fall of the White City. His resting face had long since formed a permanent scowl, but his smile and laugh contained immeasurable warmth and jubilance. Being sixty years of age, he was the oldest and wisest of Henry's High Lords.

He was dressed in a white, long-sleeved tunic with black pants and strapped sandals. Wrapped around his neck was a silver colored scarf made of fine, light silk, which he rarely left home without. He took his seat in the chair immediately to Henry's right on the level below, facing the council table.

"Perfect day to be spent inside," Urnest quipped.

"Speak fast, my Lord, or this could turn out to be a long one," Beatrice replied.

Lord Raymund entered next, sporting a satisfied smile. He had changed out of his sparring clothes into a black velvet doublet with crimson silk sleeves. Raymund nodded at Mayson and Diero as he took his seat next to Urnest. Mayson's High Lord chair would be empty until he came of age, but as Henry looked down on the second empty chair, his heart sank with the realization that Darian Carovensa would not be walking through those doors. Eight years had not lessened the pain, nor had they made Henry accept his loss.

Behind Raymund came Lord Galen, the Great Healer; Phillip

Mostyk, the Chief Architect of Astymere; and Jordyn Stone, commanding officer of the castle garrison and Lord of Kar Naron. The group conversed quietly as they entered and quickly took their seats. Beatrice and Lord Galen shared a warm smile.

Rhivor, the High Priest of Rahm and the chief religious figure of Astymere, entered then in silence. He wore a long, black satin robe with two large red eyes sewn onto either side of the chest. His grayed head was topped with a black obsidian band adorned with rubies.

Evan Mikkel, the Chief Sanitor, followed. He was a lumbering beast of a man with fists that could hammer stone to powder, but he possessed a sharp mind and savage wit that could do even more damage to a foe than his fists.

Keddra Vilzak, Chief of Commerce and Agriculture, entered next. She worked closely with the Royal Treasurer in setting prices for common goods and in handling trade networks over both land and sea. She was a slight woman with a kind, welcoming face, who always dressed in green. She kept her hair in a large bun on the back of her head, letting two strawberry blonde locks cascade down either side of her face.

She entered with Geremy Brisban, the Royal Treasurer and chief financial officer of the crown. Brisban, a rather short man with coifed brown hair and a clean-shaven face, had a look of satisfaction that never seemed to fade—too common for men in his position who had unimaginable sums of money flow through their hands daily.

The last men to enter the room were always the final in and the first out after the meeting had adjourned. Josef Benedik, Viktor Cromwel, and Patrick Lokk were as tight-knit as a woven blanket, as close as family without being related by blood. Since their first days in the military, the men had climbed the ranks together in unison, and as fate would have it, they found themselves lorded at the same time.

Astymerian soldiers had long heard the stories surrounding these three. They were the only surviving escorts to make it out of the White City and push their way to the king's camp, and the morning after the Night of Knives, the three went from enlisted men to officers of high honor. It was their success during the siege of Raelia that convinced Henry to lord each of them, making them the first lower lords to sit on the council in fifty years. They each received a Sandil for their service and bravery, a token only bestowed by the king himself.

After all were seated, the crown-bearer, a young girl dark of hair and bright of eye by the name of Elara, emerged from behind the throne. She was an orphan girl of sixteen who had been found just outside the palace walls not long after Mayson was born. Beatrice, made tender by her wounds and new motherhood, requested the staff take her in and collectively raise her. She was dressed in a flowing, black silk robe with white wool gloves, her bare feet not making a sound as she stepped. She had the sacred duty of transporting the king's crown from deep within the Mouth to the throne room.

Her charge, the crown of Astymere, was a black steel band adorned with pieces of obsidian, mounted side by side. Each piece was set in fine gold and crafted in the shape of Rahmirion's spearhead. A single large sapphire sat square over Henry's forehead.

Henry bent his neck as the girl approached, allowing her to place the crown on top of his head. Once he felt its weight, Henry looked up as Elara bowed before him. She then turned and bowed before the Royal Council, who returned a nod in good measure, and silently took her leave. Henry thought he caught a wicked smirk from Diero as she left, but there was no time to dwell on it.

"Let this meeting of the Royal Council begin," Henry announced. "First, we will address matters of State, before we open the doors to supplicants. Lord Galen, you spoke with me earlier this week. What is the update from your Healers?"

Lord Galen stood, bowing his head toward Henry. "Thank you, my King." Galen's short, grayed hair had been finely combed and his belly had grown slightly over the years under his cream-colored tunic, the standard garb for a practitioner of medicine. "Every man in this room knows of cloudstone, a terrible substance in the form of a small, milk-white pebble that is ground to a rough powder, then smoked as though it were pipe weed. The effects have been described as euphoria, severe lightheadedness, and dizziness, followed by lethargy and severe flulike symptoms once one enters withdrawal. The drug is once again circulating the streets of our capital, and I fear it is the culprit of the sudden increase in deaths among Westslope youth."

An uncomfortable silence fell over the room at the mention of the terrible substance. Ten years prior it had nearly taken hold of Westslope, killing over a thousand and grinding usual business to a halt.

"Lord Galen, there are many poisons that circulate throughout Westslope's lower rungs. Why suspect cloudstone?" asked Raymund. "We've heard nothing of it in nearly a decade, when we opened clean houses for the afflicted."

"I agree that the houses have helped many, my Lord, but when we plucked the weed from the garden, a piece of the root remained," Lord Galen responded.

"What other proof can you offer?" asked Urnest.

"I have examined many brains of the individuals known to have died from it and compared them to the recently deceased suspected of using," Lord Galen said. "The same reaction to the drug in the flesh of the brain exists in both groups—black fungus that eats at the organ. I fear that if nothing is done, our beautiful capital may have a great crisis on its hands once more."

"Very well," the king said. "Your offices shall bring any information you acquire to the Silver Shields and set up a coalition. Patrols will be set to keep an eye on high risk neighborhoods. Adverts for the clean houses will be passed to every residence in the capital. Let none be ignorant of the danger. And, from this day on, the sale and distribution of this substance shall be punishable by death."

"Death, my King?" the High Priest asked. Rhivor's face was struck with horror. "Shall the Silver Shields become executioners now? Rounding people up in the streets and butchering them like cattle? There must be another way."

"We tried another way ten years ago, your Holiness," Henry replied. As a godly man, Rhivor's sense of mercy and binding morality sometimes proved problematic, but his wisdom always carried great weight within the council. Henry wouldn't be able to shut him down without just reason. "We have tried fines and prison sentences, confiscations and rewards for turning in hidden stashes. It hasn't worked. Not well enough for a permanent solution, at least. The rats responsible for this epidemic must know that the Crown will no longer tolerate this poison circulating the

Crescent. Anyone caught in possession of cloudstone up to a certain amount, and is not afflicted by the addiction, will be held on trial as a distributor and will face a penalty of death. No one will be butchered in the streets, your Holiness. I will confer with the High Lords later this evening to iron out the details of the motion."

Satisfied with the decree, Lord Galen bent the knee and returned to his seat. Rhivor let out a heavy sigh and relaxed slightly in his chair.

Next was Geremy Brisban, who stood and acknowledged his King before circling around to the front of the table with his arms crossed before him. He told the room of the decrease in citizens requesting public relief and the crown's need to capitalize on the economic growth. Phillip Mostyk suggested that the roads in need of repair be the first to receive the excess funds from the previous year.

"I'll second that," added Lord Urnest. "The last time I approached the capital on the Royal Highway I feared I would crack my skull on the ceiling of my carriage. My skull faired well, but I am fairly certain I broke my ass." The room broke out in a chorus of laughter that could not be helped. With a nod from the king, the decision was made, and the meeting continued.

Jordyn Stone rose from his chair. Commander Stone, of strong build and sharp tongue, looked formidable in his black armor, the only man among them dressed so. His hard-lined face made him seem older than a man of forty-four, and his once bright eyes were growing dull.

"My King, I bring news from Kar Naron. Renovations on the great wall are finally complete after just a year of work." As always, he spoke to the king as though he were the only man in the room, a habit that earned him great distaste over the years.

"That's a whole year ahead of schedule, Commander," Henry said with a grin. "How did you manage this?"

"Since the White City fell, it became clear that discipline could soon wither away without the constant threat of attack from the empire, so I put the men to work in different forms," Stone said. "We have successfully installed fifteen parapets atop the wall, and we expect fifteen trebuchets from Lestora within the fortnight."

The Black Towers and the great fortress that surrounded them were practically impenetrable as they were before, but now, with the recent installations, it seemed they would be weapons themselves.

Stone then sat and the room fell silent.

Keddra Vilzak announced that the Southern Tip had produced an abundance of blueberries, nearly twenty tons more than the previous year, and the price would be affected in the market, helping the common people, but taking a small bite out of international trade profits.

At mention of the Southern Tip, Henry noticed Diero perk up and hang on Keddra's words. The Southern Tip would be his domain when he came of age, and it was comforting to know that he took interest in its upkeep. *Will he be as interested when things aren't going as well?*

Evan Mikkel briefed the council that the sewer blockages causing a horrendous stench to choke Northslope had all been cleared, and he would be keeping teams in the area to monitor the pipes. Thereafter, no one had any updates or matters to address, and so Henry clapped his hands twice.

"Open the doors to the people!" he announced.

The day was spent listening to the requests and plights of commoners. One man sought justice against a lower lord for the murder of his brother; another begged that he be allowed to raise the prices of his crops in order to feed his growing family; one woman begged for the rescue of her daughter, who had been abducted from her property and forced into a whorehouse by gangsters looking to settle her drunken husband's gambling debt; and another group of men came seeking a license to trade wine they had begun to produce on a sizable stretch of property they had collectively purchased.

Over a hundred petitioners sought aid and guidance from the crown, most getting what they asked for. Henry believed that if it was in his power to provide, no request should be denied without good reason.

As the last supplicants were escorted out, Henry could hear the sound of small bells drifting through the open doors, accompanied by the steady beat of a staff tapping against stone. *Piss. This is just what I needed today.*

An older woman came gliding into the throne room with such ease that it made her staff of dried ash, adorned with small, silver bells, seem like little more than a decoration. Her thin face was outlined by a lavender shawl that wrapped around her black hair and draped down her back. A pink gown flowed behind her, the train held by two attendants. Four guards in matching pink armor flanked her. Henry, unfortunately, knew this woman well. She was the Sesha, the Voice of the Council of Avaari Elders. Unless Henry went to speak with the Council himself, he hardly ever saw or spoke to them in any official capacity.

The members of the council were the heads of the oldest houses within the Avaari tribe, and as the Avaari chieftain, it was Henry's duty to hear their requests, announcements, and as of late, complaints. Within the last ten years, hardly a week went by without a visit from the Sesha, who refused to tell Henry her name. He prayed that whatever she had to say would be quick.

"The crown is honored by this visit from the esteemed representative of the Avaari Elders," he said. *Old hag.* "To what do we owe this pleasure, my Lady?"

The Sesha pursed her thin lips and wriggled her slightly pointed nose. With a slight bow, she spoke in a voice of absolute authority that was purely in her imagination. The tone made Henry grind his teeth in frustration. "Great Karrok-Ahl. The Council would have you hear my words."

Henry let her sit in silence for a moment before gracing her with an answer. There was nothing that legally bound him to acknowledge a meeting, but the tribe expected unity and cooperation between the Crown and the Council of Elders, and discord between the two had caused problems for previous kings.

"The crown hears you, my Lady," he said at last.

"I come with good tidings, Karrok-Ahl. The council has chosen a bride for the royal heir."

Several of the Elders had hardly said a word to or about Mayson since his birth, except to raise question of his legitimacy. Henry had taken a Dalani bride and sired a child with her. He knew when he accepted her father's proposal it would create a stir within the Elders, but it was the practical thing to do at the time. It brought Dalan and its twenty thousand elite horsemen into the Western Kingdoms, tipping the scale of power in their favor.

However, since Mayson was half Dalani, there were some within the tribe that refused to accept him as one of their own.

Henry fought the urge to both laugh and curse. "A bride, you say," Henry said, leaning his cheek against his fist. "This is quite the change in rhetoric from the wise Elders. To what do we owe this gift?"

"The royal heir will be entering the cusp of manhood soon, and before long proposals of marriage will come pouring in from the lower houses across the Crescent and beyond. The Council wishes to make sure he takes the *right* bride."

"And what is the Council's definition of the *right* bride, my Lady?" Henry asked, adding a hint of vinegar to his words.

"An Avaari bride, Karrok-Ahl. An Avaari bride from a proper Avaari family. The bloodline of Astymir the Father stands in a precarious place, and the Council means to ensure its survival. Lord Haamin of House Ahl-Kalin offers his young daughter, Sharra, to the royal heir. All we need is the Crown's consent to arrange the marriage and they can be wed as soon as the royal heir returns from the Academy."

"And what of my consent, Sesha?" Mayson said from his chair. His stance mirrored Henry's. Whether it was intentional or natural similarity, Henry did not know, but Mayson had leaned his cheek against his fist, using it as a crutch. "I also haven't seen or spoken to Sharra Ahl-Kalin in six years. What makes you think I would consent to bind myself to one who is practically a stranger?"

"Will the crown please instruct the royal heir to hold his tongue until he is addressed?" The Sesha didn't take her eyes off Henry as she spoke.

She won't even look at him. "Noble Sesha. I will discuss the matter of Lord Haamin's daughter with him personally, after I have had time to discuss it with the *royal heir*. Despite what the Council of Elders may think, the blood of the Father flows strong, and there is no need to rush this matter. The crown appreciates the Council's concern. Give my best regards to Lord Salac and the rest of the Elders. *Thank you for your visit.*" He bit each word, no longer hiding his growing displeasure. She seemed to get the message, and with an indignant snort, turned to go, her attendants shuffling to follow her with her gown's train.

"It would behoove the boy to choose wisely, Karrok-Ahl," she said, suddenly turning on the spot. "A half-breed sitting on the throne leaves a bad enough taste in my master's mouth. However, there is no force in the heavens or on all of Antheira that would make the Council accept *his* child without an Avaari mother. Mark my words." Henry didn't have time to react before she turned to leave again. The jingling of her bells burned Henry's ears long after she was gone.

Henry looked to Mayson, hopeful that he wouldn't let this incident get to him. His fists were tightly squeezed and his nostrils flared, but otherwise, he was as calm as a night sky. *Bless you boy. What kind of future have I given you?*

None of them would have been able to tell he was anything but pure Avaari, but looks weren't enough for some members of the Council of Elders. They knew he was half Dalani, and that was too much for them. As much as it pained him, he knew the Sesha was right. Mayson would need to marry an Avaari bride to assure the tribe would accept his children.

The councilmen began to stand, but Henry held them in their seats once more.

"We have one more matter to address," he stated. "My good councilors, I received a very strange letter this morning, written in golden ink." Henry watched the reaction spread throughout the council as the implication of his words took hold. As expected, Geremy Brisban's eyes lit up and he practically jumped to his feet.

"You can't mean…" he began.

"I can, and I do," Henry said. "Ladies and gentlemen, my presence has been humbly requested by Valmas Aurian, Minister of Trade and Revenue to the Gildarian Republic." The members of the council began murmuring amongst themselves in shock, skepticism, and in Brisban's case, excitement.

"We have had hardly a word from the Republic since the war ended, my King," Keddra announced, standing from her chair. "Not even a whisper since they declared the Great Plains too hazardous to cross and ended trade with us because of it. It took five years to compensate for the loss. They can't expect you to travel halfway across the continent just to fluff their gilded egos." Despite her words, Keddra's face never lost its kind sheen.

"The crown never took the closure of those trade routes

personally, Chief Vilzak," Henry addressed. "It was the right decision on their part, as problematic as it was for us. The trade routes through the plains were being raided regularly after the war. The former citizens of the empire had turned to chaos and barbarity without the emperor to rein them in. Thousands died and millions of mira worth of goods were lost or stolen. But now, King Robert has taken control of the Plains, and the rogue people of the empire have either been killed or sworn themselves to Dalan. Knowing this, it seems the Republic is now willing to reopen trade routes with not only us, but all the Western Kingdoms. Don't forget, whatever we suffered for lack of their trade, they suffered the same in turn. And now *they* come to *us*."

"So, will you go, my King?" Brisban asked, not even trying to hide his enthusiasm.

"I will, Geremy. It will take some time to confer with the other kings, but I imagine I will go shortly after the new year."

"And what if this is a trap, my King?" Lord Galen asked. Henry could see the memory of the Night of Knives in his eyes. "The kings of the west were all summoned by a foreign power once before, and the Republic had long been a vassal of Raelia. Could this not be a plot for revenge?"

"They were vassals out of fear, Galen," Henry replied, "not true loyalty. Where were their armies when we marched on the White City? We carved through the empire for nearly a year and never saw a single golden breastplate. As for security, we will be bringing plenty." Henry turned to Beatrice, who seemed visibly relieved. He then faced Brisban, who had the look of a child getting an extra slice of cake. "I seek counsel with you, Lord Brisban. Will you not join me at table tomorrow evening? I have some stipulations I would like to add to our negotiations, and they must be handled delicately."

"Of course, my King," he smiled. "It would be an honor. After all, the pen and coin have always been my sword and shield. Our kingdom will benefit greatly from our preparations."

Henry stood and gazed down at the council. "If we are all in agreement, I declare this meeting of the Royal Council adjourned."

Chapter 3

Vita Astym: Astymere
40th Day of the Tenth Month
5013 A.S.

Henry ran a hand through his graying hair as he and William rode their stallions through the streets of Southslope. That morning's council meeting had been long and tiresome. On top of that, the week had been crammed with meetings with Lord Brisban and preparations for Mayson and Diero's departure for the Royal Marshal Academy. Henry hadn't had a moment's peace.

"I still believe we should have brought at least a dozen of my men, my King. Riding about the streets unguarded always carries some risk, even here in the capital."

"I am hardly concerned, William," Henry replied, enjoying the afternoon sun on his pale white arms, exposed beneath his sleeveless black linen tunic. "We are two grown men, given the best training in the art of warfare in the civilized world, and we are both armed. Well, at least one of us is. And if you call me *my King* again, I'm going to vomit. I've heard enough *my Kings* for one day."

"Very well, my…Henry." William gripped the bridge of his nose with his thumb and forefinger, closing his eyes tightly as he squeezed the reins of his horse to remain steady in the saddle.

"I still don't see how you could have left your sword in the throne room. I've been trying to work it out since we left the palace, but nothing probable comes to mind."

"I wish I could tell you, Henry, but by Rahm's eyes, I don't know how." William moved his hand to cover his eyes, which were still squeezed shut. "I don't even remember removing it. I had it in the throne room, and when we got back to the palace, it was gone, belt and all. We haven't passed it laying in the street, so it must still be in the Mouth, unless someone picked it up."

"If someone has taken it, we will get it back. No one will want the weight of the crown coming down on them once they learn the sword's rightful owner." Henry turned to face William and finally noticed his pain. "The headaches again?"

"Either that or Golron has established a foundry inside my skull. They kept me awake again last night."

"Lord Galen assured you they would pass."

"Assured, but delivered nothing. His draughts dull the pain from time to time, but they persist, nonetheless. It's as though my skull will split open from the inside. It's slowly been getting worse ever since we took the White City."

"I will speak to Galen this evening and see if he can't get you something stronger. I'm sure there has to be something in his endless supply that can numb your head."

"I hear cloudstone is rather potent," William said, chuckling through his pain.

"Don't even joke of such things. You haven't seen the cadavers laid out on Galen's table—I have. It isn't worth it."

The worst seemed to be over since the last outbreak of the terrible substance throughout the capital, but Henry knew the damage would never be completely undone. A scar had been left on Westslope-- a scar of dead bodies and broken survivors.

"Very well, my King—Henry. It's dulling now. I think I can make it for a while, but if you don't mind, I think I will talk to Galen myself. I know what I am seeking better than you do."

"As you wish, brother. Let's tie off the horses; we're here."

William finally opened his eyes to see the Mouth of the Mountain to his left, shrouded in shadow. The base of the marble stairs still caught some afternoon sun, and tied to two posts were a pair of very familiar horses.

"Henry, where are the boys?"

"They are supposed to be at home packing," Henry growled. *They must have snuck out the west gate.*

"What in the world would they be doing here?" William asked.

"I think I have an idea."

"We aren't supposed to be up here," Mayson called after Diero as they climbed the winding staircase in the great tower of the Mouth. "Father will be furious."

"The king isn't going to know. The council let out over an hour ago. I'd bet he's already home," Diero responded, not even bothering to look back as he climbed the stairs two at a time, leaping with each pace. "The way I see it, she is your property. At least, she will be. You have the right to at least have a look. We leave tomorrow; that means you won't get another chance for six whole months. It's now or never."

"No," Mayson retorted, "it's either now or six months from now." The prince continued to give chase. "What if we just asked Father to show her to us?"

"Are you brainless? He would never bring us up here. You've heard him time and time again whenever he mentions her. *Rahmirion is no plaything. Don't ever let me catch you fooling around with her or there will be a whipping in it for both of you.* I'm sorry to say, but we are on our own. So keep up and don't dawdle."

The climb left both boys winded when they reached the chamber at the top, Diero most of all for the pace he'd set. The panoramic windows adjacent to a wrapping balcony let the afternoon light into the large round room, bathing the long, black case lying upon the floor in an orange light. The musky air of the staircase had given way to a fresh breeze when they passed through the dusty, wooden door. Mayson stood over the steel case and peered down at it. The cover, made of double-paned glass dyed gold and red, allowed him to see the weapon beneath.

He had never seen Rahmirion before, and if he was to be honest with himself, he felt rather disappointed. The great weapon of House Karrok looked to be nothing more than a staff. *This was the spear of Rahm? This is the weapon I will carry into battle as king?* It seemed he would sooner beat someone to death with it than cleave them in two. Still, though she didn't give the appearance of a great weapon, one couldn't deny she was beautifully made.

Rarely touched, only removed from her case in times of war, she still gave the appearance of being polished daily. Her smooth shaft reflected a radiant, rippling purple and deep blue. The coloring reminded him of the sight of oil floating atop a puddle, struck just right by the light. He felt the sudden urge to see if the spear felt as oily as she looked.

"Are you going to open it, or stand there staring at it?" Diero snapped from the door. Mayson jumped, for he had nearly forgotten he was in the room.

The two clamp locks sealing the case shut gave a loud snap as he undid them, and the old iron hinges made a tooth-rattling screech as he lifted the lid. As if about to cradle a newborn babe, the prince reached down and removed the spear from her black felt resting place. She was as smooth as marble and strikingly cool to the touch, weighing half the amount of a typical steel weapon of her size. To his surprise, she felt bone dry—not oily in the least.

She fit rather snugly within his hands, now nearly fully grown, though his arms were still thin and wiry. Where he gripped the staff, the metal around his hands shone a great mix of colors. Their bright glow washed the room in a newfound light. Mayson broke out into a wonder-filled smile.

DIERO COULDN'T HELP BUT BE DISAPPOINTED for a moment. The last time he had seen such a sight was the day he mourned his father, High Lord Darian Carovensa, at his funeral, and saw Morning Star for the first time.

He remembered the crowd, silent and immobile, staring into his watery eyes, and listening to speech after speech on Lord Darian's behalf. The king was the last to speak. Diero, just a child at the time, looked up toward the podium at Henry, who looked back at him. *"Your father was one of the best men I ever had the honor of knowing. He was one of the few men who always led, and never ran. You should be proud of him."* Those words rang fresh in the young lord's mind.

Diero sat there, the longest hours of his life, as by tradition the thousands of citizens who had come to honor his father said their goodbyes to a great man. Afterwards, the ancestral sword of House Carovensa, Morning Star, was bestowed upon him as the next in the bloodline. It was a moment he had been coached on since his father grew ill. All the tears that begged to be let loose, he held back to show the strength that was now expected of him.

He remembered High Priest Rhivor approaching him and kneeling while holding the sword wrapped in gold silk cloth. Young Diero unraveled the covering in Rhivor's hands, revealing the magnificent weapon within. He took her in his hands, watching the colors glow around his fingertips.

"What's happening?" asked the prince, bringing Diero back from his thought. The color was getting brighter, growing out from the circumference of his hands. "Am I doing something to it?"

Diero had no idea; Morning Star had simply glowed. Never did the weapon shine so brilliantly. Never did it seem to begin shaking in his hands as Rahmirion started to in Mayson's.

The light dimmed, and all went back to normal as the room grew darker and the weapon fell to its original color. Then, a shot of the color stretched the length of the weapon in both directions. The light sent a flash through the room, blinding the boys momentarily.

"Whoa!" the prince yelled, holding Rahmirion at arm's length. His arms and body were trembling. "That didn't happen with Morning Star!"

"And a good thing it didn't! Otherwise, we'd have had a temple full of blind people," Diero answered. "Did you feel anything? Did it hurt?"

"It didn't exactly hurt, but I felt cold. Terrible cold, the likes of which I've never thought possible. It almost felt as though my blood would freeze in my veins. I wonder if I can make her do it again."

"Give her a swing," Diero suggested. "See if anything happens."

"Are you out of your head? What if it's worse when swung? I could kill you. I could kill myself!"

"Don't be such a child. You've practiced with a spear before. Just keep the head away from you and you should be fine. As for me, I'll stand outside the door and listen for anyone coming." Diero crossed over the threshold to the landing on the stairs and gave a swift look downwards. "Alright, it seems clear. Go on. Do it!"

MAYSON BREATHED IN DEEPLY and took a mighty swing. Instead of hearing the clang of steel on stone, it was the soft thud of flesh and a sudden resistance that took him by surprise. He opened his eyes slowly to find, to his horror, his father's hand wrapped around the head of the weapon, standing there glaring at him, with Diero sheepishly by the door, keeping his eyes on the ground.

"What in the frozen hell do you two think you're doing up here?" Henry demanded. "How many times have I told you that Rahmirion is not a toy? *How many times?*"

"I know...I...I just..."

"It was my fault," Diero blurted out. Henry turned his fiery gaze upon his young, adopted son. "I twisted his arm into coming up here."

"And if you were to jump off the Commander's Tower of Kar Naron, should he just blindly follow you? You can afford to be foolish. Your brother can't. By the gods, he is going to be a king one day! How the hell is he supposed to rule if he can be bent to the wills of others so easily?" Henry crossed his arms and stared intently at the boys.

Diero seemed to slowly shrink into the floor as Henry bore into him. Their father rarely swore at them, so there was great cause to be concerned. If he didn't act quickly, Mayson knew there would be a beating in it for both of them.

"Father, please. We know we shouldn't have been here," he pleaded, trying to save their necks. He bowed in supplication, trying to appeal to his King rather than his father. "My entire life I have been raised hearing tales of Rahmirion's power and greatness. She will one day be mine, by right. How could your own blood resist? I had to look on her. I had to learn the feel of her cool steel against my hand. I needed to acquaint myself with her so one day she would serve me as well as she has served you. If you must punish one of us, punish me, for I was the only one to lay hands on her."

Mayson kept his eyes on the ground in this supplicated position. Part of him feared a smack upside the head if he looked up.

To his surprise, Henry began to chuckle. It was only after hearing this sound that the prince felt brave enough to look up. The king had a smirk on his face and lightly patted Diero on the cheek before he turned to face his son.

"You may be a young fool, but at least you have the backbone to admit when you've done wrong. And you definitely know your way with words. If you can swear to me that you two will not come up here again, and speak true, I will forget this ever happened. Do I have your word?"

"Yes," the boys quickly replied, not daring to lie straight to their King's face.

"Good. I hope you know that I will beat you both into the next Age if you break your word." They stood there silently for a moment before the pondering look on Henry's face turned to an obvious question. "Why the hell didn't you ask me to show you if you wanted to see her so badly, Mayson?"

Mayson shot a deadly glare over at Diero. To think of the trouble they could have saved if they had just gone to their father to begin with. Mayson could have throttled him at that moment, but the young prince composed himself, as he always did, and turned his attention back to the Old Bruiser.

"I'm not sure, Father. I suppose I just—thought you would say no," he admitted, with one more look to Diero.

"*No! No?* Why would I say no? The least you could do is see her in action by keeping your eyes open. Stand back, you two. I'll show you how she works."

With a sharp flick of his wrist, the god spear sprang to life in Henry's hand. The boys stood aghast at the transformation. What had been a simple staff before was now nearly twice as long, with blades aplenty. They appeared to be as thin as razors, but legend had it that she could cut straight through stone with a proper swing. Henry gave a sharp toss and caught her on the back of his hand, perfectly balanced. The boys had never seen a weapon handled that way, and they found it hard to contain their excitement. With both hands, Henry began to spin Rahmirion above his head. Faster and faster and faster she spun, until the breeze she generated began to blow the boys' hair back.

"Stop, please!" Diero cried out. "You could kill us."

"Nonsense. I have absolute control over her. I've fought with her for decades. And besides, I wouldn't kill *us* if I lost control. I would only kill *you*, Diero."

The boy's eyes went wide, unblinking. "I beg your pardon?" he murmured, visibly confused and suddenly uncomfortable. Henry stopped spinning the spear and held it out for their examination.

"It is the same principle that applies to the other Eternal Weapons. Each one is bound to the family it belongs to. When they were first forged, the founders of the High Houses mixed their blood into the ore to assure that no man would be able to use the weapons against them. Each one knows the blood of the family it serves. And as long as that blood flows within a living person, they shall remain perfect. Which means Rahmirion cannot possibly harm the prince or myself, and Morning Star could never harm you. Just watch."

Without any hesitation, Henry ran his palm across the razor thin blade and held it up for the boy's inspection. There was not so much as a crease on his skin. Mayson's curiosity got the best of him, and he too reached out and ran his hand across the blade, with the same result. He could feel a much stronger connection to her now, and a newfound confidence for the next time he would handle her.

"Does it really take just a flick of the wrist to open her?" Mayson asked.

"For me, it does. Your hand would fall off before she opened for you."

"Why?"

"She may know you, but she doesn't serve you. She serves the king, and the king only. That means that only I can open and close her. So, don't get any ideas. If you ever wish to see or train with her, you talk to me, or you are out of luck. Understood?"

"Understood, sir," Mayson replied.

"Now, that is enough for today," the Old Bruiser stated. He flicked his wrist sharply and Rahmirion returned to her original state, a harmless staff. "Put her away, and let's go home. I believe you two still have some packing to do."

The trio made their way back down the winding staircase and out the massive ebony doors at the far end of the throne room. Captain William Otter awaited them as they passed through the four gates of the Mouth and down to the street. His silver blade hung comfortably at his hip.

The day was becoming cloudy and cool as the sun slowly set. The weather watchers predicted rain for the next day, which would make their four-hour ride to the Academy a miserable experience.

As they made their way around Southslope, the boys fell back a bit for a word in private.

"I could beat you. Do you know that?" Mayson muttered under his breath.

"What the hell did I do?" Diero demanded.

"You were the one who told me not to bother asking him to show us the spear. We could have spent our first weeks at the Academy nursing bruises if I hadn't bent the knee and practically kissed the man's boots."

"I had it perfectly under control."

"And another thing, what the frozen hell happened up there? I thought you were supposed to be on lookout. You told me it was clear."

"That wasn't my fault," Diero declared in his defense. "I swear, he didn't make a sound coming up the stairs. He's like a damn cat. Before I could even make a peep, he was on me. I'm sorry—I tried."

"Well, needless to say, that is the last time I listen to you for a good long while."

"Fine, be a salty little sisswhine if you want, see if I care. Just for that, I won't help you pack."

"That is just fine with me. Unlike you, I'm almost finished. So I won't help *you* pack."

"Bastard," Diero said under his breath. Mayson punched his brother lightly in the arm as the two kicked the side of their steeds to rejoin Henry and William, who had pulled ahead.

The city bells had struck four in the afternoon before the group made it back to the palace. The four gates opened for them without a sound, and they made their way across the main courtyard to the veranda, where Beatrice sat in the hazy afternoon light in a soft gown of black silk, taking a wet stone to a curved dagger. The gold and black hilt had lost a bit of its luster over the last thirteen years, but the weapon that had nearly taken her life and the life of her son had become her prized possession. She rarely went anywhere without it. She felt it served as a reminder that she was somehow untouchable, that death had come for them both, and was turned away.

"And where have you two been?" she asked as her sons joined her on the marble bench.

"We were just—having a history lesson," Diero responded.

"I thought your father told you to stay out of Rahmirion's chamber," she said with a smirk. She had known where they were headed and why as soon as she saw they were gone—so often they had spoken of the spear.

"We have already received our lecture, Mother. We won't do it again," Mayson said apologetically.

"Be sure that you don't. Because if your father catches you up there again, when he is done with you, you will have *me* to contend with, I swear to that." Mayson shook a deep shudder that trembled down his spine. "Now, give me a kiss and go finish packing. You have a long day tomorrow."

"These two are going to make me old before my time," Henry said as he joined her, taking a cushioned seat to her left, allowing her to place her feet on his lap. The boys were gone in a flash.

"Nonsense, darling, you were old long before either of them were born," Beatrice responded, sporting a wicked grin.

"You're going to pay for that," Henry said into her ear.

"I'm counting on it," Beatrice replied as she stood and entered the palace. His eyes followed her, as they often did, hungrily. One couldn't deny that life certainly was sweet.

Chapter 4

Northrode: Astymere
1ˢᵗ Day of the First Month
5014 A.S.

THE STALLIONS TRUDGED ALONG THE HIGHWAY, their hooves clopping on the gray stones with each step. The rain fell in sheets, but not as hard as it had upon their departure, when the drops fell like stones. The deluge had made for a miserable start to the day, but as the road left the capital far behind, the weather had begun to let up. Mayson looked to Henry, riding several paces ahead, seemingly unfazed by the rain. He wore his favorite black riding suit, trimmed in golden thread, and his body was draped in a hooded, charcoal wool cloak.

Diero wore wool pants that matched his ensemble of a simple leather doublet, a cloth shirt, and a woolen traveling cloak that had already soaked through. His traveling sword hung at his hip, a blade of standard military make with a leather and steel grip. Neither of the boys were permitted to leave the capital without one. He made casual conversation with Tobias, who rode closely behind him.

Tobias Cisaer was the Carovensa Head of House, and had been in service to Lord Darian's family for over twenty years, ever since he left the Gildarian Republic in a trader's caravan as a boy. Diero often asked him what it was that caused him to leave his home at such a young age, but was always met with the same answer: "I'll tell you when you're older."

Mayson adjusted the white undershirt below his boiled leather doublet and looked out to his left at a small farmhouse in the near meadows. His hood had been up since the rain began, though not much good it did him at this point, for it had soaked through as well. Children ran into the house after being called by their mother to get out of the rain, while a farmer paid mind to his cabbages and potatoes. The first harvest of the year would be upon them soon and it all looked and smelled ripe, which made Mayson's stomach rumble slightly.

The banners of three High Houses flew in abundance, tossed and sprayed with wind and rain. Traveling with the royals were one hundred Knights of Rahm, fifty Rahmos men-at-arms, fifty Carovensa sworn guards, and one hundred and fifty soldiers of the

Black Army. To Mayson, it felt as if they were marching off to war rather than school.

A group of riders caught up from behind Mayson and Diero, who rode in formation on their destriers. Urnest had been riding with his two sons and Captain William Otter in the rear of the long train. Like Mayson and Diero, the youngest Rahmos child, Kristian, was attending the school for the first time, while his older brother, Jalen, was about to begin his third year.

Jalen Rahmos, a muscular boy of sixteen, kept his hair cut short and close to his scalp, and bore the same hard scowl as his father. His smile was also like his father's: big, bright, and full of joy. Kristian had just celebrated his thirteenth birthday three weeks earlier and had no visible muscle as far as anyone could tell. His longer hair was matted down by the rain, and his eyes were already wide and frightened of the trying times ahead at the Academy.

"You boys remember what will be expected of you?" William asked as he approached. The three first-years now rode tightly together so all could hear. "You will spend six months from home, but you will return one step closer to being a commander in your king's army. Commander Qirk will advise you about your leaves of absence, should stately obligations ever call you away. Allowances will be made for such things, however, do not expect any royal treatment. If I remember Qirk as well as I think I do, he will be as frosty as the peaks of Gol Goronath. You must remain diligent."

"Six months. Don't remind me," Kristian said with a groan.

"It's the reason we're feared, young man," William responded sternly. "First, you will learn to read maps. If you are to be an effective leader, you must be able to traverse any track of land and do it quickly. Knowing every inch of the battlefield can mean the difference between victory and defeat. When you fight, you must use the landscape to your advantage." He prattled on, discussing the demands of book work and the grueling physical tests that would take up the entirety of their first year. Kristian seemed to go pale at the thought. "Apart from basic combat training, you will be taught proper technique for riding horses, then thunder stallions if you do well enough."

"But we already know how to ride all of them," Mayson said.

"Surely we can skip over that part. I am half Dalani. By my blood alone there is hardly a horse in this world that I can't ride. That has to count for something."

"Yes, you can ride a stallion, but can you ride it when catapults hurl fireballs at you?" Jalen asked as he rode close, challenging Mayson based on his past experience at the Academy. "Or when arrows are zinging from all directions while men below swipe at your feet?"

Mayson sat silently and nodded, having gotten the point.

"The next few weeks," William started again, "will be time to settle your body and mind from the most intense riding you will have done in your young lives. You will sit and learn of the Black Army's history—all of it, not just the interesting parts your father told you. You will study strategy until you can lead men, unaided by your teachers, on the battlefield."

"Any man who fails his battle exercises has to run a mile for every man he *loses*," Urnest chimed in. "After a month or two, once you've spent some time in the classroom, you will serve as troops for the fifth years as they conduct war exercises to test their strategic knowledge. And finally, you will begin the four-year process of learning how to forge your own sword."

"I thought we inherit our swords?" Diero asked.

Henry joined Urnest. "Just like every man who passes through the school's gate," he said, "you will have to forge your own sword. Though you will inherit Eternal Weapons, making your own sword is the final piece to your education. Graduation will be impossible without it. There are few things more sacred than the bond between a man and a sword he has made with his own two hands."

The trip had been easy and uneventful, despite the rain, as the group crested the final hilltop before reaching the coastline. After taking the Northrode for about three hours, the party had forked off to the west toward the coast. Through decades of travel, Henry had learned every sight there was to see on the highway that stretched from the capital. Typically a few tavern fights, a wild beast or two, and men tending the large farms of grain or corn that kept two million mouths well-fed. This time, however, as the smell of warm saltwater blew from the west, Henry saw it all anew, as though he had never been beyond the walls of Vita Astym.

The Knights of Rahm, riding in front, paused at the top of the hill, allowing Mayson and Diero to finally see the Academy, a large cluster of buildings atop a lonely island offshore. A grass valley dropped steeply down toward the beaches, handmade by order of Karrok-Dastroltys over five hundred years before. The Academy not only served as a place of learning, but in days long gone, it was a fort to protect the sparsely populated and lightly guarded northern shores of the Crescent from the Raelians.

The descent along the lone dirt road carved into the land took an hour as the group wound their way back and forth. The path led them to a cemented stone road built upon rocks that ran for hundreds of yards. The natural-looking bridge stretched from the sandy shore straight out to the island. A massive stone portcullis, engraved with gold etchings of the four Eternal Weapons, guarded the lone entrance to the school, and was protected by twenty men at arms at all times. On no day was the gate left open.

"Good morning, your Majesty," came a voice from atop the rampart as the royals approached. An older guard sporting a long gray beard and a faded green cloak wrapped over the black armor of the Astymerian military stood at attention, taking in the royal company with probing eyes.

"We have three first-years, ready for enrollment, and a returning third-year student," Henry announced, gesturing back at the boys, who stared intently at the stone wall in front of them. Behind them sat a small army of sworn men-at-arms that practically stretched back to the beach. The warm breeze had turned into a strong wind, allowing the boys' hair to dry of the rainwater.

"Have your men dismount, if you please," ordered the guard. *I'm sure no one else gets an 'if you please.'* Henry obeyed, as was custom. His men did likewise and stood still as the portcullis slowly lifted, with a cringe-inducing grinding of stone-on-stone screeching loudly over the wind-tossed surf.

The opening revealed closely manicured grass and a meticulously maintained gravel courtyard. There were no buildings visible from where they stood; all were hidden behind a second wall that enclosed the complex. Ten guards marched through the opening, all holding a firm fist around the leather handle of their steel blades.

"Will the students please step forward?" asked a clean-shaven man-at-arms, the only one of his company to wear his black, crested helm. Mayson, Diero, Kristian, and Jalen stepped forward in a line, facing the guard. He nodded back at them, sizing them up, as if to judge how they would fare. "Say your goodbyes, latch up your horses, and be on your way."

The guard retreated as Henry and Urnest drew their boys in.

"I will write you both as often as I can," the king assured Mayson and Diero, embracing them both tightly. "I am so proud of you two. This is a big step forward, and the next time we see each other, you boys will be that much closer to manhood."

Henry watched as Urnest addressed his sons. "Jalen, look out for your brother. Let him fight his own battles, but only the ones he can win himself. Neither of you are to start any trouble here, but by Golron's hammer, if any trouble is started, you'd better finish it." The boys smiled and embraced their father for what would be the last time in months. "Kristian, remember, keep your feet light and your hands swift. Those lazy parries won't do here."

MAYSON AND THE OTHER BOYS picked up their swords and walked forward through the gate. They turned back to see their escorts walking in the opposite direction, slowly disappearing behind the lowering door.

"First things first," announced the guard who had given them entry. "Throw your swords over the outer wall, into the ocean." The boys looked at Jalen who had done this his first time and he urged them to do so. "You will all be given training blades once you are checked in."

Training blades, Mayson thought. *Gods be damned, they think we're children.*

The boys reluctantly withdrew their weapons, and in unison, flung them upward and watched them disappear over the wall. The guard then beckoned them toward the inner gate, and all stepped through onto the campus grounds.

Guards serving as lookouts patrolled the tops of the walls, twenty feet of gray stone reinforced by concrete bracings. It was said that students made up a large portion of the wall guards, each student pulling at least one watch duty a week.

Once through, there was little to obstruct their view of the wide cluster of buildings filling the island. To their left was a rectangular building of no architectural distinction, fronted by a large garden of marble statues of every great King in Astymere's history. Mayson thought he spotted a bust of his father positioned nearest to him, still only half-carved.

In the back of the open field the mess hall and barracks sat side by side, each built of heavy, sealed oak. Brick chimneys at either end of each building spat thin trails of smoke. In the far-right corner stood the bath house. It reminded Mayson of a stone pyramid that rose to hug the rim of the perimeter wall.

Jalen pointed to a large building next to the barracks made of solid marble, guarded by four men. "That's the armory. They keep both the training equipment *and* the live weapons in there. I've seen more than one first-year try to sneak their way in there. Save yourself the trouble. Even if you find a way past the guards, you'll find that the doors lock from the outside every time they are shut, and the guards only go inside to check every three days."

"That seems like an entire punishment in and of itself," said Diero.

"Only eight guards have the duty of protecting that entrance—four on and four off at a time. Each possesses a key in case of emergency, which he keeps in a secret place only he knows. They would be severely punished should they open it without leave from the Weapons Master or Royal Marshal Qirk."

To the right of the armory was a long, low structure fitted with ten chimneys, each releasing dark smoke into the strong sea wind. Henry had told the boys long ago that the fires of the forge burn so hot that the temperature inside hardly dips in the night.

At the heart of the property, far removed from the wall, rose a tall tower of black granite, built wide at the base and narrowing as it climbed. Two men in violet cloaks stood guard before the single wide entrance. Every other officer the boys had seen had worn green. At this distance, Mayson could just make out the bright outline of flames imprinted on the chests of their black breastplates.

"That's the Temple of Red Flame, where everyone takes the Final Test. Every final-year student goes in there on the day of their graduation," Jalen said. "Whoever enters is sworn to absolute, holy secrecy as to what is inside. Even the men who have been here for years don't know what is in there."

"The Temple of Red Flame," Diero repeated, musing. "Strange, I've never heard of it."

"That is because everyone who knows of it is sworn to secrecy," Jalen repeated. "Were you not listening?" He gave Diero a quizzical look, as he often did when Diero misspoke.

Mayson scanned his surroundings and found a small hole in the wall next to the classrooms. "What's that?" he asked.

Jalen chuckled and patted Mayson on his shoulder. "You'll find out in a few minutes, after the Royal Marshal's address is over," he said.

The central open field contained two hundred young men, fifty of which were dressed in the colors of their houses, some more confident than others, some with their legs trembling violently. The rest were already garbed in the traditional black uniform of the Academy. Mayson recognized the tall, thin shape of Kip Kinder, who had joined the royal family on several hunting trips this past year. Kip was holding firm, standing proud in a brown linen riding shirt and alarmingly bright yellow pants, but Mayson doubted many of the first-years would make it to graduation. Those shaking were all soft, pampered children of lower lords and wealthy merchants, sent here by their fathers to earn glory for their families.

Mayson and the others joined the crowd, gathered around a wooden platform where several teachers had already assembled. Addam Wallis, the Riding Master of the Royal Marshal Academy, was among them.

Royal Marshal Mikael Qirk stepped forward to the edge of the platform. Mayson knew of Qirk, once a great captain in the Black Army. His service in defending the borders against the Raelian Empire had propelled him up the ranks with great speed until he was considered for command of Kar Naron itself. Though he was a more qualified, reliable choice, command of Kar Naron was given to Jordyn Stone, to the objections of High Lord Wallis and the dismay of Qirk. When asked why he had made such a decision, Henry had told Qirk that both positions needed a suitable fit, and that Stone would never make a good teacher. It bore no weight on his qualifications, but it was where he was most needed. This left a bitter rivalry between the Marshal and Stone, and soured the relationship between the Marshal and his King.

He gave the appearance of a man who had been on the better side of portly for much of his youth, but military service had helped him shed the greater part of that encumbrance. His graying, brown hair was curly as sheep's wool, as was his short beard, and a small bald spot had begun to grow on the top of his head. He studied the small crowd of first-years comprised of shaking, timid lordlings, and furrowed his brow. Mayson thought he could see him sneer when the Marshal's eyes fell on him.

"New students, welcome. Former students, welcome back. Most of you have heard stories of this place and the trials you will face here, but know that the more you help each other, the easier it will be. It's the respect you give and earn here that turns into the brotherhood formed on a battlefield. Nobody will help a man they can't trust or respect, and so each day you will work harder than the day before. Each man here is considered a warrior when they leave, but I consider you one when you first walk in. You will learn, you will fight, and you will become the next generation of warriors who are feared most among the nations of the civilized world!"

He seemed to speak just as much with his eyes and eyebrows as he did with actual words. Mayson noticed the returning students standing proud at Marshal Qirk's words. "But first, new students, we have a test for you."

He ordered the new arrivals to separate to a single group and disrobe, pointing to the hole in the wall. Jalen gave Mayson a sympathetic smile as the three younger boys moved off to join a cluster of fifty first-years.

"Can you all swim?" Qirk shouted to them. His question drew mixed reactions. Most were still focusing on removing their boots. "No? Best to learn quickly."

Guards started pushing the new students toward the hole in the wall once all excess clothing had been removed. Mayson could feel dozens of pairs of eyes scan him and gawk at his scar, which was now impossible to hide. The sea wind bit at his bare skin and caused an uncontrollable shudder.

"Today we will begin your bond of brotherhood," Qirk

announced. "You will all swim back to shore. Those of you who can swim will aid those who can't, for there is only one way you are getting back on this island, and that is through the main gate. All of you. No one gets left behind, for if one of you doesn't make it back, you all fail!"

"Gentlemen!" Qirk called out as the line approached the hole. *"Welcome to the Academy!"*

Mayson took a deep breath as his turn approached. One by one, the group slid out of his sight. On the far side of the wall, he could hear splashes and panicked shouts. He closed his eyes and swallowed hard, hurling himself down the shoot and into the frigid, choppy water below.

"I can't feel my arms," Kristian said, walking unsteadily next to Mayson and Diero. Mayson nodded in sympathy. The boy's arms hung limp as he moved along the walkway connecting the island to the mainland, paralyzed with pain. "I'm not sure if they'll work tomorrow either, if they're still attached to me."

"Today isn't over yet, Kristian. I feel we're just getting started," Diero joked through thin breath.

Kristian's soaked hair dripped onto the dirt and stone below. The winds from the ocean chilled the drenched bodies of the new class until they trudged, quivering, through the outer gate of the Academy once more.

They had swum laboriously across the choppy water for several minutes while the older students watched from atop the wall with Marshal Qirk. The group moved slowly, keeping pace with a young boy, Teren of House Ashon. Being just twelve years old, he was the scrawniest of the new students and the smallest, barely reaching Mayson's shoulders. He hadn't learned to swim, so Mayson and Diero motioned for Kip, the tallest one in the party, to swim with the young one on his back.

If the tiring swim wasn't enough, guards awaited the boys on the beach, pushing them into a run along a stretch until they reached the man-sized rocks stacked alongside the Academy entryway. The boys scaled the ten-foot steep side and finally received their break on the treacherous walk against the wind blowing in from the ocean.

Thick clouds blanketed the sky, leaving the land gray and gloomy. The rain had passed, but the dampness lent an unpleasant chill to the air.

"*Faster!*" yelled Qirk, growing impatient while awaiting the boys at the open field. As the group moved closer they could see the disappointment on the Royal Marshal's face. Most of them staggered to the finish, hunched over at their knees and gasping for air. He circled around the young first-years. The elder students stood grouped behind the Marshal.

"If you were running from a battle and the enemy was on your heels, would you move as slowly as you just did?" The boys shook their heads silently. Qirk approached young Teren and tapped his shoulder. "What would you do?"

"I would push on as far as I possibly could, until my legs or even my heart gave out," he answered confidently, through deep, ragged breaths.

"Wrong," Qirk barked. "Gentlemen," he said, turning to the older students. "What is the creed of the Black Army?"

"We do not run!" they shouted in unison, their voices roaring in the wind. "We do not tire! We do not falter or weaken! We are the warriors of the Crescent! The swords of the Mountain! Our enemies will not see our backs; they will see our steel and feel our power. Rahm the Wise and Just gives me strength! The Mountain gives me purpose. Cayrian Rahma! Cayrian Karrok!"

Henry and William had made them memorize the creed as children, so Mayson and Diero knew it well.

"Now, it's time for the true test of a warrior," Qirk said. "By the looks of you, I think it is safe to say that you are all thoroughly exhausted. Some of you can barely stand. This is good. This is where we see who has the true spirit of a warrior. You *will* defend yourselves, boys, or there will be a world of hurt in it for you."

The first-years were picked out individually to face an older student in a hand-to-hand contest. The elder students stood behind their champion, while the newcomers stood behind their own. Kristian was selected first. He had a solid fight, for Urnest had taught him well, but conditioned and experienced as he was, his weary arms failed him, and he fell to a foe that was much bigger. A kick to his midsection sent him to the ground, and he did not rise until Diero pulled him, coughing, to his feet.

Most new students endured the same fate as Kristian as time passed. Kip submitted to an iron choke hold, while young Teren could barely get his hands up before a final-year student put him down with a straight shot to the mouth.

Diero went next, paired up with a dull-looking boy the Marshal referred to as Ciryl. He wasted no time, hurling himself at Diero with hellish fury in order to make an example of him. Three shots to the cheek put Diero on his knees, but as the fourth blow came for him, Diero caught it in his own grip. He twisted the boy's wrist to the point Mayson thought it would snap. With a shrill cry, and a signal from the Marshal, the melee was done. Before the older student could rise, Diero kicked him in the stomach, earning a fiery reproach from Qirk.

At last, Mayson's turn came. Despite the time it had taken for him to be selected, his breath still escaped him, and his muscles felt loose and rubbery in their exhaustion. His father had drilled him relentlessly to prepare him for this day, but swimming had been somewhat neglected. This was an entirely new fatigue.

He stepped away from the beaten, frightened group of first-years to square up against a freckled boy with a rather unimpressive build. To look at him, Mayson would have thought he was any typical man plucked out of any crowded city street. He would never have assumed that he had spent five years being trained at the finest military school in the Western world. The young man eyed the prince with a wicked grin, as if he had already beaten him, and inched forward inconsistently, trying to throw off Mayson's timing. The prince paid no attention to his fluttering and dancing about, but locked in on his opponent's eyes. Hands and feet could be deceptive, but the eyes always showed the truth. It was a lesson Henry had seared into his mind since the time he could walk.

He deflected several lazy jabs, despite his fatigue. Tired as he was, there was still speed left in his hands. The freckled boy's body language did not change, but his eyes grew more serious, and so did his shots. Faster and faster they came, with more force and frustration. But for all this new effort, the result was the same, as Mayson handily knocked each blow away. Finally, the older student could take no more and swung wildly for Mayson's head, leaving himself off balance and vulnerable.

Mayson ducked the punch and lunged forward, pulling his opponent's legs out from under him and slamming his back into the grass. The boy's breath left him in one big, explosive cough. He pounced and slammed the bone of his elbow across his foe's face, bashing his cheek and putting his lights out.

Qirk did not make a sound, but his eyes could not hide his fury. He gazed down at the fifth year, breathing heavily, his eyes shut. After stifling a look of disgust, the Marshal looked to two other students who had been standing behind him. Without hesitation, they rushed Mayson, grabbing his arms while a third moved in to finish him.

Mayson lifted his leg to block the incoming kick, then kicked straight into the crotch of one of his captors. His heart was racing and his breath felt like searing flame in his chest but he moved like a mad snake all the same. With his left arm free, he brought it straight into the nose of his second captor, breaking loose from him. With his nose broken, the boy bowed out of the fight, no longer troubling the prince.

The third to join the fight came at him again, this time with a spinning kick to his head. Mayson ducked and rolled away, finding his path to the second opponent who was trying to stand after the kick to his jewels had put him on the ground. A head butt to his belly sent him right back to the grass. His final challenger grabbed him from behind by his shirt, spinning him around.

A hard shot landed square on Mayson's chin, dropping him. Not willing to leave well enough alone, the older boy jumped onto him to finish him off. He raised his fist to send it into the prince's face again, but the blow found nothing but grass. Mayson had knocked his challenger's supporting arm away, allowing him to jump onto the older student's back and wrap his arm around his throat. After several moments of resisting, the fifth year urgently tapped on the prince's arm, signaling his surrender.

The young victor stumbled to his feet, his lungs nearly failing him, but his veins were filled with fire and his senses had become no more than animal instincts. He spun about, violently, and began to berate the crowd in his hysteria with what little power his body could give.

"Is there no one else? Come on! Send them to me! *Is there no one else?*"

Qirk no longer looked angry, but Mayson barely noticed. With a satisfied half grin, the Marshal turned to address one who stood behind him. "Allister! This *child* seeks another challenger. See if you can oblige him."

From behind the Marshal came a student that could have passed for a grown man, with a chin that looked as strong as his massive, veiny arms. His eyes were blank, and his nostrils were flared and wide. In his madness, Mayson lunged at the boy, taking the first punch before the challenger could make a move.

The prince's fist slammed into that chin, and to his horror, the hulking student's head didn't even budge. What was worse, his hand now rang with pain all the way up to his shoulder, dropping him to his knees. It felt as though his jaw had been made of granite. With an unbreakable grip, Allister took a tuft of Mayson's hair and painfully yanked him up to face him. The last thing the prince remembered seeing was that monstrous fist balled-up and reaching back before it shot forward into his eye. When he finally came to, the Marshal was addressing the student body.

"That is all for today, boys. Those injured, seek the Baths; everyone else, return to the Barracks," Qirk said, curiously eyeing the boys. Diero and Jalen made their way to the stone pyramid supporting Mayson, who staggered between them. He felt a trickle of blood swerving past his nose.

"How in the hell did you manage that?" Jalen asked.

"We just did what we were taught," Diero stammered through heavy breaths.

"Well, congratulations, you haven't been here more than an hour and you've already made enemies."

Diero didn't respond as they reached the triangular entrance of the Baths. It was formed by four massive slabs of rock meeting on an angle high above the ground. Once inside, Mayson began to come out of his fog, groaning and gripping his eye. One massive column in the middle of the open room reached to the top, with smaller support beams sprouting out like spokes on a carriage wheel. They held the four large, stone walls upright, so they didn't touch, keeping the roof open. It was thick and humid, but the heat helped fight away the chill settling into Mayson's bones.

Steam slowly rose out of twelve rectangular, glowing pools of liquid resting in a circle carved into the floor. Some were already occupied by first-years, while others were free for the taking.

Jalen and Diero helped strip the prince and slid him gently into his own pool. The liquid had no scent but touched his bare body like a wool blanket on a cold, windy night. Immediately the nausea in the pit of his stomach subsided, and with each breath, his throbbing head hurt less.

Mayson leaned his head back and closed his eyes. The next thing he knew, he was alone in the dark. The light of day had gone, and he peered up at the dense stars filling the night sky through the open roof. No torches were placed in the room, for natural heat and light came from the baths.

Qirk entered alone with his arms crossed, staring at Mayson. A look of curiosity furrowed his brow. Mayson rubbed his eye, which already was half the size of when he had entered the baths, then perched his shoulders above the surface and sat upright.

"Your father must have told you everything about this place," Qirk said as if disgusted. "I sometimes find myself doubting there would be anything for you to actually gain from coming here."

"He left much to be desired. He always said some things should be saved for formal education." Mayson looked down at the water, still caressing his eye.

Qirk knelt down next to Mayson's pool and ran his hand through the warm liquid. "It's called Eslia. It comes from a natural geyser deep within the island, and the old fort was built on top of it. They used steel pipes to funnel it into this room. Eslia has healing powers that no Great Healer could ever replicate."

"Why have we never used this on our soldiers in battle? Or for the general populace?" Mayson asked.

"Five hundred years back, shortly after the old fort was built, Great Healer Tespro deemed it too great a risk to lose Eslia to the empire, so Karrok-Dastroltys declared it should remain here on this island, and never leave. The only time it has ever been used on active soldiers was in days long gone, when the Academy was solely a fort. Besides, there isn't nearly enough of it for use on the Black Army, let alone the populace."

"How long does it take to heal in these pools?"

"A swollen eye or a concussion like you, usually a few hours. A life threatening injury could keep one in here for days. Those fights have been administered since the first year this school was opened, and never has a first-year won so handily. I wonder if it was luck, or if you and your brother truly have the skills necessary to do it again."

"We have the skill," Mayson grumbled, nursing his injured pride. "My father has taught Diero and I to fight since we were children."

"Yes, I've been waiting to see what kind of product the king would be sending me. *Karrok-Aht*, son of the great *Karrok-Ahl*," Qirk said to the prince, almost appraising him where he stood. He looked closely at Mayson's face. "So, it's true what they say about you. To look at you I'd swear you were full-blooded Avaari—not a trace of your horse blood to be seen."

Even in his exhaustion and pain Mayson had to fight the terrible urge to lash out at the Marshal. *Horse blood* was a slur against his Dalani mother. An uncreative, blunt one, but a slur, nonetheless. Though not an Avaari himself, it seemed Qirk shared the sentiment of several tribal elders who had tried to renounce him at his birth for being a *half-blood.*

"And your brother, Darian Carovensa's boy. He's the spitting image of the Golden Serpent, from the way he stands, right down to that arrogant smirk. I've known that look since long before you were born."

"Why do I feel as though we've done something wrong?" Mayson asked. "Was not the purpose of the test to defend ourselves and win the fight?"

Qirk's nostrils flared. "The purpose of the test is to teach you to stand and fight when you have nothing left. To face certain defeat, even death, without hesitation. You weren't supposed to win. You were supposed to take your licks and remember how it felt to be powerless." He trailed off and glared down at Mayson. "The king himself trained you since childhood, eh?"

"Yes, sir," Mayson replied.

"Well, I congratulate you, Prince Karrok-Aht," Qirk said with a dark smile, walking to the exit. "I'm expediting your training to the advanced courses." He let out a low, unsettling laugh. "We shall see how strong you two really are in the coming weeks."

Chapter 5

Vita Astym: Astymere
2ⁿᵈ Day of the First Month
5014 A.S.

WILLIAM AWOKE WITH A HARSH START and shot up, facing the wall opposite his bed. The morning sky was still dark, save for only a faint streak of light. His aging muscles were stiff and sore, typical of most mornings. Also typical was the incessant throbbing in his head. He stretched, then slid from his bed and dressed himself. The dream that woke him had robbed him of any rest, and he felt more exhausted than when he had fallen asleep.

It was always the same: fragmented memories and half-visions of a past he wished he could forget; a never-ending labyrinth of marble and alabaster in the dead of night; shouts of guards, alarm bells, horses braying—piercing grief. Whenever he woke from this dream, guilt wracked his heart with more pain than his aged muscles.

William held his head in his hands and rubbed the short stubble that remained after his long years of faithful service to the crown. His fingers found the scar and indent on the back of his skull, the wound he had suffered for his King. It was his *true* reward for his part in storming the White City. Fourteen years later and it was still painful to touch. *Faithful service. You keep telling yourself that, you weak imbecile. If only Henry knew. You'd both be dead. What do you feel guilty for? Is it the betrayal of your country, your King, and your people? Or is it for failing her? No, but you didn't fail her, did you? You couldn't save her, but you did not fail her.*

He walked to the window and looked out over the quadruple-layered stone wall guarding the palace in the heart of the Mountain City. His quarters looked out over Westslope, and although the captain longed for morning warmth, he never minded sitting in the shadows, watching as the city before him caught the first light of day.

By the time he left for Henry's study, his belly was full of a hearty breakfast of toasted bread smothered in blackberry jam along with six eggs, brought to his room by one of Hammund's runners. He also requested a whole pot of coffee, half of which he drank on the spot to offset his exhaustion. Galen often advised against this, but William never paid any mind.

His lieutenants, Sir Garrabed, Sir Mattis, Sir Daevin, and Sir Roace awaited him at the bottom of the winding stairs leading up to his quarters. They had donned their black helms, but he knew their names all the same. He was one of them: their brother in arms; a sworn Knight of Rahm; a dreaded Shadow Knight. It had been years since he had donned that faceless helm, for Henry preferred his company simply as a man, and not as a "moving statue," as he had put it. William began briefing them on their plans for the next few months.

Typically, there was very little variation to a Shadow Knight's daily tasks. But today, William would begin prepping his men for Henry's journey east through the Great Plains to the Gildarian Republic. The large forest nation hoped to reopen trading routes with the Western Kingdoms now that stability had returned. The other Western kings would be joining him, and William *needed* everything to run smoothly, for he would not be there to make sure himself.

"All should be clear, though as I promised I will remind you each day until the king takes to the road. We are to…we are…" His mind went dark and William stopped, staring blankly at the floor. Slowly, as though a tiny spark grew to a roaring fire, his thoughts returned, and for a moment William did not know how long he had stood there in silence.

"Right. We are to have no less than one hundred of you with him at all times, per usual. I want scouts to create a perimeter stretching a half-mile around his position. There will be guards for the other kings; leave them to it. No one but a fellow king is to get near him. If a fly so much as lands on this man's shoulder, we have failed." William's eyes bounced among the four lieutenants standing motionless, taking in his orders.

The Knights of Rahm were bound to their service of protecting the king, and should the bloodline of Astymere be broken, their holy duties were to carry out justice against those responsible, and then take their own lives. Without a living descendent of Astymir the Father, their existence would become meaningless:

If my King shall perish, I shall serve my final duty to thee.
I shall run his killer through, and I shall join him, true and true.

*When the enemies of the Mountain are gone from under the
skies,
I will have done my part, all for the Heart,
and shall be worthy in Rahm's eyes.*

William and his men traversed the labyrinthine halls of the palace, passing countless works of art collected throughout the ages depicting the great and terrible times Astymere had gone through. Busts of the most notorious Karroks in history, showcased by Astymir the Father, sat on carved obsidian pedestals placed in between the tall, arched windows. Paintings of the War of Reunification, the Battle of the Krystal River, and the Karrok Wars all seemed to be looking glasses that allowed William to peek into the deep recesses of history and myth which, after so long, had all twisted into one.

Henry's study sat at the heart of the palace. Mounted above the double doors was an obsidian bust of Rahm the Wise's head, adorned with large rubies for eyes. The entry was open, and William could see Henry sitting at his desk, scribbling furiously. William's knights fell in single file behind him as they passed through the short corridor leading from the outer doors into the room. Two remained stationed at the outer doors while the other pair took flanks at Henry's desk. The oval windows behind Henry held no glass and allowed an eastward wind to blow in, tussling William's black cloak.

"My dear Captain," Henry said before William could announce himself, keeping his eyes on the scroll. He looked up at William with a smile. "You smell of exhaustion and worry. Only one man I know has had such a scent linger about him like a thick fart." They both chuckled.

"I'm sorry to disturb you, my King, but there is something I've been needing to speak with you about. As your trek to the Republic approaches, I wanted to get it over with while there was still time."

"But of course, Captain," Henry said, gesturing to one of three chairs sitting before his desk. The thick wool carpet muffled the sound of William's steps, and William noticed the musty smell of books that had sat on the shelves to his left and right for generations, all detailing the comings and goings of the kings that sat at that desk before Henry. "I must warn you, I have a full schedule today. Many things must be seen to before I leave. It shouldn't be a surprise to you, Captain, but it is my duty to inform you that I have selected Urnest as the Guardian. I will make a public proclamation tomorrow. In the meantime, I must facilitate the moving of his essential household staff into city quarters, pass along unfinished edicts that will need his attention, and letters from supplicants will have to be organized and catalogued for his agents. In short, I will have people in and out of this study until long after the sun goes down."

"What is it that you're writing?" William asked, nodding toward the scroll on Henry's desk.

"They're notes on Gildarian law that Lord Brisban asked me to copy, as to sear it into my mind," he responded. "It feels more as if I was a first year at the Academy rather than his King. Tell me William, when was the last time a king was schooled by a man one-tenth of his worth?"

"Even the greatest of kings, like yourself, can still be taught," William reasoned. *Say it now, you fool, before he has a chance to continue on.*

"I beg your pardon, my King," came a voice from the door. Henry beckoned the newcomer to enter, and in came Tayden Habbin, Urnest Rahmos's Head of House. Hardly past thirty, Tayden was widely considered too young for his position, but all Lord Rahmos ever spoke of was his incomparable competence and organizational skills.

Tayden gained control over an unruly pile of scrolls in his arms before placing them on Henry's desk. "These are all of the forms you sent to Kar Rahmos concerning the temporary transition of power. All have been signed and stamped by my lord master. They simply await your royal approval." William watched him fidget with the clasps that held his silver cloak to his shoulders as Henry perused the seven scrolls in front of him.

"Yes, very good," Henry said as he held one up for inspection. "Inform Lord Rahmos they will be signed within the fortnight, and all will be prepared by the time he sits upon the Heart. That is all."

"My King," Tayden said with a bow. William watched him go before he turned back to Henry.

"May I speak candidly, my King?" he asked.

"You may, William," Henry replied, returning to the piles

upon his desk.

"My King, if I may," came another voice from the door.

"One moment, William," Henry said apologetically. "They have been in and out all day; I feel like I'm losing my mind. Enter!" His voice boomed out the short stone corridor to the double doors.

Geremy Brisban entered without making a sound. His feet were wrapped in thin slippers of blue silk, and a light flowing robe to match sat over a white riding jacket bound in brass buttons. William took painful notice that his insufferable coif was particularly high today. He carried a leather-bound ledger in his left hand and several old scrolls in his right. That same smug, self-satisfied grin was plastered on his face as he took a seat before Henry without being beckoned to do so.

"Geremy," Henry said, cordial, but cross. "I have been industrious on my *homework.*"

"My King, I do apologize for the intrusion, but I felt there were a few more things you and I needed to discuss before we left." His words reeked of supplication, but that grin stayed right where it was.

"We are going to be spending over a month together on the road, Geremy. You will be hard-pressed to convince me why this matter couldn't wait until then, when I have no other business to worry me."

"Because with all due respect, my King," Brisban replied, "this is a domestic matter that the Guardian will be quite powerless to handle himself, as set forth by the old laws." William watched as the argument in Henry slowly leeched from him. A citation of the old laws was always to be taken seriously, despite the inconvenience any said conversation might cause.

"You have my attention, Geremy," he replied. "But if you could please be quick about it, I have enough on my plate without constant interruption."

"Very well, my King, I shall get right to the point. As we have all been made aware, the harvests in the Southern Tip have been rather outstanding this year, which of course is cause for celebration."

"Yet you're not here to celebrate," William said. Geremy shot him a sidelong look that almost felt like reproach. William stared back at him, unmoved. Nevertheless, he persisted.

"We have been so preoccupied with the actual harvest yield that we have neglected the logistics of distributing the excess grain and produce to the local markets. Usually, the maximum tonnage sent to the smaller markets in the south is set at one hundred, and once every maximum has been met, the rest is sent here to be sold in the Bazeira, or sent north where certain crops aren't able to grow."

"Yes, Geremy, I think I am quite acquainted with the logistics of food distribution. But what is so important that…"

"What is so important, my King, is that hardly any of the excess food is making it north of the Styntas River. It is all being sold in the south and the excess will rot before it can all be bartered. I have run the numbers and the loss of product could end up costing the crown two million mira before the end of next year."

"And what do the Collectors have to say about it?" Henry asked. Geremy slapped the heavy ledger down on Henry's desk and began to leaf through the pages.

"I'm afraid the Collectors may be the problem, along with the teamsters charged with transporting the goods. With the excess goods remaining in the Southern Tip, their sale in southern markets is bringing in more tax revenue than normal, and the Collectors are holding onto more than their fair share of the pie, if you catch my meaning. You see, it seems that the Collectors only kept in line due to Darian Carovensa's close watch and quick hand. After he died, and your Majesty took on the supervision of the southern Collectors himself, they continued to stay in line, for the most part. But a king can only dedicate so much of his attention to the detailed workings of a principality. Records indicate that in the last five years, this trend has been growing, slowly. We brushed it off as a minor fluctuation at first, since the changes were so subtle, but this year it is too great to ignore. They have let their greed get the better of them, and their misdeeds can now be plainly seen."

"Bastards," Henry said through gritted teeth. "I want their names, I want their badges, and I want them brought to me. They are finished! We shall have to purge the entirety of the southern taxing offices, not to mention examine many of the public enterprises that send money through their hands. Replace them with trustworthy men. You and I will hand pick them."

"A wise choice, my King, but I am afraid, as Galen would put it, you would only be treating the symptom and not the disease itself. What the crown needs is to delegate management of the Southern Tip as a whole to one trustworthy individual, to keep an eye on the crown's agents and assure they behave accordingly with their office. Someone who can spot these irregularities as they happen and prevent them from growing out of control."

"Who would you suggest, Geremy? Lord Darian is dead and Diero is still years off from being lorded. If anything, I will just have to dedicate more of my time to overseeing the farther reaches of the Crescent, to not allow things to fall through the cracks."

"With all due respect, my King, time is exactly what you lack right now. We will have many long nights ahead of us drafting the new trade agreement with Gildar. If you take this upon yourself, you will drop before you even make it past Gol Rayna. You *must* delegate management. To me."

"Are you mad?" William asked, rising from his chair and nearly taking the smug cuss by his pretty collar. "To suggest some lowborn penny pincher be placed in Darian Carovensa's chair; that he rule a quarter of the Crescent from Kar Carovensa; to push the rightful heir of the Southern Tip aside…"

"I am neither mad nor am I suggesting pushing Diero aside. There is precedent for what I suggest."

"William," Henry interjected with a reassuring hand, "let him speak."

"My King, within these scrolls are several references to an older office known as Elavahrs. An Elavahr hasn't been named since before the establishment of the Ahm branch of the dynasty, but the groundwork is all laid."

"Ela-what?" William asked. This conversation was growing more and more nonsensical by the minute.

"It's Avaari, William," Henry said. "It means Timed Lord, to put the translation as simply as I can. What groundwork do these scrolls lay, Geremy?"

Brisban gently laid the scrolls upon Henry's desk and unfurled them, one by one.

"From what I gather, my King, an Elavahr can be any member

of the Royal Council, temporarily elevated to the governing status of a High Lord. This happens whenever a High Lord is either forcibly removed from power, is incapacitated without an heir of age, or dies without an heir of age. Lord Darian only succumbed to his illness shortly before he died, so there was no time to even consider such an appointment. If you name me Elavahr to the Southern Tip, you will be free of the added burden of managing the more minute aspects of the principality yourself. I already have a list of fine appointments to fill the ranks once we dispose of those criminals that have been robbing us blind. I have never faltered in my duties, my King, and it would be my most humble duty to serve you in this fashion."

William watched as Brisban bowed deep in supplication. *Kiss ass*. But the idea clearly held great appeal to Henry. He stood there stroking his chin, as he often did whenever giving serious thought to any matter. William couldn't believe his eyes. Henry was *actually* considering bartering the seat of a High Lord away to this coiffed puffball.

"And what happens when Diero comes of age, Geremy?" Henry asked. "How can I be assured that you will give up your hold over the Southern Tip without a fuss? You have helped me build this economy into one of the strongest in the West; I would hate to have to take your head for treason."

"The beauty of the office of Elavahr sits right in the name. *Timed* Lord," Geremy replied, placing his hands on Henry's desk. "Simply designate the appointment's expiration to coincide with Diero's lording ceremony, and I will be required by law to relinquish my power. Not to mention none of the Carovensa men would ever follow me, should I ever be so bold as to raise arms against my King." He gave a wide grin, possibly to show that his intentions were harmless, yet William felt nauseous at the sight. Something about that look made him seem like a cat that was about to be left alone with an open rabbit hutch. Henry didn't seem amused.

"Each man sworn to Darian Carovensa and his blood would personally kick your cock and balls into your mouth if they ever got so much as a whiff of such a notion," Henry said with utter seriousness. It was true, and he seemed pressed to make Brisban aware of that. "Nevertheless, you have proven yourself to be quite useful since your inclusion into the Royal Council. I will accept your offer of taking up the Southern Lord's responsibilities, under the grounds that you will immediately relinquish said power once Diero's lording ceremony is completed. Bring me your list of appointments as soon as possible, so I may approve them, and that Lord Rahmos may become acquainted with them. They will be reporting directly to him until we get back. If there is nothing else, you are free to go."

Brisban bowed quickly, like oozing mercury, and with a sharp flourish of his robe, turned to leave. William shot him the most contemptible look he could manage as he passed by, and for just a moment, William could have sworn Brisban shot the look right back at him. Ever since he was allowed to take control of the treasury and attained his seat on the council, he looked at everything, and everyone, as though they were bought and paid for—like he *owned* everything he set his eyes on. It was all William could do not to knock his perfect little white teeth out.

Henry sat and returned to his papers, the sound of his pen scribbling filling the room.

"You just gave that man more power than anyone born of his station could ever dream of," William stated, pointing in Brisban's direction. "You can't expect he will not be affected by it—unchanged. Men like him are never satisfied and you know it."

"I am no fool, William," Henry said. His voice was somehow less friendly than it had been before. "I will keep a close eye on him. Many close eyes, actually. Regardless, he is right. I no longer have the time or energy to keep every office of the Southern Tip in line myself. He will be useful, at least for a time. If he proves to be dishonest in his declaration that he will yield his power, he will have the Black Army to contend with, and that will just be the start. But I fear not. With men like you by my side, what can a man fear?" The warmth returned to his voice, and he shot a smile to William so tender it nearly broke his heart. *Do it now, man, before you lose your nerve. While you can still remember.*

"My King, that is why I've called on you today," William said. The look of confusion and worry that slowly grew in Henry's eyes was too much to bear. In shame, William looked to the floor. "I don't know how to phrase this so that it will come out as softly as I want it to, so I will just say it and be done with it. Henry, I wish to be released from your service."

"William…" Henry began, dropping his pen.

"Henry, I am no longer fit to protect you," William blurted out, severing Henry's sentence at the head. "The blackouts are getting worse. The *pain* is getting worse. I'm hardly sleeping anymore. What would you have me do? Don my helm again and become a lifeless sentry for the rest of my short life? Sure, I will serve you well, but being trapped in there without being able to eat, drink, or even rest, I will soon die. Should I have a blackout on the road, or should I be flattened by pain, I would be a liability to you. I have enough failures on my conscience, Henry, but if something were to happen to you under my watch, I would never forgive myself."

"You are not alone, though, William!" Henry exclaimed, rising from his chair and pacing about the study. William had never seen him struggle so hard to find the right words. He seemed to search for minutes before he could compose himself and continue. "You have a thousand brothers in arms that share the load with you. Every man in this city, this country for that matter, who holds a weapon, plays a part in keeping me and my family safe! It wouldn't be your failure if anything happened to me."

Henry looked uncharacteristically feeble as William stood his ground. Henry knew he was right. As the captain of his personal guard, and the Commander of the Knights of Rahm, the responsibility for the king's safety rested squarely on William's shoulders. Any failure to protect him or his family was his.

A single tear rolled down Henry's face as he turned to look out the open window. "I won't allow it. No. I won't allow you to leave me. You can do nothing unless I permit it, and I do not permit you to abandon your duty. I refuse your resignation."

"Henry, before long I will suffer a blackout while I am on *duty* keeping watch over you. Before long, I may not be able to get out of bed! If the public gets wind that one of the *invincible* Shadow Knights has fallen to illness, then the entire corps' reputation is gone, and there is no telling how long it would take to get it back. Henry, as your friend, as your Captain, I beg you to see reason. I am no longer any use to you."

"Who can I trust, if not you?" Henry's voice was hollow.

Gods, I should have died in the White City. I would rather die a thousand deaths than have to keep living this moment.

"I will personally make a list of ten men I think will make excellent candidates to succeed me. I swear on my life that whoever takes my place will have my utmost confidence in their abilities."

"And where shall we leave off, William?" Henry asked, staring out the window, almost refusing to look at him. "Do I just let you go? Allow you to ride off into the sunset to die without a word or goodbye?"

"No, Henry. I will stay by your side until my end, however bitter it may be. But I will be by your side as your brother-in-arms, not as your Captain. I will never be far, and I will never turn my back on you. On this, you have my Holy vow." Henry stood motionless for a few moments, until something suddenly released in him. His back and shoulders seemed to relax so heavily he almost slumped.

He turned from the window and returned to his chair. He picked up his pen, dipped it in ink, and began scribbling again. "Very well, William," he said in that same empty voice. "If you no longer see yourself as fit to serve the crown, then the crown is compelled to agree. As a reward for your years of steadfast service, your living quarters shall remain on the palace grounds. As of the end of this week, your service with the crown shall be terminated. A Sandil shall be crafted for you and presented to you in a timely fashion. If there is nothing else you wish to discuss, you have my permission to go."

William swallowed an enormous lump in his throat and gave a stiff bow, stifling his own tears. "As my King commands, so shall I obey."

He blinked back the wet burning in his eyes until he reached the outer corridor, until he could fight them no more. He walked back to his tower, leaving behind a salty trail of drops. As he slumped down on his bed, the justification of this horrible day took the edge off the sting. *It will be what is best for him. It will be what is best for her.*

Chapter 6

The Flat Way: The Great Plains
2ⁿᵈ Day of the First Month
5014 A.S.

"MERCY! MERCY!" PRINCE RONIN SURYN paid no heed to the captured bandit's pleas as he slid his high steel broadsword across the man's throat, silencing him save for a few pained gurgles.

"These scabs have no honor," he said, turning to his captain while wiping the stain from his blade. "They were all given the option of swearing fealty to the crown after the empire fell. And what do they do? They take to the land like wolves, preying on anyone they think too weak to defend themselves, then cry and beg when they get their comeuppance as though they are the victims. Makes my blood boil."

The bandits had been moving by horse in a group of twenty, raiding several newer villages built along the Flat Way by the Crown of Dalan. The Dalani hunting party of forty, with weapons of high steel and destriers bred for war, had made short work of them. For years, King Robert had sent hundreds of hunting groups into the vast meadows of the Great Plains to seek all those who had been preying on innocent travelers and merchants. Though catches such as this had grown quite rare in recent memory, patrols still roamed the Plains as though Dalan were at war.

"It's no wonder Raelia fell," joked Captain Eldric Faranor, a man of fifty with graying straw-colored hair down to his shoulders. His nobly built, clean-shaven face was highlighted by a broken nose, and his frame was thin and wiry, but strong nonetheless. "They're tough when you read the reports and when they attack unarmed caravans by surprise. But put them against an enemy that is ready for them and does not fear them, then they have lost before the fighting even begins."

Ronin bent down and removed the weapons of his last kill, as did Eldric and several other men, until all supplies were taken and accounted for. Prince Ronin, a young man of twenty, with his tough, tan skin, hair of deep, rich brown, and eyes as green and vibrant as emeralds, looked as true a member of the Dalani tribe as one could expect. He was built like his Uncle Roland, the first true King of Dalan, with broad shoulders and thick arms that could send a spear straight through an enemy's shield and armor.

"What are your orders, my Prince?" asked Malyn, one of the forty Sworn Hooves to Prince Ronin. His deep green cloak caught the afternoon wind, as did the horsehair mane of his winged helm. In the dull light of the overcast sun, his copper-colored steel breastplate sprang out against the darker steel of the chainmail beneath.

The prince peered ahead where the gray cobblestones of the Flat Way stretched across the rolling land and over the distant hilltops. *For all the damage they caused, I suppose we should be grateful to the Raelians for building such an efficient road system.*

"We will move forward to the Third Junction, set up camp, rest, and water the horses," he ordered, pointing north. "Then at first light tomorrow, we move to rendezvous with Commander Haledon." The hunting party had left Roleigh with eighty men and had split in two, half traveling with the prince to cover the southern plains, while the rest followed the veteran commander.

The riders took their horses at a leisurely pace several miles north to the edge of the smooth stone road, and each took turns scooping out buckets from a roadside well for their weary stallions. Every canteen had been filled and every horse properly watered when out of the north, a lone rider stormed over the top of the distant hills, terrible urgency spurring him forward.

"To arms!" yelled a Sworn Hoof who stood next to the well, watching the oncoming rider. Dirt churned and flew in chunks beneath the stallion's hooves, higher than the dry grass in the field. The rider did not travel by road and looked as though he had trekked across the rough, unkempt countryside.

"No! Stand fast. It's one of ours!" shouted Captain Eldric, his raised hand staying the sudden preparation for battle.

The captain's keen eye had proven most useful time and time again. When hunting, he had made himself famous for putting an arrow through the eye of a field hare before his companions had even known it was there.

The rider approached and slowed his horse, as Ronin noted the unmistakable red beard of Haledon's Lieutenant, Coronyn MaCairn. "A message from Commander Haledon, my Prince," Coronyn said as he handed him a rolled-up brown piece of parchment.

Why would Haledon send a rider instead of waiting for the

rendezvous? What could be so important?

The prince scanned the paper thoroughly, taking in the words in confusion. He shook his head and addressed the lieutenant. "There is no need for investigation. Our instructions were clear: *Put all captured marauders to the sword.*" He then handed the message to Eldric.

"Commander Haledon understands the orders, my Prince. But something about our latest catch has him ill at ease. They are no Raelians, and given their appearance, he doesn't think they are even Western. I believe that if the commander has doubts, then it is worth investigating," the lieutenant said in measured breaths.

They paused for a moment while the captain finished reading the message. "I agree with the lieutenant. I don't believe Commander Haledon would have sent a rider if he didn't have proper cause for suspicion." He handed the letter back to Ronin. "Haledon was never one to stay his spear. If *he* is questioning his course of action, then I suppose we must find answers."

"We move north, men," ordered the prince after a moment of thought. "Gather your gear and saddle up." He pointed to Coronyn. "You will ride with me and Captain Eldric to inform us of everything you know of these men." In a matter of minutes, the forty Sworn Hooves had their gear packed and their horses in stride, and the tight formation headed directly off the highway into the hills of the Great Plains.

The wind had grown from a bracing breeze to a strong gale by the time the Dalani party made their way past the Black City on the eastern horizon. They were back on the Flat Way after trudging through the grassy fields, and the road climbed to the top of the Bolisor hill range, less than a league from the great ruin, giving a clear view of the dead collection of melted stone and blood-soaked memories.

As the Sworn Hooves reached the summit of the first of the Bolisor hills, Prince Ronin looked to his right. The black, twisted mass that had once been the greatest city in the world still seemed to smolder and burn, with countless small plumes of smoke creeping into the sky as though they were long black fingers that sought to strangle the sun. *Nearly fourteen years, and it still burns. This place is unholy indeed.*

He was not alone in this thought. Most civilized people

avoided the Black City, fearing that the hateful spirits of the Raelian slain walked the streets seeking vengeance on the living, or that the dark, unnatural power that consumed it would somehow poison the souls of all who came too close. Whether one believed in ghosts or not, none could deny that the air of death surrounding the place encouraged any sensible man to avoid it.

The wind seemed to grow even stronger as the Flat Way passed through a small canyon that formed between the hills. The incessant howling almost drowned out the thunderous pounding of hooves upon stone. Haledon and his party had been three miles north of the hill range when they encountered the wild men, according to Coronyn. His instructions were to find the prince immediately and to return with him in all haste. Haledon had nearly yanked the lieutenant out of his saddle when he sent the man off, or so Coronyn said.

By the time Ronin and his party had cleared the Bolisor Hills, the outline of the sun had slipped behind the overlaying clouds in the west, and it was well past midday when he made out scores of minuscule figures dotting the northern horizon. "Double time!" he cried. Dalani thoroughbreds, though not thunder stallions, were still impressive, powerful beasts, and as they reached full speed, the stones of the Way threatened to shake free of their weakened, unmaintained mortar.

Commander Haledon's salt-and-pepper hair soon came into full view, as did his winged helm resting in his right hand. Haledon of House Swiftwynd had a hard face lined with scars, and eyes so dark they appeared black at first glance. He had served as bodyguard to King Robert on the Night of Knives when his brother, King Roland, was murdered. For the courageous part he had played in getting the new king and his fallen kin home, Haledon was named a Sworn Hoof to the royal family and had ridden by Robert's side during the sack of Raelia.

"All right, Commander," Ronin began as he dismounted, his brown leather boots sinking into the soft grass. "What is so pressing that it could not wait until the rendezvous tomorrow?"

"These," Haledon responded in his deep, gravelly voice. He pulled his horse aside by the reins to reveal ten animalistic-looking men in the center of a ring of Dalani horses. Each rider held their spear aloft to corral the wild men. A pile of six dead bodies lay beyond the ring of horses, alongside crude, handmade weapons.

"I will admit they look rather unwashed, even more so than the lot we usually pull in," said Ronin, "but I don't see much cause for concern here."

"Look at their weapons and armor. Look at their clothes," Commander Haledon said. "These aren't Raelians. They don't speak Altung. Their armor and swords we took are iron. There is not a single nation south of Gol Garonath that still uses iron. These men are a long way from home, whoever they are. What I wonder is, what are they doing here?"

It was quite the question. Ronin couldn't figure how men such as these could have penetrated this deeply into the Great Plains without being spotted. Though they were haggard and unwashed, they were certainly no refugees. These men had been armed to the teeth with swords, daggers, and axes, and they wore full breastplates of finely made iron. These men were killers, unmistakably.

"Has anyone tried speaking to them?" the prince asked.

"I did, my Prince," Commander Haledon said. "I tried Altung, native Dalani, I even threw in some phrases of Valkothi that I've heard before. Nothing. It's nothing but gibberish to me."

"I say we put them to the sword here and now, my Prince," Malyn chimed in. He was far removed from being a native Dalani tribesman, but a loyal countryman all the same. "Our orders are clear. I don't see why we should raise any fuss over some unwashed shit-kickers."

"You watch your mouth in front your Prince, Hoof, or I will kick your teeth in," Haledon snapped.

"That's all right, Commander," Ronin said, raising a calming hand. Malyn had a point. Their orders were clear. *Put all plainsmen to the sword.* The only complication was that these men were clearly no plainsmen. "Let me try."

The prince drew his high steel broadsword, Hashi'Elo, roughly translating to Shining Death in old Dalani, and pointed it straight at the throat of the largest detainee. It seemed as though someone, or something, had taken a large bite out of his cheek, leaving a deep indentation in his face. His beard was braided in five strands at his chin, and his hands were tattooed with fanged skulls. If Ronin could break this man, he was sure the others would shortly follow suit.

"Tallik," the prince said, meaning *speak*, utilizing what little of the northern languages he knew. The rant that came out of this wild man's mouth seemed mostly like guttural noise, as Haledon had described, but Ronin was able to discern several words and phrases. *Fonnek ak Skrimsor*, Servants of the Monster. *Hanek myljor ala*, his fist shall crush all. *Ikkerk mann flyjor*, none shall escape. These were the things that the prince was able to make out, and even so, he barely heard them, so he may have been mistaken. *Skrimsor? Does it truly mean monster, or could it mean Beast? If these men are servants of the Beast...*

By the amused smirks on the Dalani faces, Ronin could tell they couldn't comprehend a word this man was saying, which offered the prince a perfect chance to downplay the severity of these phrases. It would benefit no one to reveal what had actually been said. The men would insist that they be put to the sword immediately, severing Ronin's source of information at the neck. *Father will want to question these men himself. Best keep everyone silent until we return to Roleigh.*

"You are quite right, Commander. Not much more than throaty noise. Still, this bunch isn't quite ordinary. The king will want them questioned thoroughly, and by men who are a bit more versed in linguistics than we are. Bind them. Eldric and I will ride to Roleigh to alert the crown that we are coming. Haledon and the rest will follow in time. Understood?"

"Aye!" the Sworn Hooves cried together.

"Excellent. Captain, let us ride." As Ronin and Eldric mounted their horses, with their forty Sworn Hooves following suit, the captain met Ronin's eyes.

"What is it, my Prince?" he asked.

"I must speak to my father immediately. If I am right, this may be far worse than a few savage strangers."

"Very well, my Prince. But enlighten me, how is Haledon supposed to transport that lot? He has no horses to spare."

"They can walk, Eldric," Ronin answered. "Which gives us ample time to reach Roleigh and form at least the semblance of a plan before they arrive. But to be safe, we will be riding hard from here." Though it was all likely nonsense, Ronin had to treat any men who might be servants of the Beast as a terrible threat, and that alone made the trip to Roleigh worth it.

The young prince tore off across the plains into the west, forcing Eldric to try to keep up. There was not a horse on the face of Antheira that could have borne him with enough speed, and Ronin found himself wishing that the Wings of the Father, built into his helm, would begin to flap and bear him home on the back of the wind.

Chapter 7

Vita Astym: Astymere
3rd Day of the First Month
5014 A.S.

BEATRICE FELT A SLIGHT ACHE as she looked upon Mayson's empty seat and broke her fast with a bowl of fresh fruit. The day she had kissed him goodbye as he began his journey to the Academy was one of the worst in her recent memory, though she had been used to the boys being away for stretches of time. From the age of six, Mayson and Diero had often traveled with Henry as he visited his fellow kings of the Western Kingdoms. But this was different. She wouldn't see them again for nearly a year, and the harsh reality of their impending adulthood suddenly became clear.

When Lord Galen had sedated her on the Night of Knives, Beatrice was uncertain she would ever wake again, uncertain that her child would ever see daylight. When she finally awoke two days later, her heart had sunk to learn her husband had left to wage war on Raelia. Mayson had been her gift from the gods after so much suffering.

Henry sat at the head of the table as always, his eyes fixed on his plate. He absentmindedly picked at the blackened bacon he had requested, his own bowl of fruit pushed off to the side. For at least three days every year at this time, Beatrice noticed, Henry would grow quiet, sullen, and morose without offering any explanation. He had always brushed it off as the stress of ruling getting the better of him, and Beatrice had accepted it for far too long. This year he used William Otter's resignation as his reason. It would have been more believable if this were the first time she had seen him like this. Today, without her children around, she felt anxious and hopeful she would not be separated from her husband, too.

"Is something bothering you, my love?" she asked, breaking the silence.

"No," he replied.

"You are a terrible liar," she shot back. "I am quite used to your silences, but picking at your food like a child? That is simply worrisome."

Henry shrugged. "I suppose I just miss the boys. I am beginning to notice that meals without them aren't the same."

That much was true, Beatrice thought. When Henry returned from the Academy, he had seemed downtrodden and burdened, but he still had managed to put on a happy face in a foolhardy show for her. He was using the truth of missing his sons to lie about what was actually bothering him. Beatrice could feel it.

"If you will excuse me, my dear, I cannot eat another bite," Henry added. "I am going to take a walk. Perhaps some air will help me clear my head."

"Where are you going? I'd like to come with you," Beatrice proposed.

"I do not know where I am going," Henry said crossly. "I just need to be alone for a while. I won't be gone long." The king pushed his chair back, rose, and took his leave.

For twenty-four years Beatrice had put up with this behavior, never pressing the matter for fear of her husband's distance growing worse. *If it's secrecy he wants, then it is secrecy he'll get.* It was a gross invasion of his privacy, she knew, but after so many years of nothing but dismissals and gloomy looks, she had to learn the truth.

Once Henry had a sizable lead, Beatrice gave chase, leaving the kitchen attendants to clear the table. She discarded her shoes as she passed through the palace gardens, knowing all too well that Henry's sharp ears would likely pick up the sound of her steps if she got too close. Beatrice waited until Henry was well beyond the fourth palace gate before continuing after him.

From what she could tell, it didn't look as though he had brought any Knights of Rahm. He had ordered them to stay behind, as was his way whenever he took these mysterious walks. Only Sollyria, hanging at his hip, would keep him from harm. This would make her mission much easier. She gave a wordless gesture to the Knights guarding the inner gate to stay put. They gave their usual nod, but Beatrice could feel a certain reluctance.

With her silk cloak wrapped about her body, the queen passed through the shade of the four walls and made her way through the streets like a phantom, never losing sight of her husband, who traveled one hundred yards ahead of her.

The stone of the street was rough and warm against her bare feet, but it was immaterial to her. Beatrice had spent the majority of her life traveling without shoes, whether she was walking with her brother along the Manasq Hills on the outskirts of Roleigh, or riding with her father. It was not until she came to Astymere that she finally began to wear them wherever she went.

The sea of faces offered her perfect cover. The day was clear after a rain that lasted for three days, and everyone was taking advantage of the sunny weather. Even if Henry had suspected he was being followed, he never would have been able to pick Beatrice out of the crowd. Despite this, she took no risks and kept her distance.

The king rounded the streets into Eastslope and marched straight past the Mouth of the Mountain. *If he keeps on this road, we will come to the Holy Way. What could he possibly want in Northslope? He hasn't walked those streets of his own volition since Darian's funeral.*

Northslope wasn't that strange a destination for Beatrice; she went there often to pray and give thanks to Rahm for his continued favor toward her family, to Mahtem the Mother for a bountiful crop, and to Tyranion, the Heavenly King, to keep his protective eye upon the world of Antheira.

Her prayers to Tyranion surely would have earned Henry's ire. Though the High Faith was not banned in the Western Kingdoms, it was not kindly looked upon after the religious persecution imposed by the Raelians for centuries. Though she held little love for Tyranion, or any of the five High Gods, she understood that the power of the Heavenly and the Worldly were what truly kept the world in balance.

Her prediction proved true, for within the hour, Beatrice found they had both come to the point where North and Eastslope met each other, with the First Street becoming the Holy Way. As she followed her King in his descent, she began to smell the heavy scent of incense that served as a defining feature of the borough. With dozens of large temples dedicated to each of the ten gods, incense burned twenty-four hours a day here, for the temples were never closed to weary souls in search of guidance.

The humming activity of Eastslope significantly dropped off when they crossed into the religious heart of the city. It was a solemn place that never roused much activity, and the streets were rarely crowded. The largest mass of people assembled in Northslope in recent memory had gathered for the funeral of Lord

Carovensa. It seemed that the death of a beloved public figure was what it took to summon the citizens from their homes and temples.

Perhaps he has taken up habit of praying to a High God and wouldn't be able to bear the shame if I found out. She chuckled to herself and immediately shrugged the thought off. *The Beast will wake and Hell will ignite before anything like that ever happens.* A small fear began to grow in the back of her mind that Henry was going to meet a secret lover, but that too subsided. *The women of Northslope aren't the type.*

The Holy Way descended the slope of the mountain and ran straight to the Northern Gate. There, it flattened and split off to the west onto the Avenue of Memory. Henry took the turn and continued on. *Gods, perhaps this was a mistake.* For the first time since she had decided to follow her husband, Beatrice suddenly feared what she would find at the end of this journey.

The Avenue of Memory ran parallel to the city wall until it merged with the Trident's Way of Westslope. But Henry did not follow the road all the way through. He stopped exactly where Beatrice prayed he wouldn't: the Tombs. The sizable public cemetery held small graves, urns placed in small shrines of marble, and larger, more elaborate mausoleums for those of higher social status.

The great, hundred-foot city wall loomed over the rooftops as Beatrice passed through the iron gates of the ghostly cemetery. She had slowly closed in on her husband since they had crossed into Northslope; now, his black cloth tunic contrasted sharply with the white stone around him.

The queen could see the gray in his hair now, using the smooth, worn headstones as cover. At a distance of one hundred yards, surrounded by a sea of faces, Beatrice had been perfectly invisible. But at this proximity, and with fewer souls about, Henry's keen senses would be able to pick her out if she wasn't careful. Even with her bare feet, one snapped twig could put the king on alert. Even amidst the heavy scent of incense, one stiff breeze could blow her scent straight into his nose, and the whole trip would have been for nothing.

On their current path, Beatrice hoped he would turn right to visit the Red Wall, built in remembrance of the thousands who lost their lives in the Endless War. Built entirely of polished firestone, the curved wall sat before a reflecting pool, as smooth and clear as a mirror. The names of the victorious dead were all inscribed upon it, milky white against the blood-red tone.

But Henry turned left and made his way past the small headstones and urn casings. He entered what could have been a small village made entirely of large, carefully carved tombs. They ranged in size from modest shrines, all the way up to complex, massive mausoleums, adorned with columns of marble and painted concrete. Gargoyles and demons guarded some; others had statues of ancestors standing watch over the resting dead.

Directly ahead of her husband, Beatrice could see an elaborate, bone-white tomb with two large red eyes made entirely of rubies mortared into the stone; polished obsidian served as piercing black pupils opened wide. *The eyes of Rahm keep watch over them. Whoever is inside must have been of great importance.* Beatrice moved behind the statue of a lower lord that looked as though it hadn't been tended to in decades, covered over with dirt and lichens. She lowered herself down and began her watch.

She sat for ages as she waited for Henry to reemerge. If it hadn't been for the large tuft of grass that had gone untouched, she might have lost feeling in her backside. She began to feel foolish for the lengths she was going to in order to learn the truth about her husband's gloom. *Little girls behave in such ways. You are a queen. Surely you could have thought of a better way than this.*

Still, she was no longer in a position to doubt herself. She had made the trip and was going to have to see it through. Several possibilities flowed through her head. In order to keep herself calm and her thoughts clear, she convinced herself that the tomb belonged to Henry's father, King Harruld, Karrok-Ehl, who had died when Henry was twenty-six. She had never known him, but Henry always spoke fondly of him. Logic told her that Harruld would naturally be buried in the Dark Wood, in Karna'Sharahm, but for her nerves' sake, she held onto the thought.

At long last Henry appeared from beneath the two red eyes above the flowery iron gate. His steps were slower and more cumbersome than they had been on his way in. His eyes appeared red and puffy, as though he had been weeping.

Beatrice crouched low behind her guardian statue as Henry passed and waited until he rounded the corner. He hadn't smelled her, to her relief, for he kept on walking without hesitation. Once he was out of sight, she rose, dusted herself off, and made her way up the white steps of the tomb.

The stoop appeared to be freshly swept, and the smooth stone was so clean it shone as if it had been polished. Special care had been dedicated to this place. As she pushed the gate open, it didn't make a sound. Even the hinges were regularly oiled. *Henry has gone to great lengths to make sure this soul is taken care of.*

Beatrice grabbed one of the iron rings on the double doors, hesitated for a moment, then gently pushed her way in. The walls were all lined with the red daisies that grew in abundance under the canopy of Karna'Sharahm, and candles and two sticks of incense gave the room a faint, sweet scent. Though she was closed in with it, it seemed that the smell was not nearly as overwhelming as it was out on the streets of Northslope. The rectangular walls rounded out on the far side of the room, where two stone slabs sat in the middle of the floor.

One was a full-sized sarcophagus; the other was little more than a tiny marble slab lying less than a foot away to the right. Surrounding them were three wooden latticework windows, and above each was another pair of red ruby eyes, looking down on the resting dead. *Not only do the eyes of Rahm keep watch over the entrance, they keep a protective gaze on the souls themselves. Turn around and leave. Now.* But despite her inner demand, Beatrice continued to walk forward, the dread of her discovery urging her on instead of forcing her to turn back.

She approached the large sarcophagus with her eyes closed and laid her hand on the cool stone. With all of her will, she forced her eyes open and beheld the awful truth she had wanted so desperately to avoid:

Here Lies Emilia of the House Karrok
Princess by Marriage
Gave her Life to Perpetuate the Line of Astymir
Beloved Wife and Giving Mother
4960 A.S.-4982 A.S.

This was his first wife, his first love. Reeling, Beatrice almost felt as though she would be sick as she looked down on the woman that Henry had lost so many years ago. He never spoke of her, and any mention of her name would send him into a rage. It was a part of his past that she had never been allowed to enter. Beatrice fell to her knees to look upon the tiny slab that lay beside the Princess of Astymere:

Here Lies Harmyn of the House Karrok
Heir Apparent to the Heart of the Mountain
Passed Before His Time
4982 A.S.

At this sight, Beatrice fell to the floor and wept. Wept for the pain her husband had been carrying for over thirty years; wept for the future that was robbed from him; wept for the poor souls who were lost so she could sit beside Henry in the Mouth of the Mountain. She wept for the child who had to die before it took a breath so her son could breathe in his place, and for the first time in over twenty years, Beatrice felt like an outsider, and very much alone.

IT WAS NEARLY A WEEK before Beatrice could manage to get away from the Capital. On a typical day she would walk the streets of Vita Astym, taking in the post-storm sun and smelling the rich scent of the recent rain. Today, she had her attendants ready her carriage for transport from the palace to Kar Wallis on the southern bank of the Krystal River. The trip, usually less than three hours, had taken over four at the sluggish pace they were bound to. Despite the weather the past days, the air was thick and sweltering, causing every move to feel like a struggle.

The green fields that usually flew by had crawled past her window as the Northrode now stretched its way through the Cayne Forest of pine trees. Beatrice had practically soaked through her green-trimmed black gown by the time the carriage entered flat country once more. To the left, the road forked off through the lush countryside. Signs indicated that the city of Yarnain, the last settlement before reaching Kar Wallis, was only three miles off.

"Kar Wallis is in sight, my Queen!" yelled the driver from above as Volkysian's Hill came into view. The carriage had begun to slow, and the cracks in the stone below had Beatrice bouncing mildly with each spin of the wheel. *Will Raymund tell Henry I called on him?* Beatrice had been passing the thoughts through her mind during the course of travel, effectively ruining any peace she may have found.

She wasn't one to deal in the shadows, but she needed to know the truth. Her King was not one to keep secrets, especially of this magnitude. Beatrice knew all too well how the loss of family could make one as fragile as glass. If the wound went as deep as Beatrice thought, she might never get the truth out of him.

If anyone could help, if there was anyone she could trust, it was Lord Raymund Wallis. He had been a brother to Henry from the time he could walk, and a beloved friend and mentor to the queen since the day she first arrived in the Crescent. It was he who had brought her before Henry for the first time. His calm demeanor and raucous humor had kept her from falling to pieces that day, and he had quickly become a dear confidant.

The estate sat atop a piece of bright green land, thick with trees, the boundary of which was marked off by an endless row of tightly manicured hedges that wrapped around the property, adorned with blood red roses. In days long gone, a twenty-foot wall of iron and stone surrounded by three separate, spike-filled trenches had stood in place of the hedge. A harder barrier for a harder time.

The entrance, a bronze gate built into the hedge itself, served as the only visible opening into the property border and stood wide open. Through the gateway the road stretched on for another half mile, climbing Volkysian's Hill, upon which Kar Wallis was built overlooking the Krystal River. Bright flowers lined the path, with overhanging trees covering the road with relieving shade. The orchards were nearly at full bloom, each tree bearing a fruit of a different color than the one next to it, many nearly ripe and ready for the first harvest of the year.

Kar Wallis was the oldest of the ancestral homes, and it showed in its design. While the vast property was bright and lovely, the castle itself was a smoky gray and most unpleasant to the eye. In the days of the First Kings, the rule of the Karrok family was not absolute, and factional war had raged on and off for nearly two hundred years.

Kar Wallis had been built as a means of defending Karrok-controlled territory in the Heartlands from rebels and lesser kings in the Northern Tip, and its tall towers, spiked walls, and pointed steeples had not been changed, even to the present day. The Wallis family had gone to great lengths to beautify their land, but the castle remained a clear looking glass into the brutish past, and Lord Raymund sought to keep it that way.

He spent most of his time either inside his office or out riding along the banks of the river. The tranquility relaxed him, especially after his sparring or particularly long Royal Council meetings. He was overseeing what appeared to be an extensive renovation on the eastern wall of the castle as the queen's carriage approached. The party rolled to a stop as they passed through the southern gate and into the heart of the fortress.

The carriage door swung open, revealing a Shadow Knight already waiting, his black armor drinking in the harsh sunlight. *How these men haven't already dropped from heatstroke, I shall never know.* Beatrice reached out and took his offered aid. His grip was like iron, strong enough to crush every bone in her hand, or so she imagined. The cabin had grown sultry, but the open door let in a breeze, cooling the sweat beading on her skin.

"Thank you." She nodded to her personal guard and stepped down onto the gravel.

Lookouts in the tall towers of Kar Wallis must have seen her carriage coming, and two hundred sworn swords to High Lord Raymund Wallis had assembled within the great courtyard to receive the queen, along with all the rest of the household, including Raymund himself. The small crowd that gathered all bent the knee as Beatrice emerged from her carriage. With a smile, Lord Raymund rose to greet his friend.

"My Queen!" he yelled, rushing to kiss her hand, dust covering his own from cutting stone just minutes before. After this last courtesy was seen to, he wrapped her in his arms, mindless of the sweat that clung to him. "My heavens, for you to come here in this heat! I would be sitting in an iced bath if I were you."

"If the heat keeps up as they predict, I shall have plenty of time for that! It could be worse—I could be working myself like a dog in the midst of a heat wave," she said, jabbing at her host.

Raymund laughed, but his eyes showed an utter lack of shame, as though he would be doing no differently were the day even hotter.

"What brings you here?"

"I am in grave need of your council, Lord Raymund. I wonder if we could speak in private."

"Of course, anything, my Queen," he said, his face growing solemn. "Let's move this inside for a cup of cool water and perhaps some wine." Raymund led their way through the solid oak doors bearing the same spikes as those mounted on the walls of the keep.

Dawn, Raymund's wife and Lady of House Wallis, sat in the castle library on a lounge chair with her feet up, tapping them to a tune she hummed to herself. The Wallis library held bookshelves on two opposite sides of the room, stretching from the floor to the high vaulted ceiling. The doors leading out to a balustrade overlooking the orchards were left open to create a cross breeze.

Dawn's eyes were shut and her head back looking up at the ceiling as Raymund and Beatrice entered. She was fanning herself with the book she held, and sweat glistened on her head and chest, even dressed as lightly as she was in a thin riding dress dyed a vibrant yellow. She lowered her head and beamed at Beatrice.

"I see you're reading your birthday present," Beatrice said with a wide smile as she entered the library. Dawn rose with exuberant joy and rushed to greet the queen. The small freckles upon her nose and cheeks fascinated Beatrice. Dawn's beauty always seemed to take her by surprise.

The book, *The Tale of Andron and Ramille*, an old story of two lovers rejected by the gods during the time of their rule on Antheira, was well known, and Beatrice's favorite. She could hardly believe it when Lady Dawn had told her she had never read it and sought to rectify that immediately.

"It is a wonderful way to pass the time on days like this," Lady Wallis said, bending the knee before the queen, then kissing both of her tanned cheeks and taking her hands. As short as she was, poor Lady Dawn had to stretch as far as her toes would go in order to reach Beatrice's face.

"For the wrong reasons," the queen chuckled, jesting at the book's newfound usage as a fan.

The room held three chairs around a table in the corner, and a couch and a lounge chair adjacent to each other in the middle of the room, atop a soft red carpet. The group moved to the corner chairs and sat.

"My Queen, I must apologize," Dawn said once they were all seated. "I would have met you outside with everyone else, but it seems *someone* neglected to inform me you were here." She cast a sharp look over at Raymund. He shot a sheepish smile back at her, shrugged, looked down, and began to twiddle his thumbs. Dawn chuckled despite her displeasure, as she often did when Raymund put effort to it.

Alyd, the Head of House, walked in carrying a silver tray with three moistened glasses of water.

"My apologies, my Lord," he said as he dispersed the glasses. "I tried to keep them chilled as long as possible. I only hope they are still cool."

"It's more than fine, Alyd," Raymund stated. "Now leave us be, and make sure no one disturbs us. Our Queen has asked to speak privately."

Beatrice had only requested Lord Raymund, but knew she could trust Dawn just as well. Alyd bowed deeply before Beatrice and slid out of the room without a sound.

"What is the meaning of your visit, my Queen?" Raymund asked.

"I have recently become aware of a piece of my husband's history—two pieces, actually." Raymund looked at her blankly, as did Lady Dawn. Beatrice sipped her water. It dripped down her throat and chilled her empty stomach. Her stress over the situation had killed her hunger as of late, and she had eaten little. She returned the cup to the table and kept her elbows on her knees. "I have found Princess Emilia's tomb, Raymund. And I now know that Henry visits her and their child regularly. He has hidden them from me. I just hope to understand, so maybe, in time, our King could put them to rest."

Raymund looked to his wife, pursing his lips tightly. Then he leaned forward and brought his hands together in a fist. "Do you really want to know? I promise you; it won't bring you comfort. There is only pain to be found behind that door."

Beatrice nodded.

"Very well. They met when Henry was twenty-three and Emilia was nineteen. I was with him that day, and let me tell you, the moment he saw her in the Bazeira, he froze—truly froze, as though the gods had turned his very flesh to stone. From that moment on, he spent every free moment with her, and she often joined us on rides through the country, usually sharing Henry's saddle. If I recall correctly, I believe she even joined us on a hunt or two. She was wild and untamed, just like him, but she had a gentler, more tender heart, and she fostered the first changes that would lead him to become the man he is today. Their love was beautiful, but also quite dangerous. Emilia, you see, though Avaari, was a commoner, the daughter of a cobbler that kept his shop just outside the Bazeira. Not only that, but King Harruld had promised Henry to the daughter of one of the Elders, a girl by the name of Tamira. When word that Henry had given himself to a commoner got out, Tamira's father, Lord Genccin, demanded Emilia's head and a public apology from Henry and the king. In a fit of rage, Henry challenged Lord Genccin to a duel before the very steps of the Mouth of the Mountain. Henry won, of course, and King Harruld banished Lord Genccin after Emilia convinced Henry to spare the lord's life. Henry then proclaimed to the city that Emilia was to be his bride. They were married within a fortnight in a small ceremony, but King Harruld did not attend; it was quite the scandal at the time. Aside from the king's displeasure, they had a truly blessed two years together as man and wife.

"When we first learned she was pregnant, the kingdom rejoiced, while dear friends and distant acquaintances alike toasted to their blessing. But it was a difficult pregnancy from the start. Emilia was often weak and ill, despite the best efforts of the Great Healer. We worried she might not bring the child fully to term. When her time finally came, people were out on the streets praying for her and the child's safety. But there are some things even the gods can't give. The cord wrapped around the child's neck so tightly that the root ripped from her womb, causing her to bleed to death, and the child, poor Harmyn, he was dead before he even drew a breath. Shortly after, King Harruld died as well, and Henry wasn't the same for years. You have helped him a great deal, my Queen, but he has never truly healed."

Beatrice felt several silent, burning tears roll down her face.

"I told you that there was only pain to be found. I regret to say our King has had an unfair hand dealt to him."

"I understand why he may not wish to speak of it," Beatrice admitted.

"How did you find the tomb?" Raymund asked.

Beatrice couldn't possibly tell him the truth. She would look impulsive, irrational—like a child.

"I was paying my respects at the Red Wall," she started. It was not entirely untrue. The Red Wall was quite close to the princess's tomb, and after she had composed herself, she had gone to pay her respects before heading home. "Henry had been acting strange the entire day and I could see he needed to be alone, so I left. I was lighting a candle, praying for the souls of the fallen, when he walked past me in the cemetery, unaware of my presence, and entered their tomb. He was in there for quite some time, so I knew whomever rested there had to be of great importance. When he left, he looked notably upset—more so than I have ever seen him. So, I went in and saw the sarcophagi." Beatrice had her feet entangled the entire time she spoke. The muscles flexed in her forearm as she wrung her hands.

"You followed him, didn't you?" Raymund asked. Beatrice leaned into the back cushion, doing her best to feign being insulted. She was, of course, but not nearly as much as she would have been if the accusation hadn't been true.

"I did not," the queen declared in her defense.

"But, my Queen, you did."

"How would you know?" she retaliated.

"Yes…how would you know?" Dawn asked, giving her husband a speculative look.

"Simple, really. If you had just happened upon him in the tombs, you would have tried to join him, and he would have known you were there. The only reason he didn't is because you wished it so. Not to mention you come to me, and not him, asking for my total, most solemn confidence. So again, I ask. Did you follow him?"

Beatrice narrowed her eyes. He truly did know her too well. "I'd best be getting to that ice bath, Lord Wallis. It appears my mind has been sapped by the heat."

Chapter 8

The Royal Marshal Academy: Astymere
10th Day of the First Month
5014 A.S.

Mayson cheered as Diero slammed his elbow into Blayk's jaw in an upward swing. Mayson watched along with the rest of the class, who sat with their legs crossed under them as the two combatants sparred in the center of the courtyard. Students passed by going every which way, some circulating around the rest of the group awaiting their turn to fight, others stopping to watch the spar itself.

Blayk Mortryn was seventeen, had at least four inches on Diero, and was at least twenty pounds heavier. Nevertheless, the young lord was doubly quick, and the skills Henry had taught the boys allowed him to work circles around his larger opponent.

"A fine hit, Diero!" Mayson shouted from the ring of spectators. "Don't let him regain his balance!"

Blayk stumbled to the ground with an agonized groan and rose quickly as Diero remained still to size him up. With a furious glare, he spat into his hand, expelling a molar and a small puddle of deep red, which fell to the ground at his toes. He threw himself at the younger boy, crying out in untethered, unchecked rage. Diero darted his head beyond the reach of a wild haymaker and ducked below a second, prompting him to ram his forehead into his challenger's chest with full force. This stunned Blayk long enough for Diero to reach both hands around the boy's back and pull him into a shooting knee that found its home in his gut. Blayk flailed his arms, trying to regain balance. To finish his foe, Diero dropped his elbow into Blayk's back, knocking him to the ground. With a blow from Drill Master Perry's whistle, the session was brought to an end.

Mayson found himself nearly sitting up on his toes by the end of the bout. Their training sessions at the palace were not child's play, but the lessons at the Academy were at another level, often leaving Mayson anxious.

"Blayk! What in the frozen hell was that?" the Drill Master demanded. "You let a damn child put you on the ground, do you realize that?" Richerd Perry had been the hand-to-hand combat instructor at the Academy for nearly twenty years. As loud and brazen as he was, he had become famous for his ability to turn even the most softhearted dandy into an efficient killer.

"Did you happen to notice he is faster than I am?" Blayk asked as he slowly rose to face the Drill Master. *Crack.* Without a word, Perry unleashed a back-hand that landed square across Blayk's cheek.

"Did you notice that *I did not ask for a fucking excuse*? Get your head on straight, boy, or by Rahm's eyes, I will send you down to play at love taps with the first-years where you belong!" Perry's voice filled the entire yard, echoing multiple times and scaring the wits out of all in attendance. School legend had it that Perry didn't have a real voice, but a hurricane trapped in his throat, and no one had any cause to doubt it.

"Diero," Perry barked, but with much less bite. "I'll be gods-damned, son. It seems you and your pale friend over there are the least useless first-years I've ever seen. Well done." Diero dipped his head in thanks. "I'll only say this—you hesitate too much. On the battlefield, hesitation will get you killed. If you get a man off his feet, you are to ensure that he does not get back *on* them. Understood?"

"Yes, sir," Diero said, his breath still a bit thin from the drill. He watched as Blayk walked away, rubbing his red cheek. *Crack.* The drillmaster struck Diero upside his head, making even Mayson wince with pain.

"Well fucking done!"

The advanced combat classes had been hellish the first two weeks of term, but most of Mayson and Diero's turmoil was more predicated on the reputation of the classes themselves. They were still only thirteen, expected to compete against young men who had been studying the art of war for years. They were battered and bruised, just as they had expected to be, but to their surprise they were able to keep up with most of the older students. Some, like Blayk, they bested rather easily, earning them little love from their elder classmates. Their attempts at being cordial and civil had earned them further ire, if for no other reason than the embarrassment of being defeated by younger men.

"I heard his tooth crack from where I was sitting," Jalen said as he approached the pair, fixing his bag upon his shoulder. Both boys were packing their fighting gloves into their satchels and preparing to return to the barracks. "Your elbow must be singing to you right now."

Diero snorted. "I'm used to it. It will take more than that oaf's jaw to cause me any trouble."

"Oh, of course. How could I forget? You are invincible," Mayson said with unhidden sarcasm. Diero had a long-running habit of downplaying his injuries, brushing them off as though they were nothing but scrapes and scratches. It had always annoyed Mayson and worried Beatrice tremendously.

"You'd better believe it."

"Perry is right, though, you realize?" Jalen said.

"About what?"

"If you hesitate like that in a real fight, it could cost you—dearly."

"He was on his back. I will not apologize for preferring to beat a man when he is on his feet. I don't care if it kills me. If they actually manage to strike me down, then they deserve the kill."

"Idiot." Mayson could only shake his head, for he could see the all-too-common look in his brother's eyes whenever he would plant his foot down on a matter. Once he got that look, one would have an easier time convincing a horse it was a boar than changing Diero's mind. "Have it your way. But when you're stabbed from behind by a man you've turned your back on, don't come crying to me."

"The day I find a dagger in my back is the day I grow tits and parade around in a silk gown."

Diero was so unreservedly sure of himself. A noble quality at times, but dangerous for a man of the sword.

"I'll see you both at dinner," Jalen said as he scooped up his satchel and turned to go. "I'm off to try to stay awake for my next class."

"Which class is that?" Mayson asked.

"Battle Strategies of the First Kings and their Modern Applications. Pray for me. I'll need a miracle not to fall asleep right in front of Master Hadwyn." He jogged off, disappearing into the cluster of students milling from building to building.

The surf around the island was rough that day, and they could hear the waves crashing against the rocks even from the heart of the island. The breeze picked up, and the boys could feel the subtle touch of ocean spray on their skin.

They made their way across the school grounds to the barracks. The high noon sun felt warm, the freshly cut grass stiff against the soles of their feet. They entered the shade of their dormitory, eager to change into fresh clothes, for their combat uniforms were sticky with heavy sweat. They passed Kristian, Kip, and Teren on their way out, who asked them how the combat lesson had gone. The three of them had not qualified for the advanced courses as the royals had and were always eager to hear tell of what to expect. After a brief talk, the young three hurried off, leaving the royals to finally go inside.

The advanced class was the only one to let out at noon, so the barracks were deserted aside from the students who had just been released. As the boys approached their bunks, they could see the majority of the advanced combat class had already lain down on their own beds. They would nap before their lecture in forging started, right after the midday meal, and the class would last until dinner. But halfway down the corridor of beds, they could see a small congregation of students huddled around each other, several of whom turned to glare at the first-years who had been thrust into their ranks.

"They don't look very happy," Diero remarked as he peeled off his combat uniform and hung it on the end of his cot to dry. He wearily plucked a fresh linen shirt and pants from his trunk and slid them on, a look of sweet comfort spreading across his face. Mayson had done the same but remained expressionless. He came to notice that he was not nearly as outwardly expressive as Diero.

"Very astute of you," he replied as he burrowed into his pillow and closed his eyes. "We have been getting looks since our first day in class. Let them glare all they want. It won't make them better fighters."

"You took the words right out of my mouth," Diero said as he dropped onto his bunk. All was silent once his head hit the pillow. Even the young Carovensa lordling was too tired to keep up his usual banter.

Mayson had lain there for barely a minute before the bunk rose up beneath him, flipped over, and tossed him out, slamming him against the hard floor and knocking the wind from his lungs. He attempted to take a pained breath as the bed was lifted off him, crashing to the ground several feet away. When he opened his eyes, he found that two of his classmates had moved to pin his arms down as two more pinned his feet. He looked desperately to his right to see what had become of Diero, who had his arms restrained behind his back by two students as Blayk pummeled his midsection.

"Think about this the next time you want to act like a big hero, Bright Eyes," a familiar voice said.

Mayson turned back to look on his attacker, and he could make out the face of Brentin Kallyst, the first person to challenge him the day he had arrived at the Academy.

The prince had found himself face to face with him several times in class, all at the older boy's choosing. His anger over his initial defeat had served as fuel for his attacks, briefly getting the better of the prince, but the fights always ended the same way, with Mayson triumphant. Before this moment, Mayson had begun to feel sorry for him.

"What the hell are you doing, Kallyst? Brave man you are, attacking someone while they sleep, and not even having the stones to come at him alone. Do I frighten you that much? Do this, and everyone will know you are a coward."

The prince was so close to the older boy's face that he could make out the hundreds of small freckles across his nose and cheeks, and the mud-brown colors of Brentin's eyes.

Brentin then dug his knee into Mayson's chest, so hard Mayson thought he would crack a rib as he leaned in close. "Tell anyone, and we will make your life a living nightmare. We know where you sleep and will lose nothing in giving you some restless nights. Speaking of, you look exhausted. Let me help you get back to your sweet dreams." Brentin lifted his fist, clenching tightly.

"Don't miss," Mayson said.

Brentin snarled back. "Good night, Bright Eyes." With a powerful blow, Brentin Kallyst shot his fist into the prince's eye, which still hadn't fully healed from his first fight on initiation day. Mayson's eyes shut, and his mouth hung open as he lay upon the cold floor, gasping for breath. The only sound that kept him company as the older students returned to their cots was the labored, painful sounds of Diero's coughing as he curled into a ball, clutching his side.

"WHAT IS THE MEANING OF THIS?" A familiar voice broke the silence. Mayson wasn't sure how long he had been lying there. Diero still lay curled in a ball. The prince turned over to see Addam scanning the room. A look of worry and confusion grew on his face as he saw the dried blood around Mayson's eye. The sun was well past noon now, and though the barracks had filled slightly, none had dared come near Mayson and Diero.

"Seems our future king doesn't know how to keep his feet," Brentin scoffed from his bunk on the other end of the room. His cronies synchronized their laughter like a practiced chorus.

"And it seems to me that several fifth-years will be emptying chamber pots for a month if they don't mind their tongues," Addam retorted, mimicking their laughter.

He helped Mayson and Diero to their feet. The two boys looked upon the stricken stare of the older students' faces as they moved the cot back in place and sat upon Diero's bed. Mayson couldn't help but smile.

"You two all right?" Addam asked, placing his hands on their shoulders. Before they could answer, the door to the barracks swung open, revealing Marshal Qirk, sporting a harder look than usual.

He scanned over Mayson and Diero. "Stand at attention," he ordered. The boys stood, even Brentin and his gaggle. The wind, which had blown so strong before, seemed to hold its breath in the tense silence. Qirk cast his hard gaze on Addam. "What is the meaning of this, Riding Master?"

"I believe these first-years were attacked, sir," Addam replied. Qirk gave an indignant snort and stepped face-to-face with Mayson and Diero, looking back and forth between the two of them. Mayson could see the wheels in his mind turning as the Marshal furrowed his brow.

"Is that the way of it, Karrok-Aht?" Qirk grumbled, leaning in close to Mayson's good eye. "Has royal blood been dishonorably spilt under the protection of this Academy?" Something in his tone was too suggestive. *If I reveal what happened, it would be a smear against this Academy's reputation, and, more importantly, his. Gods, I could actually make this worse if I say it out loud.*

"It was an accident, sir," Mayson said after much inner deliberation. Diero began to raise his voice in objection, but the hard look Mayson shot him seemed to get the point across, and he piped down. Mayson shot the same look over to Brentin as the Marshal turned away, fighting his own rage at the disgusting smirk Brentin gave him.

"An accident, you say," Qirk mused. "Very well. I think tonight will be as good a night as any for the two of you to pull your first watch duty atop the walls. Removing the two of you from these barracks should prevent such *accidents* from happening again, I would think." Brentin and his thugs tried to stifle their chuckles, to no avail. The Marshal burned them with his fiery glare for the first time since he entered the room. "And you lot. I believe I heard the riding master mention something about emptying chamber pots. I am inclined to agree. We wouldn't want you all to have your own accidents, would we? You can start with mine. *Now.* Understood?"

"Yes, sir," they replied as one, every pair of eyes cast on the ground. With a snap of the Marshal's fingers, the lot of them scampered from the barracks like frightened rabbits. Mayson fought a smirk of his own.

"As for our two young royals," Qirk continued, "use the rest of the day to heal yourselves in the baths, and clean that eye up, Karrok. I expect you both atop the wall at sundown. Dismissed."

LATER THAT NIGHT THE BOYS STROLLED atop the perimeter wall. The walkway was barely wide enough to fit the two of them abreast, and some of the worn stones and mortar made for uneasy footing in spots. Mayson wondered how in times of battle any soldier had room to move, much less fight. The parapets came up to their belly, giving no relief from the brutal wind coming off the bay.

"An accident," Diero muttered as he clutched his cloak tight to him. "We could have had them out of here before sundown, and you tell Qirk it was an accident."

"And their troubles would be over, while ours would have just begun," Mayson replied. "Qirk would not have looked kindly on us for publicly besmirching his and the Academy's reputations by revealing abuse and dishonorable behavior. It would have been five years of hell for us."

"Damn reputations!" Diero said dumbfounded. "You just let them get away with dishonoring us! If you had heard what Blayk said to me…"

"I haven't let anyone do anything, brother. I am buying us time to handle this ourselves. We may have to take a few more licks before our opportunity comes, but they will pay. Rahm as my witness, they will pay for what they have done."

The boys continued walking for a few minutes in silence, stopped, and Mayson leaned against the inner parapet, looking down upon the Temple of Red Flame. "I hear students have died taking their Final Test. And some of those who live are never the same again."

"I hear that the students who die in there are left to rot for all eternity," Diero replied. "They say the stench of death is strong enough to drop a man."

"Thousands of lies build thousands more. We will never know until our day comes."

"We could always try to sneak in."

"And what?" Mayson gasped. "Risk being expelled? After all I said about the Marshal having it in for us? I'm sorry, brother, but I refuse to be the first king expelled from the Academy."

"What do you think it is? The building is so small it's difficult to imagine something larger than a classroom."

"I'm not sure, but we will find out in due time. Whatever it is, I like to think it's the reason Qirk will expect more of us. Whatever is in that building will either destroy us, or turn us into legends…I can take the wait."

Diero now faced the dark, slumbering island. It was well past curfew. All but the guards who protected the Temple of Red Flame and the armory remained indoors on this bitter evening. He jerked his head at the sound of footsteps sprinting in the wind's momentary lapse. He tapped Mayson and pointed out five figures running toward an alleyway near the blacksmith. The figures paused and stood in a circle in the shadows.

"Violating curfew. Should we report it?" Diero asked.

"Let's observe a moment and see what they do." For a few minutes they didn't do anything. Two other first-years assigned to guard duty that night had come to join in their observation, but left when nothing else happened.

Suddenly, two of the five left the alleyway and headed right for the two guards in front of the Temple of Red Flame. They were going full steam for the front of the building.

Right in front of the guards? Oh, they are definitely asking for it.

Sure enough, the boys passed right in front of the entrance, throwing small rocks and forcing the guards to give chase. The unknown runners led them off in opposite directions, the sounds of their footsteps and hollering slowly fading into the night.

Immediately after the guards left, the other three figures appeared from the alleyway and headed for the door of the Temple.

"Those fucks! They're trying to get inside!" Mayson shouted.

"The hell with this! I'm not going to let them." Diero slid his training sword from the sheath at his hip. He started for the stairway, but Mayson grabbed his shoulder.

"Hold on a moment. We can't just leave our post! We'll be ordered here every night until end of term! Let's watch them closely, note their faces or anything identifiable about them, and then when our watch is up, we will report them. We'll go to Addam. The Marshal won't want to hear about it in the middle of the night."

Diero nodded, and slid his sword back into its home, watching as the group reached the doorway without a soul to stop them. Mayson watched for several minutes as they picked at the lock and chains binding the doors. To his shock, the chains came loose, and all three shadows slipped inside.

For minutes the boys waited, leaning over the stone ledge, gazing intently at the entryway. But nothing happened. The group never reappeared. The other pair on night watch passed again, and this time, their curiosity got the best of them.

"Did we miss anything?" asked Gaven Bantenas, a first-year student from the Heartlands.

"Two of our friends down there led the guards off while the others picked the lock and slipped inside," Diero said.

"We'll inform the guards when they return," Mayson continued. "You can go about your business." After a moment's hesitation, Gaven and his companion slipped by them once again, sighing and grunting for having missed the action.

Before long, the two guards returned, empty-handed. Even at this distance, the frustration on their faces could be read plainly as they approached the steps to the Temple. When they reached the top, Mayson observed as they dropped their shields and spears and fell to their knees to examine the loose chains. They spoke to each other in hurried whispers. The words didn't travel well through the wind, but the sound of panic in their voices drifted into Mayson's well-trained ears. He waited for the wind to die down before raising the alarm.

"Gentlemen!" he called. The two guards looked around for several confused moments before Mayson waved his arms to draw their attention.

"You have three uninvited guests inside the temple!"

Diero laughed as the two guards flew through the doors, practically tripping over each other. "That'll be good! I bet they weren't expecting the guards to be back when they walk out!"

The wind picked back up again out of the north, bringing the biting cold back along with it. Clouds moved across the clear sky, covering the light of both moons in a haunting light gray. Time passed slowly as the boys continued walking, all but frozen midway through their watch. They waited for the guards to reappear from the Temple, knowing they would have the culprits any minute now.

"Where could they be?" Diero asked as he began to fidget.

The faintest of sounds began to seep through the air in between wind gusts. It was so soft that Mayson wasn't sure he had really heard anything at all. One look at Diero, his unblinking eyes trained on the Temple, told him that his brother hadn't heard anything. Nevertheless, the faint sound persisted, like the whining of a tiny mosquito's wings.

Like a clap of thunder, the Temple doors burst open, and three figures came tearing out, screaming and wailing as though they had looked into the black eyes of the Beast himself. The two guards were close behind, trying to corral the chaos.

Mayson's blood curdled in his veins at the shrieks of his classmates, as if in an agony he'd never thought possible. The three of them were frantically hitting themselves, batting at some unseen source of pain. The largest of the intruders dropped to the ground and began rolling, covering himself in dirt and ripping the clothes from his body. Mayson and Diero stood rooted to the spot, frozen by the insanity unfolding before them.

As quickly as the noise had burst forth from the darkness behind those doors, the island had gone silent once again, aside from the barking of dogs and the howling of the wind. Candles and torches had been lit in several buildings since the commotion began, including the Masters' Quarters, home to all of the teachers and the Marshal's Manse.

He had to have heard it. I'm fairly certain my dead grandfather heard it.

Torches held by dark figures emerged one by one from the Masters' Quarters, hurrying toward the source of the noise. The guards beckoned them until every flame had congregated on the spot, illuminating the three boys upon the ground.

The two could wait no more. They found the nearest set of stairs and raced down to the grounds. Their cloaks, as heavy as they were, caught the frigid air like sails as they tore across the campus to see what had happened.

The Marshal crouched over a second-year who didn't have a single hair on his face. His eyes were shut as though he were asleep, but his body was rigid as a corpse. The same was true for his companion lying beside him. The larger boy's eyes were still open, but they saw nothing. While the others gave the appearance of deep sleep, he was frozen in a horrid visage, as though something had violently sucked the soul out of him.

Addam stepped out of the crowd, narrowly missing Sword Master Giulian Archer with his torch, and passing so close to Forge Master Buchanan that the wind of his movement put his candle out. He took the boys by their collars and walked with them back toward the wall.

"Get out of here, before the Marshal sees you. Go back to your posts and wait for me." They did not move. Their curiosity was still too strong to hear the serious tone of Addam's voice.

"What happened to them?" Mayson asked, planting his feet. Addam Wallis took on the fiery look of a High Lord, and for the first time in Mayson's memory, he feared him.

"I said, *go. Now.*" It was practically a whisper but it punched Mayson in the gut with its severity. He turned and made his way toward his post with Diero close behind.

The hours flew by as the two made round after mindless round about the ramparts. As the sun began to rise, Addam came to the top of the wall with two guards to relieve Mayson and Diero.

"What was that?" Mayson asked before Addam had fully emerged into the morning air.

"It was an accident," Addam replied.

Mayson eyed him suspiciously.

"Those boys went sticking their noses where they didn't belong," Addam added, "and they have paid a terrible price for it."

"Are they going to be okay?" Diero asked.

"Why should you care about three fools you've never so much as spoken to?"

"Their screams," Mayson began. Addam nodded as if he understood; Mayson almost felt it unnecessary to continue. "I've never heard anything like that before," he went on. "Did it have anything to do with what is inside the Temple? Does it have anything to do with the Final Test?"

"Yes," Addam said gravely as he led the two down the stairs of the northern gate and out into the growing light of dawn. There was so much more he wanted to say, Mayson could physically feel it, but the young Lord Wallis simply dipped his head and sighed.

"There is nothing I can tell you that will prepare you for what you will face down there. It isn't impossible, for many, including myself, have succeeded. But if you are as careless and foolish as that lot last night, you'll never see the sun rise again. And that is a promise."

Chapter 9

Gildara: The Gildarian Republic
25ᵗʰ Day of the Second Month
5014 A.S.

"Quit squirming, young lady. How am I ever to finish this dress if you keep kicking my needle away?" Olivia winced and attempted to remain still as her mother clumsily prodded at her gown to fix a small tear on the seam of her skirt, just below her hip.

"Mother, why do you *insist* on fixing every single tear and scuff on my dresses yourself? They never look the same after you've touched them, and Father could easily buy five more to replace each."

"My mother made this dress. I wore it when I met your father, and you will wear it when you meet your husband. I swear by the Heavenly King, you will."

Now that Olivia Goldblade was fourteen, by the laws set down by the Senate, she was eligible to be engaged, and she had endured her mother Attia's obsession over cultivating her appearance for the last month. As Olivia's father had risen in the ranks of society, Olivia knew her mother was desperate to marry her off to a member of the higher echelons they were now surrounded by- preferably a senator, certainly no lower than a mid-level minister, to cement the family's place among the upper crust.

"Are you so desperate to get rid of me?" Olivia asked, half in jest. "You'll find Amy to be poor company once I am out of the house."

"All I want is to make you a good match. If you were to marry Senator Casan, you would be the first lady in the family to marry a *senator*. Imagine how it would propel our name. Don't you want to be the first lady in this family to do something truly great?"

Truth be told, Olivia did have a hunger to do something great with her life. Her father had instilled in her a deep need for success simply by being himself. As she grew, she had watched him rise from a simple coin counter in the Hall of Revenue to one of the most powerful financiers in the entire Republic. She was at the cusp of her simple beginning; all she needed was to reach for the next rung on the ladder.

Attia wrestled the bottom of the dress one last time. "That should do it. Please try to keep it intact until after you meet Casan today. And brush your hair; we are leaving for the temple in twenty minutes." Her mother swept out to prepare herself for the sermons that afternoon at the Grand Temple of Tyranion, leaving a static energy hanging on the still air in the room.

Olivia turned to look in the oval mirror standing against the curved wall, her dress half in the light as she examined the work her mother had done. Her dark, wavy hair had finally grown past her shoulders, and her light, golden brown eyes caught the reflection of the morning sun in the glass. The dress, of a fine gold fabric, exposed her stomach, cupped her budding bosom, and wrapped around the back of her neck. It fell just above her feet and hugged her ample hips rather snuggly. It was a bit racy for her taste, but still a beautiful piece of work, and one never got a second chance at a first impression, as her father would always say.

She could barely see the thread peeking from behind the patch, but no spots of the blood she felt shed during her mother's ungainly sewing. She twirled the skirt, letting it fan out all around her, silently taking in the victory that she wouldn't have to find a replacement after all. She knew this dress would catch the eye of the young senator from the northern province of Branarda. Her mother had pointed him out to her on several occasions, and despite her apprehension toward the idea of being arranged, he truly was the most beautiful creature she had ever laid eyes on.

Olivia twirled around, listening to the creaks in the old floorboards that had long since become familiar, comforting voices, then fell into her feather bed. Her head nearly hit the wall, and she propped herself up quickly to peer over the windowsill and indulge in her daily habit of people-watching.

The mists of the last week had finally cleared, and thousands of voices filled the air with an endless humming. These wood and stone streets were as sweet as any home could get, but she hadn't always felt that way. She could remember the day her father announced he was moving his family to Gildara to take work in the Hall of Revenue. If she concentrated hard enough, she could almost feel the shudder that had run up her back when she saw the capital for the first time, visible through the branches of the Golden Grove.

They had approached from the north, taking the Marian Ramp from the forest floor, climbing nine hundred feet upward to the city that sat nestled among the branches. After the first hundred feet, Olivia had closed her eyes, unable to bear looking down from such heights.

But what was once an incomprehensible spectacle was now nothing more than a common sight. She had grown accustomed to the wooden and stone platforms supported by the gargantuan branches beneath. The city didn't seem so immense here in the forest canopy as it did from below. She had grown used to the brilliant light that bathed the streets as the sun passed through the bright gold leaves of the Golden Grove. *Over a million people live among these branches. Casan can have his pick of countless women who will throw themselves at him. Will I be anything more than another face that is paraded before him?*

Olivia's musing was broken by the sound of a frantic knock at the door. "Let me see, let me see!" Amy cried as she came barreling in, her crimson stola flowing behind her. Though twelve years old, Amy Goldblade had the energy and enthusiasm of a small child. Olivia loved her sister for it, but there were days when she found her excitement quite exhausting. Today, Amy amused her.

"Did Mother finish? Does the thread match well?"

"It's mother's sewing, what do you think?" Olivia responded, lifting her hand to reveal the mismatched repair job her mother had completed above her left leg.

"Oh, no! It's as if she doesn't even look at the thread before she uses it," Amy said. "No matter. A nice belt or sash will cover it perfectly. No one will even know."

"My thoughts exactly," Olivia said with a grin.

"Care to escort a lady to the temple?" Amy asked, holding out her arm and feigning the coy expression of a lady with a suitor.

"I would be honored," Olivia said with a deep, exaggerated bow.

The sisters walked arm-in-arm through their front door, down the oak staircase of their sizable stoop, and waited at the gate with Mylas and Holto, the captains of the Goldblade household guard. Both men were tall and broad, with noble, strong chins and thick arms. Each carried a brilliantly polished broadsword of gilded steel, each hilt fitted with rubies of varying size. Both had served in the Golden Legions some years back and, like most veterans of lower station, decided to put their experience to use in guarding the elites of the city and their families.

"Any guess as to when they will be ready, Domina?" Mylas asked.

Olivia slightly pitied the poor man. It was a warm enough day, but with his thick, crimson wool cloak fastened at his shoulders over his heavy golden breastplate, the heat must have been unbearable.

"Who can ever tell with those two?" Olivia replied. "Wouldn't you be more comfortable inside, out of the sun?"

"It is quite tempting, Domina, but our orders are to await your parents here," Holto said in his deep voice. "We've suffered worse days than this."

Olivia's conscience did not have to suffer long, for her parents emerged in a matter of moments. Her father escorted her mother by the arm, much as she and Amy had done earlier. The rest of the Goldblade guards—Lukas Pinna, Balian Armonas, Emanas Navalas, and Titas Palanas—walked beside them. Each wore the gilded breastplate and crimson cloak of men of the sword within the Republic.

Eduardas Goldblade was a somewhat short fellow, stout, with a rather bulbous nose. He possessed curly hair that had once been nearly black, but now was mostly gray with some white sprinkled in. His wife, Attia, seemed his opposite in practically every way— tall, slim, auburn-haired, and always wearing a practiced look of contempt for all those she deemed beneath her, which was nearly everyone. Her husband, on the other hand, greeted every soul he encountered with a great beaming smile and an embrace that made them feel they had been friends for years.

"Well, isn't this nice? Out and ready without even having to be told twice. This must be a special day indeed," Eduardas joked. "Shall we?"

"We shall, Dominaen," Mylas replied as he unlatched the iron gate to allow Holto and the Goldblades to go before him. The others formed up behind.

Eduardas wore a strange grin as the family passed through the moving sea of gold-and-crimson clad citizens.

"You seem particularly happy today," Olivia remarked to her father.

"I am—and a bit anxious, to be honest," he replied. "Tomorrow is a very important day for my offices."

"How so?"

"The Minister of Trade has called upon me to facilitate the reopening of trade routes heading west to the kingdoms along the coast."

"Dirt-worshipping barbarians, the lot of them," Attia snorted, which earned a chuckle from their sworn guards. Eduardas brushed her off as if he didn't hear, a skill he had sharpened over the years whenever his wife had something nasty to say.

"Why do they have to be reopened?" Amy asked.

"For years after the old Empire fell, the roads across the Great Plains weren't safe anymore," her father said. "Bandits and marauders preyed upon unarmed caravans until the trade routes dissolved completely. But within the last year, things have quieted down and the Great Plains have been deemed safe to travel by the Spear Lords of Dalan, so the Ministry is wasting no time in establishing trade. We lost quite a bit of income when those routes closed."

"Yes, and we gained countless refugees, courtesy of those savages," Mylas growled under his breath.

Olivia had heard the story before. When the armies of the West had broken through the Raelian borders, countless Raelian souls had fled to the Republic, with whom they held a strong relationship. For whatever reason, the Republic had decided to stay out of the conflict, despite their close ties. Thousands of the refugees still lived within the Gildarian borders, many living in squalor as beggars, while some managed to carve out modest livings for themselves.

"I don't understand why we want any relations with those monsters after what they did," Mylas went on. "I had always dreamed of walking the streets of the White City, and those heathens took it from me."

"Mylas, we all weep for Raelia. The world is a darker place without the light of the White City to guide it," said Eduardas. "But frankly, Raelia and the Kings of the West had been at war since before the First Senate. Though we called it the Endless War, it eventually would come to an end one way or another. What's important is that the West is finally beginning to heal, and it is my job to make sure it continues to heal. A friendship with these kings could prove quite beneficial to us. Olivia, dear, if you and your sister behave in the temple this afternoon, I may bring you two with me to meet with them."

Now there was a proposition Olivia could not refuse. She had spent years entertaining countless senators and tribunes and ministers as her father rose in status, but she had never met a king before, and she began to prepare the questions she would ask if afforded the chance.

The party came to Aeniad's Square, melting into the river of people slowly navigating toward the Grand Temple of Tyranion. The litters of several notable senators flitted by, marked by white leaves painted upon the drapes shielding the occupants from the morning sun. Olivia shot a look at her mother, who was eyeing the transports with a hungry gaze. The beasts carrying them grunted by a small crowd that had gathered at the Forus Fountain, where an Oraetar stood upon a small wooden stage, reading aloud from a golden scroll. Olivia trained in on him mid-sentence.

"…and the reward for any knowledge that leads to the return of Senator Taroen's kitchen beasts shall be three hundred gilders! You hear me correctly! A caentin for each of the three beasts, straight from the senator's pocket." Olivia watched as the small crowd excitedly murmured and clamored among themselves. Three hundred gilders, three caentins, were enough to get any common person licking their lips.

"Death strikes this city once again," he continued. "It has been confirmed by the City Watch that last night, as we all slept, the Grand Seeding Officer of the Fruiters Guild, Kaelid Nirosa, burned to death in his own home. There is currently no word as to what caused the fire, or just how many perished, but Officer Nirosa has been confirmed dead. Funeral rites shall be performed here in the square at the end of the week."

His voice trailed away as they inched closer to the temple. "Didn't you know Kaelid Nirosa, Father?" Olivia asked. Eduardas furrowed his brow.

"I believe I did at some point," he replied, "but not very well. I did some accounting for a few fruiters several years back and I think he may have been one of them. Nasty way to go if you ask me. Just goes to show you can't be too careful, even in your own home."

An hour later, the family sat silently in the Grand Temple of Tyranion as they listened to the recitation of the High Testament, as they had hundreds of times before. The High Priests of the Heavenly sang their praises and read through each book within the Testament with a well-practiced solemnity. Olivia stared unblinkingly into the five-pathed bridge mounted on the wall before her, connecting the five stars of the Heavenly Gods. Every prayer service began this way. The only difference was that today, the curly-haired, tanned Senator Casan sat beside her, as part of the planned arrangement Attia had set up. It was quite the accomplishment, being elected to the senate at only seventeen, and his parents believed it was worth every coin spent. The prospect of her daughter marrying him practically made Attia foam at the mouth.

The two exchanged several nervous smiles throughout the prayers, and by the time the sermon finally wound to a close, Senator Casan had clasped Olivia's hand in his, which she squeezed in turn. After her doubt earlier that day, the gesture was exhilarating, sending waves of energy across her skin that raised goose pimples and quickened her breath.

She lay alone that night, her eyes plastered open with the excitement that coursed through her body. She had met a kind, important man who might one day be her husband, and tomorrow she would be in the presence of kings. She rehearsed the moment she might first speak to one in her mind. *How do you—No, no, no, more proper. Good day, your Magnificence. That's stupid. Do I address them as Your Majesty? Your Highness? Will their guards even let me near them?*

The mere hour of sleep that night did nothing to soothe her restlessness throughout the day. Attia kept her and Amy cooped up in the house as she spent hour after hour trying to come up with the perfect ensemble with the aid of her maids.

Eduardas was more nervous than any of his family had ever seen him. He constantly spoke of today being the day that could destroy him or catapult him to glory. He showed signs of his anxiety as he gathered everything, double- and triple-checked all papers he would need for the meetings, and loaded the family into the carriage to make their way to the center of the city.

Eduardas dabbed at perspiration that had moistened his forehead just as the Goldblades approached the Hall of Revenue.

"Negotiations commence in ten minutes. Your dawdling will be the death of me," he complained.

The only souls that could be seen on the front steps of the Hall were the sentries standing guard, which fueled the fire of Eduardas' urgency. "They've all gone inside. Gods be damned, if I am late for my own negotiations, my credibility will never recover. Heavenly King, hurry up!" As his panic boiled over, he sprang from the crawling carriage, leaving his family and guards to give chase. He had an easier time slipping through the crowd than his larger sworn men-at-arms, quickly leaving them behind.

"I've never seen him move so fast for anything," Olivia gasped as she trudged along, trying to catch her father, lifting her skirts to avoid falling on her face.

"I didn't know he *could* move that fast," Amy replied, already losing her breath. As Eduardas' lead grew larger, Olivia paused to remove her shoes, which were only slowing her down. She looked back to keep track of her mother and sister, narrowly avoiding colliding with a merchant's beast as he carried two baskets of mushrooms over his shoulders. Her head turned, and she saw only black skin followed by wide, white eyes and a cry in a strange voice. She wasn't quite sure how she had avoided him, but in less than a moment, she had left him behind.

By the time Olivia reached the bottom of the staircase, her father had already crashed through the double half-moon doors, leaving the sweat from his hands trailing down the golden paint. Amy, Attia, and the rest joined Olivia on the veranda at the top of the stairs, and together they allowed the sentries positioned there to open the doors for them, a courtesy Eduardas had ignored.

They found him in the grand solar, wiping his forehead with a kerchief and smoothing his robes. Out of character for the typical gilded décor of Republican style, there were dozens of black suits of armor positioned in a straight line across the solar holding beautifully crafted curved swords Olivia could have sworn were real, leaving just enough room for the Goldblades to pass through them. *They must have been made to please the kings.*

Mylas took a moment to look closer at one, looking up into the pitch-dark eyeholes and peering inside. A shudder crawled up his spine, and he quickly carried on.

"Well," Eduardas said with a final deep breath. "Here we go."

The four took one of two winding staircases leading up to the Chamber of Coin, a large, crimson-carpeted lounge warmed by five fireplaces positioned along the rounded walls. There were well over one hundred men and women in the chamber, some standing, some sitting. The cream of Gildarian society, draped in suits, togas, and stolas of the finest gold cloth, had come to rub elbows with their first taste of royalty in what must have been decades. Most had a drink in their hand, served by men dressed in red and gold silk, nearly equal in number. Foreign men-at-arms were positioned along the edge of the wall, keeping a trained eye on the activity. It looked as if no one had noticed the Goldblades had arrived, which seemed to relieve Eduardas.

"This is a place of business? It seems more like a bedchamber," Olivia quipped. The large feather sofas scattered throughout the room, supported by mahogany legs and frames that matched the walls, looked as if they could lull even the most energetic man to sleep. Along the east window, she could see a large desk that matched the wood of the room, and the chair beneath had been pulled out far enough to reveal a cushion nearly a foot thick, bound in leather and stuffed with what she could only assume was cotton. Nothing about this room suggested that matters of serious economic practices took place here.

"Minister Valmas has always insisted on being comfortable as he works," said Eduardas. "Though by comfortable, I think he truly means asleep. More often than not, when I call on him here, I find him on one of these couches, dead to the world. You don't see him, do you?"

"No, Father," Amy answered, though it was Olivia he had asked.

"Who are these men?" Attia asked, her usual contempt rich in her voice. "I know for a fact that Valmas has at least a hundred beasts at his disposal. Why are they not serving the drinks?"

"*Shhhhh.* Keep your voice down," Eduardas said, ushering his wife to the nearest wall to speak without risk of being overheard. "Valmas kept them all at home."

"Why?" Attia asked.

"Will you *please* be quiet? All I can say is that these coast men don't look kindly on slavery. It is outlawed in each of the ten Western Kingdoms. We want to get off on the right foot with them, and Valmas decided that would best be done by not parading *slaves* around them with collars and chains. They would be insulted. So, the minister hired these men from the best wineries in the city."

"Why would they hate slaves so much? How do they get anything done?" Olivia asked. Ever since she had arrived in the capital, beasts had been a daily sight, pulling wagons or carrying litters for their masters. This memory reached so far back she could scarcely remember any other way of living. Olivia and Amy knew their father thought it was wrong, and never had reason to fight him on it. Attia, on the other hand, constantly bemoaned not owning any.

"They were all slaves once, under the Empire, for centuries. That memory has poisoned them against the very idea. And I can't say I disagree. As for getting things done, it would seem obvious: no task done goes unpaid."

"A waste of money," Attia snapped.

"That may be, but the fact is we need to make these men happy while they are here, otherwise we can kiss the trade revenue from them goodbye. So please, darling, don't do or say anything *stupid*."

Eduardas shepherded his family to the center of the chamber, grabbing a glass of wine and offering a smile and a bow to these wild-looking men who both intrigued and frightened Olivia. On the nearest couch sat a group of some of the largest men she had ever seen, dressed in gray wool. Their king wore a crown of gray steel and spoke with a booming voice. Olivia watched as he moved to begin a rather spirited conversation with a man of strange, tan skin and a crown of white pearls. The hulking king slapped his companion hard on the shoulder with a laugh, nearly knocking him to the ground.

"Dominaen Goldblade!" came a rather raspy voice from the crowd. Out of the mix appeared a round, little man with golden brown hair that fell down to his eyebrows. At a quick glance, he almost seemed he could have been Eduardas' son.

"Tamias! I'm shocked to see you aren't drunk yet, my friend." For the last eight years, Tamias Fernum had been Eduardas' personal scribe, jotting down every appointment and keeping track of countless statements as he filled them out for his clients' ever-growing accounts. When he wasn't in the office, Tamias could usually be found in one of several taverns, each of varying repute.

"Don't worry yourself, I am well on my way. But rest assured, my dear employer, I will not embarrass you this evening."

"I'll take your word for it. They all seem happy enough for now; let us keep it that way. But tell me, why do we drink already? Where is Valmas?"

"Minister Valmas is running late from the Senate house. He instructed that drinks be served first to loosen them up. He should be here any minute now." Tamias peered closely at Eduardas' face. "You look rather flushed, Dominaen. You didn't run all the way here, did you?"

"No," he said after a moment's hesitation. "No, I didn't. I also didn't receive any notice that the minister would be late. How could he have…"

"Your Majesties!" A voice pierced the room and silenced all. From the same staircase that had borne the Goldblades came an elderly man of snow-white hair, a beard that hung down to his chest, and a flowing red robe embroidered with golden trees.

Despite his age, which no one quite knew anymore, Valmas Aurian, Minister of Trade and Revenue, had the energy of a much younger man, which he utilized in gaining the attention of the room. He scuttled through the crowd, giving each king his attention to make up for his tardiness. "I apologize for the delay, but matters with the Senate kept me longer than expected. Please, let us begin. You are all famished, I am sure, and would like to conclude our business as soon as possible. Once that is finished, we shall drink until the world spins, and we shall eat until our bellies burst."

The foreigners gave an enthusiastic cry, which gave Amy and her mother a start. Olivia could only chuckle at how meek they could be sometimes. Enough noise, or a surprise big enough, and they would nearly jump out of their skins. Olivia found these men incredibly entertaining already, and she hadn't yet spoken a word to any of them.

The sofas were drawn into a circle as Minister Valmas and Eduardas stood in the center, addressing the Kings of the West. They turned to answer individual questions and quieted small worries from their prospective partners. Olivia, and all those not directly involved in the meeting, took camp off to the side, next to a waning fire.

Most questions were about how the Republic intended to protect the investments the Western Kingdoms were going to make in reestablishing trade routes. The loss of life over the years had shaken merchant confidence in the long roads that stretched across the continent. Olivia marveled at her father, who threw back that the worst danger lay within their own territories, considering that the Great Plains had been the cause of all the trouble. If Dalan could keep the plains under control, he did not see why their investments should be at risk. She thought one of them surely would rise and strike him, but to her surprise, they accepted his retort. A man of long gray hair and green robes simply nodded in agreement. His crown, a simple golden band, caught the light of the fire like a mirror.

The sun had disappeared by the time the meeting began to wind down. The majority of those in attendance had all reached verbal agreements to be finalized the next day in written contracts.

"Well, good kings, if there is nothing else, I am sure the feast is nearly ready…" Valmas began.

"There is just one more thing, Minister," came a gruff voice from across the room. A man taller than even Holto emerged from the shadows, wearing a crown of black and gold. He had to be the palest man Olivia had ever seen, his black hair nearly melting into the dark wall behind him. The fire he stood near illuminated both the gray of his temples and his impossibly blue eyes, making him seem hardly human. He towered above her father as he approached, the muscles of his back showing through his black doublet of light cloth. Olivia hadn't seen him, not even when they first arrived, making it seem as though he had appeared in a puff of smoke. He frightened her immediately, which made her curious to know more of him.

"Ah. Dominaen Goldblade, may I introduce Karrok-Ahl, King Henry of Astymere, ruler of the Fertile Crescent and Chieftain of the Avaari tribe," Minister Valmas said with a nervous smile. *So this is the man who burned the White City.* Olivia felt her fear, and her curiosity, intensify.

"Your Majesty," Eduardas said with his usual beaming smile and a deep bow. "Your name and reputation precede you."

"As do yours, Lord Goldblade," Henry replied with a shallow nod.

"What is it you would like to discuss, your Majesty?" the Minister inquired.

"The taxing of goods crossing and being sold in our borders."

"We assumed it would remain the same as it was before the routes closed. The rate that was agreed upon nearly two centuries ago: nine percent."

"When I came into my throne, I was advised that it was not within my power to change a tax rate on trade if it had remained unchanged for more than fifty years before my coronation. Otherwise, the change would have come years ago. My royal treasurer informs me that since trade was halted between our nations, this reestablishment is to be treated as an entirely new and independent trading contract. Therefore, Astymere's new rate of tax for purchasing our goods is now seventeen percent."

One of the king's companions nodded and smiled. His brown hair looked remarkably strange to Olivia, as though it stood on end. His black suit was even finer than the pale king's.

"I beg your pardon?" Minister Valmas blustered. "Seventeen percent? That is outrageous! Egregious! What makes you think…"

"Calm yourself, Minister," Eduardas said, holding up a hand. "Good King, may I ask why you wish to increase the sales tax? You certainly don't need the money. Astymere's coffers burst at the seams year after year."

"Don't think of it as a sales tax. Think of it as a *slave* tax."

"Excuse me?" Valmas asked, shifting uncomfortably.

"You heard correctly, Minister. Your practice of chaining men like beasts leaves a poor taste in our mouths, and frankly, the Crescent does not wish to give the impression that we will be tolerating it any longer. We recognize that good relations between the nations of the West is necessary to avoid any further *unpleasantness*, but make no mistake, as long as slavery exists within the Republic, the tax shall remain and you shall be held at arms-length by each of us gathered here."

One by one, the kings in attendance rose to show their solidarity with King Henry.

"If this is the will of the Kings of the West, I see no other choice than to accept the conditions," Eduardas declared. "I can only hope that in due time, the circumstances surrounding this tax will change."

With that he raised his glass, as did the kings, their attendants, and Valmas' subordinates, to signify that an agreement had been reached.

The Minister skulked off to the kitchens to inquire how soon the meal could be served, muttering and cursing to himself, and the room went back to its lively state from before.

"That was quite a beating you gave us, your Majesty," Eduardas said, taking a seat on the sofa directly across from Henry. "I can't help but wonder why, if you hate our practices so much, you agreed to reopen trade in the first place." Olivia slowly inched closer, so as to not gain their attention. *Father is having a real conversation with a king. I'd kick myself forever if I didn't get a chance to hear.*

"For millennia, Raelia defined unity in the west, whether you were with or against them. We had no sense of purpose without the shadow of the White City looming over us all," King Henry responded. "Now that the light of the Empire has been extinguished, it is up to us to create our own unity—our own purpose. And, if I must embrace a sin or two to do so, I will do it. Plus, the extra money couldn't possibly hurt."

"Now that is logic I couldn't possibly argue with—but you aren't the one who has to dole it out," Eduardas said, sharing a laugh with the Astymerian king.

"Come now, whatever you pay, you will make it back threefold when you resell the goods to your own people and trade partners, especially if it is left up to you."

"You don't say?"

"Oh, yes. I perused some of your records when I arrived. When I heard your name, I'm sure you can understand, I needed to know more about you to know what to expect. Client investments, account managing, even lending...and do you know what I found?"

"I should hope so," Eduardas said, sparking laughter again.

"I found that not one of your clients' finances have ever seen red. And that is goddamned impressive. It makes one wonder how you manage it."

"I have always had a gift for numbers, your Majesty. They are plain, simple, and never lie. If one knows how to keep them in line, one can keep them in line perpetually."

"My treasury could use more men like you. If you ever tire of living in a tree, there is a position and a royal welcome waiting for you in Astymere."

"Most kind of you, your Majesty, but I coul never rip my wife from Gildara. Nevertheless, I think a visit would be most splendid. I have always wanted to see the Mountain City. From what I have heard, it is quite spectacular."

"There isn't any like it in the civilized world. Now that the White City is gone, it is quite possibly the oldest. I'm sure you would love it."

Olivia delighted at the sound of this. The thought of seeing the ancient parts of the world was too much to keep within.

"Is it true the walls are a hundred feet high?" Olivia asked. Henry and Eduardas hadn't noticed her standing next to them, and Eduardas shot to his feet and wrapped a proud arm around her shoulder.

"This is my eldest, Olivia." He turned to his daughter. "May I introduce you to Henry of House Karrok, King of Astymere?" With prompting from her father, Olivia dropped to her knees, rather clumsily in her rush, and fought hard not to cry out when they hit the floor.

"A pleasure to meet you, child. Yes, the walls of Vita Astym are one hundred feet high. Not quite so awe-inspiring when one has to climb all those stairs to reach the top. Such knowledge for a young girl…and such a beauty. You couldn't possibly belong to this one here."

"Now, wait just a moment," Eduardas mockingly objected. "Back before this one was born I was a veritable god among men. But once she came along, she slowly sucked the beauty right out of me, until she took it all and I was left looking like this."

Henry nearly choked on his wine at this quip, and Eduardas slapped him hard in the back, laughing heartily, taking pride that he had struck the proud king down.

"I think it is safe to say that I like you, sir," Henry confessed.

"Now, don't jump to conclusions. See if you still like me tomorrow."

"If you two keep drinking, you won't remember each other at all," Olivia said.

Eduardas chuckled nervously, "It never ends with this one!"

Eduardas excused Olivia and struck up another conversation with the pale king. She found Amy on one of the many couches positioned near the fire and sat silently, waiting for the food to arrive. She leaned her head against her hand, ignored the rumbling in her belly, and tried to imagine the Mountain City standing tall and proud to be seen for miles around. *Now wouldn't that be a sight?*

Chapter 10

Lynap: Dalan
26th Day of the Second Month
5014 A.S.

WILLIAM OTTER SAT IN A DELICATE handcrafted rocking chair, the light of a single candle bouncing off his cleanly shaven head. He rocked back and forth an inch at a time, with such gentle care that an eggshell would have gone unharmed beneath the curved legs. His daughter slept soundly on her soft mattress, covered by a handmade quilt her great aunt Susa had crafted for her shortly after she was born.

Her dark hair stood out stark against her white pillow, her breathing both slow and steady. Carefully, as to not make any sound, William rose from his rocker and inched his way over to young Lily's side. Before the sun fell the next evening, he would have to leave her yet again, hopefully for the last time.

William ran his fingers softly through her hair, wondering when he would get the chance to do so again. He leaned over and planted a kiss upon her cheek, so softly it would be nearly undetectable upon her smooth skin, then returned to the table beside the rocker to take his candle with him. As he turned to take his leave, the candlelight caught something he had not noticed before.

A bit of old cloth, unwashed and frayed around the edges, lay neatly folded upon Lily's night table. Never one to go poking his nose where it did not belong, he almost ignored it but for a shard of a memory jabbing him in the back of his dented skull. *Where have I seen this before?*

Stepping lightly, William eased the candle down upon the night table. The cloth looked as though it might fall apart in his hands, so he scooped it into his open palms, trying to preserve it. Gently, he opened the fold that ran down the center, and his heart nearly burst at the sight: flattened and long since dead and dry sat a blue-crested water lily, still rich as sapphires by some miracle of Mahtem the Mother. *Brisban. I took this from Brisban.*

The memory came flooding back to his hindered brain. William had taken it in secret during one of Henry's many visits to the Treasurer's home in the capital. Lily's eyes had grown to such a size William thought they would pop from their sockets when he presented it to her. The Great Plains were no desolate place, but flowers such as this were nowhere to be found, and she had called it a treasure. *She kept it.* The edges of William's vision blurred as he stifled tears that were desperate to come. *This is the last time, Otter. You won't have the strength to leave her again. You must settle this when you get back, and settle it quickly.*

The stairs leading down to the first floor of the old wooden country house creaked as he went, but he no longer paid any mind. His heart was pounding so hard within his chest, he was deaf to all other sounds.

Susa sat in a green armchair before a crackling fire, her feet resting on a cushioned stool with her arms crossed across her ample belly. William had brought both the chair and stool for her some years back, having had them made especially for her. She had been his mother's only sister, taken in by his grandparents when she was just a girl, and when his mother passed after his graduation from the Academy, Susa was the only family he had left. He drew up a wooden stool and joined her, rubbing his hands over the flames to fight the chill a northern wind had brought in that night.

"You're off again tomorrow?" she asked in a froggy, aged voice. Her hair was dark for her elder years, as was common for Dalani women. Only a few strands of gray caught the light of the fire, but her face was wrinkled, both by sun and worry.

"Yes. If I stay much longer, the king will start asking questions. Questions I cannot yet answer." He kept his eyes on the fire as he spoke.

"It isn't *his* questions you should worry about answering," Susa said, also training her eyes on the fire. William broke his gaze to look on her, her thinly veiled accusation striking home.

"The less she knows, the better. At least for now."

"The less she knows, the more she is in danger. The less she knows, the more her heart breaks. You don't see it. How can you? She weeps for days after you leave."

"I can't help that. It is what must be done." The crack in his voice betrayed him. His heart ached that he could cause his daughter such pain.

"She thinks you don't want her. And, as foolish as it once sounded, it's beginning to seem more and more like truth. I cannot think of any other reason you don't take her with you."

"Do you tire so much of the girl?" There was bite in his voice now, his pain turning to anger.

"I will not be around forever, William. I have done what I can to be a mother to her, but she needs you. She has always needed you."

"She wouldn't be safe with me, Susa. Were I a selfish man I would never have brought her to you. I would have kept her as I should have, and maybe I could give her a good life. But as long as she stayed with me, she would be in danger. Not to mention if Henry ever found out…"

"Do you doubt your friend's heart so? He is a good man, from what you've told me."

"And good men can be driven to do terrible things. I will take no risks with her life. Not until I am absolutely sure."

"Still, even if you don't take her with you, she can't stay here much longer. The dreams keep coming, William. Night after night she tosses and turns, moaning and crying. This is a strangely peaceful night for her, but she will have to go. I don't know where, but she will have to be taught—"

"You think I haven't thought of that? The next time I come here, I will have it all settled, unless…"

"Unless what?"

"Nothing. It's nothing. I am going to bed now, Susa. Is there anything you need before I retire?"

"Nothing, dear. I will follow shortly. Good night."

William's mind raced as he moved to his bed in the back of the house. It seemed mad, what he thought. So terrible that he hardly thought he'd have the will to do it.

He is an honorable man. He will take her in. He will take her under his protection if I ask him—if it were my final wish. William nervously fidgeted with the tiny Sandil in his pocket. It had a foul aftertaste of cowardice, but it was the only way he could be sure Lily would be safe. If he took his own life before his mind was finally robbed of him, he would be able to secure her future. As William lay his head down that night, the thought stuck with him like a fly that kept buzzing about. He closed his eyes and opened them to the morning light, not sure if he had slept at all.

William hadn't said much at breakfast the next morning but

wrapped Lily tightly in his arms as he said what would be his final goodbye.

He stepped through the door and out onto the grass quickly, but felt a hand grab his arm and turn him on the spot.

"Father, why must you leave?" Lily asked, her silver eyes peering up at him. William closed his weary brown eyes, holding back tears, and stroked the black hair that ran past her shoulders.

"My place is in Astymere, my love. It is all too complicated to explain. I have made some decisions that would make life incredibly hard for you there." He took her hand in his. Lily's soft skin felt soothing against his rough, calloused fingers. "One day soon, you will come with me. I promise you that. But under the right circumstances."

"You promised me when I turned thirteen I could come and stay with you," she pleaded. William knew that seeing her just three weeks a year would lead to this conversation, but he still couldn't bring her to the capital; it was too dangerous for reasons she wouldn't understand.

"I wish I didn't have to leave you. You know that. I can march straight into the frozen mouth of hell without a moment's hesitation and spit right in the face of the Beast himself, but saying goodbye to you destroys my heart. You don't know Astymere like I do. It's not safe for you there."

"You always tell me it's unsafe. What does that even mean? I'm not a baby. Thousands of children my age live there. Why is it not dangerous for them?"

"It's a tough thing to explain, and this is not the time for it. I am going to make sure that when you pass through those gates, it is without worry, child. I swear on my life."

As Lily pierced her father with a confused, frustrated look, distant laughter came drifting on the wind from a hilltop to the south. The house, a two-story hut in the middle of a level basin, was surrounded by four hills and sat alone for miles. The tall grass danced in the light breeze as a pack of men came wandering over the top of the hill. William stood attentively. One of the men pointed and turned the group's direction toward the house.

"Lily, go inside and lock the doors. Tell your aunt to be quiet." Something about these men left him unsettled. "If something should happen, you go out the back door, take my horse, and run."

"What?" Lily asked, turning to see the men. Her bright, pale face grew worried as the group casually approached, separating into a line formation.

"Leiliara, go inside, now!" William cried. He had never raised his voice to her before or called her by her full name without great sadness clinging to his voice. She grabbed the bottom of her long, light blue dress, went inside, and closed the door. William stood alone, listening to it lock as the group stopped a few paces away from him. The men stood silently staring. *These are no men of the West.* He slowly raised his hand and gripped the hilt of his sword.

"*Zverta! Zverta!*" yelled a man much bigger than the rest, who seemed to have a chunk missing from his face. He held his hand expectantly toward William.

"You have no business here! Let us be and go on your way," William shouted. He turned to the wooden house and saw Lily's face peering through the corner of a window.

The hulking man smirked at William, seemingly amused at his refusal, and walked toward him slowly, his large feet leaving distinct imprints in the dirt.

William, no small man by any right, only came up to this stranger's nose. He was used to fighting large men; they all thought themselves invincible, which made them stupid enough for the captain to take advantage of.

The man circled William, who stood still and centered. The big man held his hand out as the old captain assessed the situation. *Twelve men, Gods be damned. Keep your back to the house. Don't let them surround you.*

The warrior reached for William's sword, but the captain slapped away his hand. "Over my dead body," William said, stepping back and drawing his high steel saber.

The big man laughed at him, joined by the rest in his group. He quickly returned to a straight face, stared down at William, and unsheathed his own sword.

Dalani steel. The end of the broadsword, glistening in the sun, was pointed straight at William's throat.

"*Geftin zverta pyrs eythak dijark,*" said the man, no longer in a joking manner.

William took a step toward his opponent, ready to go on the

offensive, when all turned to darkness. His mind slipped beyond any trace of time and place, and by the time his senses returned, he was lying on his side, his right cheek throbbing. Before he could think to move, his lumbering foe kicked him in the midsection with such force, he could feel a rib crack.

"*Go*," he gasped, just loud enough for his daughter to hear. Lily peaked out one last time at her father, then disappeared.

The big man walked over to William but was distracted by the squeak of a door coming from the hut. He waved two men to attend to William as he strode around back to investigate. William lay coughing on the ground as the two men approached.

"No! Let me go!" Lily cried from the back of the house. William heard her struggle and gave out a choked gasp. His voice grew from a weak chirp to a furious howl as the two men reached him. He reached into his belt and quickly unsheathed a small dagger, then stood up fast and slid it through the bottom of the nearest man's jaw. He withdrew it cleanly and sent it into the chest of the other. Both collapsed to the ground. The group of warriors closed on William.

The big man reappeared from the back of the house, laughing and pulling Lily by her hair as she screamed in pain and pleaded for help. William took the small blade, his last weapon, and flung it at the big man, sticking him through the groin. His face turned red with agony and fury as he released Lily to reach down to his wound; his pants soaked red as he cried and tipped to the ground.

"*Lily, run!*" William shouted as he scooped up his sword and ushered her around the back of the house.

QERAGO, HER FATHER'S HORSE, was already saddled. Lily leapt on effortlessly and looked back to William, who followed without an enemy in sight.

"Take this!" William shouted through breaths that sounded painful. He reached into his pocket and stuffed a tiny, metal, black fork into her hand. She winced where it pricked her skin on its fine points. "This is the token of my Final Wish, Lily. Head west, to Astymere, and give it to King Henry. Tell him my final wish is for him to take you in and protect you. Tell him, give him that, and you'll never be in danger again. Go now, child. *Go!*"

He slapped Qerago on his haunch and he took off. Lily was

heading west like her father had told her. As she circled far around, she could see William, charging from behind the house into the mix of the intruders, who seemed to be nursing their leader. They quickly surrounded William. The bright silver of his sword danced in the morning sunlight as he slashed and parried. She had turned her head back to the path for just a moment when she heard him scream, before his voice was abruptly silenced. She looked back once more to see only the small crowd of wild men gathered close, and not a sign of her father's dancing blade.

She rode hard to the top of the near hills and even further, Qerago's hooves churning the soil below, galloping until she feared the animal's heart would burst.

It was past midday when Lily found herself too weak to stay in the saddle. She stopped and slid from her seat, her knees slamming into the dirt and jagged pebbles, but the pain didn't compare to the agony in her heart. She lay face down in the dirt, shedding as many tears as her eyes would allow. She wept for the loss of everything she had ever known. Her father, her home, and surely her aunt, who would not have been fast enough to escape at her age. In less than a minute, Lily's world had been destroyed, and she had been left with nothing.

Suddenly, Qerago grunted and sprinted away into the open fields, disappearing over the neighboring hills. She wanted to stand and shout, but as much fire lived in her spirit, her body had little left to give.

She stayed down for hours until the sun had vanished from the sky and the stars and moons filled the empty darkness. She finally muscled the strength to sit up and look out into the valley she had never explored.

She knew a great deal of the land around her home from her daily excursions, but she had never come this far; her father never allowed her to.

Head west to Astymere. Tell him and give him that. You will never be in danger again. She repeated those words countless times in her head and tightened her grip around the small emblem in her hand, the last piece of her father she had. William, who had never allowed her to go for being too dangerous, said she would now be safe in Astymere. It didn't make sense. But Lily had never doubted a word her father said.

After a few more moments, she stood on her shaky legs and looked up at the twin moons, which now flew high in the sky. Gazing at their beauty and mystery, she found the direction she had to go.

"West to Astymere," she declared, in a sad, raspy voice, and began her long walk to Vita Astym.

Chapter 11

Kar Naron: Astymere
30th Day of the Second Month
5014 A.S.

"Gentlemen, this morning I received a swallow from Cormyn Longbrook, Master of Borders for the Crown of Dalan. He informs me that a band of Sworn Hooves, tasked with transporting armed foreign trespassers to Roleigh, have been found murdered in the Plains, and their charge has all but vanished." Commander Jordyn Stone addressed his men from atop a wooden stage erected in the prime courtyard of Naron's Keep. "The official report is that they were able to overpower and kill every single guard as they slept. We are to remain alert and to notify King Robert if we see anything suspicious."

He eyed the men of Kar Naron, bearing shadowy stubble, not having had time to shave before this surprise meeting was called. The five thousand men stood silent, their shields and spears held at attention.

"For years I pleaded with our King to allow Astymere to dole out its own justice for trespassers and murderers, but he rejected my requests. He told me we were to let the Dalani handle the matter— that they were perfectly capable of reining in the plains on their own—but now, a band of unwashed dogs roam freely through our backyard, after hardly two years of the peace they *provided* us. The men of Dalan have failed in their responsibilities, but Astymere *will* find these brutes—and send their heads to our King on spikes!"

The men lifted their spears and fists toward the sky, cheering back at their commander, their cries ringing off the slopes of the mountain pass. Stone addressed a group of men in the front row, wearing the blue cloaks and golden sashes of Kar Naron officers, his immediate subordinates.

"First Shields Vorom, Carwick, Ramson, Kuger, Dulaire, and Ashforth will help me lead this hunt. They have each hand-selected twenty men to accompany us, but know this—these men are not wild beasts. From what I have heard, these murderers are now armed with stolen Dalani weapons. You ride in groups of ten, and no less."

Despite his stance on King Robert's effectiveness out on the plains, Stone knew that one-on-one, Sworn Hooves were some of the best fighters to be found in the Western world. If they could be cut down so easily, he would take no chances with his men's lives.

"Ready your horses and meet me at the Great Portcullis," he ordered. The attendants of the six officers went off immediately to gather their supplies and horses, as the rest of the crowd dispersed to go about their daily tasks.

"That was some speech," said a familiar voice, approaching Stone from the rear. Stone removed his black glove from his belt and turned, shaking the hand of Hann Vilamore as he offered it. "I have never seen these men so excited over a hunt." General Vilamore was one of the few Astymere had to offer who could stand him, Stone knew, much less be friendly with him. Having had a heavy hand in training and raising him, this was no difficult task for the seasoned general.

"This isn't a typical hunt," Stone replied with a smile, looking down upon his old friend who stood inches below him. "These men need to know they may die if we come across the missing savages. Since the White City fell, this is probably the most exciting thing that has happened to most of them."

"When will you return?" General Vilamore asked, watching the commander mount his snow-white stallion, Storm.

Stone had served under Vilamore for years before his appointment to Kar Naron, and the general had become the closest thing to a confidant the commander had.

"I'd like to say we will return when we bag our catch," he said, "but knowing how vast the plains are, we may never see them. In that case, we'll return before the king does."

"Where do you think they will go?"

Stone set Storm off at a slow pace with a gentle nudge to his side. "I would think if they came across Raelia, they may forage for food and supplies. The report tells me they had been heading west when they were first caught, so chances are they will continue that way, toward us, now that they are free. If so, they should walk right into our swords." He shook his head to the general, walking beside him. "Dalani fools couldn't keep a dozen savages under control while under full guard. It makes Robert look weak, and I know he has enough sense to see that."

Hann gave a dubious nod. "We don't know if they have an army backing them, so please, if it isn't too much trouble, try not to start a war. And hurry back. I will do my part to keep your little trip to myself, but from here I head south to Capany for a long-overdue holiday. I don't expect the Guardian will be calling on me to ask for a report—at least not until you get back. But if he does, and by some chance he should ask of you, I warn you, I dare not lie to him. They are likely to strip you of your command if he learns you have defied orders and led men out onto the plains."

"Only one way to find out," Stone replied with a smirk. The First Shields had assembled their men behind their commander as the massive, high steel portcullis slowly opened, allowing the party to exit into the open world.

The sun hovered just above the horizon when they cleared the mountain range, the cool breeze growing more and more stagnant the further from Gol Rayna they traveled. After hours of hard riding, the party crossed the border into Dalan, the mountains of home shrinking into the west behind them.

The heat began to bear down on them in their black armor as they trudged slowly, now spread out over half a mile in groups of ten to cover more ground. They stayed as far from the roads as possible, and even farther from any towns. If the Dalani spotted them, word would surely get back to King Henry, and there would be hell to pay.

The hours melted into each other, and with each one's passing, Stone grew more discouraged. His hopes were that their prey had somehow traveled closer to Astymere, to make for a quick hunt. As the silent search continued, he thanked the gods for the company of his men, for the endless sea of grass and roaming hills could drive a person mad if left alone among them.

Stone set the pace in the front as his group followed along in the distance. He heard no sound but the rustling of tall grass against Storm's body. No clouds roamed the sky; no mercy of shade was to be found.

"Commander!" yelled First Shield Carwick from the hill to his right. His silver blade reflected the sun, blinding Stone for a moment before he called all men to his side. As he approached the top of the hill, Stone could see what caught his attention. Looking north and scanning to the west, Stone could see a small stream of smoke from a minuscule fire, rising like white steam into the air.

"Signal the others. Draw swords, spread out, and keep your eyes open. I want the area surrounded. No one comes through these hills without our knowing." The men drew their weapons as Stone clicked his heels, and the stallions took off in stride.

The dirt sprang forth from beneath Storm's hooves as he powered his way through the flat basin between the hills. In minutes the group had plowed through several basins and made their way to the northern end of the hilly valley from which the smoke rose.

They slowed as they approached, each dismounting and going prone. The wisps emanated from behind a bend in the shallow valley that wound off to the south. The men barely moved, just far enough to peek at a small fire and a single body, hidden mostly by the tall grass. Stone turned to his men and waved a hand to spread into a line.

"It could be a trap; be on your guard."

Until this moment, they hadn't spotted any living thing, beast or man, since they left Kar Naron. The group closed on the campfire from all directions, swords drawn and silent as ghosts. Whoever it was, it seemed they truly were alone. As he approached, Stone now saw that their target was a young girl, laying on her back.

Stone returned his saber to its sheath. He walked over slowly and knelt beside her, cradling her head, as she barely had strength to lift it. She had a couple of large roots still covered in dirt at her side. She opened her eyes for the first time, revealing brilliant silver that practically glowed as the sun hit them. Her face was covered in dust, and her small feet were blackened by soil. Her dark hair was a tangled mess, matted with pieces of grass.

Silver eyes, Stone thought to himself. *Layda Arani. I come out here to find men worth killing, and instead I find a Layda Arani. A gods-damned silver seer. This is quite a day, indeed.* "What are you doing out here by yourself, young one?" he asked.

The girl looked back up at him but didn't answer. Her lips, shriveled from dehydration, parted in an attempt to speak. The commander lifted a canteen from beneath his cloak and handed it to her. She guzzled down several swallows as if she hadn't seen water in days. "What is your name?"

"Lily," she said weakly.

"What happened, Lily?"

"Men…Men came to my home and…my father." Her face twisted in agony. "My aunt…"

"What did these men look like?"

"Fur, and…iron, they just…They just…"

"Did you see where they were headed?"

"Ran…Father told me. Father. Father…"

Stone quieted her. Lily's arms were trembling as she motioned in a need to explain. It was clear there was little he could get out of her at this point. The child was half-dead.

"Where are you going, Lily?"

"As—Astymere."

"Rest now," he said, stroking her hair. He picked her up, wrapping an arm underneath her legs and around the bottom of her back. Her arms dangled at her sides. "We will take you there, don't fret. You're safe now."

With a nod from Stone, First Shield Dulaire kicked some tufts of dirt over the fire to cover their tracks. Stone laid Lily upon Storm's back, and the party made their way back to the Astymerian border with one extra in tow.

Chapter 12

Kar Naron: Astymere
34th Day of the First Month
5014 A.S.

Lily sat alone in a great hall, at the center of a long, wooden bench along the far wall, close to the commander's table. A few days of food and rest had already restored most of her strength. Warmth from the torches and hearths, lit to protect the great hall from the mountain chill, melted the cold from her bones.

Her face dripped with the broth of beef stew that sat before her. The bowl rested next to a plate of fresh fruit, and a small loaf of bread filled her nose with a mouth-watering aroma of the butter within its golden crust.

The doors on the northern wall creaked open on their old hinges, sending an echo through the cavernous room. Lily glanced up, drops of stew falling off her chin. She had lost all pretense of manners after nearly starving to death out on the plains, but now her sense of etiquette slowly returned. She patted her chin with the thick linen napkin in her lap. The commander entered, his arms crossed behind his back, and he stepped with a gait that was more relaxed than she had previously seen. "Is the stew satisfactory?" he asked as he walked, checking to make sure they were alone in the usually crowded room.

"The cooks threw together what they could find last minute," he added. "It's no palace feast, but we eat well here all the same."

"It's more than enough, my…Lord?"

"Stone. Commander Jordyn Stone. I had nearly forgotten we hadn't had a proper introduction." He sat on the opposite bench.

Lily slowly picked at her food, feeling slightly uncomfortable now with a strange man watching her. "We receive shipments of fresh food regularly from several farms nearby," he went on. "Among the many who attempt to enlist at this castle, there are more than a few that do so for the steady meals alone."

"Seems quite the incentive."

"It never stays that way. Once men don their black armor and pick up their spears for the first time, something changes in them. Their service becomes much more than a regular meal. The honor of manning these walls supersedes any number of comforts."

Lily bit her lip and looked down at her cooling stew. *I'll find no comfort here. No real comfort, anyway.*

"I'm sorry for your loss," Stone said. "The feeling is indescribable."

"You speak as if you know what it's like," she snapped. Her father would have been furious to hear her speak that way to an elder, but the trauma of the last days had left her emotions raw and inflamed. "No one knows what it's like."

Stone frowned, but not unkindly. "Countless souls, just as unfortunate as yourself, know what it is like, girl. I, too, have lost more than I was ever willing to part with."

"What is it you have lost, Commander?" Lily twirled the stew with her spoon.

"My father…just as you have."

"To die an old man tucked into bed is an easy death. At least that is what my father always told me. That is the natural way of things. My family was *taken* from me. There is nothing natural in that."

She was not so much angry with the commander as she was with the unfairness life had dumped at her feet, but there was no separating the two. Unfairness had no ears to hear her ire, and the commander did.

"Who ever said his death was natural?"

Embarrassment reddened Lily's cheeks. "I'm sorry. I figured…"

"You figured since I am old, he had to be old as well. Well, I am sorry to say, but he was quite young when he died. Not even as old as I am now."

"How did he die?" The question was too blunt, but the commander hardly took notice.

"He was stabbed in the back, quite literally, by a man he called his friend. Jaran Stone, my father, had been a thorn in the side of the Raelian Emperor Arulian IV, or so I am told. The last time the Empire tried to invade these borders, my father led the king's army through the Pass of Gol Ain to meet them in the open field. He slew over a dozen imperial officers, and Gods know how many of their men, before the Raelians grew desperate. Story has it, the emperor sent spies to call on the one man who was closest to my father on the battlefield, Layn Vilamore. I don't know how long they kept at him, but by the end, they found his price: eighty thousand gold Raelian coins, two hundred acres within the empire, and a holdfast. On the slopes of Gol Rayna, Vilamore drove his blade through my father's ribs from behind and slipped away into the Raelian ranks."

"What happened to him? Did you ever find him?"

"No, unfortunately, I did not. But there was one I suspected who knew what became of him. His brother, Hann, who had an equal hand in raising me as my own father, refused to speak of Layn for years afterward. Whenever his name was mentioned, he would go silent. 'He is dead to me' were his last words on the matter. But his eyes always hid something. After many years, when I could take no more of his silence, I nearly strangled the truth out of him. Through gasps and chokes he told me the last he'd heard of his brother was that he had drunk himself to death, unable to live with his shame. I felt empty that day, knowing I would never have vengeance."

"As bad as what he did was, he still knew right from wrong, it would seem."

"It seems we all have perfect hindsight. But for those who have the gift of *foresight*, hindsight just doesn't quite seem necessary, does it?"

Foresight? Lily wondered. She fidgeted in her seat, not quite sure what to say.

"If I had the gift of foresight," he continued, "I am sure I could have saved my father. But I don't, and I have long since come to peace with that fact. So, I cannot imagine the shame one must feel if they have the gift, and still fail to save those they love."

"Why are you saying this? I did not fail my family! How was I supposed to know what would happen? There was nothing I could do! I don't know the future."

"Oh, but you do, girl. You do." His tone went dark and cold, like a night wind that carried heavy snow in its wake.

The words hummed in her ears like the incessant buzzing of bees. He had jumped beyond not making sense, straight into pure lunacy.

"Do you hear yourself? That's impossible!" Lily cried. She had intended to try to convince him, but when she heard the words, it felt as though she was trying to convince herself.

"They didn't teach you much out there on the plains, I see.

You are a Layda Arani."

"A what?" Lily wanted to tell him he was mad. She wanted to tell him the obvious truth, that there was no such thing as a… whatever he had called her. That to see into the future was impossible. All these things she wanted to say, but the dreams—the dreams gave Lily pause, and it seemed Stone could sense it.

"No one ever told you?" He waited for a moment, then shook his head. "I am not surprised, to be honest. Who would want to burden a child with such things? To be a silver seer means you carry the weight of the hopes and fears of all those around you. Haven't you ever wondered why your eyes are silver, child? Any man with half a brain could tell you that silver eyes make a silver seer. They allow visions into the future."

"I've never been able to do that…"

"Don't lie to me, *witch!*" the commander shouted, dropping his façade of the concerned caregiver. "You have knowledge no man could ever hope to have! A power that no person should ever be able to hold over another! Tell me what you have seen!"

"Please, leave me alone…"

"Out with it, witch, what have you seen?"

Lily thought she might collapse from fear and anger, but the blast of the Spire Horn rattled the wooden rafters of the great hall, along with each table and bench. The deep, rumbling note made Lily feel as though her teeth would shake right out of their roots. Cries and commands could be heard from the courtyard below as chains rattled on the western side of the fortress, and the thunder of approaching horses grew louder by the moment.

Commander Stone rose as his personal page came scuttling through the open doors, his face a wide-eyed visage of panic.

"What is it, boy?" The page stood frozen for a moment. "Out with it! Who comes here?"

"Commander…" he began. "The Guardian has come."

"What? What could Lord Rahmos want here?"

Lily detected fear in his voice, and from what she could tell of her new host, he did not strike her as a man who frightened easily.

"Take her back to her room and watch the door," Stone ordered. "I don't want anyone speaking to her without my leave. Understood?"

"Yes, sir. If you will follow me, miss."

After a moment's hesitation and a stern look from Commander Stone, Lily rose and made her way out the doors and up the stairs of the Commander's Spire to her room, with the page boy following close behind.

Lily slammed the door shut behind her as she entered her chambers, nearly splintering the old wood. She ran to the bed and planted her face in the soft feather pillows propped against the carved wooden headboard and wept for minutes, sobbing a puddle into the fabric.

If all men are like the commander, my father may have been right about Astymere.

The silence grew unbearable as she tossed and turned, then stood to pace about the room. She stuck her head through the thin, glassless window for a sign of life. The view looked west, through the remainder of the Pass of Gol Ain, to reveal a sliver of the rich green country beyond. To the right, the mountain slope blocked her view to the north. If the wind allowed, she might be able to hear the conversation of the men in the courtyard below.

Kar Naron was usually abuzz with activity, but there was no noise, to her dismay, not a single sound anywhere. The small fortress city was silent as a snowy night.

She pulled herself back through the stone opening and slid down the wall until she sat on the hard floor. Despite the chill of the mountain air, she found that the walls and floors were quite warm. She gazed blankly into the black stones across the room, thinking of her father. His cries and shouts rang perfectly in her head. She hardly ever saw him, and she began to wonder if she truly knew him at all. *Did he know? Did Susa know?*

Minutes passed, and still no sound broke the serene quiet, the silence leaving an empty void in the room that seemed more like a prison with each passing second. Lily's view of Kar Naron had changed the instant Stone turned on her. *Can I really see into the future? Is that why the capital is so dangerous? Is that why my father didn't let me leave? Is that why we were attacked?* These questions flooded her thoughts before she could even begin to think of answers for them. But the last to come pierced an icy dagger into her heart. *Did I really fail my family?*

Tears began to well as Lily feared the worst. None of the past few days made sense to her. Usually she gardened, did chores, and cooked with Susa. The most exhilarating times of the day were watching the sun rise and set on the plains. She had taken it all for granted. One never imagines having to go through the remainder of their days never seeing a familiar face again, or hearing their voice, or feeling their touch, she realized. Her old life was now as dead as her family, and she hadn't a clue what to make of the new, uncertain one that lay stretched out before her.

STONE STOOD ALONE IN THE ECHOING HALL after the girl took her leave, deep in thought. Despite his panic, he kept his composure, as was expected of a man of his authority.

His eyes settled on a dim fire against the wall and squinted, taking in the light, giving him warmth and settling his nerves. *This is my fortress, my men. I am the commander. I am the authority here.* He knew Lord Rahmos came with urgency, for the Guardian would not leave the capital without just cause. He suspected what his visit entailed and prayed silently that he was wrong.

Then, with a deep breath, he left the hall, took the wide, straight staircase downward, and made his way to the rear courtyard, where his men stood at attention.

High Lord Urnest Rahmos had dismounted his gray and black stallion and settled his two hundred silver-cloaked men behind him, separated from the guards of the old fortress. The proud sigil of House Rahmos, a broken silver chain upon a field of black, danced over their heads in the wind. Stone found Lord Rahmos among the mass of men, handing his stallion by its bronze reins to a man of his party. When Lord Rahmos turned, his eyes bore deep into Stone's soul.

He approached with slow, menacing steps, and Stone could make out the scar upon his face, accented by the light gray streaks his hair had accrued over the years. Beside him stood his eldest son, Tyrel, equal to his father in height and hardness of face, but practically stick-thin to the untrained eye. Many had paid the price for mistaking his frame for scrawny. Beneath his black armor and silver cloak was lean, wiry muscle that moved with lightning-fast agility, making him one of the deadliest fighters with sword and fist in the West, at only twenty-one.

Commander Stone bent the knee, as did every man in

attendance who hadn't ridden in with Lord Rahmos. After several tense, silent moments, Stone stood upright from the soaked earth and lifted his chin to meet Lord Rahmos' eye.

"Do you know why I am here, Stone?" Lord Rahmos asked in a flat, curt tone, as if he were restraining himself.

"I haven't the faintest idea, my Lord, but we are honored by your presence. We shall prepare rooms for you and your party immediately. If we had had more notice, they would be prepared already."

"That won't be necessary, Commander; we will not be staying the night."

"My Lord?" Stone looked on as Tyrel handed his father a roll of parchment bearing the seal of King Robert of Dalan, which had been broken.

"I received this letter from Roleigh this morning. It would appear that Dalani scouts spotted a sizable force of riders wandering through the Great Plains without leave from King Robert."

"What business is it of mine that careless men should wander over Dalan's borders, my Lord?"

"*Business?* It's your business because the riders were described as black-armored and led by men with blue cloaks. Can you think of any other group of individuals who match that description, other than the officers of this fortress?"

Stone looked to the ground, desperate for any explanation or ruse that could deflect this accusation away from himself. "My Lord…"

Crack! The sound of skin on skin rang like a bell through the quiet courtyard. Stone's cheek, now reddened, snapped in the opposite direction from Lord Rahmos' powerful strike.

"You piece of scum," Lord Rahmos said. "You *willfully* defy your King's orders and…"

"Lord Rah…" *Crack!* The same hand, hard as iron, now reddened the opposite side. The disfavor he had earned from those in the capital over the years was now plain for his men to see.

"Do not interrupt me, Stone!" Lord Rahmos shouted, his voice so loud it could make the dining hall rafters shake just as well as the Spire Horn. "You led the forces of this castle to trespass against our neighbors! I always knew your arrogance would taint the decision of giving you command of this fortress. The name of Kar Naron seems to have given you the impression that you are above the law. Having been raised by a man as honorable as Jaran Stone, it is hard to grasp how you could have gone so far astray."

Stone glanced quickly at the soldiers in the yard, who stood aghast at their leader being dethroned from the small kingdom he ran within the walls of Kar Naron.

"Perhaps we should take this to my quarters?" Stone said, hoping to escape further humiliation in front of the garrison. *Crack!*

"Do not dare presume to hide this! Your men are going to see you for what you are—a selfish, overreaching fool who acts as if he rules. You don't rule a damned thing. Everything your King has granted you can be erased without a trace with a single word."

Stone looked down. Lord Rahmos followed him down, dipping his body lower to adjust to Stone's new point of view. He snapped his fingers and pointed Stone's attention back up.

"Are you the king?" he asked the commander sarcastically when their eyes met again. Stone hung his head and shook it.

"Commander Jordyn of the House Stone, by the power bestowed upon me by the Crown of Astymere, you are hereby charged with insubordination, dereliction of duty, and low treason. You know as well as I do that the typical punishment for such a crime is ten years imprisonment. But, I am nothing if not merciful. I, Urnest of the House Rahmos, Lord of Kar Rahmos, and Lord Paramount of the Crescent Coast, shall waive this punishment in light of your years of faithful service to the crown. Instead, I offer you a choice."

Stone looked up. "Choice?"

"Either you will be stripped of your command and dishonorably discharged from the Black Army, or you shall receive twenty *public* lashes, so your men may never forget your shame."

Stone gaped up at Lord Rahmos in disbelief. Surely he would find satisfaction in this. The High Lords and much of the council had never tried to hide their disdain for him. It seemed this was their golden opportunity to finally be rid of him, to pluck the thorn from their sides. Everything he was he had earned through service in the Black Army. Without Kar Naron, without his command, he was nothing.

Thoughts raced through his head, and while there was little hope left for him if he lost his command, the thought of his own men watching him whipped made his skin crawl. His authority, as it had existed for years, would be forever tarnished. The only thing keeping his mind from unraveling was the reality that redemption was much closer to his reach if he took the lashes and retained his post. If he allowed them to force him out, he would never be able to live down the shame. He would be the first commander forcibly stripped of his post in over five hundred years.

He silently looked up at Lord Rahmos and gave a shallow nod, accepting his fate.

"Tie him to the flogging stand."

Stone unlatched his cloak and removed his shirt, revealing the scars that covered his pale, muscular body. He stepped solemnly toward a wooden pole in the middle of the courtyard fitted with shackles for both the hands and feet. With a snap of Lord Rahmos' fingers, one of his men-at-arms produced a long, single-tasseled whip from his saddlebag. He silently extended his hand as his eyes stayed on Stone. His fingers tightened around the leather handle of the whip as he stood in the clearing of soldiers and guards surrounding him.

Minutes passed, each feeling like a year between successive lashings. The men around the courtyard grimaced, some even showing signs of pity and sympathy for the man they had grown to respect.

Crack! The tan, leather weapon whistled. *Crack!* Stone, a bloody mess from behind, stared at the ground, unable to meet anyone's eye. He didn't move, he didn't flinch, and he didn't make a sound. There was barely a wince in his face with each passing blow.

The physical pain, though agonizing, was nothing alien to him. But the thought of having his reputation destroyed, beaten out of him like an insubordinate child as the men he commanded watched, brought a single tear to his eye. That pain could not be swallowed so easily.

Nothing would be the same after this, but Stone clung to the idea that even this degradation would be easier to live with than losing Kar Naron and having his cloak stripped from him. He would never survive that. Either by drinking himself to death, or by his own sword, Jordyn Stone would be no more.

After Lord Rahmos had carried out the sentence of twenty lashes, he commanded that Stone be released and left to collect himself, ordering that no one was to aid him until he climbed the steps of Naron's Keep and made it inside on his own strength. The pain had not seemed so bad during the torment, but now that it was over and the pole no longer supported him, Stone found he did not have the strength to stand. The pain and loss of blood sapped him of all energy.

He began to crawl through the mud, burying his hands in it, squeezing it through his fingers in angry fists. Inch by inch, he moved toward the steep steps of the massive, towering castle.

"You!" Lord Rahmos demanded of a lad who had entered the courtyard just as the whipping was about to commence. "You are the commander's personal page, are you not?"

"Ye...yes, my Lord," the boy said with a hasty and clumsy bow, fouled by fear. "Worner, at your disposal."

"The message I received from King Robert stated that the riders trespassing on his lands had been spread over nearly a mile, but suddenly converged on one spot before turning around and crossing back across the border. What did you find?"

"With all respect, my Lord, I wasn't actually there."

"I *said*, what did you find?" Lord Rahmos demanded.

"Commander Stone found a young girl on the plains, my Lord. We have been resting her here. She was half-dead when she arrived. She..."

"Yes?" Lord Rahmos pushed.

"She has silver eyes, my Lord," Worner said softly, practically whispering.

Lord Rahmos' face remained as stoic as ever, but his eyes erupted as though the fire in his mind would spew forth from them, consuming his entire body in flame.

"Show me."

THE DREAM WAS THE SAME as it had always been, as far back as Lily could remember. Try as she might, she could never make it out, at least not clearly. It was as if she had gotten water in her eyes, and her vision had failed her. She could see something…something falling…falling endlessly, but for the life of her, she could not see what it was. On the nights when the dream came to her, she would wake exhausted, as though she hadn't slept at all.

The door opened quietly, but it woke her all the same, for she had not been sleeping very soundly. Through the opening walked a man with the darkest skin she had ever seen. Her father and aunt had told her many times of the dark men and their prevalence in other parts of the world, but in her little cottage on the plains, she had never seen one for herself.

"Did I wake you, child?" the dark man asked, with a voice holding a deep resonance that reminded her of the old Dalani harp Susa had played for her on rainy nights. She found his voice soothing, like slipping back in time and wrapping herself in a warm, happy memory.

"No, sir, I was resting my eyes," she answered.

"And what eyes they are," he said, stepping closer and sitting on the bed next to her as she began to rise from the floor. The scar over his own eye was unnerving, but she made her best attempt not to stare at it.

"My name is Urnest, child. What's yours?" His soft tone made her feel safe, even more so than the commander's voice had, at least before that afternoon. Even when Stone was kind, he had looked at her as if he wanted something—but this dark man looked on her with nothing but tenderness and curiosity.

"My name is Lily, sir."

"*My Lord*, child."

"I apologize, my Lord."

"Very good. Now tell me, how does a girl your age find herself alone in the middle of the Great Plains without food or water?" At the forlorn look on her face, he added, "It's all right, child. Whatever it was that drove you out there, you are safe now. I give you my word."

"My father had come to visit me at my aunt's house near Lynap," Lily said. "Ten men dressed in fur and iron came from out of the hills and attacked us. He told me to run, so I took his horse and ran until I fell from it. I couldn't catch it after that."

"Did he not come to find you, child?"

"I heard his screams as I ran, and then silence. My aunt is

surely dead, too."

"From Lynap to where you were found? On foot it had to have taken at least a week. How did you make it that far?" He seemed genuinely impressed, compelling Lily to want to tell him more.

"I followed streams as far as I could before they took me off course. And I picked wonyk berries wherever I could find them. I finally found some gola roots and used stones and dried long grass to make a fire to roast them, but making the fire took what was left of my energy and I collapsed. That's where Commander Stone found me."

"It sounds like quite the harrowing tale, child. But why travel so far? Why not go to Roleigh? I'm sure King Robert would have helped you."

"My father told me to come here. He said King Henry would protect me and take me into his home."

"Why would your father make such a claim?"

"He was Astymerian, my Lord. He gave me this." Lily reached into her pocket and withdrew her token. "He said to present it to King Henry when I arrived in Vita Astym."

Urnest took the token from Lily and examined it closely.

"This is a Sandil, child. A replica of the godspear, Rahmirion. It is a token of a Final Wish. If this truly belonged to your father, it shall be honored. I swear on it."

After the last week, these words were music to Lily's ears. The comfort was short-lived, though, for Commander Stone's words still jabbed at her. *Silver seer*, he had said. *What have you seen*?

"My Lord?" she asked, not quite sure where to begin.

"Yes, child?"

"Commander Stone said I was a…"

"Layda Arani," Urnest said without missing a beat.

"Yes," she said, worried for what would follow. "He's wrong, right?"

"I wish I had some comfort to offer you, child. But unfortunately, Stone is right. Silver eyes make a silver seer. There is hardly a man alive who hasn't heard the name or the stories. Before long you will look through a portal into the days yet to come. The mists of tomorrow that hover over all our eyes shall be lifted from yours, and those silver eyes will see things others can scarcely comprehend."

The room began to spin as the dark man spoke, and Lily felt feverish. One hundred thoughts flew through her mind as she reached desperately for something to hold onto. She turned again and again on the spot, spinning nearly as fast as the world around her, reaching for anything that would root her to where she stood. *It isn't true. I won't believe it. I can't believe it. There is nothing I could have done.*

Lord Rahmos' words made her failure real, and her stomach began to heave and churn. Her head felt as though it would burst open from within, blinding her with pain to the point her legs would no longer support her. The last thing she remembered before darkness was the feeling of falling and being embraced by a strong grip. Falling. *Falling...*

Chapter 13

Royal Marshal Academy: Astymere
37th Day of the First Month
5014 A.S.

Mayson and Diero sat with their fellow first-years at a long wooden table in the mess hall, stuffing food into their mouths. The banging of pots and pans in the kitchens ran countermelody to the chorus of voices swirling about their heads. Chicken stew warmed their bones, chilled from the harsh ocean wind. Kristian dipped a soft piece of fresh bread in gravy, as little Teren tediously removed peas from his bowl. Diero didn't lift his head from his stew, but Mayson angrily spied Brentin Kallyst and his minions from across the hall.

The third beating had happened two weeks past, landing the boys in the infirmary. This time, Brentin, Blayk, and their cronies had cut open Mayson's right eye, knocked out one of his molars, and split Diero's lip. Their injuries were not severe enough to be sent to the Baths, and so the pain robbed them of sleep for two nights. Diero was unable to eat for another three.

Blayk had broken two of Diero's ribs in the first attack, leaving him in too much pain to even notice being hungry. Now that he was beginning to heal, his appetite was coming back with a vengeance. Brentin took one look at Mayson's stitched eye and said something to his group that the prince couldn't hear. Whatever it was, it made the lot of them burst out laughing.

"I wonder if he will laugh while emptying my chamber pot once I'm king?" Mayson asked, staring down his nemesis.

For three days, the boys had been separated by conflicting schedules and guard duties. Mayson had sat alone in the mess hall during his off hours and Diero was forced to dine alone as well. To have everyone together again was a small but welcome comfort.

"I should stand up and kick his stones into the roof of his mouth," Mayson spoke out.

"Come now, Mayson," Kristian said with disappointment. "It isn't like you to be petty."

"It isn't like him to get seven shades of shit kicked out of him either," Diero replied between bites.

"You think they'll come over today?" Kip asked through a

mouthful of chicken and rice.

"I doubt it, but I've been wrong before," Mayson replied, gingerly touching the stitches over his eye. "I've been thinking...we should confront them and finish this once and for all."

"What are you saying?" Kristian asked

"I'm saying we take the fight to them—go on the offensive."

"That's brilliant," Diero said as he emptied his horn mug of ale, washing down the last of his stew. "Be sure to remind me how it went after they put our skulls back together."

"We've already proved we could destroy them one-on-one, so let's take advantage of that. We hunt them down one at a time and send them to the infirmary, while making sure their injuries aren't bad enough to be sent to the Baths. There is not a single one of the lot that can take us alone, much more both of us together. I'd wager we can do some pretty gruesome damage if we get them separated."

"Why not just go to Qirk?" asked Teren. "I'm sure he could end it in a moment. Why risk it?"

"Qirk *could* end it in a moment, but he won't," Mayson replied. "He's made that clear. To openly acknowledge abuse at the oldest and most prestigious military school in the kingdom would irreparably scar its, and his, reputation. He wants this done quietly, and if we get this right, there will hardly be any fuss."

Diero ripped himself a large chunk of bread, spilling crumbs upon the table. He held the piece before his mouth as he thought for a moment.

"What did you have in mind?" he asked, a spark of wicked curiosity in his eyes.

"Well, what good is a leader with no one to lead? We work from the bottom up. Save Blayk and Brentin for last. That way they won't have anyone to back them up," Mayson replied with a sly grin. "I went to Addam the other day and asked for access to the schedules for every student at school, which he reluctantly obliged, given the state of things."

Mayson pulled several large rolls of parchment from his satchel, marked with names, locations, and times. "We now know where they're going to be, and when they're going to be there."

"And who they're going to be with," Diero added.

"Just be careful," Kristian said, shooting a sidelong glance over to the final years across the dining hall. "One miscalculation and you'll bring the whole lot of them down on you at once. You'll have to move quickly in order to get to each of them before they catch on."

"Trust me, cousin," Mayson replied, the seeds of regality in his voice finally sown. "We can't fail."

The next morning, Mayson exited the forges, covered in soot from the burning coals and sweating from the sweltering heat of the furnace. He slowly removed the now blackened bandage protecting the wound over his eye and walked from the main entrance to the side of the building, away from the heavy flow of student traffic.

Ciryl Zagar, a skinny tall boy of seventeen, absently ran his fingers through his mustard-colored hair, removing the tiny black particles. His buckteeth stuck out beyond his lips as he lumbered out after Mayson. He was separated from his clan, putting finishing touches on his unimpressive practice sword. Diero bolted out of the entrance and shoved Ciryl hard, knocking him to the ground with a soft, dull *thud.*

"Come here, you little shit!" He shouted, giving chase around the corner of the foundry. Mayson was close behind, treading as lightly as a mountain cat stalking a deer. They turned left once in the back of the forge, entering a dead-end corridor between the back of the building and the border wall of the school. "I'm going to teach you a lesson you won't soon forget."

"Wait," Diero stopped. "Aren't you just a scrawny weakling who can't get it up?"

Ciryl's eyes widened as he walked over, cracking his knuckles and stretching his arms, preparing himself for satisfaction. Mayson closed in from behind, blocking the alley entrance. The gravel crunched beneath his feet, causing the older boy to turn and face him, allowing Diero the chance to lunge forward and place him in an iron-tight hold, restraining his arms behind him.

"Not so much fun when the numbers are against *you*, is it?" The prince asked, slowly approaching. "Be sure to tell Brentin about this when you wake up," he said, now looming over his hunched foe. "I will put it to you simply. This ends *now*."

Mayson grabbed Ciryl's chin, forcing him to look into his ice-blue eyes. "Understood?"

Ciryl nodded, wide-eyed, and watched as a swift overhand swing struck his jaw with a deafening crack, knocking him unconscious. Mayson and Diero stood over his limp body huddled on the ground.

"One down—on to the next," Mayson said.

They spent the rest of the day picking off the three other members of the group. Daniel Skarton, the lookout, was asleep in the barracks for a midday nap. Mayson sat on top of his chest, pinning his body and arms, as Diero laid into his midsection with continuous punches. Daniel swore to not aid Brentin any further, and for good measure, Mayson broke the boy's forearm to let the message sink in.

Cecil Arin was alone in the mess hall when the prince sent his head into the plate of fruit that sat before him.

"This could go on and on, or it could end now!" Diero yelled before slamming his head into the splattered juices once more. He hadn't even allowed Cecil to answer before ending the conversation with a slap across the face. The foggy look, along with the ever so subtle shake in his eyes, suggested the boys had concussed him, sending their third mark to the infirmary as planned.

Mack Razin had held Diero's arms back the first time Blayk savaged him. The pair found him relieving himself in the latrine, where Diero swept his legs out from under him. The two swiftly picked Mack up and stuffed his head down the privy hole. Mayson held Mack's legs on his shoulder, wrapping his arms around the boy's knees, while Diero delivered a series of merciless kicks to his midsection, earning one or two unmistakable *cracks*. The last they saw him, he was lying on the floor whimpering and cursing them with what little breath he had left.

As they expected, the older students had little ability to take the two without numbers on their side, and the small amount of fight the buffoons had was quickly overmatched. It felt good to finally let their enemies know what it was like to feel helpless. The sweet prize of justice was so close, Mayson could taste it.

Later that day, the boys sat outside their history class, where they learned more of Astymir's final victory over the old empire on the slopes of Mount Karrok. Students filed past them as they rested upon the steps, surveying their surroundings. Brentin stood with what was left of his posse on the other end of the courtyard before strutting across the yard, Blayk trailing behind. Fury fueled his steps. Digging his feet into the dirt, he left a trail of dust in his wake. Mayson and Diero rose from their perch, and calmly marched to meet him in the center of the open yard.

"You little shits think you're clever?" Brentin shouted as he neared, the freckles on his face appearing like targets to Mayson.

"*Silence*," Mayson ordered, surprisingly bringing the older student to a halt.

"What did you say to me, you puddle of horse spunk?"

"I said, silence. I've heard just about as much as I'm willing to tolerate from you. It's over. Your friends will spend no less than a week in the infirmary. Your advantage is gone. We can end this now and let bygones be bygones, or we can do things your way. Take your pick. Either way, things are about to change."

Brentin stood still and silent. Mayson hadn't thought he would hesitate so long. He hoped he would either stand down quickly or lunge at him, but the fool just stood there for what seemed like minutes.

The silence was soon broken by a sharp *pop*. Mayson turned to his right to see that Diero had silently gone over to Blayk and struck him in the mouth while he'd been focusing his attention on Brentin. Blayk fell like a bale of hay, and Diero was on top of him before he even hit the ground, apparently taking note of Perry's instructions not to hesitate.

Seeing this, Brentin turned to flee. Mayson normally pitied men overcome by such cowardice, but today, blood was in the water, and for the first time since he arrived at school, Mayson was the shark and not the seal. Mayson quickly overtook Brentin and kicked his legs out from under him, causing him to skid to a stop on his face. As the prince turned him over, he could barely hear his pleas for mercy over the shouts of the crowd of students that had gathered to watch. His cheek was already scraped open from the impact, and dirt had turned his teeth a muddy brown.

Blow after blow, Mayson sent his fists hammering into Brentin's face, knocking a tooth loose and cracking the bridge of his nose. He could hear himself cry out words of anger over and over in a strange voice that seemed like it did not belong to him.

Mayson couldn't tell how much time went by, but when Drillmaster Perry came to break things up, he could barely move his arms. He looked over as Addam attempted to pull Diero off Blayk, whose nose was squirting blood, and a large cut over his eye ran into the middle of his forehead. As Diero began to walk away, he slipped out of Addam's grip to kick Blayk in his side one last time.

Perry had to drag Mayson away by his arms. The exhilaration of his victory began to ebb as Brentin shrunk into the distance. All sound was an indistinguishable murmur as Mayson's thoughts raced to process what he was feeling. Euphoria, fatigue, burning in his lungs, and, to his shock, fear. It was a fear he'd never known before, sharp and clear as a shard of glass slicing skin. He didn't fear any consequence nor acts of revenge. He feared himself and his overwhelming satisfaction with the damage he'd done. He had awoken a beast within and now worried that if he didn't cage it properly, it would consume him from the inside out.

CHAPTER 14

Lynap: Aldan
37ᵗʰ Day of the First Month
5014 A.S.

RONIN FOUND HIS MEN BUTCHERED in the thickets of tall grass along a roadway on the Plains. The lot Commander Haledon had charged with transporting the Northern haul had fallen just a day's ride from reaching their destination of Saskawna Prison. The Dalani prison was a lone island in the center of a sea of grass. Once inside, there was no hope of escape, even if a prisoner were to slip beyond the wallless compound. With no cover for miles, it was easy work for a patrol to ride any escapees down. Only, the Northmen had never made it inside; the guards never knew they were there; therefore, they vanished into the green sea like ghosts.

Ronin and his party scattered the vultures and prairie wolves picking at his men and organized a proper burial just outside Saskawna. *The blood left in this grass will not be in vain.* By the grace of the Winged Father, the prison hounds hadn't taken long to pick up the trail. They had barely gotten the search underway when, from out of the north, a thunderstorm of hellish strength blew in and forced the party to make camp. The winds howled through the night and the rains practically blew in sideways, making sleep a most elusive, slippery thing—but the men wearily packed up and rode on.

"Thank the gods," Eldric piped up as he trot in stride with the Dalani prince. "If the storm hadn't broken the heat, I think I might've already fallen off of my horse." The wet suction of hooves being pulled from mud could be heard in abundance, as the trail of the Northerners led them off-road.

Ronin grumbled. "It would be miserable, but we would have reached Lynap by now, well rested."

"My Prince, you sound like a whining child—no disrespect intended, of course."

Ronin shot Eldric a seething glare. The winds of the night had sucked the energy from him, his usual wit drained. *I'll repay him for that in my own time.*

A featherbed awaited each of them in Lynap. That was all Ronin could focus on—perhaps he was growing soft. A year ago, one sleepless night wouldn't have bothered him so much. *To grow old and weary while still a young man—what a sorry fate indeed.* Ronin drew himself up straight in his saddle and shook his head as if to clear the sand and webs from his eyes.

The storm wiped away nearly all traces of a track in the endless grass, but by some miracle, the hounds kept the scent and the trail held true, leading the company straight for Lynap.

Though it was no great city, Lynap was home to over one thousand souls and well guarded. If the Northmen had come this way, they did not linger. *They wouldn't risk raiding this town. They are wild, not stupid.* Ronin hoped they would avoid people altogether, though he knew it unlikely, for they'd need supplies for their long trek home. Lynap itself would be safe, but the smaller, surrounding communities would not be.

The hounds began to bay ferociously and darted off toward the top of the hill, disappearing over the other side before anyone could react. *Could it be they stayed here?* With a snap of the reins, Ronin and Eldric tore away from the Sworn Hooves, climbing the southern side of the hill while their men fought to catch up.

When they reached the summit, Ronin and Eldric stopped suddenly in their tracks, so much so that their Sworn Hooves nearly barreled into them from behind.

Below them, in the basin of four hills separated from the endless ranges beyond, sat a burnt out black husk. From what Ronin could figure at this distance, it could only have been a house. *No smoke. They are long gone by now.*

The air, which had been alive and cool with breeze after breeze all morning, felt still and empty. The hairs on Ronin's forearms began to rise. *Death has come here.* The hounds could still be heard baying and crying down at the base, where they appeared as nothing more than five black dots closing in on the dismantled, blackened structure.

With a kick to his thoroughbred's sides, Ronin was off again, followed by the thunder of Eldric and his Hooves keeping pace. Less than a minute later, the party came upon a much more horrific sight than they could have imagined. From the top of the hill, they could barely make out this blackened shell of a cottage, let alone what stood before it. The hounds stopped their yowls and let out only soft whimpers and whines as they sat before the horror.

Before them appeared to be two scarecrows erected on large

stakes dug into the ground in the shape of an *X*. Ronin surmised that the wood had been taken from the house before it was burned, for they wouldn't have found it anywhere else. But as the prince and Eldric dismounted and approached the scarecrows, the overpowering stench of rotting flesh overtook them.

From what they could tell from the grayed, bloated bodies, they had been a man and a woman once. Their legs seemed to have been gnawed upon, most likely by prairie wolves. Ronin nearly gave an order for them to be cut down, but closer examination revealed they were not merely tied to the stakes, but impaled on them. The beams had been shoved into their sides just above the hips and had emerged from their rib cages, piercing the undersides of their arms. The woman's dress was tattered and half removed, exposing a large, dangling breast. Her face showed signs of a terrible beating, and just below, her throat had been cut. The man, however, appeared to be in much better condition. The only visible wound beyond the damage to his legs seemed to be a deep piercing wound over his heart.

"Take them down," Ronin ordered after a long, grave silence. These new deaths pushed the prince beyond fury and into the grips of desperation. *There will be no more bodies. By the High and Low Gods, there will be no more bodies.*

Ronin explored the property as his men began taking down the crucifixes. He had been so preoccupied with the slain residents that he did not notice several ashy funeral mounds ten yards off until he was practically on top of them. There were three separate piles, each adorned with a small *X* made from smaller pieces of lumber. Before the pyres, planted firmly into the ground, stood a sword that was neither the crude iron make of the Northmen, nor the fine, straight steel of Dalani Hooves. Ronin deduced the curved blade belonged to the man impaled on the planks. *They left him his sword. Why steal the others but leave this?* It seemed that the saber stood guard over the pyres, as if forever reminding the dead who it was who had sent them into the beyond. *He claimed a few before they cut him down. Impressive for a country hermit.*

Ronin pulled the saber from the soft earth and wiped it clean on his green cloak before holding it aloft to examine properly in the light. The hilt was banded and segmented, much like the shell of a Tirani armadillo his father had acquired as a wine bowl during his travels to the other Western Kingdoms. But it was the blade that gave Ronin pause. The blue ripples, like so many veins in a man's arm, and the vibrant silver in between revealed just one possibility: high steel.

The prince was no stranger to high steel. His father and many of his closest guards had weapons made from this top-quality material, but only one nation produced high steel blades in such a shape.

"Check that man!" Ronin cried. Saber in hand, he charged over to the bodies, now lying flat as the Hooves attempted to remove the stakes from their sides, gagging and coughing from the odor. Ronin grasped a handful of the dead man's clothes and pulled them close to examine, oblivious to the smell as his mind focused on his revelation. *Black silk. An Astymerian. Eiruashte, Winged Father, help me.*

His heart began to race at the thought of King Henry scouring the plains with his black knights, taking this hunt away from him. But as he looked hard on the rotting face of this poor soul, his heart seemed to stop in his chest. The beard, the bald head, even the sword now seemed familiar. *I know this man.*

"Coronyn, I want you to take ten men and bring this body to the Crescent. Then, I want you to return to Roleigh and await us there. Hostran, you are to give this lady a proper burial with full Dalani tribal rites; then you are to ride hard for Lynap and send a swallow to the Crescent. Inform King Henry we have found one of his men on the plains. Understood?"

"Aye, my Prince," the pair replied.

"The rest of us follow the trail. We leave now. *Mount up!"* New life was breathed into the Hooves as the hundred men clambered onto their destriers and plucked their spears from the mud.

"Are you sure about this, my Prince?" Eldric asked. "How can you be certain this man is Astymerian?"

"Can you name any other man who carries a saber of high steel and wears black silk clothes? He is from the Crescent, I'm certain, though I feel there is something else. I know this man, Eldric. If I am not mistaken, he is William Otter."

"Who?"

"He was Captain of King Henry's personal guard for over

twenty years. I met him several times when my father would bring me on his visits to Vita Astym."

"What do you think King Henry will do, my Prince?"

"I can't say for sure. But I do know that whatever it is, it will not bode well for us. Let us hope we find these bastards before word reaches Astymere. I will not have this kill taken from me."

Ronin kicked his steed into full stride to pick up the trail once again. *Hell with featherbeds. Hell with sleep. I'll sleep after I've washed their blood from my hands and my blade.*

Chapter 15

Vita Astym: Astymere
2nd Day of the Second Month
5014 A.S.

BEATRICE SAT IN THE LOW SHADE of an arash bush as late morning sun drifted behind the tall steeples of the palace, throwing long shadows across the grounds. The feeling of grass beneath her bare feet, which had always been enough to settle her mind and nerves, did little to dispel the dark shroud cast by the thought of Henry's dead wife.

She had gone outside to watch the clouds go by but there were none to be seen, and so she sat alone with her thoughts of Emilia and Henry's need to keep her a secret. She had come close, on more than one occasion, to broaching the subject. Despite all that Raymund had told her, her intuition said there was far more to the story. Grief was a weight that all must bear, and all bear it in their own fashion. She understood it was natural not to talk of things that cause too much pain. But only those also marred by the weight of shame will keep secrets as closely guarded as this. *What happened to her, Henry?*

Shouts near the eastern gate broke her from her reflection. She stood, brushed her skirt clean of leaves, and stepped through the hedges onto the gravel walkway leading from the gate to the eastern veranda. She walked without a care for the heat or uneven jabs of the stones. There was little, short of hot coals, her Dalani feet could not handle.

A party of riders displaying the broken-chain banner of House Rahmos filed through the open gate as the Knights of Rahm watched closely from the ramparts. A dark, bald head leaned down out of the saddle to speak to one of the many attendants who came rushing to relieve the Rahmos party of their horses. Once Urnest dismissed him, a young officer Beatrice did not recognize gave a hurried bow as he flew past her, crunching the gravel as he went. Beatrice watched as Urnest dismounted, revealing someone had been sharing his saddle: a young girl no older than thirteen, by the look of her. Urnest took her by the hand and set her on the ground as his eldest son, Tyrel, emerged from the troop to join them.

Beatrice stiffened her relaxed pose and raised her chin, giving the formal appearance of a queen, as the trio, accompanied by ten silver cloaked Rahmos guards, approached. They bowed deeply as they drew near, and the men-at-arms behind them bent the knee until Beatrice beckoned them to rise.

"My Queen," Urnest said, stepping forward and removing his riding gloves. His bald head shone like glass in the unobstructed sun. "My most humble apologies for arriving unannounced, but is the king within?"

"My dear Urnest, you have bowed before me. I think we can dispense with the formalities, don't you?"

A wide grin spread across his face as he began to chuckle, relaxing his stance and speaking in a more personable tone.

"You know I have never been able to refuse you anything, Beatrice. Well, how about it? Is the Old Bruiser in there, or am I going to have to tear across the city to find him?"

"He was in his study, the last I saw him. To what do we owe this unexpected pleasure?"

Urnest was always welcome at the palace and frequently came and went as he pleased. But rarely was there such pomp and circumstance, with a full array of men at arms and waving banners.

"To be frank, my Queen, it is our guest," he said, gesturing behind him. The girl who waited with Tyrel stood clasping her hands with hunched, timid shoulders. "Come, child." The girl hesitated, fidgeting in place. Tyrel gave her an encouraging nudge and she slowly made her way to them, looking at the ground. "Lily, may I introduce Queen Beatrice Karrok, Lady of the House of Suryn, Spear Maiden of the Lords of Dalan, and Wara Ahiashte, Daughter of the Wind."

The girl lifted her long blue skirt and gave a deep, clumsy curtsy. "It is an honor to meet you, your Majesty," she said, barely more than a whisper.

"The honor is mine, child," Beatrice said with as much royal grace as she could muster. Formality would have to be maintained with this stranger for now. "Any friend of Lord Rahmos is a friend of the Crown. Such a lovely young thing you are. Lily, is it? Come, let me see you." With a firm but gentle finger, Beatrice raised the girl's chin to look her in the eye. Her breath caught in her throat at the sight, and her cheeks flushed hot. *He brings one of them to my door. A Layda Arani.*

Beatrice remained locked on the girl as a booming voice came from behind, quickly approaching. "There is only one head in all of Astymere that can fit to blind a man at fifty yards! Urnest, my most faithful Guardian. I hope no one misbehaved while I was gone."

Henry planted a kiss on Beatrice's cheek, breaking her concentration, else she likely would have stared at the girl until the Second Flame. He wore a suit of white linen with coal black buttons, collar, and pants, decked with a gold and silver sash. He always dressed well for company.

"My King," Urnest said, bending the knee. Tyrel and the girl followed suit. "There was a slight…incident. But it has been dealt with in accordance with your laws."

"So I've heard. I imagine Stone will now wet himself whenever he hears your name," Henry said with a smile. He beckoned for Urnest to rise, and the two came together in a tight embrace. "I don't know if I should thank or curse you. You have saved me a great deal of trouble by seeing to the matter, but I have been robbed of the pleasure of knocking Stone back into place."

"The next time Commander Stone defies orders in your absence, rest assured, I shall wait for your return," Urnest said, tapping Henry in the shoulder with his riding gloves.

"We'll have to keep an eye on him from now on. Perhaps a Crown-appointed liaison would do well…"

"My love," Beatrice interrupted, crisp and clear. "Urnest has not come here to discuss Commander Stone."

"Hasn't he?" Henry said, looking on Urnest with curious eyes.

"I bring a guest, my King." Urnest gestured toward the seer. The girl took a deep breath, and for the first time since she dismounted, seemed to stand with pride.

"My King, this is Lily," said Urnest. "She has been through hell to make it here to you."

"Is it as cold as they say?" Henry asked, unable to mask his amusement at his joke. The girl stood silent, uncertain of what to say, or to whom.

"It's alright, child," Urnest said warmly. "You may speak for yourself. Tell him why you are here."

Yes, please do, Beatrice thought.

"Your majesty," she said in a meek, innocent whisper. She

might have passed for a common girl, had Beatrice not seen her eyes. "My father was in your service. He told many stories of how he fought by your side and looked on you as a friend. Before he died, he gave me this." She pulled something from her pocket and held it out for Henry's inspection. The tiny black object reflected the sunlight in bright flashes as she turned it over in her fingers.

Beatrice had seen enough of the tokens of the Final Wish to know what they signified. *What man worthy of such a token would associate with* them?

Henry took the tiny black emblem and gingerly rolled it about in his open palm, staring in disbelief.

"It's been a long time since I've had one of these brought before me," Henry said. "I bestow them hoping I never see them again, blinding myself to our inevitable ends. Tell me, child. What wish comes borne on the back of this token?"

"My father's final wish was for me to be fostered here, to be brought under your protection." The girl sounded much surer of herself now.

Sly witch. Using one of Astymere's most sacred traditions to get next to the king.

"A very touching tale, my dear," Beatrice said, stepping forward and placing herself between the Layda Arani and her husband. "Tell me, who was your father? How can we know that this token was *given* to you, and that you did not simply take it from one of this country's greatest heroes?"

"Yes, child," Henry said in a steady voice, as though a fog had been lifted from him. *That's it, my love. Don't fall under this witch's enchantment.* "What was your father's name?"

Trumpets suddenly blared out in the streets beyond the palace's four walls, as the sound of hooves on stone and the creaking of wheels carried from the gatehouse, where a company of green-cloaked riders in dazzling copper-colored steel breastplates gathered. The green and white banner of Dalan heralded their entry, and Beatrice momentarily forgot about the young witch trying to infiltrate her home. The rare occurrence of her countrymen in their presence always warmed her heart. She counted ten riders, one of whom pulled a small cart. He sallied forward, still mounted, while the rest of his group made way toward the king on foot.

"Tyrel," Henry said. "Stay here with her. Don't let her out of your sight."

"Yes, my King," Tyrel said as he shot a sheepish, almost apologetic look toward the girl.

Henry, Beatrice, and Urnest walked to the gatehouse to meet the Dalani party, accompanied by the Rahmos men-at-arms and several Knights of Rahm who had silently fallen into step.

Beatrice grasped Henry's hand and walked close to his side. She glanced up at him, trying to gauge him. His face had grown unnaturally hard and stoic and had looked that way for days, ever since Ronin's letter arrived. Even having grown up with them, Beatrice was still amazed by the speed with which the Dalani thoroughbreds had bore the body to Astymere. *Such hard riding. We will give those horses comfort they have never dreamed of.*

"Perhaps he was mistaken, my love," Beatrice said softly as they walked. "Ronin had met William only a handful of times. There is still hope."

"No one has seen or heard from William in weeks, dearest," Henry said in a grim tone. "The more I hope, the more my heart will break if I am wrong. Stay with me." The last bit was hardly more than a whisper.

Beatrice's heart stood poised to break as well if the letter proved true. *At least I can bear some of the load with you this time.*

The lead rider removed his winged helm, releasing a cascade of long, ginger hair. His wind-beaten face was frozen in the dark expression of one trapped in the company of death for days. He took point at the front of the cart and bent the knee. The Sworn Hoof leading the cart hopped down with a soft *crunch* and fell to his knee as well. Henry silently beckoned them to stand.

"Your Majesty, I am Lieutenant Coronyn MacCairn, Sworn Hoof to Crown Prince Ronin Suryn. I come before you with the deepest of regrets, to bring you the body of one of your own. Would you look on him and give him your mark?" The lieutenant did not look Henry in the eye—whether out of respect or shame, Beatrice did not know.

Henry walked to the cart, which sat about chest high, and looked in. His stone face visibly drooped and sagged as he slowly closed his eyes. Beatrice couldn't bring herself to go near the cart, lest she burst into tears and crumble before her countrymen.

"Where did you find him?" Henry asked, his voice cracking and weak.

"Outside of Lynap, your Majesty, near a burnt down hut. He had been…" The lieutenant faltered.

"Tell me," Henry implored. "Don't let me imagine all manner of terrible things."

"When we found him, your Majesty, he was impaled on a crucifix, next to an older woman who suffered the same fate."

"Susa? I didn't know she was still alive. William hadn't spoken of her in years." Henry gazed into the cart as he spoke, his voice trailing off.

"We figure it was the fugitives Prince Ronin had been tracking. We were part of his hunt until he sent us to you, your Majesty. Prince Ronin seemed to think your man killed several of them before perishing. There were funeral pyres as well, and they left him his sword. They stole the swords of the men they killed on the plains, but they left his…I imagine he was very brave, sir."

"I've never known any that compare," Henry said, laying his arm against the rail of the cart to rest his head upon. "I want to build a pyre for him. He often told me that was how he wanted to pass on. A funeral pyre so bright they could see it across the Krystal River. Rahm as my witness, he shall have it." Henry sniffed and wiped his nose on his sleeve, wiping away the few tears that managed to force themselves out.

The Hooves moved in to remove the body from the cart as Henry stepped away. Beatrice wanted to go to him, to take him in her arms and allow him to release his pain, but she stood still. The queen was never one to shirk her duty. It was, after all, why she was in Astymere in the first place.

Henry stopped in his tracks and lifted his eyes from the ground, his brow furrowed in serious thought. He suddenly cast his gaze along the yard toward Tyrel and the witch. A single, silent tear fell down his face as his mouth fell open.

"Tyrel!" he cried. "Bring her here, now."

Tyrel led the girl to the cart by the arm. The Hooves had finished assembling a litter and had placed William's body on it, covering it with a sheet. Henry met them halfway and Beatrice watched as he took the witch by the arms, grasping her around her biceps. He drew her in close and dropped down to her level to look in her unnatural eyes. *Has William's death touched him? What is he doing?* The queen stepped lightly as she approached, careful not to agitate Henry further.

"Your father's name," Henry kept saying. "His name. Tell me his name!"

The girl shrank back in terror, on the verge of tears. Tyrel stepped in and silently pleaded with him, communicating some unheard appeal. Whatever it was, it seemed to do the trick, for Henry looked away and softened, his back hunched from emotional strain. "Tell me, child. What was your father's name? I swear no harm will come to you. Just tell me his name."

The girl took a few moments to gather and compose herself. After much effort, her trembling lips began to move.

Beatrice could not make out what she was saying, but what happened next shocked her to her core. Henry released his grip on the girl's arms and planted a kiss upon her forehead. *She's entranced him!* She grasped her Raelian dagger within the folds of her skirt to strike the witch down before she could do any further harm, but Henry took her under his arm, providing his symbolic royal protection. *How do I break him from it?* He led the seer over to the litter, where their dear William lay silent and still. Beatrice trembled with anger, but until she could prove Henry was under some foreign influence, she could do nothing.

Henry instructed one of her countrymen to lift the sheet and reveal William's face. Beatrice could not see him from where she stood, but as the sheet was pulled back, the seer dropped to her knees and threw herself upon the body, wracked with violent sobs as she clung to William's stiff, silent form. In that moment, Beatrice understood and slowly felt her anger ebb away, replaced by shame and heartache. *Oh, child. You poor, poor child.*

Henry stood on the balcony of their bedchamber, the warmth of the torches and braziers within the room radiating onto his bare back. All around him the city was sleeping, save for the occasional dog barking or the distant sound of the Silver Shields marching. The weary king ran his fingers through his hair, searching for some measure of peace. The sight of William's gray, withered corpse sucked the life straight out of him. Even now, he could feel the icy cold of William's hand; smell the thick scent of death; see William's lifeless face. The latter was what kept him awake.

"Can't sleep?" Beatrice wrapped her arms around Henry's waist from behind and began rubbing her hands across his belly. Her voice was sweet and lilting.

"Not tonight, dearest," he said, lovingly patting her hand. "Today still weighs heavily on my heart."

"William haunts me as well, my love. To see him like that— it wasn't right. And that silver witch being dropped on our doorstep…"

"Her name is Lily, Beatrice. Growing up under Raelian rule left the mark of their stigmas upon you, and the Red Vision's nonsensical campaign after the Night of Knives only emboldened your superstitions. The girl is harmless, and our new ward."

"Must she be *our* ward, though? William sought to have her protected and we have the resources to make that happen. Why must we keep her under our roof? I am not the only one 'emboldened by nonsense.' People will talk. Dissent will spread."

"Don't be ridiculous," Henry chided. He delicately removed Beatrice's hands, then pushed through the curtains and threw a few coals on the braziers. "Rhivor has kept such poison in check. Things have gotten better with the Order since I appointed him. As for Lily, William's final wish was for *me* to take Lily under my protection. That is exactly what I intend to do."

"There are ways you can protect her without ever having to be near her. Send her away, set her up in a good, safe home, give her a royal allowance, post Knights of Rahm on her for both her protection and the protection of others—just don't bring her into our home, I beg you!"

"Enough!" cried Henry. "I know you want someone to blame for what happened to us, to you, to Mayson. But blame *me*—not the Layda Arani, and certainly not the girl. She played no part in it, Beatrice, she is William's flesh and blood. She is as much our family as he was. Her place is here. With us. Please do not make this difficult for me. The grief is more than I can bear." He sat on the edge of the bed and held his head in his hands, breathing deeply to try and compose himself.

"If I had as many heartbreaks as you, I, too, might lose my sanity." Beatrice's sympathetic voice sounded almost like music.

"As many as me?" Henry picked up his head and narrowed his gaze. "Have I had many?"

Beatrice's eyes widened so subtly that an average man would never have noticed. But to Henry, it was as brazen as a loud cough. *She thinks she's said too much.*

"Well…your parents. I never knew them, but I know you loved them dearly."

She was an honest woman, but even Beatrice had a few tells. Her most obvious, which she currently tried to hide, was to suck in her bottom lip. *That isn't what she meant.*

"You fully know the grief of losing both parents, and yet here you are completely sane." He rose and straightened his back, stretching to his full height to tower over his queen. She stood strong, but Henry could see uncharacteristic desperation in her eyes. She had let something slip—something she had gone to great lengths to keep to herself. If he was going to get it out of her, it would have to be while she was rattled, before she could raise her ironclad defenses. "What grief do I know that you do not?" *It couldn't be. She wouldn't.*

Her stance relaxed in resolution.

"After you brought the boys to the Academy, you fell into one of your dark spells," she answered. "I grew tired of asking you year after year why this melancholy gripped you so and got no answer. So, when you went on one of your *walks*, I followed you to the Tombs. I followed you to her grave…"

"You had no right!" shouted Henry with such power that a sharp pain shot down his throat. His stalwart queen cowered a bit and stepped to the other side of the room. "You had no right," he said again, this time in a soft, hoarse whisper.

"I had *every* right. When I married you, I received claim to you, as you received claim to me. *All of you.* For over twenty years, I thought you were mine completely. Now I realize I was married to a stranger—a stranger whose heart belongs to a ghost!"

"Don't speak of her that way! Whatever your quarrel is with me, you leave her out of it. She never did you any harm. She never did *anyone* any harm!" Henry stared into the fire of the nearest brazier and lost himself to the past. Emilia's blue eyes, like mirrors to his own, gazed out at him through the coals. Her flowing black hair cascaded and blended with the black iron frame. Henry swore he could hear her sweet laugh in his ear.

He tore his eyes away from the fire to look upon Beatrice. There she was, in all her glory. Her wild brown hair had been let down out of its braids, as her taut, slim muscles created shadows on her arms and legs. The scar across her bare belly, revealed by her nightclothes, was hard and pale against her smooth, tan skin. She was a vision. She was a goddess in her own right. And she was very much alive.

Beatrice's eyes began to well. The look of betrayal on her face turned Henry's stomach.

"You're right, my love. I *am* haunted. But my heart belongs to you. Whatever heart belonged to her, died with her."

"How could you keep such a thing from me? My heart breaks for you, Henry, it truly does. To lose a husband and a child is a pain I've never known and could never understand. But my heart also breaks because I thought, after all we've been through…"

"My heart belongs to you until the day I die, Beatrice. I never speak of her because of the shame it brings me. I never told you about her because I didn't want you to think less of me."

She walked to him and grabbed his hands in an iron-tight grip. Suddenly, it all seemed to bubble over and burst from his chest. His knees crumbled with the exertion of releasing over thirty years of agony, and he fell, pressing his head against her belly and weeping uncontrollably.

"It's my fault," he said through heavy sobs. "It is *my* fault. They died because of me. Great Healer Calewys told me they were in distress; that something was wrong. He begged me to allow him to open her, as they opened you, and remove the baby safely. Gods, my son. My poor Harmyn. I wouldn't listen. I wasn't the same back then, Beatrice. I was a hard, stubborn fool who thought he knew better than everyone else. I can still hear myself saying it. I can still feel the words in my mouth and throat. *No child of mine shall be born with knives and tricks. He shall be born the proper way, and I will hear no more on it.* My Emilia bled out in less than a minute. Harmyn, my brave boy, strangled by his own cord. It was *my* fault…Mine…"

"Henry," said Beatrice, stroking his hair and rubbing his arms. "You said it yourself—you are not the man you once were. You are no longer that arrogant boy. You are a king—a great king, and a wonderful father. I love you, and I promise that from now on, I shall honor her with you. You are a man worthy of her forgiveness and if you have not yet earned it, I will see to it that you do before your time has come. Please—look at me."

Henry met her eyes to feel the first true peace he'd known in years. To have Beatrice know and still see that same fierce love in her eyes was so overwhelming it nearly made him weep again. "The man I was never deserved you—I'm not even sure I deserve you now."

Beatrice pulled him into a kiss with such ferocity, it hurt. Henry rose to his feet, facing her, as he ran his hands up her thighs and cupped her firm buttocks. She broke from him and pulled his breeches down, revealing his stiffened sex. She took him in her hand and began kissing him again, biting his lip, wrapping her free arm around his neck. Henry's fingers trailed between her legs, reveling in how wet she was.

She stretched her head back and moaned as his finger entered her, while Henry kissed her exposed neck and throat. All the while her hand remained fully wrapped around him, stroking and driving him mad. With passion-filled strength, he scooped her up and held her close, letting her feet dangle above the ground. He brought her down, entering her slowly and feeling her arms tighten around his neck and shoulders. She was never one for soft, delicate whimpers. From their first night together, she had always lit a fire in him. Her moans filled the halls as he filled her. There was no telling how long he held her there, sliding in and out of her, feeling her clench and squeeze around him. It nearly made him burst.

Beatrice laughed as Henry dropped her onto the bed and climbed on top of her. She gazed up at him with hungry expectation and unwrapped her nightclothes from around her chest and waist. Her nipples were erect as she rubbed her petite breasts, waiting for him to continue. *Goddess. You are my goddess.*

She groaned in his ear as they lay there, coupling for hardly a minute before both their bodies began to tense and stiffen. Her back arched as Henry's thrusts became more powerful and desperate. He could feel it churn and push within him—he could hold back no longer. Together, they climaxed in ecstasy, their cries sailing through their open bedroom window into the dark, quiet night.

Beatrice closed her eyes and bit her lip. Henry dropped to the sheets next to her, completely deflated. He lay there for ages, taking in her smell, feeling the beautiful effects of age on her tan skin as he ran his fingers along her back. The last thing he could remember was kissing her forehead before he fell into a deep, dreamless sleep—the first he had known in decades.

Chapter 16

The Dead Lands: The Great Plains
12th Day of the Second Month
5014 A.S.

Ronin watched Eldric guide the Sworn Hooves as they broke camp under the heavy, dark clouds of the afternoon. The party had crossed into the Dead Lands two days ago, and the mood had grown tenser by the hour. In the shadow of such desolation, the memory of unspeakable bloodshed pressed heavily on their minds.

The men were all too familiar with the stories of the Dead Lands' destruction. They had been raised hearing about how King Golrik of Ilbaan and King Hermann of Lupfur had crushed the Imperial Legions in one of the bloodiest battles in the War of the Fall. The tall stalks of grain that had once grown in a thick sea of gold had been stained red, churning the soil into a foul, dark mud before the Raelians finally pulled back. Golrik had hoped to lay claim to the vast granaries once the war was over, but on his way home, he discovered they had been consumed by the same hellfire that wiped the White City from the face of the world. Endless fields of gold, laid to waste in a single night.

All the Dalani men could see now was endless gray dirt and countless black and white husks scattered like pebbles. Though thick clouds constantly hovered, rain never came to this place, leading wary travelers to believe it was as haunted as the ruins of Raelia.

"We can't be more than a few hours behind them now," Ronin said as he strapped his pack to the back of his saddle. The prince shook the loose, powdery earth from his green cloak, set his winged helm upon his head, and mounted his horse to resume the chase. It had been nearly two weeks since they had picked up the trail, and every day, the endless grass seemed to stretch on beyond them.

"Are we sure they are still alive, my Prince?" Eldric asked. "I can't imagine they would make it very far through the Dead Lands on foot."

"If the gods are with us, they're alive. It is possible they reached the Acrontian River, if they took the long way around the southern edge. The Raelians used it to water the granaries before the war. If they made it there, they would have access to water and river trout. *If* they made it there."

Ronin and his men set an energetic pace in an attempt to reach the river before nightfall. The one hundred Sworn Hooves, whose thunder usually rang out into the emptiness of the plains, silently charged through the loose soil, sending a massive cloud of dust billowing into the air as though a great inferno raged around them. Ronin, Eldric, and those at the front of the formation paid no mind to the dust they created, but the prince could not help but sympathize for the men in the rear, no doubt on the verge of suffocating.

"Spread out!" the prince shouted with as much force as he could muster. "Single line!" The Sworn Hooves disappeared beyond Ronin's peripheral vision as they loosened formation, but Eldric rode close, keeping stride and taking care not to collide with him.

"We can't keep this pace forever, my Prince!" he cried over the sound of the wind. "We are running low on food and water, and the horses will drop from beneath us if we don't turn back. This hunt will kill us all!"

"Once we reach the Acrontian River, we will water the horses and stock up on trout. They run thick this time of year! It should be more than enough to get us home."

Satisfied, Eldric took formation once again, the armor of his horse jingling and creating a beautiful chorus with the rest of the company.

The heavy clouds made it difficult to judge the time of day, but the light was just beginning to wane, along with the horses' strength, by the time Ronin and the Hooves reached water. The land was so flat in this stretch of the Dead Lands that they almost rode straight into it. If not for the sound of the current roaring over their muted hoof-beats, they never would have known it was there before they charged over the southern bank.

The river was wide where they found it, cutting across them as it head southeast. Ronin followed it back to its source, scanning northwest before it sharply turned. The mountains of Gol Garonath were beginning to rise from the northern horizon, inspiring awe in the company, most of whom had never traveled this far north before.

Ronin achingly dismounted and knelt in the cool mud to wash his face in the fresh water. He hadn't been able to tell, but the soot that washed away in the current revealed the prince had several layers of filth clinging to his skin. The brisk water felt harsh at first, but was soon relieving to his wind-beaten face. He turned to look downriver, where trout were leaping out of the water in droves as they made their way south to spawn.

Once the canteens had all been filled and the horses properly watered and rested, the men spent the remainder of the day's light collecting fish. Each had removed their emerald cloak and used it as a net to catch the trout in bundles. After an hour, their stores replenished, the Hooves used the remainder of the wood they had brought to smoke the fish, preparing it to last their long journey.

"Eat your fill, gentlemen," called Ronin. "We won't be rationing again for a while. Tomorrow we change course, follow the river north, and fish only when the need arises. The Northmen had to have followed the river. It is five hundred miles to the next water source." He addressed his lieutenants Coquun, Bardel, and Tanna. "I want fifteen men posted at fifty yards around camp at all times. Eldric and I will join the second watch. We go in two-hour increments."

The Hooves began erecting tents once they were dismissed. As the last light of day vanished into the western sky, the prince settled into his perch on a lone hilltop fifty yards south of the riverbank. His mind raced as though he were still in hot pursuit. *I don't want to have to cross the mountains of Gol Garonath, but Gods be damned, I will.*

Two hours later, Ronin switched guard duties with a few of his men. He embraced the howling wind and the biting chill of the air on the walk back to his tent, for these hardships would make his victory and earned comfort all the sweeter.

"RONIN," ELDRIC SAID WITH BITING URGENCY, breaking the prince's uneasy slumber. "Wake up—it's time." Eldric kicked him gingerly in the side. Ronin forced one stubborn eye open to see his captain standing in the opening of his tent, the dull light of dawn flooding in behind him. Despite his body's exhaustion, he rose to face the day, determined to put this business behind him. He had meant every sentiment that came to his head the night before, but frankly, if he could finish this without crossing the Great Divide, he would certainly try.

"Break camp!" Ronin shouted as he emerged from the tent, shaking the weariness from his voice. His sore legs sang to him with each step. He and the Sworn Hooves broke their fast on the remaining portion of dried peaches and smoked trout. With a splash of cold river water to the face, Ronin felt alive and ready to give chase once more.

The river wound its way north toward the Great Divide like a monstrous serpent, each bend stretching over two miles to the east and west, making the trip slow and tedious. The Dead Lands had given way to the dry plains of Tuun, filled with cold and harsh grasslands that hugged the river in its northernmost stretch. After the company had traveled sixty miles north, Kal, one of Ronin's forward scouts, spotted a pile of trout carcasses along the nearest bank. They hadn't been cooked, but they had been cleaned and gutted properly.

"They are still moist, my Prince," Kal said as he dismounted to observe more closely. "They can't be far."

"*Double time!*" the prince cried. He could practically smell his prey now; his very soul was aflame with a thirst for blood. *Keep moving. Keep moving.*

The mountains of Gol Garonath were no longer a distant mirage on the horizon, but a looming behemoth that hovered over the party, filling all with strange desperation.

A light snow was beginning to fall, though the clouds were much thinner than they had been that morning. It was blowing off the top of the mountains, carried by icy winds that had grown stronger throughout the day. As the cold grip of the wild lands closed around the throats of the Sworn Hooves, Ronin spotted his mark.

Trudging along the river at no more than two hundred yards off were nine fur-covered figures moving erratically over the rough landscape. Ronin's eyes widened.

"*Charge!*" Ronin bellowed with terrible force, startling the men behind him. The Sworn Hooves lifted their spears and formed into a tight wedge, with Ronin at the center. He could hear the Northmen's panicked voices as they shouted to each other, each feebly attempting to separate from the group as the horsemen closed in.

With a savage thrust, Eldric speared the back of the slowest man, skewering iron, fur, and flesh like a wild boar. The blow sent him flying into the man in front of him, and both slammed into the dust from the impact. Eldric drew his high steel bastard sword to cut down another, who attempted to hack at his leg with an axe.

The rest of the party circled and surrounded the group as Ronin, Eldric, and Kal dismounted to finish the survivors. One man rose from the ground to pull Eldric's spear from his companion's body. He had only one hand but fought with fierce strength, lunging at Ronin, who now stood directly in front of him, with reckless abandon. The young prince parried with his own spear, swinging the shaft back around his head and slamming the wood into the side of his foe's neck. Another sweep to the Northman's legs took his feet out from under him. He barely had time to catch his breath before Ronin thrust his spear into his eye, burying the steel tip in his skull.

The prince turned to see Eldric with his arm wrapped around a man's throat from behind, as he parried another's strike with his sword. One Hoof broke from the surrounding circle and finished off the attacking enemy with a spear to the back. Eldric was now free to drop his sword and use his free hand to grab a dagger from his belt. He slid the steel into his victim's back between his ribs and let him drop limply to the ground, the air sighing out of his lungs.

"Spear!" Kal cried, as the last survivor attempted to charge the ring of horses surrounding them. Ronin tossed him his weapon and watched with glee as Kal sent it sailing into the air, piercing his target through the leg. Ronin drew his broadsword, and before the man could roll over, drove it through his back, silencing him.

The chaos lasted mere moments, but Ronin's heart was pounding with both exhaustion and exhilaration, his hot breath trailing like smoke in the frigid northern air. With this business finished, he began to feel his spirit settle and his nerves release.

"Search them," he said through heavy breaths.

The Hooves moved from body to body, rooting through the tattered, filthy pelts the Northmen had been wearing. There was nothing of any particular value besides the handful of weapons they had stolen from the Hooves they'd murdered. The rest was a bunch of barbaric idols, as well as bone tokens they had carried with them from the start.

"My Prince," Kal called, his clean-shaven face beginning to grow red and frostbitten in the frigid cold. "Look here." He held a befouled, filthy piece of parchment that seemed to have been crumpled up for weeks in the dead man's pocket.

Ronin fumbled to smooth it, his hands slightly numb from the sharp mountain winds sweeping down over the plains. It bore a design that was beginning to fade—a spear etched in black ink.

The prince nearly tossed the parchment aside, but thought twice about it. It was no more than a flicker of familiarity, but upon closer scrutiny the prince realized he knew this spear, and knew it well. He had seen it once when he was a boy, when King Henry stayed in Roleigh on his way back to Astymere after the White City had fallen.

He then recalled he had seen it many times since. Every time he looked upon the banner of Astymere, there it was, staring him proudly in the face. The unmistakable shape of Rahmirion had been painstakingly sketched onto the tanned paper with surprising skill for a barbarian. *Father must see this... Immediately.*

The prince carefully folded the sketch and tucked it under his shirt beneath his breastplate. The others were still preoccupied searching the dead.

"*My Prince!*" cried Willard, the newest and youngest addition to the Sworn Hooves, from the top of a hill overlooking the riverbed. Being only seventeen, his thin beard did little to protect his face from the temperature. Ronin and the rest of the party hurried along the slick grass and mud to join him at his perch.

Twenty yards off, just climbing out of the water onto the opposite bank, was a lone straggler who had likely slipped down into the river before the fighting began. Ronin could see him fall to his knees as he reached shore and began to slowly crawl up, the energy sapped from him as he crossed the ford.

"What do we do with him, my Prince?" Eldric asked, the blood of his kills still steaming off his face.

"Let him go," Ronin replied, his thirst for blood satisfied. "He won't make it far. The chill will cut him down, as it will us all if we don't get moving."

"What do you wish of the slain, my Prince?" Kal asked.

"Leave them for the wolves. We need to get south before the snow worsens." Ronin sheathed his sword and leapt into his saddle with what little strength his legs had left. "*Mount up!* We're going home, boys. I will see to it that each and every one of you gets the hero's welcome you deserve once we return to Roleigh. We ride!"

Chapter 17

The Great Temple of Rahm: Astymere
30th Day of the Second Month
5014 A.S.

LILY APPROACHED THE GREAT OAK DOORS of the Temple of Rahm and looked upon the god's face engraved in the smooth wood. The rectangular cathedral, black as night, was unnerving to behold at first, but as Lily drew nearer, she felt a strange sense of calm wash over her, the tension in her shoulders melting away. One pointed steeple towered high above, casting a great shadow on the streets below. The unblinking red eyes of Rahm painted above the doors drilled into Lily's heart.

She had been here once before. King Henry had led Lily past the temple for the first time on a tour of Northslope. The king told her all he could about it and the Order of the Red Vision, the Priesthood of Rahm, before the building passed out of sight. The Order pre-dated Astymere itself, with some saying it pre-dated even the Raelian Empire. Legend had it the Order had existed in one form or another since the days of the Dawn of Man, and had put their faith solely in Rahm the Wise, in contrast to the ways of the Balance, which ruled over mankind at the time.

The temple, however, only stood for six-hundred years or so, commissioned by King Solym, Karrok-Dastroltys, to centralize and unify a religion that had begun to splinter and fray into chaos.

The first day she awoke after collapsing at Kar Naron, Lord Rahmos had explained what little he knew about Layda Arani and their history. But he'd said few besides the seers themselves could tell her much, for they were a secret people who kept mostly to themselves. The Order of the Red Vision were the only ones with *any* knowledge of seers, and were unlikely to even look at her, let alone tell her.

Lily had begged for an audience with the High Priest, but to secure a meeting with him would take time, especially given she was Layda Arani. Any liaison between the two would have to take place under absolute secrecy. After a week, Henry had called Lily to him and said the High Priest would see her in the Great Temple late in the afternoon, when it would be empty except for himself.

The day had been a blur as she raced to properly dress herself and travel to Northslope. Three Knights of Rahm, by order of the king, had accompanied her as she made the walk from the palace. The people rarely saw the Knights of Rahm unless they accompanied a member of the royal family, but they were not an unfamiliar sight. To see them escorting a stranger earned many quizzical, if not judgmental, looks from the northern citizenry.

The Knights waited outside while she entered the cavernous cathedral, where even the slightest noise radiated throughout the entire room. A girl in the corner blew out a candle as she finished her prayer.

She can't be much older than me. What is she doing here by herself? I thought King Henry said it would be private. The girl's eyes widened as they fell on Lily's, her black robe tangling beneath her as she tried to scurry out. Instead, she stumbled and fell at Lily's feet. Lily bent down to retrieve the girl's candle, and as she held it out for her to take, the look she gave suggested Lily was pointing a dagger straight at her heart. She snatched it out of Lily's hand with the speed of a mantis and shot to her feet, backing herself up toward the wall.

A central aisle led to the altar. A single man sat in the second row faced the front of the room, his head bowed low in prayer. He had hardly moved when the girl fell. "Elara, collect yourself and leave us, my dear," he said.

Elara shot one last icy look at Lily and burst through the wide cathedral doors.

"What is it you seek, child?" The man remained seated with his eyes shut, his forearms pressed against the back of the pew in front of him, and his hands tightly clamped together.

"High Priest Rhivor?" Lily asked, her voice hushed and shaky after the strange encounter.

Rhivor, the leader of the Order of the Red Vision and the religious figurehead of Astymere, rose from his seat and stepped into the aisle in silence. Even in such a cramped space, he moved effortlessly—as though he were made of air. He wore a long, black satin robe with large red eyes sewn onto either side of his chest. He solemnly held his hands together as the two met near the end of the wooden bench.

"That is what people keep calling me," he said with a smile.

"King Henry told me you would see me. I'm Lily."

"He did, child, but I must begin by saying I do not often grant private audiences—and, forgive me, but if my brothers discovered I allowed a seer within these walls, they would not rest until I was excommunicated, or worse. Your friends outside will ensure we are not disturbed, but you must keep what we discuss between us. Can you do that?"

"Should we worry about Elara?" Lily asked.

"I trusted her enough to let her be here at the time of your arrival, did I not?" he asked with a knowing smile. "She is an agent of the crown and would not dare incur Henry's wrath if she led you to harm. It really all comes down to you."

Lily nodded, looking sideways and down. "I don't understand why you'd be excommunicated. King Henry says you are a true and faithful servant of the gods."

Rhivor smiled in an unexpected, genuine way. "Walk with me."

They moved toward the wall lined with windows, each depicting tableaus from the Age of Gods. The first showed ten stones sitting in a circle upon a rocky plateau, with a beam of light shining on them from the heavens above.

"What do you know of the gods, child?" he asked.

"Mahtem makes the grass and trees grow; Patreonar gives us a bountiful hunt; Amarra brings the rain…"

"Yes, we all know what the gods *do* for us, but what do you *know* of them? What do you know of how they first came to be?"

"Nothing, I suppose," Lily replied, sullen in her ignorance.

"For eons, the light of the First Stars shined on these stones," Rhivor began, pointing to the tableau. "They were the first beauty known to the world, and from these stones, endowed with the powers of the Spirit of Creation, were born the Ten. Even they were young, innocent, and ignorant of their paths once, just as man is in some respects. Just as *you* are."

The next glass mural depicted a group of gods, each with a finger outreached, pointing at a blank landscape. A single ray of light emanated from each of their fingertips.

"Upon their birth, the five Worldly looked upon the empty canvas of Antheira and filled it with their wonders. The Goddess Mahtem, whom men now call the Mother, covered the world with green forests and fields of the most beautiful flowers. Golron, whom men affectionately named the Immovable, erected great mountain ranges across the globe. Patreonar, whom men now call the Father, populated these forests and mountains with an assortment of wild beasts. Amarra flooded the lowest pits of the land with water and formed the Great Marranthyne Ocean, which Patreonar gave creatures that could live beneath the waves. And Rahm, who wanted no vast wonders or colossal monuments to his power, created a forest he called home. With Mahtem's aid, Rahm willed into existence a forest of trees whose wood was black as pitch, but whose leaves were as white as pure snow. These gods, the low gods, filled this world with life and beauty. Their brothers and sisters, however, looked only to the heavens. Tyranion, Estrelda, Auberan, Ariel, and Selayjia found no joy or wonder in their siblings' creations, and instead longed to join the stars to bask in their light."

The next window showed a lightning bolt dividing the ten figures into two groups of five.

"They split?" Lily asked.

Rhivor nodded. "Long after their birth, the strength of the Ten gods grew immense. Each day they fed on the stars' light and power, until finally there was no longer any limit to what they could do. If they willed it, it would be. So, Tyranion, Estrelda, Auberan, Ariel, and Selayjia decided it was time for the low gods to abandon their 'prison' and take their rightful place in the heavens amongst them and the stars. But the low gods were drawn and bound to the world they created, both in spirit and in heart, and condemned their brothers and sisters for their arrogance in thinking they'd ever abandon the world that had birthed and fostered them."

The final tableau showed Rahm front and center with the other four of the Worldly staring over Mount Karrok, with five stars shining in the night sky above. "After endless arguing, both sides realized that neither would convince the other to abandon their cause, creating the event known as the Rift. The five high gods we now know as the Heavenly left the physical world and created their own kingdom amongst the stars, Strai'Alara.

"Despite this rift, men looked to all Ten gods to guide them. The wisdom granted to them by Rahm allowed them to see the truth. This world, and all the Dominion of Creation, is kept together by the power of the Ten. This was in the days before kings, when men lived with each other and the gods in harmony."

"So, for all their power and wisdom, the gods were just as susceptible to pride and foolishness as men?" Lily asked, disappointed. *I thought the gods were supposed to be perfect. How can people hope to be any better?*

"Precisely," Rhivor said with a sad smile. "And, unfortunately, there was nobody to help them find peace with each other, as they once did for men. The Ten were living on two paths that could not be joined together. Even the Spirit of Creation could not impose its will to change it."

"You guide men based upon the word of these imperfect gods?"

"*God.* In this temple, we pray solely to Rahm, for he has kept Astymere under his protective arm for thousands of years. It was he and he alone who attempted to bring the two factions together and prevent the Rift, but his words fell on deaf ears. We still hold to the will of the Worldly, but people honor certain gods above others. They are all here for a specific purpose, just as we are."

Lily moved toward the window and gazed up at the smooth black face of Rahm imprinted in the colorful glass.

"The reason I tell you this, Lily, is because you are not here without reason. Your path has led you to me, and shall take you far beyond."

"How do you know that?" she asked, jolted by his sureness.

"The paths of those touched by the gods are always the longest, their destinations always the most difficult to see."

Lily couldn't help but smile as Rhivor led her once more to the pews. They sat in one of the back rows, looking upon the altar at the far end of the room. Rhivor patiently waited, watching Lily twirl her fingers around one another. Part of her had been too frightened to seek Rhivor out. Part of her still wanted to believe it was all a mistake. But she was here now, and there was no longer any doubt.

"I was wondering if you knew anything about…" For some reason the rest of the question would not come to her, no matter how hard she tried. *He must know. Everyone else seems to know so much about me after just one look.*

"Layda Arani?" Rhivor asked gently. Lily nodded. "It isn't difficult to see, child. You want to know, and yet you don't want to know. You feel you aren't prepared for the ramifications."

"Yes," she said in a forced whisper. The release of her confession loosened something tight in her chest, and she felt free to spill the contents of her mind. "Ever since I came to Kar Naron, I have heard the words Layda Arani thrown around like some kind of curse. When I first met the queen, she looked as if she wanted to murder me. What am I, Rhivor?"

"To put it as simply as I can," Rhivor began, leaning his elbows on the pew in front of him, "from what little I know, Layda Arani are the select few chosen by Rahm himself to bear a small fragment of his power of foresight. They possess the ability to look further down the current of time than other mortals- and even most of the gods- are allowed."

"But why me, Rhivor?" Lily asked, staring down into her lap. "Rahm could have chosen anyone."

Rhivor hesitated for a moment. "Why, yes, he could have. And he chose *you.* Whatever his purpose was, I cannot say. It is a responsibility, I fear. A terrible one to put on the shoulders of someone so young. But you must also see it as a gift. Simply being what you are makes you closer to the immortal beings than even I could ever hope to be. People like you are legends, child."

"Then why does everyone look at me like I'm cursed? And why are you willing to speak to me even though you could be excommunicated?"

"Child, imagine you dedicate your life and every fiber of your soul to serving a god—to try to get close to him, and have him grant you his blessings and knowledge. Now, imagine after swearing your life away for the love of said god, someone comes along who was granted a piece of that god's power, chosen at random with no real purpose or reason. It is enough, I fear, to sow terrible jealousy and bitterness, and it is that bitterness that has taken root for thousands of years. It began in Raelia, quickly spread to the four corners of the world, and eventually, the Order. They've spent years convincing anyone who would listen that Layda Arani are witches who are in league with the Beast—that their vision is a *challenge* to Rahm himself. It has gone on so long I fear the Order now believes it to be fact. The last seer known to the West fell victim to their propaganda. And we may have lost valuable wisdom for it."

"Why? What happened to them?"

"She turned her back on us. Nearly twenty years ago, she came to the palace saying we were not safe. Her vision told her that King Henry's life was in danger, and that entering the White City would bring disaster. After Tiberian, the last Raelian Emperor, tried to assassinate the Kings of the West, the Order and the previous High Priest, Baleccor, called for the seer's head. They said she caused the Night of Knives and had been in league with the Emperor to strike the kings down. In Henry's absence, a mob led by priests of the Order came for her. She fled to Karna'Sharahm, where she now resides under Rahm's protection."

Lily had heard the tale of the Night of Knives from Lord Rahmos. He had not been in the White City that night. As Guardian of the Heart since the death of his father, Urnest remained behind to rule in Henry's stead. He had been awakened in the dead of night with a message carried on the swift wings of a wind swallow, bringing word of the horror that had unfolded out on the plains. He hadn't even waited until morning before he called for his armor and his great sword, Chain Breaker, before mustering the Black Army from the fields of Astymere.

"Perhaps the people would understand if you explained," Lily pleaded.

"I have done what I can. The Order sought to block my appointment because of my stance on your kind. But after Henry learned what happened with your…predecessor, he used all the power at his disposal to have me placed at the head. Despite my teachings, the stigma the Order helped to perpetuate still grips the souls of our countrymen and much of the civilized West. The people won't call for your head, but rest assured, child, they hate you for what you are. The Order has seen to that."

Lily felt disgusted. *I must find a way to prove myself and redeem my kind.*

"I must go see her."

"Indeed, you must. For if true knowledge is what you seek, the only proper teacher is another seer. Once you reach Karna'Sharahm, she will seek you out, for it is said that the older, more attuned seers can feel the presence of their own kind. Her name is Vytria."

Lily beamed. For the first time since she left her hut, her path seemed clear and certain.

"But be warned," Rhivor told her. "When you step inside the branches of Karna'Sharahm, you are in Rahm's domain. He has but two Holy laws that *must* be followed. Do not willfully cause any harm to the trees or plants, for they are sacred gifts to him from Mahtem. And, most importantly, you must not utter a *single* word. To break the pure silence of Karna'Sharahm is a grave crime. May the heavenly and worldly help you if you break it.

"Go now, child. Your journey towards clarity is just beginning. It may be nothing, or it could mean the difference between prosperity and utter destruction."

Chapter 18

Royal Marshal Academy: Astymere
1st Day of the Sixth Month
5014 A.S.

THE ENTIRE SCHOOL WAS PACKED into the gymnasium as the ocean winds howled outside. Mayson and Diero sat beside each other, their legs crossed beneath them. It seemed Diero could barely control his excitement, his eyes darting to and fro among the crowd sitting in the bleachers that surrounded the advanced combat students. Word had spread quickly through the student body after the boys' encounter with Blayk and Brentin, and the pair had noticed that still, even months later, their classmates showed an air of fear whenever they were near.

The two were nearly expelled after word got out they were also responsible for the injuries inflicted on the rest of Kallyst's group. When Addam reminded him of the incident in the barracks, revealing the abuse hadn't stopped, Marshal Qirk begrudgingly allowed them to stay but sentenced them to two months of double physical training, a fate they graciously accepted. Kallyst and the rest were assigned nightly guard duties until the end of term, after spending days recovering in the Baths. They also were barred from participating in the Final Fights due to behavior 'unbecoming of an Officer of the King's Army.' Blayk, however, proved more clever than Mayson and Diero had given him credit for. He convinced the Marshal that Brentin had coerced him into participating in the abuse of Mayson and Diero, and under extreme threat of violence, had no other choice. Blayk therefore only had to perform a public apology before the entire student body and staff, and pledge his services to Diero once he came into his Lordship. Diero, needless to say, was not satisfied.

The Vigrei, or Selection in old Avaari, was one of the most anticipated days of the school year, when the students of the advanced combat courses would be chosen by chance to face each other in the Final Fights. Every school year at the end of the sixth month, a crowd of tens of thousands would gather at the Kastigra, the largest public stadium in Astymere, to witness these young warriors pit their skills against each other.

Mayson and Diero were the first pair in decades to fight in their first year. Typically, combatants ranged from third-year students to final-years, though some considered it unfair for them to fight in the Kastigra before taking their Final Test just days later. It was a true crucible for a final-year student to make it to their graduation day; those who made it were rightfully elites.

Diero rocked back and forth, soaking in the dull roar of the two hundred students eagerly waiting for the ceremony to begin. Mayson kept his eyes on the floor, his hands clasped together supporting his chin. His own excitement was soured by relentless wariness. Fighting in the Kastigra had been a dream of his since the first time he went with his parents to watch as a boy. A victory there as a first-year would make him a legend to his people. What plagued his nerves was the random nature of the Vigrei. He could be paired with anyone—which made him wonder why Diero was so giddy.

"Are you okay over there?" he asked, keeping his gaze on the floor.

"I'm marvelous, thanks for asking," Diero replied with a large smile he couldn't have held back if he tried.

"You seem rather confident you'll get a good pick."

"I'm not confident—I'm certain," Diero said slyly.

"Certain? How?"

"I convinced Kaleb to mark Blayk's submission. A small indent in one of the corners can easily go unnoticed to one not searching for it. When I draw my opponent from the bowl, I'll know which is his."

Mayson couldn't think of a reply before Marshal Qirk made his way through the crowd and took his place on the rounded stage erected in the center of the gymnasium. All stood at attention as he stormed by. Qirk looked as cross as ever, his green cloak trimmed in gold thread flying behind him, clasped to his leather jerkin with two silver pins in the shape of Rahmirion. As he reached the center of the stage, a soft smirk overcame him as he turned to the circle of students who waited below. As salty as the Marshal could be, he took joy in the school's ancient traditions.

Qirk summoned the combatants with a wordless gesture. They marched forward and took the high step to circle around the Marshal on the edge of the stage.

"You may be seated," he said, and the students plopped back down. The fighters sat along the edge of the platform, facing in toward Qirk.

"Good morning. I'm sure you are all itching to get this ceremony underway, so I will make this brief. Sitting before you are the finest this Academy has to offer. They have spent years here, crafting their bodies into the best instruments of combat in the Western world."

He couldn't be sure, but Mayson thought he saw Qirk shoot him and Diero a sidelong look.

"Today we witness the Vigrei, the Selection. These young men will discover who they shall face as they enter the Kastigra at the end of the month. I demand that you all remain silent for the duration so the selected may hear their names clearly. Now, my esteemed warriors, let the Vigrei *commence!*"

The prince hung on the Marshal's every word, making an exception to snicker at the thought of spending *years* crafting their bodies into killing machines. *There's time.* The irony quickly vanished from his mind as his eyes met the boy sitting across from him, and he felt his stomach twist. Mayson had tried avoiding him since the day he'd arrived at school, but his head began to ache from the memory of their first encounter. *Hold fast, Karrok. He is just a man.* A man indeed, whereas the prince was still a youth in most respects. Mayson was most thankful this hulking student hadn't been involved in Brentin Kallyst's abuse, for it was unlikely Mayson would've seen the Vigrei if he had been.

Sitting opposite him was Allister Bullvine, a final-year student and the top-ranked fighter at the Academy. He had given Mayson his first taste of defeat, and he hadn't forgotten it. At eighteen, Allister hardly seemed human, with thick, light brown hair and eyes to match. His rippling muscles seemed to be carved from stone, and his jaw could have easily been molded from iron. During classes, the prince and Diero had never been allowed to join the small group of elite students to which Allister belonged.

The vast majority of the advanced combat courses all trained together, with Allister and four others separated into a much more demanding subsection reserved for those who passed the Steel Trials.

The Steel Trials were nearly as secretive as what lay within the Temple of Red Flame. Whereas most final-years liked to boast of their exploits, the Steel Class simply smiled and laughed quietly among themselves whenever asked about the Trials. There was Mikael Desion, an Avaari boy who served as Allister's lieutenant, swift of hands and hard of face; Kevven Mohain, taller by a head than any student on the island, even Kip; Jon Kasserin, who seemed to find everything funny; and Vin Zarrad, the smallest of the bunch, but from what Mayson observed from the hits he absorbed in training, seemingly indestructible.

The night before, the advanced combat students had been summoned to the heart of the island at nightfall to draw straws, determining who would be pulling names in the Vigrei. The prince had drawn the second pairing and stared at the blank space next to his name, hoping to Rahm that Allister wouldn't be filling the void. He didn't want an easy fight. He didn't even want a fight he would necessarily win. All he asked was anyone…*anyone* but Allister.

Mayson's name, just above Diero's, Jalen's, and seven others, comprised a vertical list written in chalk upon the black slab mounted on the stage behind the Marshal. While Mayson had been trying to compose himself, the personal attendants to Marshal Qirk, Commandants Grein and Barton, had carried in the stone basin containing the combatants' names. They held it with grace, but by the time the large vessel was placed with a great thud, the two men were red in the face, dabbing their foreheads with handkerchiefs. They stepped away winded and joined the Marshal on his flanks.

The first student to be matched with a challenger was Daniel Skartyn, a fourth-year boy from the heartlands whose father had made a small fortune in beehives and honey farming. He was a rather unimpressive boy with a hard face, the kind of look that attempted to convince everyone around him he was dangerous. He rubbed his hands absentmindedly as he rose to stand before the basin, remaining still as he awaited instructions.

"Combatant," Marshal Qirk said, now acting on ceremony. "You will close your eyes and place your hand into the basin. You will remove one piece of parchment and read the name upon it aloud. You will then return to your seat. Understood?"

"Aye, sir," Daniel replied, staring blankly ahead, standing straight and rigid with his chin up. He closed his eyes and reached blindly into the basin, mixing the random names until he finally closed his grip, accidentally crumpling one. He opened his eyes and looked down as he carefully unfolded the wadded parchment. "Airyn Rothkys!" he proclaimed to his fellow students. He was met by a chorus of chants, hoots, and foot-stomping as he offered the name to Commandant Grein, who wrote Airyn's name next to his on the slab. *This should be interesting.* The two had often been paired in drills and exercises, and had been fostering a growing rivalry since the start of term. This fight would be personal.

Next was Mayson's turn. The crowd grew silent, and he swallowed hard before forcing himself to his feet. He could feel every eyeball in the room upon him as he ran his fingers over the edge of the rough stone bowl, taking his allotted position. The prince closed his eyes before he was instructed to. The Marshal's words seemed distant and hazy, and Mayson found himself fighting the urge to search for the marked parchment indicating Blayk.

The sound of his heartbeat thundered in his ears. *Which one? Gods, there is no way of knowing. Just choose. Choose.*

Mayson closed his fingers, capturing a handful of slips in his grasp. With a gentle shake, one by one they fell from his hand until a single piece of parchment remained caged in his grip. He unfolded it slowly, rubbing his thumb across it as though he could feel the script upon it. He waited until the slip was completely flat before he opened his eyes and studied it carefully for a few moments. He raised his eyes to the crowd, and cleared his throat. "Allister Bullvine."

The chalk scraping against the board, scratching Allister's name next to Mayson's, was the only sound that could be heard in the crowded hall. Two hundred voices remained silent and still; the prince could hardly breathe, the air of celebration gone from the room.

Diero stood and continued the sequence, closing his eyes and searching. He took a few extra moments to search the bowl and nearly smiled when he grazed over the indent. "Blayk Mortryn." The cheers erupted once more, if slightly more reserved.

Minutes later Jalen picked Karmine Tal'Por, a fierce fighter from a noble Southern Tip family. Jalen's large pool of friends in the stands had raised hell when he spoke the name, hollering until the Marshal himself had to silence them. When the selections had been made and Qirk spoke his final words, the remainder of the students filed out, abuzz in thrilled conversations rife with expectations and predictions. Mayson remained behind, unnoticed in the squirming current of bodies. He had been mentally preparing for this day for weeks, but in the light of his fortune, Prince Karrok-Aht's active mind had gone blank and silent.

THE GYMNASIUM SOMEHOW seemed much smaller now, after the stage and most of the seats had been cleared away. The prince sat at the top of the raised benches in silence, facing the northern window, the overcast light of the late afternoon flooding the room. Allister and the other Steel Trial students were going about their drills without an instructor. This was an open period, and the group often used it to review the lessons from earlier in the day.

As the room emptied, Mayson had taken his perch and remained there, trying to convince himself it was all a bad dream. Allister and his crew hadn't even noticed him.

Kallyst and his goons were one thing. Their age and status had granted them ranks in the advanced classes, but there was nothing advanced about them. They only caused him and Diero so much trouble because there were so many of them. The Steel Trial group was another matter altogether.

If they had to, these young men would be able to lead men into battle on a moment's notice. Their minds and bodies were the pinnacle of what this establishment expected of students, and Allister was their leader in both practice and in spirit.

Mayson looked on as Allister drilled the group in grappling, twisting the wrist of Jon Kasserin and throwing him into Vin. Kevven attempted to wrap his arms around Allister's neck and was promptly flipped forward, his back slamming to the floor with an echoing *bang*. Mikael managed to shove his leg behind Allister and trip him over it to the ground.

As he descended on the bigger man, he found himself rolled onto his stomach, his arm bent behind him. The joint looked to be on the verge of dislocation, prompting the boy to tap the mat and beg for mercy. *Gods, he is strong. You'll never match his power. But, he is slower than you, and a lot sloppier than expected. You will have to beat him with speed and precision.* Mayson took notice of one final, possibly life-saving, detail as the sparring continued. *Their stances…none of them are left-handed.*

Allister addressed the group as they composed themselves and gathered around, giving them notes on what had gone wrong. Still, he spoke in a soft voice, and even in the cavernous gymnasium, the prince could not make out what was said over the wind outside.

After an hour of this, Allister's group gathered their belongings, wiped their sweating brows, and took leave. Only Mayson's foe remained in the center of the room, sitting with his legs crossed beneath him, eyes closed, breathing deeply. The prince took the steps as quietly as he could, stepping on the balls of his feet as his father had taught him to avoid alerting Allister of his presence. He felt as though he were a babe trapped in the lair of a giant, and one missed step would be his last. He reached the ground and turned toward the exit, ready to make a mad dash.

"Was that entertaining, boy?" Allister said without opening his eyes, stopping Mayson in his tracks and sending a chill up his spine. "I imagine being stuck in company with the likes of Kallyst and the others—you must have wanted to see how it's really done."

"Something like that," the prince replied. "My apologies. I didn't mean to disturb you. I was just leaving."

"No apology necessary. It's I who should apologize to you. I've never had to participate during the first test. I didn't want to do what I did, but it seems you offered the Marshal little choice. How's the eye, by the way?"

"It still works," Mayson said curtly. *No thanks to you.* "I've hardly thought about it. I look forward to being able to truly test myself against you, at my best." Mayson drew courage from every inch of himself to hide his discomfort.

"Do you realize this will be as unpleasant for me as it will be terrible for you?" Allister asked. "Stomping a first-year into the dirt is not how I wanted to leave this place. I suggest you make an appeal for a change of opponent, for this can't end well—for either of us. There is nothing but humiliation in it. You will be brutalized in front of your father and future kingdom, and I will forever be remembered as the man who earned his great final victory over a child. So, I say again, make an appeal."

"And be remembered as a coward who disgraced the Vigrei?

The appeal is never meant to be used and you know it. It's there to weed out the cravens and see who will accept their matching, whatever the cost. I know what I am in for. I may be young, but I am no fool. I know what you can do to me. But, for the chance of a victory against you, I am fully prepared to die. So you *must* be willing to kill me, because it is the only way you'll be able to stop me…Have a pleasant evening."

Mayson turned to go without allowing Allister an opportunity to reply, his stomach churning and grinding as he walked. The words had just flown out of his mouth, and at a moment when he should have been at his most confident, he felt he had just signed his own death warrant. *Of all the things Father taught you, the one thing he missed was a lesson on how to keep your big mouth shut.*

His feet seemed to float over the moist grass as he jogged back to the barracks, trying to leave the moment behind. The sun had already fallen below the horizon, but the sky held its light all the same. The incessant waves, which had always helped to ease his mind in times of trouble, now sounded like the scratching of the chalk on the slab. Mayson's head was practically spinning by the time he made the cross-island trip back to his bunk.

The barracks were half empty, with many students still attending their last classes of the day. The prince could see several groups of his classmates talking amongst themselves, eyes darting from him back to their friends. *You're a dead man, and they all know it.* Feeling defeated, he dropped to his bunk like a sack of potatoes, burying his face in his pillow and letting out a deep groan he'd been holding back since the Vigrei.

"There he is. The most regal corpse I've ever seen," said Diero, who was lying on his bunk. He had his face buried in *A History in High Steel*, part of the assigned reading for the first-year sword-forging course.

"Shut. Up." Mayson replied from his pillow.

"Don't blame me. I'm not the one who made you pick his name out of the bowl. If I were you, I would have just taken Blayk's marked slip and been done with it."

"Diero—just—don't." The empty, weak sound of his voice was enough to call off the onslaught, and Diero went back to reading in silence.

As the minutes passed, Mayson could detect the distinct smell of candle smoke growing stronger as the rest of his classmates returned, reading their letters that had arrived that morning. He hadn't received one. He had written the king a week ago, seeking his words of guidance on the Vigrei, but to no avail.

As his spirits began to sink to new depths, Mayson felt the weight of someone dropping down onto his bunk. He rolled over to see Jalen sitting at the foot of his bed, flashing a wide, brimming grin.

"I've got to give it to you, Karrok," Jalen said. "That had to be the boldest thing I've ever seen. If I had drawn Allister's name from the bowl, I would have soiled myself right there in front of everyone. He is a beast, if ever there was one at this school."

"You know me, Jalen," Mayson replied. "Bold as brass and dead as a doornail."

"The Marshal wasn't pleased, to say the least," Jalen said. "Things are bad enough between your father and him. The last thing he needs is to present the king with your busted, unconscious body."

"Thank you for the vote of confidence. It's most reassuring."

"You need to relax, cousin. The way I see it, this can only go well for you."

Kristian, Kip, and Teren joined them as Jalen spoke. Kristian sat with his brother, Teren sat on Diero's bed, and Kip stood, towering over the rest. As tall as he was, he was still growing.

"That's funny," Mayson said, his patience wearing thin.

"What are you talking about, Jalen?" Diero asked.

"My Prince, you need to look at the situation from a new perspective," Jalen answered. "So what if he beats you? You're a *first-year*. I don't think there is anyone alive who can remember the last time a first-year set foot in the Kastigra, let alone against one of the greatest warriors the Academy has ever seen. You'll still be lauded as unshakeable: a man who backs down from no opponent, no matter how great. Your pride might be hurt, but trust me, you'll get over it quickly. And consider this for a moment: what if you win? You might! It's not impossible. If you beat him, you will be a *legend*. Historians who document your reign will paint you in the most glorious colors, naming you indestructible, invincible—cousin, you have far more to gain than you have to lose."

The prince squinted at Jalen, rather perplexed. He wanted to believe him. Jalen did make a sound argument. Still, Mayson was unsettled by the thought of dying in front of his father and mother. To have the eyes of the kingdom fixed upon him as he failed would be the last thing he remembered, bringing shame into the afterlife.

"And what if he kills me, Jalen?" Mayson asked, choking back fear. "There is more than a fair chance he could."

"Don't dwell on it too much. Keep your mind clear and trust in what you have learned…I'm off to bed. Physical training at dawn. Should make for a wonderful morning." With a sigh, Jalen was gone, and Diero returned to his reading.

"He's right, you know," Kristian said. "You have an opportunity to do something no one has done before."

"It may not mean much, but we believe in you, Mayson," Kip said. "Even if you don't believe in yourself." Kip never spoke much, giving great weight and value to the words he saw fit to share before they all dispersed.

Mayson lay there long after the candles had gone out, contemplating everything Jalen had said. Win or lose, he had everything to gain. The problem was losing without getting himself killed, for he would never submit as long as he was able to stand. He closed his eyes, trying to escape the starkness of reality for a short while.

Mayson could not remember falling asleep, but from out of the darkness, he saw Allister's face and brick-like fists flying at him with deadly purpose. He could feel each blow hammer into him, shattering bone and pulverizing organs. The pain, though agonizing, was numbed by soul-crushing shame. He and Allister were within an immense pit, the light of day barely visible above their heads. The eyes of all of Astymere were upon him, watching as he was crushed and his royal blood spilled. As he fell for the final time, he landed at the feet of his father, who looked on the young prince with disgust, his eyes cold, dead—unforgiving. Henry kicked his body, rolling him over the edge of a precipice to send him hurtling through emptiness into the dark, frozen depths of hell.

Mayson sprang upright. The sensation of falling had dissipated, but the darkness and cold remained. It took several moments and a few deep gasps for him to realize where he was.

His bed sheets were soaked through with cold sweat that still clung to him, chilling him to the bone. *This is perfect. A month of sleepless nights to look forward to. At this rate, I'll drop dead of exhaustion before I even enter the Kastigra…I can't do this.*

Mayson found himself outside of Vaun Hall the next morning, as lessons focusing on the history of Astymere's greatest generals droned on. Addam had told Mayson he could find Allister there.

"Karrok!" Behind him, walking briskly through the warm, green grass, marched Emma Scholyn, Postmistress of the Royal Marshal Academy, a sheaf of letters in hand. Her short-cropped brown hair just barely caught the breeze as she moved, the golden feather pen pinned to her doublet catching the morning sun and her saber swinging to and fro at her hip.

"Postmistress," Mayson said as she approached with a formal bow. He stood at attention. "How may I serve you?"

"I need nothing from you, my Prince. A satchel of letters was misplaced yesterday, and fifty messages went undelivered. I have my staff tearing about the island taking care of the rest."

"You decided to bring a letter to me yourself? I'm honored."

"Don't let it go to your head. It is a formality. You will be my King some day and rituals must be observed…Also, I figured you needed to see a friendly face after your luck in the Vigrei."

"I appreciate the effort, Postmistress," Mayson said as he reached out to accept a letter from her hand.

"As you were. Be well." Emma took leave as Mayson sat beneath a nearby willow to examine the missive. The envelope was held fast by the royal seal, Rahmirion's black spearhead. Mayson broke the seal with great fervor, his heart lifting to see his father's hand upon the page:

Mayson,

Imagine my worry when I realized how close the Vigrei was upon you. Your mother and I have fretted since the day we learned Qirk stuck you and your brother in the Advanced Combat courses. Part of me worries that you will have to face someone you are not prepared for—but then I remember how you improved every day under my tutelage, and I can only imagine the things you will learn under the guidance of your teachers. You are the Blood of the Mountain; there is insurmountable strength in you.

Whomever fate brings before you, they will fall before you. He is just another enemy. Study him, know him, learn his patterns, and you will surely have victory. I know that this could not have been easy for you, but I have faith that your strength of heart will hold true. As you prepare over the next month, let this truth carry you: Win or lose, I am incredibly proud of you. All love from your mother and me.

Until we see you again,
Father

One tear fell upon the page, spilling from the prince's overwhelmed heart. The voices of doubt and fear plaguing him had at last been silenced. These words of confidence from his father put him at ease, and he began to laugh at himself for even considering making an appeal. After he finally collected himself, Mayson looked to the rich, blue sky with a new sense of purpose. *Get off your ass, Karrok. You have work to do.*

Chapter 19

Northrode: Astymere
38th Day of the Sixth Month
5014 A.S.

HENRY HAD KEPT IN CONSTANT CONTACT with Mayson throughout the last month, providing him tips on how best to study his opponent and his weaknesses. Since the fall of Raelia, Henry had led a rather peaceful, quiet existence, and he began to feel exhilarated by Mayson's training. He warned his son not to stay too close to Allister, lest studying him should begin to look like spying.

Every other day he sent a letter, including words of encouragement from the queen and news of Vita Astym. The forty days seemed to fly by, and now here he sat, bumping along the cobblestones of the Northrode, following the mass pilgrimage to the Kastigra.

The highway was packed and the small army the king had brought with him did not help. Fifty Shadow Knights surrounded the carriage and behind them marched two hundred men of the Black Army, followed by another one hundred Silver Shields. Then there were the security forces of the High Houses: three groups of one hundred black-armored men draped in cloaks of brilliant gold, sharp silver, and bold crimson.

The first three hours of the trip from the Mountain City were smooth and easy, but as the final hour approached, their pace grew stagnant. It seemed as though every man and woman in the Kingdom would turn out this year, for it wasn't every year a prince fought, especially in his first year at the Academy.

Henry sat and listened to the wheels turn and hiccup with each crack in the pavement. Despite the bumps, the road had been much improved in recent months. Lord Brisban had followed through on his promise to put the people's money to good use, and Henry envisioned him snickering while counting coins and bills stacked to the ceiling atop his desk.

We just passed the sign for Aldegin. Another ten miles. Opposite him, on their own leather bench, sat Queen Beatrice and Lily. They hadn't said much during the ride, confining the majority of their conversation to simple pleasantries and Lily's complimentary observations on the passing countryside. Beatrice smiled warmly enough to fool the girl, but Henry could still see distrust and wariness in her eyes.

"You're going to love the Kastigra, Lily," the king said, breaking the silence. Beatrice turned to gaze out the open window at the lush countryside. "Urnest tells me you take special interest in works of architecture. The Kastigra is more a work of art than a building, really."

"How much further?" Beatrice asked while turning to Henry, wearing an innocent face like a thick layer of makeup. Henry couldn't tell if she had truly meant to cut him off.

"Not far, my love. Should be no more than an hour." Beatrice turned back to the window as if unsatisfied by his response. "As I was saying, Lily, it is a marvel of not only engineering, but of artistry. The exterior is adorned with statues carved with painstaking accuracy, and the manner in which the building has been expanded over the generations will astound you. You'll see our boys fight on the same dirt that I fought on in my youth, and my father, and his father before him."

"I'm not sure I'm ready for this," Lily admitted. "I wished to stay in the Capital. With all due respect, my King, I feel as though I've witnessed more than enough violence for one lifetime."

Henry could have sworn Beatrice nodded with a smirk. *Does she not respect this girl's convictions?*

"Child, if you cannot handle this, you will not be able to venture to the Dark Wood on your own when the time comes," Beatrice confidently advised. *Well played.*

"Though, I do worry," the Queen continued. "Word has reached my ears of this Allister our son will be fighting. They say he is the finest warrior the Academy has produced in recent memory and is ready to lead men in battle. Practically a man grown. You allow our child to step into the arena with him?"

"Breathe, my Queen. Mayson will be all right," said Henry. "I taught him myself, as did nearly a dozen other great warriors. If I did not believe he was ready, I would not allow it. There is immeasurable strength in him."

"And Diero," she interjected, her nerves visible. "The boy he fights could crush his bones—I can hardly bear the thought."

"They will be men of the sword when they leave the Academy, my dear. You must embrace the risk or surely, you will go mad." Henry leaned forward and placed a loving hand on her knee.

"And should one win and the other lose? Do you not fear they will resent each other? Do you not fear a rift?" Beatrice asked.

"Those boys are joined at the hip. I'm sure if one wins and the other falls, the victor would feel no joy. These boys, Beatrice— you've watched them grow. They are not like others their age. They hunger for greatness and today, win or lose, greatness is upon them. I do not have the heart to take that away from them."

The sun rolled high into the morning sky as the Northrode descended a hilltop into the town of Aldegin. Unlike many communities that found their prosperity in lumber and mining, these people made their wealth off the countless souls who trekked north to visit the Kastigra. Entire businesses had been born from the arena's popularity. Inns were nearly always full. Masons had settled for miles around in order to maintain the great structure. Hunters and farmers appeared by the dozens to keep the larders full for visitors throughout the year. The arena was the town's lifeblood, and that blood was rich indeed.

The taverns were fit to burst, with many of the inhabitants leaking out into the streets, carrying mugs and cups in the road. Many of these people had likely been here for days, drinking and eating themselves stupid in preparation for the coming spectacle. Bargainers hoped to make a fortune over these couple of days, selling jugs of wine, meat skewers, candied almonds, and fresh fruit off carts on both sides of the road. Lily swung her head from one side of the carriage to the other.

The town consisted of a single main road going west to east, flanked by thick clusters of shops and homes the whole way. The homes were smooth-cut stone and roofed with perfectly placed red clay tiles. The streets going north or south were all narrow in comparison.

On the left, a deep, gray plateau jutted from the roaming, green hills to the north. Lily's silver eyes lit up at the sight of the carved behemoth as Henry looked on with a wide smile of his own. Beatrice couldn't help but gaze in awe as well. The road traveled east to the outskirts of Aldegin and circled back around to the north toward the arena, where foot traffic became so bad that many abandoned the road and trekked the rest of the way through grass and fields.

"I told you it was a marvel, child," Henry said. Lily nodded in agreement and continued to stare as the building drew closer. People now lined both sides of the road, strolling to the gates. Some bent the knee as the carriage passed by, accompanied by its small army. The rest simply shouted and waved, for in the wealthiest town of the Northern Tip, the people were not quite as formal as in the Heartlands.

The road soon turned to close in on the arena, with much of the traffic being diverted to the north and south entrances. The royal carriage rolled around to the eastern side with hardly a reveler in sight.

The carriage door swung open, letting in a soft breeze. Beatrice took the hand of a Shadow Knight and stepped out first. Lily followed, and Henry emerged last, donning the face of a king and adjusting his posture accordingly.

The group approached the open concourse, where thick concrete pillars nearly three men wide ran to the top of the Kastigra, supporting it upright with steel arches in between each. The metal had been twisted into dazzling floral patterns, and each arch held two straight poles that proudly flew the banner of Astymere. Lily approached the base of one upon which was a carved relief of a cloaked, bearded man holding the spear Rahmirion, leaning on it as though it were a staff. There were many others like it wrapping around the edge of the arena, each in a different pose.

"It is custom that when a king passes, they engrave his likeness into one of these pillars," Henry told her.

Beatrice led the way into the shadows, her white gown shining brightly in the dimness. Henry looked up to the rafters and viewed the waving flags of every house that would fight in the arena that day. The queen waited for Ladies Dawn and Illysha of Houses Wallis and Rahmos as they left their own carriages, accompanied by their husbands. Droyan Wallis rode his own horse alongside Tyrel and Kristian Rahmos. She kissed each gingerly as they entered the arena together, surrounded by guards of each house cloaked in many different colors.

The king entered flanked by Lords Urnest and Raymund, each

telling of their experience with the terrible traffic around the city. Lily followed behind in the crowd of attendants, keeping to herself as the group climbed dark stairs to the second level, with many vomitoria leading out into the light.

They were ushered to a lounge shaded by a grand tarp of white linen. The benches were wider here and covered in thick, deep cushions stuffed with soft cotton. Henry walked out with Lily to the balcony and began pointing out places around the arena. The pit below extended three stories deeper than ground level, enhancing the Kastigra's immense size. The stands had already begun to fill as the king listened to the young seer's rapid-fire questions, asking some before he could even finish answering.

Beatrice stepped out of the opening of the lounge and watched them silently. Henry simply smiled at her, wide and bright.

MAYSON COULD HEAR THE THUNDER of the crowd in the stony depths of the arena as he attempted to meditate. The low rumbling was beginning to creep into his bones, making it difficult to relax. The wooden bench caught every vibration coming from above, as though he were sitting on a living beehive. Through his closed eyes, he could still make out the light of day streaming in through the five portals in the wall.

The cavernous waiting chambers of the Kastigra sat two stories below ground. It had only been three-hundred years since King Henry's ancestor, Karrok-Ahm, deemed smoky torchlight obsolete and even hazardous for the athletes waiting to compete. Karrok-Ahm decreed the chambers should be opened to the air above and commissioned the construction of twenty large ducts fitted with reflecting mirrors to bask the four chambers in daylight, reserving torches for the stairways and corridors.

Mayson shared the chamber with Diero, Jalen, Airyn Rothkys, and Ciryl Zagar. Diero stood near one of four square pillars against the outer wall, shadow boxing. From the moment he woke that morning, he had been abuzz with a manic drive. Jalen stretched in the corner to Mayson's left. Airyn and Ciryl sat at the far side of the room near the door, speaking to each other in low voices.

The prince kept his eyes closed as he attempted to quiet his mind. This day was going to stretch on for years. Marshal Qirk had declared his fight with Allister to be the main event, and therefore, he would go last. He would have counted himself fortunate had he been able to fight first and get this dirty business over with, but alas, he was doomed to stew in dread for the next several hours.

"I hope he's scared," Diero said, his voice straining in the exertion of his drills. "I hope he's good and scared."

"I'm sure he is," Jalen replied. "After what you did to him in the yard, I'd say he wishes he were anywhere else today. Don't you feel the beating you gave him was enough?"

"He broke two of my ribs, practically suffocated me with my own blankets, and spat on my father's memory," Diero replied through his combinations. "No, it wasn't enough. Not nearly enough."

"I hadn't heard that. He insulted your father? What did he say?" Jalen asked, aghast at the audacity of insulting a High Lord. He sat beside Diero on the smooth stone floor to better hear.

"One night, as I lay on the floor trying to breathe after one of his beatings, he whispered in my ear," Diero said. "'You *are* your father's son. Weak and arrogant. If he were half the man everyone claims he was, he would still be alive. If you ever make it out of here, be sure to wear plenty of armor, or you will end up just like him.' He's lucky if I don't kill him today."

"I don't think anyone who knows you would lay blame on your shoulders. But this day isn't about revenge," Jalen said. "It is about showcasing how you will represent the Crown with skill and *honor*. If you kill him, you would probably get the satisfaction you seek, but you would forever taint yourself in the eyes of your country and your King."

Mayson didn't stir, but he could feel Jalen's eyes fall upon him.

"Diero will conduct himself accordingly," Mayson said. "I have absolute faith in that. Isn't that right, brother?" Mayson cracked one eye open to look at Diero.

"Blayk will live to graduation," Diero said, clenching his jaw. "But that's *all* I promise. I will have my satisfaction today, reputation be damned."

"You are the last of the Carovensa blood. That *means* something in this country," said Jalen. "Don't squander your family's good name for the sake of a few minutes of gratification." With this, Diero grew sullen and still, weighing Jalen's words.

"After today, Diero will have his own reputation to rely on," said Mayson, "one *he* will build for himself." He wished the conversation would end. He could feel Diero's tension as the conflict between his desire and his duty raged within. He hoped his own vote of confidence would settle Diero's mind long enough to allow him to continue preparing. One moment of carelessness could mean disaster.

"*My* reputation?" Diero asked, returning to his jovial, joking self. "What about yours? When this day is over, the Western Kingdoms will be abuzz with your name—I envy you."

"You're more than welcome to switch with me," Mayson chided. "Say the word and it's yours."

"No, that's quite all right," Diero responded. "I don't want glory *that* badly."

"I didn't think so." It was easy for them to talk. Both Diero and Jalen had been paired against opponents they could easily handle. He was the only one being put in grave danger to test himself. *If you make it through today, that reputation will taste sweet indeed*, he told himself. *If* he made it through the day.

The pale light bathing the deep chamber had grown strong and bright in the endless stretch of time that seemed to roll on before them. The prince had finally managed to find a degree of peace, shutting out all thought and outward distractions. Diero and Jalen had even been compelled to join him. Ciryl and Airyn stopped whispering as well, and simply sat near the door, lost in thought.

The tranquility Mayson found was abruptly shattered by the pounding of distant drums, pouring down the stairway and flooding the room, each resounding strike reverberating along the stone floor and walls. A thin layer of dust shook loose from the rafters as the beat carried on, showering the room in a light, gray drizzle. Mayson strained to adjust his vision to the light. It was midday, and within minutes, the fights would begin.

"All right, boys." A voice pierced through the dimness. "On your feet."

Mayson hadn't heard Drillmaster Perry come in. The roar of the crowd and the persistent drumming had completely masked his footsteps as he descended from the arena with three guards. Perry had always seemed an imposing man in his training uniform, but today, in full military garb, he looked like something out of an old tale. His black plate-armor had been freshly polished, as had the silver scales glinting brilliantly along his upper arms. His green silk cloak, fastened about his shoulders, hovered just above his ankles.

He pushed open the door as the five youths formed a single-file line, each standing at attention. "You will follow me up the stairs and out into the assembly. There you will join your classmates and present yourselves before the king and queen." Mayson could have sworn Perry shot him the quickest of glances, but dismissed it as a trick of his uneasy mind.

"Keep your heads and remember your training," Perry went on. "The cream of the Astymerian crop is here to watch you execute what we've taught. Don't disappoint them—and *don't* make your teachers look stupid. Some of you are lucky enough to be graduating in a few days, but others are not so fortunate. Make me proud, or I'll make your lives miserable from now until you graduate."

The group gave a slight chuckle at this. It was true any poor representation of the Academy would be met with punishment, but Perry had personally trained each of the combatants who would be fighting today; it was easy to see that most of them had his confidence.

"This way, gentlemen. It will all be over before you know it." *If only that were true.*

The air became close and stuffy as the party entered the stairway which, in comparison to the waiting chambers, was poorly ventilated. Torches mounted on the walls filled the confinement with the sweet smell of applewood.

If not for Jalen behind him, pushing him forward, Mayson would have stopped altogether, watching Diero and the rest disappear into the afternoon sun. His father's words rang in his head. *I trust you. I believe in you.* They were soothing, yet with each step he felt as though he were marching toward the executioner's block, his head not long for his shoulders. Still, he stepped out of the shadows and into the brilliant noon sun.

The crowd erupted into a deafening roar that overwhelmed

Mayson's thoughts and sent chills through the young fighters. A sea of banners waved in the light breeze, blending with the colorful outfits of the citizens holding them. Mayson noted the black bull wrapped in golden vines upon a tan field for Allister, many banners for House Tal'Por, with vines of green beneath a golden star upon a field of gray and white, and, of course, the banners of the High Houses: the black shape of Rahmirion on a field of white for Mayson and House Karrok; a broken silver chain on a field of black for Jalen and House Rahmos; a black tree adorned with white leaves upon a field of crimson for House Wallis; and a golden star upon a field of magenta for Diero and House Carovensa.

Mayson had seen many fights at the Kastigra, having accompanied his parents over the years, yet had always been astonished by the view. However, immersed in a sea of chanting revelers tens of thousands strong, he'd never seen the view from ground level, gazing up at the countless faces.

The Kastigra had originally been built to hold ten thousand. But as the popularity of the Final Fights grew, so did demand for seating, and the arena had been built up higher and higher until finally the head count reached sixty-five thousand. The arena stood over ten stories, the largest structure in the Crescent—even bigger than the palace.

The flat arena floor was separated from the lowest level seating by a ten-foot wall of sand-colored concrete. These lower seats were reserved for the upper class: men of business, lower lords, and wealthy merchants. The King's Box was located in this section, along the eastern side of the stadium, visible beneath a canopy of white linen. Just behind that was an entrance to the lounge where Mayson, along with the royals and High Lords, had once feasted on luxuries like Kyprean olives and sunfruit of Pele'Dis from the ample kitchens.

The remaining four sections climbed higher and further away from the action, but they filled quickly enough all the same. The combatants, though minuscule from such heights, all wore standard black so as to stand out against the sandy pit. The Final Fights always drew a sizable crowd, but today they were frenzied with anticipation. Mayson would have much rather been in that box now.

The people were always eager to see how their future king would fare in heated contest. But this was no ordinary fight. The crowd, as big as it would have been had Mayson chosen an easier fight, had grown to monstrous proportions as word spread of the promised spectacle. The prince, a boy with hardly a hair on his chin, had been pitted against someone in his manhood, a crowd favorite, having ground boys like Mayson into the dirt for years already.

Many, no doubt, hoped to see their Prince stun the kingdom with a glorious upset. Still, others came to these events for the blood sport, and surely hoped their Prince would get his teeth kicked in. They wished to see someone who had spent his life on a pedestal knocked down into the muck.

The center of the grand stage was cordoned off by a black velvet rope supported by ivory stands, creating a great ring over one-hundred feet in diameter. The velvet just grazed Mayson's shoulder as he bent at the waist to pass under it, causing his tightly wound nerves to jump half an inch. He looked up to see the rest of the combatants, three other groups led by Addam Wallis, Master Forger Varin Buchanan, and Sword Master Giulian Archer. He hadn't even noticed them, as they'd all approached the ring at the same time. His eyes had been locked on the crowd.

Rahm himself could have stepped in front of him without the prince knowing as Mayson's eyes fell on Allister. His massive arms were crossed behind his back as his black silk tunic stretched tightly across his chest. The young prince tugged at his own tunic, which hung rather loosely about him in comparison. He quickly averted his eyes before the feeling of panic got the better of him and looked around for anything to take his mind off the fight at hand.

He found the King's Box in a matter of moments, the sight of his parents sending soothing warmth throughout his body. He hadn't seen their faces in months and was even happier than he'd expected to have them here today.

They were dressed extravagantly—even Henry, to Mayson's surprise. He wore a flowing black robe that hugged him tightly about the neck and a light cloak clasped under his chin by a ruby brooch. Beatrice wore a moon-white gown, and around her neck, a jet-black cowl crafted in a marriage between the shape of

Rahmirion's spearhead and a strange flower. Today, his mother looked absolutely singular.

Lords Urnest and Raymund sat just in front of them. Raymund wore a blood-crimson shirt beneath a black leather doublet, and Urnest wore a white linen shirt that flowed over tan riding breeches, his famed silver scarf hanging loosely about his neck.

Mayson couldn't make out the finer details at this distance, but while his mother was stiff as a board, his father sat completely relaxed. The queen sat at Henry's right, but an unfamiliar face sat to his left. *This must be his new ward I've heard so much about. This must be William's daughter—the silver seer.*

The news that William had been killed had struck Mayson within the deepest reaches of his heart. He had been raised to embrace the fact that all men must die, but despite himself, he'd become convinced of the notion that some men were invincible. This group contained his father, the High Lords, and William Otter. To have such a man cut down only made Mayson more aware of his own mortality and had seriously shaken his faith in his abilities.

Despite this heartbreak, Mayson was still quite curious. He had never seen a silver seer before, and his mind raced with questions aimed at replacing myth and conjecture with real knowledge. Of course, his curiosity wasn't purely intellectual. Even from this distance, he could see she was a rare beauty.

Sitting a few rows in front of his family at the edge of the King's Box was another familiar face. Lord Haamin Ahl-Kalin and his daughter, Sharra, sat with a small entourage. Though they were removed from the king, they were within the box, which meant they were both there at Henry's invitation. *Gods, he must mean to consent to the arrangement. Why would he do this without speaking to me first?* He looked just long enough to catch Sharra's eye, and though he was too far away for her to tell where he was looking, he quickly looked to the ground in embarrassment. When he gathered the courage to look up again, she was still looking at him, now smiling wry, proud, and knowing—as though he were a horse she knew she was going to buy.

He turned to strike up a conversation with Diero in an attempt to forget that he was being watched so closely, but he found him to be miles away. He, too, was transfixed upon the King's Box, as the silver-eyed girl peered back. They held each other's gaze so long that Mayson could have sworn they both smiled before being taken aback by the roar of a voice. The crown bearer, Elara, stood directly behind the seer, still and tense, as though she were standing guard.

"Ladies and Gentlemen! I welcome you to the Kastigra!" The announcement filled the vast space, flying out beyond the last seats high above. The crowd erupted once again.

The voice belonged to Marshal Qirk, dressed in a long-sleeved, white cloth tunic that fell just above his ankles, adorned with the black shape of Rahmirion imprinted upon his torso. Once again, Mayson's attention had been so focused on his parents, he hadn't seen or heard the Marshal approach; instead, it seemed as though he had simply appeared.

"You are all here today to witness the culmination of the finest military training in the Western world! These twenty young men are the future of the Black Army's leadership, and they stand before you prepared to demonstrate why they are worthy of such honor." He bowed toward the King's Box. "My King," he said curtly. "My Queen. I present to you—your combatants."

The crowd resumed its booming cry and did not stop until Henry stood from his cushioned seat and raised his arms. The people were in the palm of his hand, and for nearly a minute, one could hear a pin drop.

"Gentlemen," Henry began, his voice just as powerful as Qirk's with much less effort. "I salute you for the service you have rendered to this nation. And I salute you for the service you shall one day give as commanders of the Black Army. I wish you all well—may Rahm the Wise keep his ever-watchful eye upon you."

He believes in you. Believe in yourself.

The combatants moved from their circular formation and formed a straight line before the King's Box. Elara moved forward solemnly and placed the crown atop Henry's head.

"We, the youthful militant, salute you, our King! Cayrian Karrok!" the group shouted as they extended their right arms into the air with their fists clenched. They had been drilled for weeks to ensure their response to the king's address was perfect.

Cayrian Karrok was a phrase Mayson had known since he

was a baby. It had been shouted at him in the streets of the capital nearly every day for as long as he could remember. It meant "glory to the House Karrok" in old Avaari. Truth be told, the literal translation leaned more toward "glory to the Mountain," but the mountain and the Karrok family had become one and the same with regard to Astymere's identity, given they had taken the name of the mountain as their own. Mayson had been used to hearing it, but felt rather strange saying it himself. It seemed too narcissistic for his liking.

Henry surveyed the group for several moments before answering their salute with one of his own, raising his right arm and clenching his fist. "I declare these fights...*OPEN!*"

"Combatants, to me," the Marshal said, no longer projecting to those in the farthest seats. The group formed a tight circle around Qirk as he ran over the ground rules with them. "Today is treated like true combat. You fight until you can fight no more, or until you've decided you've had enough." That last bit came out with disdain—no attempt to hide the fact that dishonor would fall on anyone who forfeited the fight while physically able to continue.

"There will be no blows to the groin, no biting, no scratching, and no eye-gouging. Take your places on the other side of the rope and wait until you are called. You will meet your partner in the center of the ring and await further instruction. May the gods be with you, boys. Good luck."

The prince sat in the dust on the other side of the rope, crossing his legs beneath him, and watched as Airyn Rothkys crossed back over the rope to meet Daniel Skarton. The pair bowed to Qirk and to each other before the Marshal began the match. Mayson watched for several minutes as the two threw hurried jabs, conservatively probing at the other's defenses. He soon grew bored with the inaction and found himself closing his eyes to meditate again.

The roar of the crowd snapped him back to his senses. He opened his eyes to see Daniel Skarton with his legs wrapped around Airyn's ribs, leaning back and stretching Airyn's arm to the point where it seemed it would snap in two at the elbow. Airyn frantically tapped at Daniel's leg with his free hand, and with a signal from the Marshal, the fight was over. With a look of painful dejection, Airyn shook Daniel's hand with his good arm and took leave to join the rest. Qirk raised Daniel's arm in victory and faced the cheering crowd.

Mayson hardly paid attention to the majority of the other fights. He cared little for the combatants; the results meant nothing to him. One by one, the scheduled fights worked through the queue- impressive bouts, but nothing truly spectacular. Of the twenty boys, there were only a small handful of great warriors, and those fights were reserved for the end of the day.

The first of this final lineup to fight was Jalen, who had been paired with Karmine Tal'Por, a fourth-year student whose lean arms were covered in winding vine tattoos. The designs danced with each other, eventually meeting at a large star in the center of his toned back. It was tradition for the men in his family to show honor to the Two Queens: the Mother of Man, Low Goddess Mahtem, and the Queen of Starlight, High Goddess Estrelda. He had removed his tunic, for Karmine never wasted an opportunity to reveal his tattoos, and this was the perfect audience for it.

"Kick his painted ass into the dirt, Jalen!" came a wild voice from the crowd. Mayson knew the owner without needing to think. Lord Rahmos sat dead still in his seat, with all the dignity of a High Lord on his emotionless face, attempting to pretend it wasn't he who had just cried out. Lady Illysha gave him a soft blow to the arm and Kristian held his head in his hands. All Tyrel could manage was a nod and a smirk in Jalen's direction. Jalen laughed aloud as he approached his opponent in the center of the ring. With a bow to the Marshal and to each other, the fight began.

Karmine wasted no time, throwing several spinning kicks at Jalen's head, which he dodged. Jalen was quick, but Karmine had true speed on his side. The prince's apathy had disappeared, and he was completely drawn into the action. Mayson knew Jalen's immense strength could win the day for him, but anything could happen with an opponent that fast. Mayson watched uneasily, holding his breath.

The painted boy had now begun a barrage of lightning-fast jabs that came painstakingly close to their target. One even grazed Jalen's jaw, to no effect, as his thick, muscular frame allowed him to absorb such attacks without much consequence. Where Karmine was loose and erratic, Jalen was as still as a millpond, conserving his energy, ready to channel it into one devastating shot when the opportunity arose. However, each time Jalen attempted to approach, he was met by a sweeping kick or a shot from his opponent's fists.

After nearly twenty minutes of dodging, and several light jabs taken to his sturdy chin, Jalen found his opening after Karmine found himself off balance after throwing a punch and poorly executing a straight kick to the midsection. As he struggled to regain his stance, Jalen pounced with a devastating left hook that collided with Karmine's jaw, sending his elder crashing into the sand. Karmine began to rise unsteadily, but before he could get both knees off the ground, a straight kick from Jalen struck him square in the face, sending him flying and ending the fight.

The crowd had been enthusiastic from the beginning, but for a son of Rahmos, the throng was on its feet with pride fueling their cheers. They expected no less from the son of a High Lord. *Rahm only knows what they expect of you, Karrok.*

"My turn," Diero said with a devilish grin, springing to his feet with giddy energy. "Be careful," Mayson said, sounding more like a father than a friend. "One misstep and he'll put you in a world of hurt."

"Relax—that oaf won't last two minutes. I'm untouchable," Diero replied as he rose to take his place with the Marshal.

Diero was already standing in the middle of the ring by the time Blayk Mortryn even crossed over the black rope. As the lumbering boy reluctantly made his way to the center, the young Carovensa was hopping up and down in anticipation.

The pair bowed to the Marshal and turned to each other. Blayk gave a begrudging bow, while Diero simply stood still, staring at his opponent with blind hatred. *Bow, you fool. Bow.* The Marshal cleared his throat suggestively, shooting Diero a seething glare. After a few moments of tension, he gave the slightest of bows, just enough for it to be considered legitimate.

Hot-headed bastard. All the good it would have done to be disqualified before you could even throw a punch.

Diero gave a flinch forward, immediately trying to unsteady his opponent's mind before dedicating energy to an attack. Each lurch forward was met with a defensive flinch from Blayk, who was developing a thick film of sweat on his forehead. The exchange seemed so ridiculous it was all Mayson could do not to laugh. Diero was as wiry as they came, and barely standing over five feet, he looked like a child in comparison to his foe.

After several minutes of this back and forth, it seemed Blayk could take no more of it, and in a fit of desperation lunged at Diero with a straight kick aimed at his gut. Diero sidestepped the attack, grabbed hold of the leg, and used his whole body to twist the much larger boy to the ground. He was on his prey in an instant, showering him with a barrage of hurried blows to the head and midsection. But to Diero's clear frustration, Blayk was prepared this time, with each shot unable to find a home. He managed to get a foot under Diero's belly and, with a mighty push, sent the smaller boy sailing through the air. Diero landed on his back with a resounding thud that made Mayson's spine ache, but Diero swallowed the pain and was on his feet in time to brace for Blayk's counterattack.

Despite his size, Blayk was deceptively athletic and had jumped to his feet before Diero even hit the ground. Diero was able to block the first four shots of the furious combination, but the fifth caught him in the cheek, sending him stumbling into the ivory rope-stand. *Gods, I can't watch.*

Blayk approached slowly, grinning as though the fight were already over. He grabbed a tuft of Diero's hair and lifted his head to look him in the eye as Diero knelt before him, blood dripping from the corner of his mouth. Blayk pulled him up to his feet. Once Diero stood upright, he sent a darting kick to his attacker's knee, catching him just behind it with a sharp *pop*. A cry of pain wrenched itself from Blayk's throat as he dropped. Diero wiped the blood from his mouth, and, grinning at his opponent, shot his heel straight into his chest, knocking Blayk onto his back. Diero pounced once again, but this time, he brought his skills *and* his mind with him. Instead of throwing thoughtless punches, he demonstrated proper Kataar technique. Using his elbows to knock the defending arms away, he brought his fists down on Blayk's face in a hammering fashion.

Blayk managed to block one or two shots at a time, but Kataar, being adaptive, allowed Diero to invent new patterns to knock away the defense, hammering Blayk's face over and over. This went on for half a minute before Marshal Qirk stepped in to pull Diero off his victim. His fists and forearms were covered in blood from the attack, and Blayk could hardly move. Between the damage to his knee and practically being beaten unconscious, Blayk had to be dragged off the arena floor.

As the Marshal raised Diero's arm in victory, the boy seemed to bathe in the adoration of the crowd, screaming back at them and beating his chest like a wild man. *What a piece of work he is.*

After soaking in the cheers for another moment, Diero glanced up at the King's Box and suddenly went still. The silver-eyed girl again held his gaze with unfamiliar intensity.

"Well done, brother," the prince said as Diero finally joined him, his lip stained red with his own blood. "You almost got your head kicked in, but well done."

"Were you watching the same fight?" Diero spat back. "I had him right where I wanted him! I told you, I'm untouchable."

"It looks to me you were touched quite…" He stopped mid-thought. The crowd had gone silent, and the Marshal was staring at him from the center of the ring. Allister stood beside him. *Rahm, if you have been with me through my days, stay with me today.*

"Say a prayer," Mayson said to his brother as he rose. The grin vanished from Diero's face. With a firm shake of the hand, Mayson left him to join his opponent in the ring. As he approached, he looked to the King's Box for one last glimpse of his parents for reassurance. Henry looked as calm as ever, but Beatrice was now leaning forward, her elbows on her knees and hands clutching her mouth. He stood next to Allister, half as wide and a head shorter. He knew he must look like Allister's toy to the audience in the highest seats. Not a sound could be heard. Even the wind couldn't muster enough life for a small breeze.

Cocking his chin upward, he locked eyes with Allister before the two turned to bow to the Marshal, then back to each other. The Marshal raised his arms, and the battle began.

Mayson extended his arms in a guarding position, keeping his right foot forward. *He hasn't trained against anyone who is left-handed. Use it.* He had elected to wear a short-sleeved tunic to give Allister less material to grab. *Use your speed, use your stance, and you just might make it.*

He crept slowly toward his opponent, who held the same guarding stance, though much more relaxed. *He doesn't see you as a threat—use it.* Mayson sent a probing jab into Allister's concrete jaw, to no effect. *Damn, he's made of stone!* Allister smiled at the effort. *Hell with him. You are the Blood of the Mountain; you will break him.*

Allister's hulking arms suddenly went into killing mode, sending potentially devastating blows to Mayson's head in clusters. Mayson's speed was all that stood between him and a shattered skull, each punch ending less than an inch from him. He could feel the breeze generated by each swing, causing his heart to jump each time. *Keep swinging, big boy. Tire out those tree trunk arms.*

The prince attempted a swing of his own, but his thin arm was caught in a steel trap, and before he knew it, Allister grabbed hold of his chest and tossed him to the ground. Instead of pouncing, like anyone would onto an opponent lying on his back, he strolled over to the prince with the same casual nature as one walking into a park.

Fear was overcome by fury, and as soon as he was in reach, Mayson swung his legs around, completely sweeping Allister's feet out from under him. Seeing the look of shock on his face, combined with the explosion from the crowd, Mayson felt like a giant as he sprang to his feet, ready to continue. *He'll try to finish it quickly now. He will make more mistakes.*

Allister leapt to his feet, his sly look now replaced with an intensity that made Mayson uneasy. With a rapid flurry of Allister's hands, Mayson found himself confused just long enough for his foe to grab hold of his neck and push him down into a knee shooting straight for his face. With all the strength he could muster, the prince put his forearms between himself and the knee, and with a mighty heave, pushed it away. Wasting no time, Mayson freed himself and began a frantic flurry of punches to Allister's midsection that he didn't bother to block. He took them all, laughing at the attempt.

"Go on," he whispered. "You can swing until your arms fall off. It will do you no good. Your father is going to have to watch me pummel you into the dirt."

Allister struck him with a back-handed smack across the face, earning a gasp from the crowd. Mayson found himself on the ground once again, the taste of blood filling his mouth. He was slower to rise this time, only getting to his knee by the time Allister reached him. He now strolled with more drive and more sinister energy.

Driving his heel into the ground, Mayson shot his entire body skyward, driving an uppercut straight into the underside of Allister's imposing jaw. His fist sang to him in pain, but Allister fell back several steps, and the prince went in for the kill. Hook after hook collided with the stunned Allister, who continued to lumber backward. Mayson's arms were half the size of Allister's at most, but there was power in them that his opponent had overlooked.

His training to increase his speed was paying off, as Allister barely had time to react between blows. An uppercut to the gut made him double over this time, and a spinning back-kick sent him stumbling into the ivory stands. The entire crowd was on its feet, practically frothing at the mouth. *The shadow of the mountain falls upon all.*

The rest of the fight seemed to meld into one long moment for Mayson. He funneled all of his energy into each combination, hoping to chip away more and more at Allister's tough outer shell. But as much as he gave, he received in proper fashion, and before long, he could feel his ribs and nose had been broken. With busted, bloody knuckles, he desperately took advantage of any slip in Allister's defense, made easier by his reversed stance.

This pattern was repeated no less than a dozen times, until both boys stood toe to toe. Mayson's right eye had swollen shut, and a deep gash poured blood over Allister's left. Allister's ribs had been broken as well. He couldn't hide the way he kept his left arm clutched tightly to his side.

This was a fight to end the day for sure; it was what the people had hoped to see, and Mayson couldn't tell how long the crowd had been on its feet, nor could he make out any noise. There was only Allister…Allister and the victory that waited just beyond him.

Mayson grasped a jab from Allister on his right side and pulled it in as he dropped his left elbow to ruin his opponent's injured arm. But before he could make contact, Allister crashed into the side of his face with a murderous head butt, knocking him to the ground for what seemed to be the hundredth time.

Everything was a blur. The shapes around him blended together and the light of the sun was blinding. The shadow of Allister appeared over him, and as his large, wounded fist came seeking its target, time seemed to slow to a crawl. Mayson moved his head out of the line of attack at the last moment, forcing Allister to punch the earth beneath. He could hear bones cracking as Allister cried out in agony. With all the energy he could muster, Mayson spun out and sent his right elbow slamming into Allister's eye, knocking him to the ground.

The only sound the prince could hear now was his heartbeat, as the smell of his own blood filled his nostrils. The taste of victory was on the tip of his tongue. With what little he had left, Mayson climbed to his feet using the nearest ivory stand to aid him, and limped back into the center of the ring, his left knee having been twisted in the fall.

Allister was on his knees now. Between the blood in his left eye and the strike to his right, he was effectively blind. *I am the Blood of the Avaari—of the Dalani. I am the Blood of Astymere. I was born to rule. Before me, you rightly tremble. Before me, you rightly kneel.*

Mayson had lost control of his thoughts. He stood on the cusp of victory and this, along with his injuries, overtook him. He planted his good leg into the ground as he threw every last bit of will and power into a spinning kick that caught Allister in the side of the head, putting his lights out.

When he did not rise after several moments, Marshal Qirk waved his arms, signaling the completion of the Final Fights. It seemed the very mortar that held the stones of the Kastigra together would come undone as the crowd exploded. Mayson couldn't feel it, but he could see the Marshal raise his numb arm in victory, shouting something unintelligible to the crowd with a look of pride on his face that seemed so alien and strange to him.

He turned on wobbly legs to see Diero and Jalen leaning over the velvet rope, jumping about like madmen, reaching to embrace him. Mayson took two feeble steps before the ground rose up to meet him.

Chapter 20

The Dark Wood: Astymere
10th Day of the Eighth Month
5014 A.S.

Lily hadn't ventured out much on her own in months, but the king insisted she go to Karna'Sharahm by herself. He would have gone with her, but it was all too possible that Vytria might not see her if she were escorted by royal guards or anyone else that represented the Crown. The Knights of Rahm had ridden with her as far as the Palagh Hills, two leagues south of the Dark Wood, stopping and setting up camp as she continued on. The crown-bearer, Elara, had insisted on coming as well. King Henry had found it odd, but gave his consent, so long as she did not try to enter the wood with Lily. He was hard pressed to get her to agree, for she seemed adamant about following her every step of the way.

Lily couldn't deny the safety she felt being surrounded by the Shadow Knights, as daunting as they were. After months of being near them, she had grown accustomed to having them around. She would often pretend to engage them in conversation to pass the time. It always made her laugh, especially when she would create foolish voices for her companions. Elara didn't find it at all amusing. As she approached the wood, it felt strange being without the knights—like she was missing a piece of clothing. She was more than relieved to be rid of Elara.

It was a perfect day for riding, a clear, sunny day with only a few thin trails of clouds above and hardly a breeze. The wood was just close enough to the ocean to benefit from cooler temperatures, but not so close as to be subjected to unpredictable winds.

She took the Northrode, passed over the last hilltop of the Palagh Hills, and finally laid her eyes upon the vast expanse of the Dark Wood, Karna'Sharahm. The trees were not as tall as they were wide, and there wasn't empty space to be found as far as she could crane her neck to see. The leaves, a pure white, fluttered off the night-black branches in endless bunches.

Lily urged her horse toward the sacred grounds, gripping the reins in forceful apprehension. The fallen leaves carpeted the ground under the winding branches, nearly fooling her into thinking they were snow until the wind lifted them off the ground to dance wildly before wafting back down again.

The branches, which constantly lost leaves, never seemed to expose any more of the sky above. *How is that possible?* She watched as a leaf wiggled and detached from its base. Immediately, a small white bud appeared where its predecessor had fallen, and within moments, the tiny bud grew to a round, snow-white leaf. Lily couldn't say how long it would remain before it, too, fell, but she didn't have the time to find out.

A single path ran through the forest, constantly swerving and dipping, rising and tilting to accommodate the trees and their wild roots. Lily hopped down from her saddle and after examining the way ahead, decided it would be safer for both her and her horse if she tried to find her way on foot. She couldn't risk the poor beast slipping or tripping over some unseen obstacle, possibly crippling itself with a broken leg, or crushing her in the process. It was a prudent decision, for as she planted her shoes on the ground, they disappeared in a sea of white. She walked her courser, Guardian, to a low-lying branch, where she tied the reins. She smiled and gave the horse an affectionate pat on the nose.

"Wait here," she instructed before stepping under the canopy of the great trees, reminding herself to speak no more once in the forest.

Lily had never heard a silence so absolute, so all encompassing. Her breath sounded like thunder in her ears, and if she held it, she swore she could hear her own heart beating. The king had warned her that the shadows of the Dark Wood would give her a deep chill, and this proved to be true; the sun hadn't even gone down yet and already she felt a shiver run up her spine. She wrapped her cloak of black bear fur about her.

She wandered aimlessly into growing darkness, avoiding the bigger, thicker trees. When she lost the path, she could not tell *where* she had lost it, and her mind raced. She argued with herself as she kicked leaves, looking for the dirt pathway. Every way she turned in her search for where she'd gone astray seemed to pull her deeper and deeper into the wild brush, until she was surrounded by snarling, claw-like branches and a swirling rain of falling flower petals. She dwelled on thoughts of her brief stay at the palace after the Fights, when the young Lord Carovensa guided her through the twisting paths of the royal gardens.

They had wandered for hours, for some reason at a loss for words, just happy being in each other's presence. Diero looked on her as though she were some unspeakable treasure, and something in that look woke her from within—where she hadn't even known she'd slumbered. He was a treasure himself, a golden serpent that seemed to shine just for her.

Lily clung to that shine as she wandered through the shadows. She figured she only had a few hours of daylight left, and she worried she might never find Vytria—or her way out. Her confidence vanished as she reverted to memories of her days alone on the plains, feeling hopelessly lost and pressed upon by unyielding danger.

Everything looked the same as she scrambled through the darkening wood, trying to get her bearings, frequently stubbing her toes on roots hidden beneath the snow-like leaves.

A flash of movement from within the thick trees, sharper and quicker than the falling petals, just barely caught her eye. Something was out there.

You're seeing things. She tried to keep her eyes on the ground before her, but some unseen force kept pulling her eyes upward into the trees. A minute would go by with no activity before she would catch the slightest movement in the corner of her eye. *It's just the leaves.* A twig snapped behind her and Lily pivoted on the spot, fear cementing her where she stood. There was nothing. Only the dark trees, falling leaves, and the all-consuming silence.

She turned to continue on her path and froze. Two red eyes peered at her from out of the darkness. They burned into her, glowing like two coals fresh from a furnace, and try as she might, she could not see what they belonged to. Within these blazing red eyes, large pupils in a shape she could not describe stared at her— a hard glare, she could tell, despite having no face to show. She inched back, her mouth agape, trapped by those eyes. They looked deeply into Lily's heart, as though they saw everything within and turned her body and mind inside out. She slowly inched backward until she could feel her heels on the edge of a drop. Lily stopped, trapped in the gaze of the otherworldly eyes. The soft soil and layer of leaves along the edge crumbled at her feet and, arms flailing, she tumbled backwards down the hill.

She somersaulted for what seemed like eternity over rough

roots, lumps and bumps buffeting her body. Then everything went black.

LILY WAS NO LONGER IN KARNA'SHARAHM, but surrounded by sharp, icy mountains with light snow falling from a thick blanket of morose gray; shattered stones already had been dusted in a layer of white. The mountains looked almost like Gol Rayna at first, but these were far more jagged and unforgiving, as though they were the white-tipped fangs of some gargantuan beast. She felt an unimaginable cold pierce her, as though her heart itself had been gripped with icy fingers, and the air in her lungs nearly turned them to glass. At first, she saw nothing and felt nothing besides the snow and rocks. Slowly, as though they were born from smoke, she found herself surrounded by soldiers in the midst of a terrible battle.

Despite her initial fear, she soon realized these men paid her no mind. It was as if she didn't exist. Lily moved freely through the mob, observing all that occurred around her without hindrance or obstacle. Pure mayhem strangled the landscape as far as the eye could see in any direction. There was no order, no formations, no semblance of control—these armies were completely interspersed in a massive, deadly, free-for-all. Men armored in gold steel, fur and iron, silver, green, gray, and black, were all hacking each other to pieces at a pace slower than life, as if she were watching the event unfold underwater.

Lily recognized the armies of the Kings of the West from books she had read and the stories King Henry had told her. Their combined strength was mixed with a sea of iron-clad barbarians, the very same that had come for her and her father. She wandered for what felt like ages through swords and spears. The only things that seemed real were the frigid snow and the sharp rocks beneath her bare feet, now completely soaked in blood. She came to a small clearing and paused as a nightmarish castle loomed through the fog, dripping rivers of blood from its dark mortar. Its walls were lined with jagged spikes, many of which supported skeletons in varying states of degradation, and it's cavernous portcullis stood half-open, the iron bars baring down like snarling fangs. The rest of the terrible structure was encased in thick clouds and sheets of whirling snow, with the fighting seemingly growing more intense and wild the closer she came to it. In the middle of the chaos, a warrior dressed in black armor stood face to face with a giant.

The great foe was over seven feet tall and wielded a sword nearly as long as the warrior. He was dressed in a thick, dark-gray iron suit, crowned with a helm fashioned in the shape of a horrific skull with two great bull horns long enough to rival spears. He appeared more monster than man.

The warrior, dressed in the black armor of the Crescent, wielded the spear Rahmirion with a ruthless, bloodthirsty sense of purpose. He wore the crowned, masked helm of an Astymerian king, and his eyes seemed to be nothing more than two black holes, lifeless and unknowing. As they hacked at each other, Lily could see dozens of dead bodies lying at the iron giant's feet. The horrendous nature of their wounds—missing arms, sprawling innards, shoulders cleaved down to the sternum—told her that only this monster could have caused them.

The faceless king carried on, paying no mind to Lily or the slain that lay around him. He seemed dead set on his opponent, with not an ounce of fear showing in the way he held himself. Only hatred emanated from within his body. As the king raised Rahmirion in preparation for another attack, Lily felt the world begin to spin. The warriors around her began to blow away with each gust of wind, returning to the smoke that bore them. A dark whirlwind of shouts, cries, and her father's voice telling her to *run* pushed and pulled at her, carrying her away over the cruel, icy mountains, until she found herself back in Karna'Sharahm.

She awoke against the base of a tree at the bottom of the hill. Her head felt as though it would split from within as she lifted her dirty hand to rub it. A large bump had grown, and a cut had left a trail of blood in the pitch-black mud on her face. She wanted so badly to cry out in pain, but she heeded the warning Rhivor had given her. *Pure silence. Not a sound.*

Something stirred to her right and slowly emerged from the brambles. Nerves fired up and down Lily's body. She wanted to run, but couldn't move. Her legs locked in pain when she tried to stand. The figure approached slowly, pausing in the light a few paces before Lily's battered feet. It was an old woman with unkempt, frizzy hair that sprang wild on her head, tangled down past her shoulders, and ended abruptly, as if it had been axed off. Her long, black robe draped down past her feet and trailed behind her.

"Are you Lily?" she uttered in a deep, angry tone. Lily nodded, unable to decide if she should also risk speaking and incurring Rahm's wrath. She half-expected the old woman to burst into flame or explode into a thousand pieces, given the severity of Rhivor's warning, but even through the darkness, she could see the woman's eyes clearly. The bright silver couldn't have been mistaken—not for a moment.

"My name is Vytria, but surely, you knew that already. Follow me." Her voice was much softer now.

Lily could only sit, dumbfounded and too frightened to break Rahm's silence.

"It's all right, child. We have an understanding, the Watcher and I. You may speak, but now is not the time for talking. You must come with me at once."

"I...I can't," Lily admitted. "My legs—I think they're broken."

The old seer regarded her silently, her tall, lanky body looming over her. She waved in the direction from which she had come, and from the shadows emerged a small, blue, glowing orb that hovered above the ground. As it grew closer, Lily could see the orb sat atop a slender staff, crafted from one of the black branches of Karna'Sharahm.

"We must get a move on," Vytria said, nodding to herself. "I shall give you a quick fix so you can walk, and then something more permanent when we reach the Delves."

"The...what?" Neither King Henry nor Rhivor had mentioned anything about any delves.

"The Whispering Delves, child. It has long been a place of refuge for our kind, built by Rahm the Watcher himself."

The staff began to whistle a low *hum* and floated closer, dipping towards Lily's kneecaps. The blue light seemed more of a mystic fog as it pressed closely to her skin. When Vytria motioned her hand over the orb, it glowed brightly, forcing all darkness away and encasing them both.

She tapped both of Lily's feet lightly with the bottom of the staff, but the pain in her legs remained.

"Better?" Vytria asked. Lily shook her head and winced. The orb shone brighter, and Vytria motioned her hand once more. The *hum* grew much louder as a stream of bright fog flowed from the glass and danced to the motion of Vytria's hand; she conducted it like a sweet symphony. It circled above their heads and took a nosedive toward Lily's legs as she pointed to them. Instantly, Lily lost all feeling. In fact, she felt as if her legs weren't even there—as though they were part of the fog and she was missing half her body.

"How about now?" she smirked.

Lily wiggled her toes inside her shoes and felt no pain, though the only way she knew they were moving was to see that her brown shoes were being punched from within.

"Much better," she said with a smile. She stood and followed Vytria. It felt strange walking without legs, as if she was tipping over, but she continued onward, avoiding roots and sticking to Vytria like glue—so close she had to avoid stepping on her billowing train. Lily bombarded her with questions, though the same response was issued every time.

"In due time, child. You will understand what it means to be a seer—to be a Layda Arani."

They slowed as they approached a circular clearing, the largest opening in the forest that Lily had seen, though it was only about ten paces in diameter. They stopped in the middle and stood silently.

"Vhodul!" Vytria uttered, and the trees surrounding them danced to life, swaying in a sudden gust of wind. They came to a halt when the bark directly in front of Vytria grew a pair of red eyes—the same red eyes Lily had seen in the darkness.

"What are those?" Lily whispered, alarmed.

"The eyes of Rahm, child. They keep the Delves hidden from unwanted visitors. Only He allows passage. I'm surprised you didn't know…having been in Astymere."

They approached the tree and Vytria peered into the red eyes, placing a hand on a knot beneath them. To Lily's awe, the knot gave way and disappeared into the side of the tree. The branches and leaves all shuddered as if the tree had taken a breath and fell back into place. The bark on one side of the trunk split down the middle and separated with a strange grinding noise, as if it were moving upon wheels atop a track.

They entered through the narrow opening. Vytria ducked as they began descending a spiral staircase for several stories, each step carved from the black wood of the tree.

"Are there other seers who live here with you?" Lily asked.

"No—none stay as long as I have. They come for as long as they must until their vision is clear. Some for weeks, some for months, a few for years. They are the unfortunate souls that did not reach me in time and were too old to master Serenti, the Quieting. Their visions remained foggy and distant, and the relentless dreams drove them to madness. You, however, are young. I have faith Serenti will come to you, but your mind is wild and troubled, which will make this quite difficult."

"How long do you think I will be here?"

"That is entirely up to you, isn't it?" Vytria replied matter-of-factly. "One cannot see how far the road goes upon taking their first step. But I will only keep you for mere spans of months at a time. I feel a great force pulling you back toward Vita Astym, a force beyond my reckoning, and I dare not try to oppose it. This setback may add great stretches of time to your training."

At the bottom of the staircase, they started down a dark tunnel carved through the deep soil. Every few yards a new tunnel opened on either side, spreading the subterranean network like a complex spider web beneath the forest.

On the arched ceiling above, Lily saw white stones sprouting baby roots and, to her displeasure, worms. Glowing worms were half-sticking out of the soil overhead, squirming as they walked. She cringed at the sight. Lily had never given much mind to worms above ground, but hated their slimy nature all the same.

They veered right when the main tunnel split in two. At the end of the dark, cool pathway, Lily could make out an ominous, ghostly blue haze. They entered a large, cavernous room carved from the stone and earth. Thin, sharp rocks jutted down from the ceiling and sprang up from the ground all around them. In the center of the cavern was a large pool of shimmering, rippling liquid—the source of the glow.

Vytria approached slowly and ran her fingers through it. "Do you know what this is?"

"No." Lily bent down and took a small scoop in her hand. The blue substance felt warm and thicker than she thought, almost like jelly.

"This is what we call Afina. It is relatively unknown to the world of man. Nobody but the seers who venture down here know of its existence, and none have ever spoken of it."

"What does it do?"

"As a gas, it has incredible healing properties, as you've seen, though it is quite rare—even rarer than the liquid state, though luckily, it's recyclable. Speaking of…"

Vytria motioned her hand so that the blue gas reemerged from beneath Lily's skin, floating in the air to find its home in the orb atop the old woman's staff. The pain was nearly gone, and Vytria assured her it would soon disappear, along with her bruising. Lily had forgotten about the lump that had swelled to the size of a fist on her forehead.

"What does it do for seers?" she inquired.

"It dispels the mists of uncertainty. It acts as a bridge between your waking mind and the current of time, allowing it to ride the waves and sail over the ripples to see what lies far beyond you."

"People have been drinking this for hundreds of years? How do you not run out?"

"Perceptive girl, you are," Vytria said, now sitting next to Lily beside the pool. "But hundreds of years? *Hundreds* you say? More like *thousands* of years, child. Thousands upon tens of thousands. Since the first silver eyes were opened, Afina has run beneath Karna'Sharahm in rivers. Legend says it is linked to the power of Rahm himself, though none know for certain. The only certainty is that every seer alive would have to drink for eternity to drain these pools."

Vytria stood and walked to a single shelf carved into the wall behind them. It was lined with dark cups the size of a small bowl, of a wood Lily somehow knew came from Karna'Sharahm. Vytria chose one and headed back to the Afina.

"Lie down," she told Lily. Lily tucked her cloak underneath her and stretched out on the ground.

"You will not be able to move or speak," Vytria said as she bent and filled the cup. "But I will be with you, guiding you through whatever you may see. This is a small portion, so your body can adjust. Too much at once may have some unpleasant effects if you are not careful. I will gradually give you more, but for now, I just want to see where the smallest ripples in the current of time take us."

She handed Lily the cup and watched her drink it. The warm liquid tasted sweet, like freshly squeezed juice from a fruit she could not name. She finished the cup in a few gulps, having had little water since entering the forest.

"When will I begin to feel the effects?" she asked.

"Immediately," Vytria replied, as Lily's eyes slowly closed, and she found herself in a blank space. She felt a pervasive stillness as her breathing slowed, and she began to slip beyond the confines of the present.

Chapter 21

Gildara: The Gildarian Republic
1ˢᵗ Day of the Seventh Month
5017 A.S.

Eduardas Goldblade paced before the large windows of his office chambers looking out over the streets of Gildara. On a typical day, he could see for nearly a mile through the large clearing in the canopy over the heart of the treetop city. Both the wooden buildings carved into the bark of the trees and the artfully constructed concrete ones lining the street were painted in gold and crimson, all shining in the sunlight that sparkled down through the golden leaves above.

Winding off into the east, the Caerian Aqueduct carried water from the forest floor to the million souls living upon the great platform, and less than half a mile away, it wrapped around the Senate House in the center of the city. Of the architectural wonders Gildara had to offer, the Senate House stood apart from the rest in Eduardas' mind. Suspended over the only opening in the city platform, it was hung by over five hundred steel chains fastened to a great branch high above. As the center of government, it was both the physical and figurative heart of the forest city.

But today, Eduardas had no such view. He could barely see ten feet beyond the window, as the city had been engulfed in a low-lying cloud. The mist, whenever it came, made the old ones uneasy. It was long said in the Republic that the coming of the mist always preceded ill fortune. Eduardas typically thought it nonsense—but these were uneasy times for the Republic.

"Death strikes this city once again." It was a common line to hear in Gildara as of late. Eduardas had first heard the Oraetar say it in the middle of Aeniad's Square on the day he struck a deal with western royalty. Guild men had been burnt with no culprit; handfuls of military leaders and politicians went missing without a trace. It was the first time in the Republic's history that a serial killer systematically worked their way through high-end officials. The men and women of Gildara had begun to whisper that the criminal underworld had a new 'king' by the name of Vasur, a demon spawn of the Beast sent to wreak havoc on the innocent. The only trace of him left at the scene of the crimes was a black *V* etched nearby.

While the Republic around him seemed in chaos, Eduardas was otherwise distracted. It had been three years since he'd reopened the roads heading west to the coast and agreed to King Henry's demand that the Republic pay nearly double the sales tax for their trade- his popularity with the people had increased exponentially. He had worried he would be blacklisted and the Ministry would attempt to ruin him- that his offices would be closed and his properties seized to be offered as gifts to the oldest senators and their sons- or that his clientele would abandon him upon coercion from Minister Valmas, or even the Consularas himself.

To his surprise, however, his dealings with the Western Kingdoms had the opposite effect. Though the Ministry was displeased, the commoners were astonished and curious about the man who had done business with kings. They came to him in droves with their money, looking to stash it away or invest it. The influx was so great that many of Eduardas' leading competitors were put out of business, and those who remained were half as powerful as they'd been before. This made Eduardas Goldblade the second most powerful man of the coin in the entire Republic, behind the Minister of Trade and Revenue. He was even considering running for the position himself when Valmas' term was up.

This left an unsettling feeling in his stomach. Whenever his excitement got the better of him, he reminded himself that the higher he rose, the more tempting a target he became for Vasur. He didn't fear being killed outright, but he knew that sooner or later, Vasur would show himself and, one way or another, it would not end well.

The tall clock to his right chimed seven in the evening. *I was supposed to be home at six. Who do these people think they are, keeping me waiting?*

In years past, Eduardas had been used to waiting hours on end for prospective clients to arrive, for he'd suffer any slight if it meant earning more business. In his humble beginnings, he had to do what was necessary to keep a roof over his family's heads, but now, at the top of the financial world, he had no tolerance for tardiness.

Having had enough of staring out into the gray abyss,

Eduardas moved back to the heavy oak desk facing the double doors of his office and sat in his deep armchair with a groan. He had bought the building less than a year ago and already it seemed he'd worked there for decades. Bookshelves stretched from the marble floor to the high, vaulted ceiling on the wall opposite the windows. Each was stuffed to the brim with scrolls and books documenting the financial information of his more important clients.

He had taken a blank roll of parchment and dipped his quill to write a note to be sent to the tardy solicitors, expressing he was no longer interested in their business, when a knock came at the door.

"Enter!" Eduardas barked, his frustration getting the better of him. The doors inched open without a sound, and in poked Tamias' apologetic face. "This had better be good, Tamias."

"Dominaen," he said with an encouraging grin, his cheeks reddened by his trip up the stairs. His years cavorting in the taverns had done little for his health. "They are here."

"It's about damn time. Send them in. I want to get this over with."

"Yes, Dominaen." In a flash, Tamias was out the door, his hurried footsteps trailing down the stairs.

Not long after, Eduardas could hear three sets of feet climbing the staircase. *This had better be worth it, or I swear by the Heavenly King, I will have Mylas and Holto throw them out into the gutter. That will teach them some manners.*

The thought suddenly terrified Eduardas. It was the exact kind of thing his wife would say; this nearly made him ill. Another knock sounded on the thick, double doors, and this time, Dominaen Eduardas Goldblade was a bit more gracious.

"Do come in," he called, attempting to rid his voice of anger. He smoothed the front of his golden robe and adjusted his red leather belt as the doors opened to reveal Tamias, followed by two of the strangest men Eduardas had ever laid eyes on.

The first odd thing Eduardas noticed about them was that they moved in unison. The pair stood nearly a head taller than Tamias, looking like giant praying mantises, gaunt and thin, with pointed chins. The cloudy green color of their togas, clinging tightly to their frail builds, only strengthened the image.

"Dominaen," Tamias began, slightly winded from his trips up and down the stairs. "I present the brothers Tarbous and Junar of the Spicers Guild. If there is nothing else, I will take my leave."

"Thank you, Tamias. That will be all," Eduardas said with a curt nod. "Gentlemen?" He gestured to the two cushioned chairs facing him. "Please be seated." Masters Tarbous and Junar sat in unison. Eduardas found their slow, deliberate mannerisms vaguely repellent, as did the finer details of the twins' appearances.

At this distance, he now saw the two men had mismatched eyes. Each had one black eye and one white eye, without a pupil in either. *Gods, what kind of spice are these two snorting?* To top it off, in the center of their foreheads—right where their hairlines should have been, if their heads had not been shaved clean—were the smallest of tattoos, too small to make out in the fading light. Something about the mark was oddly familiar. After several silent moments, Eduardas realized he had been staring at the pair and jumped into business.

"Gentlemen," he began once more. "I don't know how the Spicers Guild does business with the local financiers around the outlying territories, but in this office, when an appointment is made…"

"Our most sincere apologies," the pair said in unison, cutting Eduardas off. Their voices seemed to melt into one, as if a single thought drove both of them.

"I realize we are quite late, Dominaen. But I assure you the Spicers Guild places the utmost value on punctuality," Tarbous said alone.

"Yes, Dominaen," Junar chimed in, practically on top of the end of his brother's sentence. "Surely though, as a man of business, you can understand that certain matters can take up more of one's time than expected."

"The Spicers Guild does not wish to imply we do not value your time," continued Tarbous. "These offices have become the standard of safe investment in this city, and we would not want to take our business anywhere else."

"Very well," Eduardas said, attempting to not let his ego dictate the conversation. All flatterers whose numbers didn't add up had been turned away. "But if the Spicers Guild wants to do business with this firm, tardiness will not be tolerated. I must insist on that."

With a look to each other, the brothers smiled as if dazed, revealing impossibly white teeth. *I have never met a stranger pair in all my days. How do two airheads like these become representatives of one of the most powerful guilds in the Republic?*

"To be honest, Dominaen…" Tarbous began.

"…we do not speak for the guild itself. Not today," Junar finished.

Eduardas grunted. "That is quite misleading. I was under the impression that the Spicers Guild was looking to invest a portion of its profits from the last year with us."

The guild had opened three new trading routes with several kingdoms along the eastern coast, and it was no secret they had been raking in mountains of gold ever since. Until today, Eduardas had been more than eager for their business.

"A half-truth, Dominaen," Junar said.

"We represent one of the guild's most generous benefactors," said Tarbous, "and he was worried you would not see us unless we told you we were speaking for the Guild directly."

"A generous benefactor? All right gentlemen I think we have wasted just about enough of my time today. I'm sure you can find your way out." Eduardas began to rise from his seat. Tarbous slammed his hand down on the desk, stopping Eduardas in his tracks. The empty-headed smile was gone, and the glare from those mismatched eyes seemed to emanate from the pits of frozen hell.

Tarbous removed his hand from the desk, where he had slapped a small piece of parchment, seemingly blank.

"What is this?" Eduardas asked, shaken.

"It is our master's planned deposit," the pair responded in unison. With cold hands, the nerve having been sucked right out of him, Eduardas scooped up the tiny piece of paper before him, turned it over, and examined it closely.

"This can't be correct," he sputtered. The figure before him nearly crossed his eyes.

"Oh, but it is, Dominaen," Junar answered. "Seven million. Down to the last zero."

"In what form is this amount? Sistras, I suppose?" This amount in sistras was far more likely for any single, private investor.

"No, Dominaen," the pair replied. "Our master wishes to invest seven million gilders with these offices." *Seven million gilders. Dear heavenly King, could it be possible?*

"If I may," Eduardas said, clearing his throat and attempting to remain calm in the face of such fortune being dumped at his feet. "How has your benefactor come by such funds? He must be a senior senator, or perhaps a lord of one of the old families from the first Senate?"

"We are not at liberty to discuss such things, Dominaen," Tarbous stated. "Our instructions are to bring you the amount and make the deposit. No more. Surely you understand. Our master is a very private man. The fewer who know his business, the better."

"Very well," Eduardas said, taking a kerchief from an inner pocket of his robe and dabbing his brow. "Unfortunately though, I will be needing his name. It isn't as though I can open the account in the name of the Spicers Guild, as I had hoped. With a private benefactor, the individual's name must be on record, in order to assure the deposit's legitimacy."

The pair exchanged an uneasy look, as though some unseen eye kept watch over them. Tarbous then lit up, the excitement in his otherworldly eyes making him look frightening beyond logic.

"We have several names to give, Dominaen, each bearing a portion of the load of such a large deposit."

"I will only be needing one, sir," Eduardas said with a polite, unsettled smile.

"Dominaen," Junar said with a gracious nod. "The deposit shall go under Kaelid Nirosa, if that will suffice?"

"Of course, gentlemen, of course," Eduardas replied, still trying to compose himself. He was both overly excited and absolutely desperate to get these men out of his office. He pushed away from his desk to fetch a fresh scroll to begin the proceedings, but before he could reach the shelf, the name sank into his bones and lit his nerves on fire. *That name. Kaelid Nirosa. Where have I heard it?* The answer hovered in his mind like an infuriating sneeze that wouldn't come. Eduardas looked into the light of the lamps upon his wall, and just as he expected, the answer came flying out. *Kaelid Nirosa, the Fruiters Guild officer that went up in flames in his home. Now, I remember.* Eduardas sank his eyes deep into the small tattoos on their head once again. *Gods, those are Vs. Vasur. He has infiltrated the Spicers Guild!*

"My…good fellows," Eduardas said with a cough, turning back to them. "I believe this concludes our business for today."

"We don't understand," the pair said in unison once again, agitation creeping into their single voice.

"I am going to be plain with you. You have taken time out of your busy day to come seek my business, and I respect that. That being said, I have spent my entire adult life clawing and scrambling my way out of a coin counter's closet to get where I am today. I have dedicated all my energy and sacrificed all my spare time in order to build what you see around you…I cannot jeopardize my job and reputation by consorting with a known criminal."

"Our master is no criminal, Dominaen," Tarbous said through a clenched jaw. "Many unsolved crimes have been unfairly branded with his name simply because the authorities find coincidence in the spelling of his name. Such charges would be laughable in court."

The thought of the consequences, both social and legal, for being associated with a common gangster filled Eduardas with seething rage. "You work for Vasur! Has he not been killing his way through the seedy underbelly of the Republic for over three years now? Senators, the military, the Armorers Guild, the Fruiters Guild, even the Spicers Guild, whom you claim your *master* represents—Gods know how many more before the City Watch caught wind of his name. The only reason Vasur has not been brought to trial is that every witness seems to disappear or lose all memory of the events. Not to mention the fact there isn't a soul in this city who has ever seen his face. Many in my own office wonder if he is even real! For these reasons, gentlemen, I firmly request you leave my office, and take your money with you. … *Now!*"

The room fell silent. Eduardas was now sinking into the shock of having refused such men with dark connections. Rising as one, the two stared unblinkingly into his eyes. Eduardas was so ensnared by their death glare that he didn't hear Mylas and Holto before they flew through the doors, their hands on the jewel-encrusted hilts of their longswords.

"Is there a problem, Dominaen?" Mylas asked, his muscles tense and his eyes wide.

"We heard someone shouting," Holto added.

"No," Eduardas said with a sigh. "These fine gentlemen were just leaving. Would you be so kind as to see them safely outside?"

"If you would follow us," Holto instructed, beckoning to the open doors, not taking his eyes off the strange pair. With one last narrow-eyed gaze at Eduardas, the Spicers reluctantly followed the Goldblade guards out of the office, gripping their togas with as much dignity as they could muster.

Eduardas stood in that very spot for several minutes, frozen with fear. The carrot had been offered. Now, surely came the stick. *What have I done?*

Eduardas' walk home, however, was peaceful and silent. Hardly a soul wandered outdoors when the mists rolled in. Only the lamplighters dared to walk the eerie streets in such conditions. Each tall lamp emitted a large halo, growing smaller and smaller as Eduardas and his guards moved north along the Street of Ballots that would take them home. They could barely see the house through the dense fog by the time they'd reached the iron fence, and Eduardas would have walked right past it had Mylas not pointed it out. He had barely put his key in the door when a sharp realization hit him in the stomach.

"Damn!" he cried, getting a start out of his guards.

"What is it, Dominaen?" Mylas asked.

"Are you all right?" said Holto.

"My apologies, boys. I didn't mean to startle you. I left my ledger back at the office, and I hadn't finished putting my numbers in for the day. It must be done tonight before the meeting with Minister Valmas tomorrow. I'm sorry, but I must go back and get it. Could I trouble the two of you to come with me?"

The two accepted without hesitation. Eduardas could not help but feel a pang of shame grip his side. It was a chill, damp night, and these two more than deserved to go home and get warm, instead of holding the hand of an old coward like himself.

The trip back down the Street of Ballots seemed to take much longer than their first, for the light of day was gone. The conditions had grown so severe that they lost their way more than once, and a twenty-minute walk now took them an hour. Even the lighters had finished for the night by the time Goldblade's Coffers came into view, a magnificent marriage of stone, wood, and glass. Eduardas felt his nerves unwind once they'd finally gotten their bearings.

"Here we are, boys, I told you I'd have us here in no time."

"You said that half an hour ago, Dominaen," Mylas grumbled, his crimson cloak beginning to cling to him in the damp air as they approached the property.

"Never mind. You two stay out here while I grab my ledger. I will be in and…"

Before he could place his hand on the gate, the building was ripped apart and consumed in wild flames. The blast sent the three flying backwards into the street, as large chunks of stone and shards of glass hurled out into the night air. The chaos died in an instant. Once the rain of debris settled, the air was still once again. The imposing fog flowed violently back into the empty space, kept only at bay by the heat of the lingering flames.

The world around him shook violently as Eduardas rolled onto his back. With all the strength he could muster, his ears ringing and his torso aching, he propped himself up on his hands to sit upright and view the destruction. Goldblade's Coffers was no more. The large square tower that adorned the heart of the building had been completely destroyed, strewn across the city for hundreds of yards in every direction. What remained of the building had been completely engulfed in flame, and was withering away before Eduardas' eyes—his life's work snuffed out in a blink.

Fighting physical and emotional agony, Eduardas forced himself to his feet, as did Mylas and Holto. Blood dripped from Holto's ear and Mylas had half a dozen cuts upon his face, but all were alive. The crackling flames were joined by the barking of dogs in the night, followed by ringing bells in the distance.

"Dominaen," Mylas stammered. "Are you all right?"

"Yes, I suppose, though…"

The voice in Eduardas' throat was snuffed out like a candle in a sharp wind. *It can't be. Gods, protect me.*

A dark figure emerged from the flames and slowly made its way down the front steps, its black cloak dancing in the heated air. The fire seemed to part and bow to him, offering a clear path out of the wreckage. As he reached the street, two eyes of a haunting, ghostly green glowed from beneath his deep hood. *Vasur.*

Swords drawn, Mylas and Holto had already begun to approach the shadowy figure before Eduardas could get any words out. He stood frozen as his guards closed in.

Mylas charged Vasur and lunged to take him to the ground, but as he came into contact with his target, the man turned to black mist before Eduardas could blink. Mylas crashed to the ground, the clang of his armor hitting stone ringing through the crackling of the flames. Drifting as if on a breeze, a black cloud rematerialized behind Holto. With a great swing of his gilded sword, Holto pivoted and slashed the stranger's throat—or so he intended. Vasur melted into the cement that bound the cobblestones together, running between them like a filthy, black liquid. He reappeared on the steps of the ruined office, eyes glowing with hellfire, yet his face was completely immersed in shadow. Eduardas could feel in his bones that he was smiling under that hood. Mylas and Holto moved in again, determined fury in their faces.

Whatever power it was that had been crippling Eduardas, rooting him to his spot disappeared. He shouted to his guards. "Run, you fools! Away! Away, with me! Come!" He had to yank their cloaks back before they would obey. With a backward glance, Eduardas could see that Vasur was not giving chase—only standing there before the flaming rubble, victorious and proud, those glowing eyes boring after him. *I should have foreseen this. What else could have happened once I crossed that man? That…thing?*

The street lamps, soothing only minutes before, all seemed to watch him now, serving as eyes for Vasur. Every time the group passed through an orange glow, Eduardas could feel eyes hovering over his skin. It felt as if they ran for hours before he realized his legs were on the verge of failing, and his heart was pounding out of his chest. He also realized he had not been paying careful attention to the direction they were running and was once again lost.

The group found themselves standing underneath a street sign, pausing to catch their breath. Between his aging eyes and the fog, Eduardas could not make out a single word written on it.

"Mylas," he said with as much air as he could gather. "Your eyes are better than mine. What does this sign say?"

"We are on the Ramproad, heading toward the western gate."

"And if we take this right turn here? That should put us on the Vaurian Way, shouldn't it?"

"Yes, Dominaen, I believe so. That will take us back to the Street of Ballots, back to the house."

"Then let's be quick about it!"

It was a slow trip, for there were over a dozen taverns on the Vaurian Way, all of which were still open. Each had an open patio with tables and benches all warmed by brick firepits, and even on a night like this, they all boasted fair crowds—whose conversations now all pertained to the large explosion nearby. The three walked as casually as they could manage, for the last thing they wanted was more attention.

Once they passed the last of the taverns before coming to the Street of Ballots, the trio took off running once again. One thought kept racing through Eduardas' mind as he pushed himself along. It was not a pleasant notion, but it was now his only option to keep his family safe.

"We need to leave," Eduardas said through puffs and gasps as they tore along the foggy cobblestone road, a cool dampness accumulating on his forehead. "We need to get my wife and the girls, pack up immediately, and get out of the city."

"Where shall we go, Dominaen?" Mylas asked. "Your villa in Araiti to the north? Or your home in the southern woods in Seltinum? It is much farther."

"No, my friend. The Republic is no longer safe for us. We must *go*—farther than any of us have gone before. And we must pray that even the long reach of Vasur cannot find us there."

Chapter 22

Range of Gol Rayna: Astymere
1st Day of the Seventh Month
5017 A.S.

Mayson's belly rumbled as he attempted to build a fire using the last of the field kits, his numb hands fumbling with the flint. The final night of the Steel Trials stretched out before them, and at this rate, none were certain they would make it past the last challenge. So trying and dangerous were the Steel Trials that those who dared attempt them were branded the Forsaken. The group of eighteen had dwindled to fourteen after five days of wandering through the snowy wilderness of the mountaintops of Gol Rayna. Each day held a new challenge and a strict timeframe in which it was to be completed, leaving little time to eat or sleep.

The first challenge had been to scale the Cliffs of Kalrima in order to reach the Pass of Ehstes and the one-hundred-mile trail that would end the Trials. Commandants Grein and Barton had rounded them up after the midday meal the day before and marched them through the Northern Tip to the cliffs. By the time they got there, there was nothing to see but the full moon Aviora and the waning light of Yildun. The two officers then told the Forsaken to climb. Anyone who did not reach the awaiting liaison by dawn would be forced to turn back. Once they gave their instructions, the Commandants turned their backs and abruptly departed.

Kip, with his long, gangly limbs, took to the rocks like a mountain goat, gripping the jagged stones that jutted out from the cliffside like countless spikes. At twenty feet, Emmin Park, the youngest of the Forsaken, lost his grip and fell, slamming into the boulders below.

"Emmin!" Mayson called out. "Are you all right?" At this height, it was hard to tell whether or not it was his head that had slammed to the ground. To lose someone in that way would have haunted Mayson.

"My leg, my Prince. I think it's broken," he managed to squeak, his voice feeble and shaky. He sat up, groaning. Those looking down on him could only see the top of his curly head in the darkness as he kept his eyes on the ground, shamed. He gripped his shin and let out a sharp cry. "I've failed. Couldn't even get through the first damned challenge!"

"There is no shame in failing, Emm," Kristian told him. "You already earned great honor by simply qualifying to take the Trials."

"You know the rules, my Lord," he answered back, on the verge of weeping. "When you elect to take the Trials, you either pass or you're expelled. I'll never graduate now. I'm a failure!" he cried, burying his face in his hands.

"Emmin, dry your eyes and remember yourself," Mayson instructed. He mimicked his father as best he could: a marriage of motivation and harshness. "I give you my word that I will not forget you when I come into my crown. You will be held with honor and the highest regards, I swear. Hold tight. I'm sure someone will be along to collect you soon. We will see you on the island in a few days." Then he was off, not bothering to wait for a reply, conquering Kalrima foot by foot.

Halfway up, Cordarion Tyne pulled a rock loose of its anchoring against the cliff, nearly crushing Kristian Rahmos' head below.

"Watch where you reach, you damned fool!" Kristian barked, glaring up at him as he clang to his own perch for dear life. There would be no bumps and bruises from a fall at this height. They now risked death if they made a mistake.

Their hands were raw and bloody by the time Mayson and Diero reached the top. Kip was already waiting for them and Cordarion followed close behind, with Kristian on his tail. One by one, they reached over the ledge to pull their brothers up.

Phylip Hempher hadn't needed much aid; neither had Teren Ashon. Foran Pleke needed the most help, his sweaty, bald scalp looking pale in the growing light of dawn. He'd shaved it clean in anticipation of the Trials, thinking it would toughen him up. Mayson knew it would cost him precious warmth.

Most were already spent, doubled over, and moaning about the next five days. Before them laid eighteen field kits: each man had a canteen; a fire starter; five meals of dried meat, fruit, hard cheese, and a loaf of bread no bigger than the palm of a hand; the map they had personally drawn; and an old, iron training sword meant to get them through the last test, which remained secret. Other than that, all they had were the clothes and cloaks on their backs.

The top of the cliff was unusually flat in comparison to the mountains around them, the plateau rising in a shallow incline to the east. To the west, the evergreen forests of the Northern Tip stretched on for miles. To the north and south were the endless snow-capped peaks of Gol Rayna, sprinkled with green patches where the evergreens, tall and proud, climbed the slopes.

"Up there! Along the ridge!" cried Naron Haladronihn, a fourth-year Avaari tribesman who took great pride in being named after Karrok-Naronei, Naron the Indomitable.

"What do you see?" Kristian asked, slinging his pack over his shoulder.

"I see black. That is our first liaison, I'm sure of it."

"Why doesn't he come down to meet us? We have to go all the way up there to him?" Terman Eronsen, the skinniest among them but none the faster for it, had Mayson worried he would not make it more than two days.

"That is definitely a rock," Kip said, holding his hand above his eyes to help focus in the weak, predawn light.

"I'm telling you; I swear on the Indomitable, that is our liaison," Naron insisted.

"You're seeing things!" cried Durk Neel, a strong, young man of the Southern Tip and a capable fighter, but dumber than sin, having the lowest marks of the fifth-years. His physical prowess alone qualified him for the Trials.

Naron turned on him, enraged to have his eyesight called into question. They went back and forth, even drawing Terman, Kip, and Cordarion into the debate, before Mayson saw a sliver of orange fire peek above the mountaintops.

"Quiet," he said, turning back to them. "Quiet!" The argument went on; they hadn't heard a word. "*Gods*, will you all shut your fucking mouths?" That did the trick, though Mayson now worried he might've caused an avalanche or rockslide. He paused for several moments, then sighed in relief when nothing stirred.

"Naron is right," he told the others. "That *is* the liaison. So, unless you want to go down in history as the first class where no one passes the Trials, I suggest we get moving. Look. Dawn comes!" Their seventeen green cloaks caught the air like sails as the Forsaken climbed the shallow incline of the plateau. The many large, loose rocks made careless stepping treacherous. Ballyn Farrish fell three times in his mad dash to reach the tiny dot upon the ridge. Diero, light as a dancer, sailed ahead of the rest as Mayson and Cordarion raced to keep up.

The sun was halfway above the peaks by the time the Forsaken reached the ridge where the plateau ended, giving way to the rougher slopes of the mountains around. There sat Drill Instructor Sellid, a thin man with an ingrained look of misery and a forehead made large by the retreat of his hair. His nose stood out, large and hooked, as he wickedly grinned at the group.

"Already lost one, eh?" He chuckled. "We aren't off to a very good start. It seems Commandant Barton owes me a few mira—he said you wouldn't lose anyone until tomorrow."

Mayson's stomach twisted at the obvious pleasure he took in their misfortune. "Why are you here?" barked Karam Lorina, a Tirani native with skin tanner than Diero's, and hair nearly as black as Mayson's. His chin hair was bound in a thin braid, a Tirani custom. "If you're not here to help us, then you're just in our way."

"Mind your tongue, boy, or you'll be going home in pieces." Something told the Forsaken Sellid meant it. "I am here to escort any who fail to reach the second challenge back to the island. For some reason, Marshal Qirk seems to think young men deemed worthy to take the Steel Trials are still incapable of looking after themselves. Which means I have to stay in this blasted place until tomorrow. Then you're the next lout's problem. Now, get going. You have twenty miles to cover before nightfall. I'm sure I'll be seeing some of you soon."

They couldn't get away from the instructor fast enough. Once they were out of earshot, the comments began to fly.

"Fucking prick," Diero said, starting off the barrage.

"He's never happy unless someone else is miserable," said Ballyn.

"I hear he can't get it up, and that's why he hates everyone," Doun Lundin joked. "Poor man is probably backed up from balls to brains."

"Horseshit," Zak Valey replied. "He gets his rocks off watching people get their heads busted. You can see it whenever anyone catches a savage shot in hand-to-hand. His pants raise up—not very far, but I've seen it."

"No, no," Gabel Castegan threw in, stroking the five hairs upon his chin that he so proudly called a beard. "He prefers girls. My brother told me. Says he seeded some merchant's daughter in her final year. Took her right over there on that ridge after she failed the second challenge."

"Enough," Mayson said, disgusted by the petty gossip and hearsay. "Sellid is a miserable cuss because he used to be an officer in the Black Army. He was discharged and got reassigned to the Academy after getting drunk one night and pissing all over General Vilamore's quarters at Fort Hilliac. He thought it was the privy."

"How do *you* know, my Prince?" Naron asked. Mayson's blood boiled at Naron's dismissive tone.

"Addam Wallis told me, and being both a member of the faculty *and* a commander in the Black Army, I'd say he knows better than any of you," Mayson answered. No one had anything to say after that—except for Zak, several minutes later.

"I still say I saw him spring one after Olyn Sander got his brow split open," he muttered.

"Shut up, Zak," Diero said.

The rest of the day was spent in silence, all energy bent on reaching the daily required twenty-mile mark before sundown.

The Ehstes Pass wound much further south than the one hundred miles required of them, only cutting off a league north of Kar Naron and the Pass of Gol Ain. Their way was little more than a goat path, much like Gol Ain had been before the Raelians crafted it into a highway. The mountains encroached on either side and, for most of the day, the path remained level with no dramatic dips or drops.

It wasn't until the sun finally dipped behind the peaks on their right that the path began to climb. It was sharp at first, but soon it became downright dangerous. Ice clung thickly to the ground before them, making each step a gamble. They stuck to spots of thick snow for some chance of traction. When this, too, became difficult, Mayson used his training sword like a walking stick. The rest followed suit.

"How much further?" Diero asked, his voice thin and weary.

Mayson stopped to consult his map, bits of snow and ice falling from his shoulders as he moved. Diero and the others were beginning to show signs of windburn, but Mayson and Naron, having Avaari skin, did not burn from the sun or wind. He even removed his leather gloves to handle the map more carefully, the sharp, harsh mountain air chilling them instantly.

"If we keep pace, we should reach the second challenge with more than enough time. We just need to keep moving." He pointed out a small arrow he'd made in red ink the night before, marking twenty-mile intervals to signify the challenges that lay before them. It would only be two hours if they could keep up.

The path opened up to the slopes on their right. It had taken them deep into the heart of Gol Rayna, and the green country beyond could no longer be seen. They were now encased in a prison of stone and ice without end. Their course would take them down the slope into a shallow canyon to their right, a steep drop covered in thick, light powder. The ravine traveled wide for three hundred and fifty yards before narrowing further south, back down to little more than a thin path.

"Stay away from the center," Cordarion instructed. "Stick to the eastern side. The maps I consulted when I drew up my own showed there's a stream that flows through this canyon. If anyone falls in, the chill will cut them down before morning."

The trek was hard going until they reached the rocks of the thin path to the south. The powder in the shadow of the eastern slope was loose, and the footing unsteady. They couldn't see the stream, but every map they read told them it was there, buried under white.

When they set foot on sure stone again, they found a dip in the rocks to their right, where the stream, now free of its snowy cover, could be seen flowing off to the west. Knowing there was no longer a potential hazard of losing a foot to the hidden waters eased their spirits and loosened their movements.

They soon found themselves cutting west, staring straight into the setting sun, which hovered over the snow-capped horizon.

At the western end of the canyon, having traveled downhill for half a mile, they found their way blocked. A rocky hill stood before them, impossibly steep. The towering pile of boulders and gravel plateaued right before the top, where a little ledge sat like the rim of a cup. It seemed to be the only true, solid piece they'd be able to stand on before the second half of the climb. It wasn't much—and it wasn't natural. A small wall blocked the ledge from the solid, flat land beyond.

Their legs were heavy and frozen, and their hearts sank into their pants at the sight of it.

"What in frozen hell is this monstrosity?" Aeveri Burnit grunted. Nearly as tall as Kip, the young, dark man had hardly said a word all day. This was his breaking point.

"It's the second challenge," Diero said through squinted eyes and heavy breaths. "The Perch. We climb the hill and scale the wall. The only problem is the top wall isn't mortared. The rocks are all loose. We need to somehow get ourselves over without knocking any rocks down. Anyone who disturbs them will fail."

"What the hell is the point of that?" Durk wailed.

"Stealth and control over your body," Mayson explained. "I'm sure our second liaison is up there beyond the wall. If we reach him before sundown we'll likely be able to get some extra rest before we need to get moving again."

Kristian led the way up the solid, rigid part of the hill, nearly losing his footing more than once. The rest scrambled up after him, making their way as best they could, but before long, everyone found themselves on their hands and knees, crawling up the cold stones.

The top of the hill leading up to the peak was solid rock that shot up another twenty feet. It felt like another two hundred after trudging through ice and snow following their climb that morning. There was less to hold onto than at the Cliffs of Kalrima, but the task was not impossible.

Kristian reached the narrow ledge first and examined the base of the wall of loose rocks. Standing at full height, he called back that he could see clear over them to a wide, flat landing with stairs carved into the stone, leading down to his left. He attempted to grab a handful of a rock near the top and place his foot as a brace near the bottom, but the slightest touch made the whole wall tremble and wobble. None of them were going to *climb* over this wall.

Mayson, Diero, Kip, and Teren joined him on the narrow landing facing the wall. "If anyone touches this more than a tap, the whole thing will come down," Kristian said with despair.

"What if we try vaulting over?" Teren asked.

"Kip and Aeveri can get over that way," Fran replied. "Maybe even Cordarion. But no one else has the height or can jump high enough to get over alone."

"Then our course is clear, isn't it?" Mayson replied matter-of-factly, sounding smug despite his best intentions. "We toss each other over. Kip and Aeveri will have to go last."

"But, what if we can't do it?" Aeveri protested. "My legs feel like jelly. I don't know if I have it in me."

"You pulled yourself up two cliffs and traveled twenty miles in a day. Now you're trying to tell me you're afraid of a pile of stones?" Mayson asked. The question was simple, but it worked. Aeveri resolved to go last.

The Forsaken were up and over the stones in a matter of minutes, some landing more gracefully than others, but not a single rock was moved. Finally, it came down to Kip and Aeveri. With all the power his long legs had left, Kip shot himself upward and vaulted over the wall, flipping head over heels and landing on his upper back. He used his momentum to roll to his feet and spring up on the other side.

"Come on, Aeveri," Kip called. "There's nothing to it. Your legs are stronger than mine; you can make it." Aeveri stood, uncertain for a moment. "Stop overthinking and do it! Too much thought is the seed of fear, and fear poisons the power of will. It is a mind killer. Think only of what must be done, and then do it! Come on!"

He will make a fine leader when the time comes, Mayson thought.

With mad desperation, Aeveri hurled himself into the air, his torso clearing the barrier by nearly a foot. His legs, however, hung lower, and as his feet passed over the wall, they caught several stones, which came crashing down with him. He lay there for a few moments, taking in the gravity of the situation, and then sat up and looked straight ahead.

"Aeveri," Diero said. "I think…"

"I don't care what you think, Diero. I'm going." He didn't look at anyone, and slowly rose and took the stone stairs to the left, pushing Teren out of his way.

Mayson had been right. The liaison sat in a chair at the bottom of the stairs. *Who brings a chair this deep into the mountains?*

Mayson recognized him as Blade Instructor Pelegrin, a squat little man with hands like lightning. He appeared to be sleeping and woke with a start when Aeveri kicked his foot, mumbling something the rest couldn't hear but which sounded unpleasant. Pelegrin gestured before him, and the two head off true south — the path would take the others to the east.

"Aeveri!" Mayson called. Aeveri cast a begrudging look up to his Prince and the rest. "Vahs gozileri ca Rahma astani dishma!" *May the eyes of Rahm fall upon you.*

Aeveri took two fingers of his right hand and touched them to his forehead, extending them again to his Prince in a solemn salute.

After that, the days all blurred together. The demands of the Trials required they be nearly constantly on the move, only allowing them to make a fire and rest during the coldest hours of the night. This did little to restore their energy or mend their injuries.

The second day consisted of nothing but traveling and talking. They found the more they talked, the more it seemed they were just out for a walk, and the miles and hours seemed to fly by. Even Mayson, who had reviled the chit-chat at the start, had thrown himself into the thick of conversation.

The third day brought the third test, which was to slip past their liaison undetected. Zak was spotted after sneezing and falling from his hiding spot. The liaison, Eric Kirn, treated him as if he'd been captured in battle, dragging the boy off bound and gagged.

On the fourth day, in order to cross a stone bridge to reach their camping ground for the night, their liaison, a tall, hulking sentry that none of them had met before, demanded the answer to a riddle: what is everything to you, and nothing to everyone else? Mayson gave *your mind* for an answer and was allowed to pass. They were each forced to go one at a time, so the others couldn't hear.

The group lost Durk that evening, rather unsurprisingly. They slept one hour that night before the liaison woke them and told them to get moving.

By the morning of the fifth day they were empty. *The*

challenge will come in the night. That is what Addam said. We must cover the twenty miles as soon as possible. The day saw nothing but walking, and unlike earlier in the week, the conversation fell dead along with their energy and spirits. It was only by miracle that they reached the tree line upon the lower slopes of Gol Rayna, the green land of Astymere visible once again.

Now, as the fifth day came to a close, Mayson's fire began to crackle, sounding like sweet music after the group had been caught in a considerable snow flurry that buried them up to their shins. He was half frozen, his hands shaking as he held them over the small, struggling flames. Whether it was from the cold or exhaustion and malnutrition, he could not tell, but he rubbed them together anyway before stuffing them under his armpits. His ribs and jaw ached with the memory of the injuries Allister had given him three years prior. He longed for the Baths, not only for their great healing qualities, but also for their warmth. It was the closest to bliss he could remember feeling. He scraped pieces of ice from his short beard as he gazed into the flames.

"Do you think it will really be like this out there?" Diero asked, lying on his side as he watched the fire. Kristian and Naron sat beside him, staring at the prince, awaiting his answer. Most of the others were asleep.

"I believe in most cases, no," Mayson said through chattering teeth. "But it *can* be like this, which is why they push us so hard. If we can make it through this course, I think we can make it through just about anything."

"Gods, if real war will bring us conditions like this, I say we do away with the practice altogether," Karam said, looking around to whomever would listen.

"Yeah." Diero stood and stretched slowly with a great groan. "Let me know how that goes." He turned and walked beyond the light of the fire.

"Where are you going?" Mayson asked, propping himself up.

"For a piss. Want to come hold it?" Diero replied, not looking back.

"Don't go too far. We don't need you getting lost before sunrise."

"I'll get lost if I please." Mayson thought that was what Diero had said, but he was too far away at that point to tell. The fire wasn't nearly enough to keep them as warm as they would have liked, but they found small comfort in it nonetheless.

"I wonder when it will come," Naron said. "The final challenge, that is."

"It won't be long," Mayson said. "They will wait until most of us are asleep, I'd figure."

He was wrong. Out of the night, on all sides of the slopes and through the trees, came the simultaneous light of nearly two dozen torches. His exhaustion had robbed him of his wits, and it wasn't until the intruders were close enough to be seen by their own torches that Mayson raised the alarm.

"To arms! To arms!" His voice barely had any power left, but it did the trick in waking his comrades.

They formed a ring around the fire, drawing their iron training swords as the torches approached. *Where the hell is Diero? If they catch him alone, he will surely fail.* Thirteen weak, stumbling bodies grouped tightly together around the small fire, blocking what little light there was to be had. The approaching torches danced in the night as their carriers charged through the white powder. All were dressed in black.

Their swords were already drawn, dripping a dark substance into the pristine snow. Adrenaline had given Mayson some of his brain back. *Their swords will mark where they strike us and determine if we would have lived or died.*

"Swords of Rahm, with me!" he cried into the night, charging headlong into the fray, slashing at any man who came his way. A storm of iron-striking music filled the chilly night air, as the stars shined above and the mountain winds howled. Naron was struck hard in the belly, knocking him to the ground as he sucked for air. Mayson picked up Naron's sword where it lay and hurled himself back into the fight. There was no telling how many blows the prince caught on his swords, each seeming fit to knock them from his hands and strike him down into the snow. His arms could barely handle the severity of the attacks. His bones felt as though they would shatter, and his muscles all felt rent and torn. Through the chorus of metal on metal, he could hear the cries of his classmates, each of them feeling as though they fought for their lives. Another assailant approached from his rear to the right. He ducked a savage blow aimed for his head and sliced his foe across the belly. *That would have been an ugly kill.* Five others followed the first, and he took them two and three at a time, surrounding himself with his iron blades, using the Dragon Stance, fighting with beastly ferocity.

His swords danced without thought or hesitation, flying with minds of their own. Mayson found himself within a ring of attackers, and whether by divine providence, blind luck, or true skill, his two shining friends always seemed to put themselves between him and the next blow, spinning and turning him like a cyclone until the world turned into a blur.

Mayson's mind had gone blank and before he knew it, it was over.

"Yield!" cried the man on the ground before him, lifting his hood to reveal Commandant Grein himself. Mayson looked around. Most hooded men were picking themselves up from the snow or separating the students into two groups of nearly equal size. Doun, Ballyn, Karam, Naron, Terman, and Gabel had all been marked up terribly by the black substance covering the assailants' training swords. Kristian, Cordarion, Foran, Kip, Phylip, and Teren didn't have a mark on them, and neither did Mayson once he checked himself.

Commandant Grein beckoned to Mayson's group while the others were immediately spirited away.

"Well done, gentlemen," he said. "I must say, this year has been most interesting. Karrok, do you realize you are the first student to put me down since I've been involved in these exercises?"

"I did not, sir." Mayson replied with what little breath he had left. His eyelids felt as though they were filled with sand, and his legs shook from exertion and cold.

"Well, then, now it's time to…"

"Wait," Kristian said, cutting off the commandant. "Where is Diero? He never came back."

Diero's breeches had been around his ankles when he heard the commotion from the fire. He ducked behind a thick thrush when the torches burst out of the darkness in order to keep out of sight. He redid his belt, hoping to come up behind the attackers and take a few by surprise.

He crouched behind a tall pine and watched the action unfold around the fire in the distance. It was little more than shadows dancing around a few lights from where he stood, but it was more than enough for him to make his bearings. He unsheathed his iron sword, dull as a butter knife, and prepared to move in.

"Ere's a pretty boy!" came a voice from behind. Diero whipped around. This newcomer wreaked of stale ale and wine, and his voice carried a foreign accent. He didn't carry a torch like the others, and Diero had been so focused on the fighting that he didn't notice the stench that clung to this man until he was right on top of him. He was draped in an old gray cloak, lined with white stripes in an argyle pattern. His pants were tattered, but his boots looked to be expensive and hardly worn. Diero couldn't make out a face out from under the hood, but saw a smile of crooked, yellow teeth.

"What the hell do you want?"

"Now, now, be a good lad an' poin' me to one of yer lil' friends. Name's Carovensa. They call him the gold snake."

"The golden serpent, you glorified wet nurse. You want him? You're looking at him. Now come on, get on with it."

"Well ain' this my lucky day? Heh! When I'm done wif you, you won't be goin' nowhere, snake boy."

The man drew a blade from a sheath hanging under his arm. A piece of parchment fell from inside his gray cloak that he didn't seem to notice. The sound of steel against leather was unmistakable, and Diero found himself breathing a bit heavier.

"What do you want with me?"

"Oh, nuffin much. Jus' fa you to die." The foul stranger lunged for Diero, knocking him into the snow and ripping his training sword from his hands. Fight as he might, the Trials had robbed him of nearly all his strength, and the young lord squirmed and kicked like a helpless child. The stranger easily overpowered him, a feeling to which Diero was not accustomed. The steel bit him harder than the snow and ice had, and sudden warmth poured over him in the cold night air.

The pain became unbearable by the time the foul stranger had done his work, slowly carving a deep line from the lower side of his belly to the center of his chest, pouring hot, steaming blood into the snow. A grimy hand covered his mouth as he attempted to scream, and darkness began to creep in.

"Diero!" Voices called. *"Diero, where are you?"* Over a dozen torches were headed their way, apparently too close for the man's comfort.

"Sweet dreams, snake boy," he whispered before slipping off into the night. The sounds of crunching footsteps and distorted calls washed over Diero as the darkness grew, and his senses slowly slipped away from him.

The Forsaken had each taken torches from their instructors, hoping to find Diero before the elders did. He would surely be punished and called a craven for being absent from the most important moment of the Trials. Mayson began to speculate as to what would happen to him. *If he has any luck, they will still test him—only harder than the rest of us.*

Mayson found the edge of the pool of blood just within the tree line, and his torch fell over Diero, totally still. *"Diero!"* He removed his cloak and pressed it hard over the gash across his brother's belly, still pouring a crimson river into the white snow. "I need a field kit, now!" Mayson shouted, cradling Diero's head.

Commandant Grein and another he didn't bother to recognize began to dress the wound. "We need to get him out of here," said Grein, panting from the exertion of the fight. "The cold might slow his heart enough to give us some time to get him to a Healer, but we must move quickly."

"I'll go with you," Mayson said, resolute and unyielding.

"No—you stay here with the others where it's safe. You barely have the strength to stand, let alone ride. Let us take care of him. Your part will come soon enough."

Before Mayson knew what was happening, Diero was plucked from his arms and he was powerless to stop it. Grein shouted commands to several of his men, but he could not hear them. The snow had turned to fire and the trees had turned to ash. His classmates gathered around him. The prince saw their lips moving, but he didn't hear a sound. The only thing he could see was Diero's limp, bloody hand dangling over the side of a horse. The only sound he heard was Diero's heartbeat fading away as they bore him off.

Mayson collapsed in front of a low thicket, burying his face in his hands to shut out the world around him. Something tickled his leg, and though he attempted to ignore it, it persisted and grew more irritating, striking every nerve he had that still worked. He looked down to see a folded piece of parchment that had been sitting on some leaves atop the snow.

He picked it up gently and unfolded it. Suddenly the world's detail came flooding back to him—every sound, every sight, every feeling. New life was breathed into Mayson's weary body as fire filled his veins and his great thirst for water was replaced by a thirst for blood.

Diero Carovensa, the Golden Serpent. Tan skin and fair brown hair. Destroy him. Be sure of it. By any means necessary. He must die, or you get nothing.

Chapter 23

Vita Astym: Astymere
10th Day of the Seventh Month
5017 A.S.

Mayson slept uneasily upon the armchair in Diero's bedchambers. He hadn't had a real night's sleep since he arrived back at the capital seven tempestuous nights ago, and it was beginning to take its toll. In the old wooden chair he could feel his neck cramping and stiffening, and every time he closed his eyes, he was back on the mountainside, up to his knees in red snow, clutching that wretched roll of parchment.

A sharp knock at the door stirred him as Galen and two of his aids entered without summons. One held a roll of bandages and several instruments, and the other carried a small bowl of water that spilt little drops here and there as he stopped short of Diero's bed.

"I didn't say you could come in," Mayson grumbled, rubbing his eyes and his aching neck.

"Apologies, my Prince. But I am working for *him* today," the Great Healer shot back, keeping his gaze on Diero. Mayson welcomed Galen's candor—a sense of normality in this dark time. The only king Galen seemed to bow to was medicine, and Mayson admired him for that. A man with his directness and experience would be quite the asset to him one day. Then again, he'd already done more for Mayson than the prince could ever repay him for.

The Great Healer had traded his robes for a white cloth shirt with short-cut sleeves. He dipped his hands into the bowl and dried them on the front of his shirt before lifting the thin, linen sheet off Diero's chest, which rose and fell more steadily now. Diero's first three nights after returning home had been the worst. It was a constant struggle to keep him breathing, and whenever he stopped, getting him to breathe again without making his wound worse was both challenging and traumatic. The immediate danger now passed, but Mayson's watch remained stringent nonetheless.

"I thought you weren't supposed to check on him again until tonight," Mayson said as he strained to stand up. His legs had gone stiff and his feet felt tingly with pins and needles.

Galen shrugged. "I didn't like the look of his dressing, and I always err on the side of caution. *Especially* with an injury this severe. If we don't stay on top of it, an infection could spread and a fever could burn him into the grave before we even realized something was wrong."

"It's a wonder your career advanced as slowly as it did," Mayson said, fixing his hair and stepping out onto the balcony. Mayson clung to biting humor these days to keep from sinking into despair.

Westslope seemed leeched of color on this overcast day, and the usual mind-numbing pace of the goings-on seemed subdued. Mayson thought he heard Galen snap something back at him, but a sharp mountain breeze drowned it out.

He stepped back into the room to observe the Healers' work with silent curiosity. Diero's belly looked gruesome, still caked with bits of dried blood and the remnants of Galen's salves and cleansing ointments. *Get a good look. This won't be the last, or the worst.* Seeing Diero this way never got easier, no matter how long he sat with him. He tried to remember the last time he'd even left the room.

"Yes, good," Galen said to himself, scanning the wound. "Very good indeed."

"This is *good*?" Mayson asked.

"This is just about as good as we could hope for," Galen replied. "The dressing definitely needed changing, but the wound itself is no worse for the wear. There are no signs of internal bleeding, and there doesn't seem to be any infection—no puss, abnormal swelling, redness. If things hold as they are, I'm certain he shall continue to improve."

"I thought he was dead when I found him," Mayson said, half to himself.

"He may as well could have been, had anything gone differently," Galen said, gently placing his hands under Diero's back and lifting to wrap the new dressing around him. "The frigid mountain air slowed his heart significantly, which kept him from bleeding out. And had the knife gone just a hair deeper, it would have completely severed his abdominal wall, slicing into his intestines. At best it would've caused an infection that even I doubt I could've fought off; at worst, he would have been eviscerated. I think he will have *several* offerings to make to all the gods once he wakes up."

"Any word from my father? Have they turned anything up?"

"Nothing yet, my Prince," Galen replied, stopping what he was doing to look at Mayson directly.

Mayson spent the waking hours he wasn't worrying for Diero obsessing over the note he'd found in the snow next to him. This wasn't some country brigand looking for an easy mark; it was an assassination attempt on the last living member of House Carovensa. If word got out, the whole country would be up in arms. Luckily, the king had kept the incident under wraps, and had every spy and silver shield at his disposal out hunting for any clue.

It was only a matter of time before the bastard was caught, but that was too much time for Mayson's liking. His father had been to see Diero at least once a day since they brought him home, and every day, he said his spy networks found nothing. Aside from the note Mayson had given them, there was no trace of the perpetrator. It was as though he had melted into the snow.

"How is that possible?" Mayson demanded. "It happened right under us. There were thirty of us not a stone's throw away, and yet we heard nothing. The pool of blood was still growing under him, and yet we saw nothing. One man was able to slip in and out of the watch of the Academy and then drift away like smoke on the wind, and all we have to show for our efforts is one Gods damned note that's led us *nowhere*?"

Mayson opened his eyes. He could not guess how long they'd been closed, but he found his fist lodged in the door of Diero's wardrobe. He pulled it out to check if he'd broken anything, but there were only a few superficial scrapes. *Thank Rahm that wasn't the wall. Gods, Karrok. Get a hold of yourself.*

The three Healers stood motionless, staring at him wide-eyed and unblinking. Galen moved first, dismissing his attendants, sending them off with old bandages and used instruments in a small burlap sack. Once the door closed behind them, Galen placed the sheet back over Diero before firmly grabbing Mayson's shoulders.

"We are all scared, Mayson," he said. "We are all angry. *Especially* your father. Something like this hasn't happened within our borders in centuries, Mayson. It is weighing heavily on him that something like this could happen under his watch. Word is he nearly decreed Qirk be removed from his post and even brought up on charges, until your mother made him see the folly in it."

Mayson cast his eyes to the floor and fought his tears back, swallowing the growing lump in his throat. *I shouldn't have let him go off alone.*

"Now is the time when all the things your father has taught you will become real. These aren't just *lessons* anymore. You must put them to use, and remember yourself. He will need to rely on you more than ever now. We all will. Your time is coming, and you *must* be ready. *Well-rested.* Do you understand?"

Mayson nodded and wiped away the single tear that managed to slip his guard. He wanted to scream, to throw something, to tear the entire room apart—but now wasn't the time. He had to think of Diero, his father, and his kingdom. *The Mountain does not crumble.* "Yes," he managed to say. "I understand."

"Good. I'll be back later tonight to check on him. I'll send someone this afternoon to make sure you both get some water; we mustn't let either of you dehydrate. In the meantime, I strongly suggest you go back to *your* room and get some rest, before doing something, *anything*, productive. You need to take your mind off this while he recovers."

Mayson opened the wardrobe and picked up the chunks of wood now scattered over Diero's clothes. The chamber door opened, and two startled yelps tore him from his task. Hammund stood outside clutching his chest, as Galen rubbed his brow.

"Gods," Galen grunted. "Don't you ever knock?"

"I was about to, my Lord, before you *yanked* the door open." Hammund straightened his robes and stood as tall and dignified as possible, still trying to catch his breath.

"Well. Who better in this city to make your heart stop, eh?" Galen replied, his smile growing. Hammund chuckled himself.

"If you'll excuse me, my Lord, I need a word with Mayson."

With a sweeping bow, Galen took off down the hall and out of sight. Hammund entered, leaving the door open behind him. He looked on Diero for a moment before turning his attention to Mayson.

"My Prince, I…" Hammund took a step toward him and stopped in his tracks, his eyes going wide at the sight of the wardrobe. "What in Rahm's name…"

"I fell into it," Mayson blurted. Hammund looked at him as

though he'd grown horns, but quickly shook it off. It seemed after seventeen years, there was little Mayson could do or say to faze the seasoned Head of House.

"Right, well, why don't we get you out of this room, lest you *fall* again, eh?"

"I'm not leaving him, Hammund," Mayson said firmly.

"I will stay with him, my Prince. And I will have guards posted at the door and on the balcony. No one will touch him, I swear it."

"That doesn't solve anything," Mayson replied.

"It does, Mayson," Hammund cut in, waving his hands as though shooing a fly. "Your father told me what you told him. You let him wander from the group that night. You may never have said it out loud, but he could hear it in your voice, and he could see it written on your face. You blame yourself." Mayson stared, half-tempted to strike the presumptive, all-knowing look off his face.

"You weren't there, Hammund," was all he managed, feeling the fight leak out of him until his shoulders slumped and his arms hung. "You didn't see."

"I've seen more than my fair share in service to your family, rest assured. Your father has watched men die all his life, some of them right in his arms. He *knows* the look. But you have done all you can for Diero, and he no longer needs you. Your king does."

"What?"

Hammund drew a tightly bound scroll from his long sleeve, waxed and bound by the royal seal, and handed it to Mayson. The wax was still warm as he gently ran his thumb over it, and he could still smell the ink that had not yet completely absorbed into the parchment.

"His Royal Majesty has given you an assignment, my Prince," Hammund said with a proud smile. "As he continues to head the investigation into Lord Carovensa's attack, he will be needing some clerical aid. He requests that you report to the Mouth and sort the public pleas."

"He wants me to read '*I want*' letters? Isn't there anything more…*pressing* that needs attention?"

"Are the needs and concerns of your future subjects not *pressing*, my Prince?"

Hammund, so slight and unassuming, gave Mayson a look that seemed to chop him down by over a foot. He swallowed hard. "No, of course they are. But I thought maybe he would need extra help with the investigation."

"Your father has all the help he needs. Don't concern yourself further with this business. This task is specifically meant for you. It's been a while since he's given you an official assignment, and acquainting yourself with the needs of your supplicants seemed to be the perfect job."

Mayson shook his head and exhaled. "As my King commands," he said with a shallow bow. "I'll go wash and dress myself. I should be able to start before midday."

"Very good, my Prince. Will you be requiring anything of me?"

"Just send word to the kitchens that I will need something I can take with me to eat. Beyond that, you are dismissed."

"As you wish, my Prince," Hammund said, bowing as deeply as his aging back allowed. He scurried out of the room in his usual gliding manner and left the door open behind him. The cloaks and boots of two Shadow Knights flanked either side of the entrance; even Mayson hadn't heard them approach. He took one last look at Diero and, satisfied he wouldn't drift away if he left, Mayson stepped out into the palace halls for the first time in ages.

MAYSON STUFFED THE LAST FEW BITES of the fresh roll from the kitchens into his mouth as he climbed the stairs to the Mouth of the Mountain. Today they had cut the roll and stuffed it with eggs, potatoes, onions, and peppers. A peculiar culinary experiment, but it certainly did the trick. If he had the time, he would have gone back and asked for another. *I shall have to make this a regular request.*

His black satin cloak pinned to his white linen shirt flapped limply at his sides for lack of any breeze, though the mountain air was still cool and crisp under the heavy clouds. He could have picked something more stately to wear, but if he was going to be stuck in a stuffy room reading letters all day, he was going to be comfortable. Six Shadow Knights marched with him, silent as ever.

The throne room was empty; not even the Crescent Council

table was present. Seeing the Heart of the Mountain, his future throne, made Mayson's palms sweat. No matter how long he stared at it over the years, he could never see himself sitting on it. The unchanged face that always looked back at him belonged to his father, with hair as black as night and eyes filled with blue fire. But it was a lie; Henry's real face no longer matched this vision. His hair grew grayer by the year, and the fire in his eyes that once burned so intensely now felt more like candlelight. Mayson shook thoughts of the inevitable out of his mind and continued walking past the Heart, taking a door to his right into the chambers and corridors that lay beyond the throne room. He bid his guards to wait for him there.

His office, where he had acted as his father's representative in all manner of tasks since the end of his first year at the Academy, sat two floors above the Heart. His only solace in the tight, enclosed space was one small, north-facing window that required him to stand on his tiptoes to see out. There were several satchels sitting beside his desk, and a fresh quill and ink bottle left behind for him. He was rarely disturbed when he did his *chores*, as he liked to call them, and he preferred it that way. The quiet helped him concentrate.

The first sack of letters was simple enough: aspiring business owners seeking permits, requisitions from lower lords for public works in towns under their care, invitations to his Majesty from the upper nobility, and over a dozen complaints from the citizenry that they'd been denied access to the Public Relief Fund despite qualifying. He marked each with his initials and sorted them by means of importance and time sensitivity. As he pushed away the tidy piles, Mayson began to feel better about his prospects. If he could keep this pace up, he would likely be done with this business by sundown. He cracked his knuckles, shook the stiffness from his left wrist, and got started on the next sack.

More of the same: people complaining there were too many deer near their property eating their crops, lodgers wanting to know when this year's bear hunt would be authorized, and nearly three times as many complaints about the Public Relief Fund. Mayson moved that pile closer to him as he initialed and sorted the messages for the king's inspection. He hadn't heard anything about the fund being low, but he did not sit on Lord Brisban's financial council; any number of things could have been going on without his knowledge.

The third satchel finally made him pause: within the entire sack, only ten letters did not have to do with the Public Relief Fund. In all, there had to be over one hundred appeals begging for reconsideration. "What in the frozen hell?" he asked aloud.

The smaller details, circumstances of the families, and where they lived all differed, of course. But the overall message was clear: they all qualified for relief and were denied. Each came with a financial profile, always provided by the agents of the Fund, along with denial letters sent from the Treasury. Brisban's mark had been made on all of them, though it could have been made by anyone in those offices. Geremy Brisban had no time to take his pen to anything other than receipts of payment, and often used an ink stamp to quickly pass things along with little effort.

Mayson found a spool of string after puttering about in one of the desk drawers and bound all the Treasury notes and letters together, marking them *"Most Urgent"* in his own hand. He, too, had an ink stamp, but this could not be mistaken for anything the king might deem as typical—having the words written would most assuredly grab the king's attention. He even underlined the words three times for good measure. Mayson then tucked his charge under his arm and flew down the stairs, leaving the other stacks on his desk. *They can wait.*

When he reached the throne room, Mayson thrust the papers into the hands of a Shadow Knight standing to his right. He was several inches shorter than the others, the only way of marking him. "Sir Dirrin," Mayson addressed him. "Bring these straight to my father's office and be sure to put them *directly* in his hands. Should he ask where to find me, tell him I am going to the Vaults, and may not be back until after sundown. Understood?" Sir Dirrin nodded wordlessly and fell in line with his fellows as Mayson led them out the enormous double doors and down the street to their horses.

Mayson gave his coal-black destrier, Taronax, an affectionate pat on the white spot directly in the center of his snout before hurling himself into the saddle and making for the lower levels of Eastslope. Sir Dirrin took his leave of the group and rode hard for the palace, easily weaving his way through the sparse crowd that chose to leave their homes on this dreary day.

The party made good time. Not only were the streets practically barren, but any one who stood in their way quickly removed themselves, shouting *"Cayrian Karrok!"* as the riders passed.

The Vaults, where most of the public money used by the crown was stored, sat nestled in a secluded corner of Eastslope, guarded by tight, narrow streets and four Silver Shield barracks in the surrounding blocks. The building was long and slim, with high, narrow windows lining each side. The only way in or out was through a granite door just wide enough for one man to pass through at a time, and was guarded from above by murder holes, where private guards sat ready to fire arrows and bolts down on any who tried to force their way in.

Mayson rang the large brass bell mounted in the doorway, for the door only opened from inside.

"Who goes there?" came a gruff, authoritative voice from above. Mayson could hear the bowstrings straining.

"Inform the Vault Masters that Prince Karrok-Aht demands entry on official crown business," he replied. Mayson had long since worked on perfecting his 'princely' voice, and found there was little he couldn't accomplish when he used it properly.

There was no reply, but not even half a minute passed before Mayson could hear the gears and levers within the door working and cranking. The granite began to inch to the side, and two slim fingers poked out from within. Someone groaned and strained on the other side of the door, his voice acting in harmony with the granite scraping against its stone frame. The door was half-opened when a small man popped his head out into the evening air. His eyes were wide and darted to and fro like a rodent, which matched the appearance of his face. It was as if a spell had been cast upon a groundhog to transform him into a man. He ran his trembling fingers through his thinning hair as he eyed the royal party nervously.

"My Prince," he squeaked. "I must apologize, but we are closed for official business for today. The Masters are all about to leave, their ledgers closed. Perhaps we could fit you in first thing in the morning?"

"Tomorrow won't be good for me, I'm afraid," Mayson

replied. "If the Masters are still here, then they have time to see me." The doorkeeper shot a nervous look behind him and bit his quivering lower lip.

"My Prince, I have very clear instructions…"

"That's correct, sir," Mayson interjected. "Your instructions are to open the door and let me pass. Otherwise, I may leave my friends here to make sure no one leaves and come back in the morning with one hundred men to drag you all out of here by whatever hair you have left." The poor fellow looked as if he would weep, and after a few moments of looking at the ground and muttering to himself, put all of his weight against the stone door to push it fully open.

Mayson marched down a long aisle in the center of the room, his Knights filing in behind him. Each step landed with a practiced, regal authority. The two sides of the lobby were filled with desks, benches, and plenty of empty scales, but not a soul in sight. Though the windows let in plenty of light, they did not open and the place was poorly ventilated, leaving Mayson to fight the urge to cough as the smell of coin grease and turpentine overwhelmed his sensitive nose. He approached two doors that sat behind a polished wood counter at the far end of the room.

The door to his right flew open as Mayson approached the counter, and four men in robes came scurrying out. They were older and grayer but, to Mayson's relief, far less rodent-like than the first. He locked eyes with the first man out, and all stopped in their tracks; Mayson found himself wishing he had picked something more stately to wear after all.

Mayson hadn't quite acquainted himself with the entirety of Brisban's staff within the Treasury, but truth be told, few appointments lasted more than a year or two ever since Lord Brisban had been declared Elavahr. Fresh faces constantly filled various roles, and it became impossible to track them all.

"My Prince," the leader saluted with a deep bow. His voice seemed far older than his body, weak and wispy. "To what do we owe this pleasure?"

"Pleasure is not what brings me here this evening, gentlemen." Mayson kept the regality heavy, for he could not appear the slightest bit weak or easy-natured.

"Allow us to formally introduce ourselves," the elder Vault

Master replied. "Bern is my name, Master of Accounts. I used to help manage the household ledgers for your grandfather, King Harruld. Gods, I haven't seen you since your father presented you before the city after the fall of Raelia. Oh, how you look like him."

The Vault Master to Bern's left stepped forward. "I am Abanad," he croaked in a deep, throaty voice that seemed stifled by a nose that hardly let any air through. "Master of Interests." The two men to Bern's right were both slightly stunted, both plump with necks like tree trunks. It seemed to Mayson that the only difference between them was their amount of hair.

"I am Joffrey, Master of Loans," stated the hairier of the two.

"And I am Zander, Master of Public Funds," said the other with a proud bow, or as much as his protruding belly would allow.

"Ah," Mayson exclaimed, his bright eyes lighting up. "Just the man I needed to see." The man's smile disappeared, replaced with confusion and worry.

"*Me*, your Majesty?" Zander asked, swallowing as Mayson approached. Even at his age, he had half a head on the man at least. *He doesn't need to know you won't hurt him— but step carefully.*

"Yes," Mayson said grimly. "You."

"How can I be of service to you, my Prince?" he asked. Small beads of sweat began to form on his bare brow. *Don't push any further. You've got him. Turn on a bit of charm.*

"I was wondering if I could commandeer your services for a few minutes, Master. I am in need of your knowledge, and preferably, your records." Zander seemed to loosen a bit and began to form an answer when Bern cut in.

"Our ledgers are closed for the night, my Prince," he replied with a condescending smile. "They cannot be opened again until morning."

"Is that so?" Mayson asked, returning the smile in kind. "They can only be opened when exposed to sunlight? What powerful magic that must be." He stared unblinking into Bern's eyes. Bern then looked to the floor, his cheeks reddening.

"No, my Prince. *Physically* they can be opened, but it wouldn't be-"

"At all difficult to open them, since they aren't bound shut by witchcraft, wouldn't you say, Master?" Mayson interrupted. He turned back to Zander, who was now dabbing his forehead with his sleeve. "If you would be so kind as to fetch me the ledger for the Public Relief Fund, Master."

"My Prince," he sputtered before he managed to get the words out. "It is a fairly large, heavy book, and my aides have all gone home for the day."

"Not to worry," Mayson said with a warm, dangerous smile. "Two of my friends here will aid you. We will wait." He nodded to the Knights at his flanks and watched as the three left the room.

He strolled about, inspecting the stonework in the walls and floors and examining the carpentry of the tables and benches. He crossed his arms behind him as he walked, pulling back his cloak and revealing his sword at his hip. A subtle gesture, but necessary. The other Masters whispered among themselves. Mayson couldn't make it all out at first, but as he trained his ears on them, he could hear enough.

"What could this be about?"

"This is most unusual."

"Does the king mean to appoint the boy as Treasurer? What would become of Lord Brisban?"

"He couldn't possibly mean to have us answer to a boy, green as grass."

"Not to worry. Lord Brisban will go before the Elders before it gets too far. They will put the little half-blood in his place."

Mayson felt a flush of anger fill his cheeks, and he approached the trio, his right hand gripping the hilt at his hip tightly. Before he could get a word out, the door opened once again. Out came the two Shadow Knights carrying the monstrous ledger between them. It was over a foot thick and bound by old, decaying, black leather. Zander came after them, gripping the ends of his sleeves and shooting his companions a nervous glance. *This should be good.* The Knights set the ledger on the nearest table with an echoing *bang*. Zander and the rest gave the slightest of starts—enough for Mayson to notice.

"Master Zander," he beckoned. "If you please."

Zander approached and wiped his hands on the front of his robe before taking a great handful of the many pages and opening the great book with a thud. After several moments of leafing through individual pages, he finally landed on the fund's final entries. He stepped aside and beckoned Mayson to see for himself.

At first glance, everything seemed to be in order. It tracked an influx into the fund over the last few years, but then a gradual decline with no contributions to replenish it. Now, it seemed the fund had only a total of twenty-thousand mira. The arithmetic was precise; the error couldn't possibly be there. But none of the entries made any sense. How could there not be any contributions made? Payments had been made regularly each month since the fund was established.

"Why has no one informed the king there have been *no* contributions made to the fund in nearly a year?" Mayson demanded.

"Lord Brisban was made aware, your Majesty," Zander replied, folding his hands and hunching his shoulders. "He directed the contributions be distributed to public works projects—building new roads in the Northern Tip and renovating the capital's irrigation pipes. He believed the fund would last without it."

"Even if contributions had stopped for this long, the fund should have been solvent for at least a decade. Is he taking money *from* the fund for these public works projects as well? And why are messages being sent out that the fund is overdrawn when there are thousands of mira left?"

"My Prince, it is not my place to say…"

"You have your answers, Karrok-Aht," Bern barked. "We *must* bid you goodnight." Mayson stood unflinching. The longer he waited, the longer Bern's momentary confidence began to wane.

"Take me to the relief vault. Now." The four stood their ground, as well as any unarmed, old men could. Mayson raised his right hand, and the five Shadow Knights at his side drew their blades. *Who will call whose bluff?* "Take me to the vault."

Bern relented and gestured for Zander to lead the royal party through the second door. He and the others didn't move as Zander frightfully scuttled past the counter, hanging his head low. The others watched him go and snorted derision as Mayson walked by. Before passing through the door, he turned to the Masters. "I'm sure the three of you can manage putting that back. I won't be needing it any longer."

Mayson followed Zander and his knights down several flights

of stairs, winding downward in a tight square. Each landing was fitted with five torches that cast their light both up and down the stairs on either side of them, leaving little shadow. The bottom of the stairwell split off in six different directions, each corridor as dark as night. Mayson took several torches, handing two to his Knights and keeping one for himself, as he walked close to Zander, never letting him out of arm's reach.

Their guide chose the path straight ahead at the bottom of the stairs. They passed many doors, most no bigger than the one leading down into the stairwell, but several with wide, iron seals bound in chains and heavy padlocks. Near the end of the corridor, they came upon a steel door ten men wide, with no discernable lock or mechanism to be seen.

"No key?" Mayson asked. "How the hell are you supposed to get in?"

"It is a trace lock, my Prince," Zander replied. "Running a finger along a specific pattern will open it. If you'll please turn around." With a roll of the eyes, Mayson obliged and bid his Knights to do the same. It sounded as though Zander were running his fingernail across a taut fly screen, a zipping that unpredictably rose and fell in pitch. After several moments of this minor irritation, the floor and walls began to rumble. Mayson turned to see the ponderous door sliding upward of its own volition. When it finally stopped with an echoing *clang*, he took a step forward.

Zander grabbed his arm with fierce desperation before he could enter. The Knights drew their blades, and only Mayson's lightning-fast reflexes stayed their blow on the poor fellow, shooting his hand up to halt them. He looked on Zander with pity. His eyes were wide as the twin moons and sweat poured down his face.

"Please, my Prince," he whimpered. "It wasn't my fault. I only did what I was told." Mayson pulled his hand free and entered the imposing vault.

Where there should have been endless waist-high piles of gold coins, organized into neat rows as far back as the light could touch, there was nothing but empty floor. Three stone shelves carved all along the walls on either side that should have been filled to the brim were as bare as the Dead Lands. Mayson kept walking, waving his torch from one side of the cavernous chamber to the other, hoping to find some glint of gold, or anything other than cobwebs and dust. His torchlight finally hit the back wall—not a single Gods damned coin to be seen. He tightened his grip on his torch and took several deep breaths before starting the long walk back to the vault door. His heavy footfalls echoed through the desolate chamber as he approached the trembling, sweating Fund Master. Mayson took one last look at the vast emptiness and breathed in the damp, musty vault air before addressing him.

"Arithmetic has never been my strongest field, Master Zander. But I am fairly certain this is *not* twenty-thousand. Start talking."

Chapter 24

Vita Astym: Astymere
15th Day of the Seventh Month
5017 A.S.

THE SCENE WAS UTTER CHAOS as Henry scanned the room, looking for Mayson, who hadn't been seen all day. Everyone was arguing, screaming, pointing, cursing—some at each other's throats. The Old Bruiser had just about enough of it. The deafening squabbling was leading them nowhere, and he could not afford to waste any time.

"Silence!" he barked over the dozen voices all trying to be heard. The king's voice filled every inch of the throne room, and all in attendance obeyed his command without hesitation. The last time he'd seen King Robert of Dalan, it had been under similar circumstances, bringing dark words and troubling news. He could still see the crumpled drawing Robert brought him three years earlier. It seemed so nonsensical then. Rahmirion had been well known across the world since the days before any king ruled under the sky, and it concerned him little that some wild men had taken note of her. But now, after what happened on the Plains, it was much more unsettling.

"King Robert," Henry said to the now silent room, "you were saying?"

The King of Dalan stepped forward. Aside from new scars and deep gray hair, Robert Suryn looked no different than the night he had fought alongside Henry in the streets of Raelia. His copper-colored steel breastplate clung to its shine in spite of age and use, and his eyes reflected his stern demeanor. He was a hard man, less boisterous than his brother had been, but the slaughter of his men had turned his body to stone and his heart to fire.

"One of my scouting parties was ambushed along the Acrontian River, north of the Black City. Only two made it back alive."

"And what they described sounded exactly like the men I encountered three years ago," Prince Ronin added, now standing at his father's right side, as was his fashion. "One of them bore the crude parchment we brought you. We'd tracked a party of ten to the Acrontian River, just within reach of Gol Garonath, and killed all but one."

"What happened to this man?" Henry asked from his seat, gingerly rubbing the arms of the Heart of the Mountain.

"He crossed through the river, Henry," Robert replied. "The chill surely killed him before the sun set that day."

"How can you be sure?" Urnest demanded from his high seat below the Heart. "It is common logic to assume any one of us would have succumbed to the cold after passing through the river. But if these men are from beyond the mountains of Gol Garonath, as you say, then they were reared in the harshest environment known to man. The lands north of the Great Divide are covered by ice and snow—winds that could freeze the blood in a man's veins rule the night air. If you are right, then it is safe to say there is significant chance he lived."

The room fell silent once again, all eyes on Lord Rahmos, who glared disapprovingly at the Dalani prince. Ronin had clearly never considered this possibility before, and it could be read plainly on his face.

"Thank you, Lord Rahmos," Henry said, taking back control of the conversation. "What do you suggest, Robert? What do you wish of me?"

"For the most part, Henry, I need only your vigilance. I am assembling a force of one hundred riders to track down these trespassers and destroy them. Out of respect for your friend William, and for you, Henry, I am here to ask if the Crescent wishes to send representatives to join us on this expedition."

"I am honored you thought of us, Robert," Henry said, deeply moved by such a gesture. "As much as I would like to send the entire Black Army out to hunt with you, I regrettably cannot offer much. I cannot declare war on a group of trespassers, but will send fifty of my best men to join you."

"My King…" Geremy Brisban said from his High Lord's perch. "Long-standing military code forbids such action. The only military maneuvering in peacetime that doesn't involve the king's personal detail may never exceed twenty men. With all respect, of course."

Henry inwardly rolled his eyes. In the years since Brisban had been appointed Elavahr, he had embraced the role from head to toe. He dressed in solid black suits of only the rarest silks, as outward representation of his newfound status. His hair, once long and coiffed, had now been cut short, set off by the ever-present shadow of a beard that was never fully allowed to grow. His carefree expression remained only to those who paid close attention. Nowadays, he hid it with a well-practiced look of grave consternation. But neither Henry nor the Council were fooled. The core of the man remained entirely unchanged.

"Thank you, Lord Brisban, for that clarification," Henry replied, narrowing his eyes in annoyance. "My apologies, Robert, but it must be twenty men."

"My King," came a voice from Henry's right. Before Henry could turn his head, Raymund had swiftly moved in front of him, bending the knee and bowing his head before the Heart of the Mountain. "William was as much my brother as he was yours. I beg you for the honor to represent you on this expedition." Raymund Wallis spoke truth, and Henry could hardly argue. "Allow me to bring a dozen of my best household guards to join Robert. I beseech you."

"If you insist so strongly, Lord Wallis, the Crown sees no need to refuse. You have my leave."

"My deepest gratitude, my King." Raymund lifted his chin, nodding with satisfaction.

"You are to report back within a month's time to divulge all you have learned," Henry directed. "And I charge you with one special task. If it be possible, bring one of these men back to Vita Astym alive. I intend to thoroughly question him myself. Do you so swear to carry out the task bestowed upon you by your king?"

"I swear, my King."

"Rise." Raymund gave the slightest of groans as he straightened his aging knees to look Henry in the eye once more. "When we have concluded our business here, you shall ride immediately for Kar Wallis and assemble your party. You shall have leave to pick eight riders of the Black Army to join you as well. Tomorrow, you'll join King Robert at Kar Naron, and from there, you shall ride for the Plains. You may be seated."

Henry watched as Raymund stepped away and sat upon his heavy, dark oak armchair. He trusted Raymund absolutely, but his heart felt uneasy. *Find them, Raymund. Bring William justice. Above all, be safe, my brother.*

"If there is nothing else, the Crown shall declare this meeting closed," Henry said, breaking himself from his thoughts.

The ebony doors at the far end of the chamber swung open with thunderous groans, letting in the afternoon light and a single shadow. Mayson sprinted into the throne room, every muscle tight with urgency. "My King!" he called as he approached. "I beg an audience with Crown and Council, if I may."

"May the Crown remind Prince Karrok-Aht that he was expected here over an hour ago?"

"My deepest apologies, my King. But I assure you, my tardiness is not without purpose."

Mayson presented himself before the Heart, standing in front of his cousin and great uncle. He bent the knee to Henry and remained there until his father spoke.

"Step forward and present your case to the Heart, young man."

"Thank you, my King." Mayson made his way around the Council table to stand in the center of the group. The wind outside the throne room had calmed slightly, but whistled as the Council awaited the prince's speech.

"Esteemed Councilors of the Crescent- you were all granted your positions by the Crown because you have proven yourselves the masters of your trades. But just as important, you have proven your loyalty to the Crown. To sit at this table and aid the king in governing this land is the ultimate reward for faithful service. The Crown has the utmost trust in each and every one of you, and the king's trust is a terrible gift to waste."

The room had given the prince their undivided attention. He was not yet officially a member of the Council, but they all knew he would one day sit before them as their King, and so he received the respect expected of such a future. As he continued, though, the attitude of Mayson's audience changed from obligatory attention to genuine curiosity. Chief of Sanitation Evan Mikkel leaned forward and rested his chin on his large fists, his brow furrowed in concentration.

"Last week, I was summoned to my office here in the Mouth of the Mountain to review supplicant letters. There were several satchels waiting for me. At first, there was nothing out of the ordinary, save a few grievances, but as I continued, I found more and more until there were over a hundred. Would you happen to know what those grievances might be, Lord Brisban?"

The prince crossed his arms behind his back, in Henry's fashion, and swiveled slowly on the spot to look the Elavahr in the eye. Geremy Brisban kept his relaxed posture, but his face twisted in confusion. He turned in his seat to glance up the stairs behind him into the king's probing eyes, then reversed quickly back to Mayson—faster than Henry would have liked.

"I have received no grievances, my Prince. If my staff has neglected to place them before me, then I give my word they shall be dealt with."

"Your *word*," Mayson said. "I am not sure how much that is worth, quite frankly."

"My Prince?" Lord Brisban bristled.

"Those grievances were not meant *for* you, Lord Brisban. They were written *against* you."

"*Against* me? Why, that is impossible, my Prince. I live to serve the people. What offense could I have given?"

"I'm glad you asked. You see, each letter begged for an appeal of Treasury rulings. I read how over one hundred families who qualified for acceptance into the Public Relief Fund were outright denied. They were told the fund was dangerously low and could not support any more recipients—that they should cease their inquiries for the foreseeable future. Each family claimed their letter of rejection had been marked by the stamp of *your* office. Naturally, once I finished reading the letters, I personally checked the coffers of the fund. The ledger tracking the fund's balance painted a disturbing picture. Despite a system put in place to ensure the fund does not lend at a rate exceeding contribution, the fund only registered twenty thousand mira, and no contributions had been made to it in over a year. This, by itself, made no sense. But when I checked the vault, do you know what I found?"

"I would imagine twenty thousand mira, if that is what the ledger counted."

"No, Lord Brisban, I did not. I did not find a single coin. The Public Relief Fund has been *completely* drained. Before you say the fund has been doling out to more families than usual, let me stop you. I ran the numbers and, given the amount of working people paying into it and the rate of expenditure—according to the number of families supported by the fund— there should be over eight million in the coffers. So, I ask you, *trusted* Elavahr and Lord of Coin—where has it all gone?"

Lord Brisban straightened his spine and pulled his shoulders back. "Most of my time has been spent with your father over the last few months, overseeing the expansion of several cities in the Northern Tip. Torant, Camdyr, and Kailyn's Point have all needed severe upgrades to their town walls, and I have not been able to spend as much time at the treasury as I would've liked. But rest assured, my Prince, once we have concluded business here, I will head directly there to investigate any discrepancy and find the money. Mismanaged funds will not go unpunished, as long as I sit in this chair."

It was comfortably cool in the Mouth of the Mountain. Nevertheless, Henry could see sweat forming on Lord Brisban's neck.

"The question was rhetorical," Mayson snarked. "I know *exactly* where the money has gone."

"Well, that's a relief." Brisban's voice had become shaky, his shoulders hunched, as he rubbed the shadow under his chin.

"I wouldn't be so sure, *my Lord*. A great deal of effort had been put into hiding it, but that much money tends to leave very plain trails. I combed through all expenditures exceeding one million mira in the last few months and, believe me, there weren't many. What I did find was that two orders had been made to two separate shipping guilds, each for three million mira, to build four dozen blade galleys. These two fleets of ships would be fitted with shadow silk sails, making them some of the fastest vessels in the civilized world…"

"Get to the point," Lord Brisban snapped, no longer minding his manners. He was biting his nails now, as the whole Council scowled at him.

"Lord Brisban, I checked who placed these orders, and I found two separate names—a Master Van Amfirth and a Karl Prostyn. Not trusting my untrained eyes, I brought these orders to three of the best graphors in the Capital to analyze the handwriting, and they each confirmed my suspicions. These two names were written by the same hand. I then brought one of *your* letters addressed to my father to these graphors, and each one told me the same thing: You wrote all three."

"Preposterous!" Lord Brisban cried.

"But that is not why I've made my case before the Council, Lord Brisban," Mayson continued. "I could easily have you arrested in your home, by the power vested in me by the Crown, but no, I come before the Council today to reveal a crime so monstrous, I could hardly believe it myself. By order of your King, this has not been made public knowledge, but there was an attempt made on young Lord Carovensa's life during the Steel Trials."

The Council erupted again; gasps of shock and shouts of anger rang up through the stone pillars into the great dome above. A raised hand from Henry cut the voices short, but their echoes lived on.

"What the king does *not* know is the extent of your unspeakable treachery. When I found the link between the orders of the blade galleys and the Elavahr, I realized I had seen another letter written in such a hand. It had been scribbled on a dry piece of parchment, carried by a man who tried to slay Lord Carovensa. It ordered his immediate death, by any means necessary. I took the message back to the graphors, and they unveiled the *horrid* truth."

"Liar!" Brisban shouted, but he could hardly be heard over the deathly roar of the Council, who now called for his head.

"You, Geremy Brisban, attempted to assassinate the rightful heir to the Southern Tip before he came of age, planning to cement your position by ransacking public funds and building a fleet. There is hardly a clearer example of scum and villainy that has ever disgraced the Crown in living memory."

Brisban's face swelled with anger. "Do you know who you are talking to, boy? You forget yourself!"

"You forget yourself, sir," Mayson shouted. "You speak to Karrok-Aht, Blood of the Mountain, and heir to the throne! You will be silent, or I will cut your tongue out myself!" Brisban went silent.

"I have instructed that the orders for these fleets be cancelled, and the money paid immediately returned to the Crown. I have ordered every man-at-arms you have hired be arrested and questioned. A quarter of the money is still missing—which is why I've sent fifty Shadow Knights to your home and other properties you own around the city to search them thoroughly. A man such as you would never keep that much money far from reach."

"You have no right! I am a High Lord, and I shall not suffer my honor to be slighted by some power-hungry, little tyrant! I will not have my loyalty questioned by a half-blooded mongrel!"

"You dare call yourself a High Lord? You are a fill-in—a spare wheel used to prop up the cart until a true replacement can be found. I act with the power of the Crown, and the Crown may use any means necessary to exact justice. It is only a matter of time before the money is recovered and one of your servants reveals your secrets. Then, your fate is sealed."

"This is an outrage! I will not stand for this!"

"My King, my Queen, great Councilors whose wisdom guides the will of the Mountain, by the authority granted to me by the Crown, I charge that Geremy Brisban be arrested and taken into custody immediately. I charge he be stripped of all formal rank and title; torn from the post of Elavahr; and removed from the Council as Royal Treasurer. I denounce and attaint him, and hereby charge him with high treason!"

"Geremy Brisban! Rise and present yourself before the Heart!" Henry shouted. The idea of cold-blooded murder now dangled before him like a worm on a hook. *Don't take the bait. A quick death is far better than he deserves. See if any more can be learned.* Lord Brisban rose slowly and stepped before the great stone throne, begrudgingly glaring into Henry's eyes.

"You are hereby charged with grand theft, falsifying official documents, embezzling from the Crown of Astymere, and the attempted murder of the last living blood of the House Carovensa. You will await trial in Canlon Prison, far from your offices, and any who may be so foolish as to try and aid you. I hereby launch a full investigation into the Royal Treasury and your household, to see just how deep this corruption goes. All property of your estate shall be seized and the contents sold to be funneled back into public relief. You have made a *fool* of me and this Council, and you have forced me to call my own judgment into question!"

Henry looked down on Geremy Brisban as one would a gutter rat, practically gagged in disgust. His knuckles had gone white gripping the carved armrests of the Heart of the Mountain, attempting to maintain control of himself. "Get this thing out of my sight."

Two of the ten Shadow Knights who flanked the throne

sprang forward instantly, grasping Brisban by the arms to drag him from the room. Brisban, at first paralyzed by fear, suddenly sprang to life as the group approached the double doors. He fought like a madman to escape the iron grip of the Knights of Rahm, to no avail.

"You would be nothing without me! You hear? Nothing! Without me, you're finished! You're all finished! None can do what I do! None! The Southern Tip is mine!"

He continued to shout as he was dragged outside, but the wind choked his voice dead. Once the last traces of his cries vanished within the throne room, even the howling wind seemed to be swallowed by the uncomfortable silence creeping into the hall.

"Prince Karrok-Aht," Henry said, his anger ebbing, and slowly being replaced by pride. Mayson, who had watched the two Knights drag Brisban out kicking and screaming, turned and knelt. "You have the thanks of the Crown, and surely, the thanks of the people and your beloved brother. I am now left to deal with two considerable problems. A High Lord's chair is once again empty, and our treasury is now fit to fall into complete chaos. I suppose at least one of those problems can be easily fixed."

"My King?" Mayson asked.

"It is not without precedent that the heir to one of the great families be lorded before his eighteenth birthday, and Diero is close enough to it. I will not have any more snakes in my garden. This seat before me is meant for a High Lord, and a High Lord shall sit there from this day until his last." After a moment of thought, Henry turned to the Captain of his Guard, who remained helmetless in William Otter's fashion. "Captain Saldren, I have a task for you."

"Yes, my King?" Nolan Saldren presented himself before the Heart and knelt before Henry. Henry looked on his black hair and saw William Otter's bare scalp instead. He had never quite gotten used to the sight of another man standing before him.

"You are to ride for the Royal Palace, immediately. You will find young Lord Carovensa there. He should be well enough to sit in a carriage by now. Bring him here at once, with all care and haste."

"Aye, my King." Captain Saldren seemed to glide across the smooth, reflective marble as he sprang toward the exit with two of his men in tow. Their black cloaks of light silk trailed after them like the sails of blade galleys.

Not mere moments later, a heated discussion broke out. If a man like Geremy Brisban could succumb to such treachery, who among them could be trusted? The question wasn't given much thought before another arose. Lord Josef Benedik suggested the problem lay within the appointment itself. The seed of treason had been brewing in Brisban for years. What forced his hand was his sudden rise in power and social standing. Once he had secured one of the High Seats, he likely felt desperate as Diero's imminent lordship drew near. He would have done anything to maintain his position.

After debating over whether or not it had been wise to give such power and standing to a man not of a High Family, the conversation turned to the upcoming expedition. The most driving question was where these intruders in the Plains could have come from. There were countless peoples living north of the Great Divide, and many of their cultures were indistinguishable to outsiders.

"They couldn't have come from any further than several hundred miles beyond the mountains," Robert said. "Most Northmen don't take kindly to strangers passing through their land. And, though the first ten may have slipped through unfriendly nations unnoticed, fifty is far less subtle."

"The ones I caught spoke Ikkar," Ronin added, "from what little I could tell. But over fifty tribes and nations speak it. And they bore some general ink markings, but it is nearly impossible to tell them apart without being a Northman yourself. The only way to identify their origins is to bring one of these new ones back alive and question him, thoroughly, as the king said."

Robert had just opened his mouth to continue the discussion when the great double doors once more let in the waning light of the late afternoon, and a sudden gust of wind sent the many torches hanging from the walls and pillars flickering. Marching out of the wind came Diero, Captain Saldren, and one of the guards.

Diero was wearing a silk nightshirt, stained ever so slightly with a thin streak of red across his belly. The urgency with which Nolan retrieved him clearly hadn't allowed him time to dress himself properly. His sleeves had been rolled up to his shoulders, revealing his lean yet muscular arms. Henry took in a sharp breath as he relived the images of Lord Darian in his last days; even several members of the Council went pale at the sight.

"Diero," Henry called to him. "We've been expecting you."

"My apologies, my King," Diero said, rather hoarse and weary. As the young lord approached the throne, aided by Captain Saldren, Henry noted the light beard on his chin, making the Old Bruiser feel quite old indeed.

"I would have washed, but I was told you needed to see me immediately," said Diero. He stopped as he came before the four seats of the High Lords, finding two of them empty. "Where is Lord Brisban?"

"Lord Brisban has been arrested, Diero," Henry said, squinting knowingly. "He has been stripped of all offices and charged with high treason."

Diero rounded on Mayson in clear frustration. "I thought you said I could be here when you presented your case?!"

"I couldn't just sit around and wait for you to get better. What if he came after you again? What did you think I was going to do? Give that snake another week to prepare his next move?"

"I was sort of hoping you would," Diero said rather sheepishly. "Is this what I was needed for?" he asked Henry. "To be disappointed and slightly humiliated?"

"No, Diero," Henry replied with an amused grin. "We have summoned you here for a greater purpose." The doors opened yet again, allowing the wind to nearly blow each torch out. Through the opening came the black form of the second Shadow Knight who had accompanied Captain Saldren to the palace. In his arms, he cradled a white silk bundle, held aloft with delicate grace.

"What is this?" Diero asked, his voice shaking subtly.

"This is your day of reckoning," Henry said with pride. "For too long we have been subjected to a false lord while you sat bound in the chains of adolescence. This chair you see before you is meant for one man, and one alone. In hindsight, I would have much rather left it empty and untainted until this day, but I cannot change that now. You are practically a man, and that seat is empty once more. It is time for its true master to take his place."

Henry and Beatrice rose as the Shadow Knight approached, placed the white bundle in Henry's arms, and returned to his post behind the Heart. All rose with them, for in this room, when the king and queen stood, nobody sat.

"Diero Carovensa," Henry declared. "Present yourself before me." Diero took many slow, uncertain steps toward the throne, keeping his eyes trained on Henry. "Kneel," he said when Diero finally stood before him. He had to put a hand down to the ground to steady himself, but Diero obeyed as quickly as his body would allow.

"Diero of the House Carovensa, last of your blood and son of this Crown, do you swear undying loyalty to your King?"

"I swear," he said softly, as if trying to grasp the immensity of the situation.

"Do you swear to uphold the laws of the Crescent from this day until your last, on your honor?"

"I swear," Diero replied, a bit stronger.

"Do you swear your faithfulness and unwavering character shall remain steadfast in the face of hardship and adversity? That the people of your lands will be granted safety and justice?"

"I swear," Diero said with full vigor, his voice now beginning to fill the room.

"And do you swear that you will honor the legacy bestowed upon you—that it may be even greater when you pass your title down after you are gone?"

"*I swear!*" Diero cried, emotion finally overwhelming him.

Lords Urnest and Raymund moved to join Henry, flanking him as they all looked down on the boy. Henry slowly unwrapped the object in his arms, allowing the white silk to fall to his feet.

Morning Star was just as brilliant as the day of Darian's funeral. She almost seemed to come alive and dance with light, as if she knew what was happening around her.

"Then, by the Holy power gifted to this family by Rahm the Wise…" Henry began, passing Morning Star to Urnest at his right.

"And by the brotherhood that has bound our families together through the ages…" Urnest continued, tapping Diero's left shoulder with Morning Star before passing her to Raymund.

"And by the love we have all felt for you from the day you were born, and will feel until our last days…" Raymund said, tapping Diero's right shoulder with the blade before passing her back to Henry.

"I charge that you rise, Diero Carovensa, High Lord of Astymere, and Lord Paramount of the Southern Tip," Henry concluded, tapping the top of Diero's head with the blade.

Diero rose with silent tears pouring down his face and extended his hands to accept the sword of his father, and his father before him, stretching back into the mists of history. The same light that emanated from her on the day of his father's funeral burst forth in a spectacular display, as if elated to finally be back in the hands of her true master. Flanked by Lords Urnest and Raymund, with Henry in the rear, High Lord Diero Carovensa was guided to his seat for the first time. As he dropped down into the deeply cushioned ebony chair, so long occupied by a traitor, the room burst into thunderous applause.

Diero drank it in, seeming to transform from a boy to a great High Lord who already had lived a lifetime of glory. As he held Morning Star high above his head, a chant that had not been heard in decades rang throughout the hall, and would linger there for days: *Vabas Carovensa! Vabas Carovensa! Vabas Carovensa!*

One problem is solved, thought Henry. *Now I must replace Brisban before my treasury goes up in flames.*

Chapter 25

Kar Naron: Astymere
10th Day of the Eighth Month
5017 A.S.

Eduardas pulled his cloak tightly about him to brace against the chill of the mountain air, leading the way as Mylas and Holto rode on either side of the doublewide carriage that carried his wife and daughters. Attia had scoffed at her husband when he decided to ride out in the cold, saying that the *help* were just fine on their own. This only made him more eager to get atop his own horse, though he did regret leaving the girls in there to suffer her incessant griping. As cold as he was, he thanked the gods and stars above that their journey of over a month had finally come to an end.

They started by traveling north to the Goldblade estate in Araiti, which had taken three days. Having had no time to saddle horses or pack anything heavy, they had to walk this leg of the journey. As they made their way through the forests of Gildar, Eduardas swore he had seen those ungodly green eyes peering at him through the thick underbrush, making his skin crawl and his knees shake. The flames of his burning business seared their way into his mind like black spots after staring into the sun.

Beyond the Golden Grove, the trees quickly shrank. Within a day there was not a remarkable thing to be said about them, save for the subtle golden veins that ran through their deep green leaves.

Eduardas would only allow them to stay one night in their spacious villa, much to the chagrin of Attia and the girls, who had hoped for more time to rest before moving on. The sun had barely peeked over the canopy of the trees before the carriage was packed, and all attendants not necessary to maintain the house were rounded up for the westward leg of the journey.

Araiti had been built in one of the largest clearings the forests of Gildar had to offer, and the flat, fertile land was not wasted. Vegetables such as corn were a rare commodity this far north, and the town had grown wealthy through its sale. The stalks were still short, but Eduardas spied hundreds of slave workers tending to the fields in the early morning sun, picking weeds and watering the soil. *I'll be glad to put such sights behind me.*

His nerves began to calm in large company, though he was still wary of being followed by that *thing*. At least his eyes were no longer playing tricks on him, and the occasional snap of a twig didn't stab at his every nerve. The only green he saw was glistening grass and the light sneaking through the foliage above.

The road rolled on through thick, green country once they left Araiti behind. Aside from over a dozen villages built in harmony with the forest, the scenery did not change for days.

The party made good time on the meticulously maintained forest road. Their way had been straight and unyielding, and Eduardas grew more confident with each mile put between them and Gildara.

"If we haven't had any trouble by now, I think it's safe to say we aren't being followed," he said to Mylas on the eighth day of their travel. It was on this day the Goldblades and their attendants came upon the rare sight of open, empty country.

The patches of forest grew thin on the outskirts of the Republic, and the road flew out of the tree line without much warning, opening onto the vast emptiness of the Wave Lands. This stretch of empty, hilly territory separated the forests of Gildar from the mountains of Gol Garonath to the north and wrapped around to the west and east. Eduardas could still see the look on his daughters' faces as they fought to get both their heads out the small carriage window, their hair blown by the unobstructed wind. Neither of them had ever been outside the forests and both stared, unblinking, taking it all in.

"Get used to it, ladies," Holto told them with a weary smirk. "This is going to be your home for the next month."

"Thrilling," Attia said through pursed lips. "I trade my warm featherbed for a stuffy carriage, empty, ugly land, and incessant howling winds. Why? Because my lionhearted husband saw a ghost."

"*Mother,*" Olivia scolded.

"Dominaia," Mylas said, ushering his brown destrier closer to the carriage. "If you had seen what happened that night, you would understand."

"What *did* happen?" Olivia asked, forcing her head and shoulders out the window. "No one has spoken of it since you ripped us out of bed that night. You were all babbling and yelling over each other—one would think you'd been possessed. What are we running from? Where are we going? How long until we can go back? When can I send word to Casan?"

"Domina, please," Mylas replied, holding his hand up in an effort to get a word in. "There—there was an incident…"

"Do you *want* the truth, child?" Eduardas cut in, riding in next to the window. Olivia's eyes answered the question before her mouth could even form the words. "I need to know you are ready to face whatever I tell you and accept it. I need to know you will not fight with me, or argue the matter. Can you do that?"

"Yes, Father," she said.

She seems so much more ready for this new world than I am.

"Olivia, my office was destroyed. The glow you saw through the mist as we left the house was Goldblade's Coffers. It was burning."

"*What?*" Olivia whimpered, her eyes beginning to well.

Eduardas thought he could see fear growing in Olivia's deep gaze, but as her tears began to roll, he realized it was pain. *Sweet child.* She knew exactly what his work meant to him, and her empathy nearly brought tears to his eyes as well.

"I refused a man's business," he forced out, stifling his tears before they could come. "And to strike back, he burned my office to the ground."

Eduardas took a moment to scan the grassy hills before him, trying to collect himself in silence. The road traveled straight to the west for over a mile before it curved around the base of a low hill.

"Father? Are you all right?" Olivia asked.

"Yes, love, I'm all right."

"Who would do such a thing? Who *could* do such a thing? The Ministry protects you. There isn't a soul in the Republic who would risk bringing the Hall of Justice down upon them."

"There *is* one who would, child, only one, and as luck would have it, he found me."

"Who?"

"His name is Vasur. I'd heard his name in certain circles, and I knew he was dangerous, but…Gods, I've never underestimated a man so greatly. If he can even be called a man."

"What else could he be?" Olivia asked.

Eduardas gave his guards a hard look and made sure the other attendants riding behind the carriage were out of earshot. They were all talking amongst themselves, commenting on the rock face of the low-lying hill that had come up on their left. They paid the carriage no mind. The fewer who knew the truth, the better.

"We don't know what he is, dear child," he began. "But after that night, I am certain of one thing. He is no man. He is something else—something out of a nightmare. I have feared men in my time, but the terror that gripped me could only have come straight from the frozen pits of hell. I am certain of it."

He was suddenly aware of the weight of his words and began to feel as if the hills had eyes and ears, watching and listening to his every breath. In days past, such a thought would be gone before it had time to form, but after facing Vasur, nothing seemed beyond possibility. He turned his attention back to Olivia, trying to focus on her face alone.

"I don't understand," she said.

"When I returned to my office that night the building burst apart, consumed with flame," he told her. "Not a soul could have survived a blast like that. If someone had, they would never last in the inferno that nearly consumed the three of us. Dear child, Vasur *walked* out of the flames. No…he didn't even walk now that I think about it…he strolled, as though he hadn't a care in the world. The flames *parted* before him."

"That isn't all, Domina," Holto said as he rode in close to Eduardas. The brown traveling cloak wrapped about his shoulders hid his gilded breastplate from the increasingly damp air. "Mylas and I tried to cut him down, but with each swing of our blades, he dissolved and became immaterial—like smoke."

"He then became liquid and ran along the cracks in the pavement," Mylas added. "I saw it with my own eyes, Heavenly King as my witness."

"Impossible," Attia chimed in from within the carriage. "Your heads were all rattled by the explosion. What happened to your office was a terrible accident, but running from shadows and whispers is ridiculous."

There was something different about her usual harsh tone, Eduardas noticed. Her words held the faintest touch of fear. Regardless, he had no patience for her ignorance.

"You weren't there, Attia. You know not of which you speak. Kindly keep your *opinions* to yourself." Dominaia Goldblade gave a derisive snort and leaned back in her seat, crossing her arms and looking away from her husband. Eduardas turned his attention back to Olivia. "Naturally, Gildara isn't a safe place for us anymore. Nor the Republic, for that matter."

"For how long will we be gone?" Olivia asked.

There was no simple answer Eduardas could give. This was the last thing the poor girl needed, her wedding to Casan barely a month away. He knew that wherever they went, she expected to return home to him eventually. He wanted to tell her they would be gone for at least a few months, but he also doubted he'd ever see the Republic again.

"These are troubling times, and there is much to think about. First, we must reach our destination. Then we can worry about going back."

"Where may that be, Dominaen?" Mylas asked. "You've neglected to mention."

"For good reason," Eduardas said with a nod. "I wouldn't risk saying it out loud as long as we were anywhere near that *thing*."

"So where are we going?" Olivia asked, once more with childlike eagerness. "Kana? I've always wanted to see their capital. They say Torrin has one of the largest libraries in this part of the world, with books that date back to the days of the Old Empire, before Raelia took to the High Faith."

"We are of like minds, my love. It would warm my heart greatly to see Torrin, and to walk through the endless aisles of books and scrolls within the Kallan Library, but we would have to turn north to get to Kana from here. Our road continues west."

"But to go west would lead us into the Dead Lands," Attia added, eyes as wide as saucers.

"Calm yourself, dear," Eduardas said, squeezing the reins of his gelding. He was tempted to let her keep thinking they'd cross the Dead Lands, but he was not cruel. "We shall turn south."

"Will we see Raelia on the way?" Olivia asked, a sharp eastward breeze blowing her hair in her face.

"Perhaps we will. I can't say for sure. Many believe the city is home to ill fortune and dark spirits. Those are the last things we need at the moment."

"Don't tell me you've become superstitious, Father," Amy said, finally squeezing her head out the window to join her sister.

"All my life I wasn't. Not a wink. But the night my office was destroyed changed all that. Now, if there is even one tale of dark goings-on about a place, I will think twice about visiting."

"Please, Father?" Amy pleaded. "I want to see if the walls are as big as they say in the stories. They say they have stood for over six thousand years!"

"So they have. Well, they did—at least what's left of them," Eduardas said, surveying the road now visible once again as they rounded the base of a hill. It stretched off for over a mile to the southwest before it vanished again.

"You still haven't said where we're going," Olivia pressed. She would not rest until she knew.

"Astymere, love. We make for Astymere," Eduardas said with a smile. He kept his eyes on the road a moment, letting the information sink in before looking upon his daughters. He wasn't disappointed. Their mouths were agape; both seemed completely dumbfounded. Even Mylas and Holto seemed perplexed.

"You mean to take that pale king's offer, don't you?" Olivia asked.

"As a matter of fact, I do. It is half a world away from the Republic and Vasur. It is a thriving country with plenty of coins to count, and it is said to be protected by ancient magic."

"Devil magic is more like it," Mylas said, half to himself. "These men of the coast are all savages; it is well known. They worship trees and dirt and rocks—and the Astymerians are the worst of them! They put their faith in a black-skinned, red-eyed demon."

"Yes, Mylas, we've all heard what the High Testament has to say about the Low Gods. I, for one, prefer to take the teachings of the good book with a pinch of salt. Have you not ever thought the Testament might be wrong about certain things?"

"No, Dominaen. I am not one to question the Testament," Mylas said incredulously.

"I didn't think so," Eduardas shot back, shaking his head. "Regardless, that is where we go. I recommend you either start warming to that idea, or you can turn around and go back."

"Where you go, I go, Dominaen."

The matter was settled. They would grumble and complain, but it made no difference. Attia might attempt to convince him to turn south to Colembria, for it seemed a more sensible destination; Colembria was a close vassal to the Republic, while relations with the Western Kingdoms were shaky at best. Still, the trip to Colembria would force them to travel well over a thousand miles around the southern tip of the Republic to avoid going back through it, and nearly just as far to the east. A straight journey to the western coast was more pragmatic—and there was no royal welcome awaiting them in Colembria.

Then again, if the king did not remember his offer, there would be no royal welcome in Astymere either. It had been three years; Eduardas had nothing but blind faith King Henry would remember him.

They spent the next month winding through empty country on the vast roads the Raelians had built millennia before, stopping at whatever towns they could find. On nights where there were none in sight, the party would make camp on the side of the road. Eduardas and his family, Mylas and Holto, Taimin, the Goldblades' Head of House, and his five subordinates, three maids, and the other Goldblade guards would gather around a large fire each night, one man always assigned to keep watch in the shadows beyond the flames.

Despite the gravity of their situation, the company managed to maintain high spirits, except for Attia, of course. Once they crossed the border into Dalan, they received their first taste of the West, stopping at the city of Manaqan to resupply and rest for the night. The green banner of Dalan, bearing two white spears crossed beneath a white crown, fluttered above the stone wall of the border city as they passed through the gates.

Olivia and Amy were fascinated to see horses in the street everywhere they turned. Horses were no strange sight in the Republic, but they were not nearly as abundant. It often seemed as if there were more souls on horseback than on foot traversing the wide cobblestone roads. The square, stone buildings did not seem to be all that different from those in Gildara, but where the buildings of their old home were all painted in gold and crimson, these were plain and dull in comparison.

They had stayed one night in a small inn on the northern side of the city called the Thundering Hoof. Though not even half the size of a typical Gildarian tavern, no one seemed to mind once bread, beer, and potato stew fresh from the pot were put in front of them.

Attia had scoffed at the establishment at first, but once her head hit the pillows that night, she was fast asleep in moments. This was the way the family lived for weeks, though most grew to accept these conditions. Each mile they traveled west was another mile between them and danger.

This sense of wonder soon leeched its way out of the Goldblades, though, as every new town looked the same as the one that came before. The trip was beginning to feel mundane now that they felt secure and had grown used to their surroundings.

On the forty-ninth day of their journey, the rising sun hit more than the Goldblades' backs. As the light seeped into the sky, Eduardas could make out tiny snow-capped peaks just inching over the horizon. If he was reading his maps correctly, it had to be the Range of Gol Rayna, which spread across the entirety of the western coast. Hardly anyone paid them any mind, for at such a distance, they looked like nothing more than the hills they'd seen every day since they left the forest. Eduardas, however, felt great comfort knowing their journey would soon come to an end.

The company struck camp later that evening. The moons Aviora and Yildun were nearly full, and the girls had all settled into the carriage for the night. Eduardas sat around a fire with Mylas, Holto, Lukas, Balian, Emanas, and Titas. The older guards told war stories to which the younger men and Eduardas eagerly gave ears. Then began the distant howling of wolves.

Emanas, the oldest of the Goldblade guards, brushed them off, stating they were likely leagues away and that prairie elk ran thick in these parts, or so the local hunters in the last inn told him. So the group continued with their stories. To everyone's surprise, even tiny old Taimin had served a short term in the Golden Legions some forty years past. He had lied about owning land and borrowed old armor and weapons from a neighbor in order to enlist. He was found out and discharged before he ever saw combat.

But the howling returned, now much nearer, loud enough to send chills through every spine and spook the horses. Even

Emanas thought it was a good time to strike camp and get moving. Everyone lit a torch in the fire and saddled up, the six guards creating a perimeter around the carriage.

They rode hard through the night. Though they never saw the wolves, the howling didn't cease until morning, and by that point the party—men, women, and horses alike—were exhausted. By the time the sun rose again, the mountains loomed over them, dominating the western sky.

"Well, I'll be damned," Eduardas said in awe. The summit of each mountain as far as the eye could see in either direction had been carved into a great statue, all looking toward the rising sun, each holding a great spear in its right hand.

"How old would you say those are?" Holto asked Mylas, his eyes locked on the colossi before them.

"I would bet my life they are older than the Republic itself. It feels as though they were always here—that they were never *not* here."

"They don't seem very welcoming," Amy said, her hand working its way down Olivia's arm to clutch hers. "They're… eerie."

"They're beautiful," Olivia said, a smile tugging at the corners of her lips.

"I agree," Eduardas commented, gazing upon the mountains. After a few moments, he found the will to tear his eyes away to study the road ahead, which crawled through the only pass in sight. "Shall we press on? If we make good time, I believe we may each rest in our own bed tonight…with a bath."

"Say no more," said Mylas, snapping out of his trance. "You heard the man!" he shouted to the group. "Let's get moving, unless you want to stay here for the wolves!" With a groan, the wheels of the carriage began to turn, and Attia pulled the girls inside with a sharp yank.

They spent all morning traversing the pass. What began as a narrow path quickly became a respectable highway. The stone at their feet had been carved flat, and the slopes of the mountains on either side had been chipped away to make a sizable road out of what was once an old goat path. *The Raelians did this—and by colonizing the Crescent, they unwittingly sowed the seeds of their own destruction.*

"This is the only way in?" Amy asked, her head once again poking out the carriage window.

"By land, it is," Eduardas answered. "These mountains are impassable, and they wrap around the entire eastern border of the Crescent. It is one of the reasons no army has ever crossed onto Astymerian soil."

"*One* of the reasons? What are the other reasons?"

"Many of the merchants I've met over the years tell of a large fortress that…" The words were stolen from him as his horse rounded the bend. Roughly four hundred yards ahead, the pass widened further yet to accommodate a colossal obstacle that stood before them.

Blocking the pass from slope to slope stood a great wall of pearl-white stone, roughly one hundred feet in height. Two massive guard towers soared high above the ramparts where the wall met the slopes of the mountain on either side. Their tops were rounded and artistically crafted, fitted with dozens of narrow slits and murder holes.

Across the base of the wall, spaced at every thirty feet, large buttresses curved upward to the halfway point between the ramparts and the ground. As the group approached, they could see the wall did not stop as it met the slopes of the mountain, but climbed the slopes another one hundred feet, where there were two more sentry towers just as tall as the first pair.

At the heart of the great wall stood a gate larger than any Eduardas had ever laid eyes on. It looked less like a gate and more like the mouth of a cavern of monstrous proportions. Spanning the opening was an enormous portcullis of shining steel, blocking the way like a radiant spiderweb.

Beyond the white wall stood three sky-touching towers, all connected to one another. Two stood side-by-side, twins in every respect, while between them and slightly behind stood a tower even larger than the others. All three seemed to bare terrible, jagged crowns at their peaks, and whereas the wall and sentry towers were of bright, spotless white, these towers were of the deepest black. Eduardas felt a chill of dread. There was not a stone he could name that would give such appearance. From this distance, they seemed to be more shadow than stone—as if the shadows the mountains cast down into the pass had raised into this looming colossus.

"What in the Heavenly King's name is this?" Attia asked, her voice hushed for a change.

"This, my dear," Eduardas said, "is Kar Naron. Amy...*this* is the other reason no army has ever set foot in Astymere."

"I believe that," Olivia interjected, unable to take her eyes away from the black towers.

"Dominaen," Taimin said softly in the growing silence, "might I suggest we get moving? At this rate, it may be dark again by the time we gain entry. With all respect, of course."

"Yes, Taimin, you're right. We will have plenty of time to stare once we are inside, *if* they let us inside. All right everyone, let's finish this blasted journey, shall we?"

As they approached, Eduardas examined the gate more closely. Even in the shadows of the mountains, the bright silver color mixed with rippling blue could not be mistaken. *High steel. By the stars. This entire portcullis is made of high steel. Only a fool would try to fight their way through that.*

The sound of voices snapped his attention back to the ground, where he was shocked to find a rather sizable crowd of wagons and horses, all waiting to cross the border. Eduardas was perplexed that so many people escaped his notice for so long. *I didn't see any of them come in with us. They must have been camped here all night.*

The overwhelming scent of spice forced its way into his nose as his group sought to mix into the crowd. He traced the aroma to a caravan of spice merchants' wagons arranged in a half circle, where several men were wearily putting out the last embers of a small fire. *Spicers—just what I need.*

Olivia stuck her head out the window to regard the crowd. Aside from the spicers and several dozen carriages bearing metal cages filled with small, colorful, chirping birds, most transports were empty. Each was branded with the same black symbol printed upon the white banners that flew above the great portcullis: Rahmirion.

On the other side of the portcullis, through the cavernous opening, the silhouettes of men running here and there flickered in the light. Obscure commands echoed as the fortress within the gate slowly sprang to life.

"*Stay clear!*" shouted a voice from the far side of the tunnel.

The ground began to shake, and a deep, earth-shaking groan emanated and echoed through the Pass of Gol Ain, soon joined by the grinding of metal upon stone as the portcullis rose. Foot by foot, the hulking steel lattice crept upward until it was locked in place with a thunderous *bang*.

"All agents of the Crown follow the gatekeeper for your pay," barked a clean-shaven man in jet-black armor. He had stepped out of the shadow of the tunnel as the portcullis was secured, the mountain breeze catching his sky-blue cloak and brown curls. Fifty guards marched in formation behind him, spreading out across the span of the opening as morning light hit their spears and black shields. "All traders follow these guards to Goods Inspection, and any visitors, follow me! I want orderly lines, patience—no shoving!"

The guards split themselves to accompany each group as the crowd organized itself. The empty branded wagons, which Eduardas surmised were the agents of the Crown, had already formed their own line, as though they'd gone through this routine one hundred times before. As many people as Eduardas had seen to begin with, nearly double the amount sprang from the carriages, sleepily rubbing their eyes and politely taking their places in line.

The traders, on the other hand, were all scrambling over each other, as though the first ones into Astymere would be the first to sell their goods. One of the guards even had to break up a fight between a spicer and a dried-fruit merchant, threatening both with his spear to force them back in line.

Besides the Goldblades, there were few other visitors—only about twenty or so—each one different from the last. Five seemed to have hand-woven their garments from wool and looked as if they hadn't bathed in a year. Eight were undoubtedly Kanans; the white cloth of their clothes embroidered with a silver ram's head was impossible to miss. Three seemed to be monks, brown-cloaked and wild of hair, serving a god Eduardas could not figure. The last four rode horses he could only describe as regal, each blanketed in a bright pink, reflective blanket. Their riders wore flowing silk robes of magenta and gold, with deeply tanned skin.

"All visitors, this way, please!" the curly-haired guard ordered.

The Goldblades skillfully weaved their way through the small crowd without jostling anyone or causing a commotion. It was not long before they found themselves right behind the guard, who continued on foot.

"What is your name, sir?" Olivia asked. Attia gave a low *hiss* to try to silence her, but it did no good.

"Captain Edmin Toraf," he responded, turning briefly to look upon the girl. "But it's Captain to you. Understood?"

"Yes, Captain," Olivia said respectfully. "Where do the visitors go? Why do we all have to split up?"

"The traders have to have their goods inspected before they are allowed to cross the border, to be sure their wares are worth selling and to make sure they aren't smuggling anything in. Visitors like you must go through one security checkpoint, submit your belongings for searching, and answer some questions before being on your way."

Once they emerged from the shadow of the tunnel, the full fortress came into view. The three black towers were only the centerpiece of a much more complex keep that sat within a vast courtyard enclosed by the white walls. Two enormous buttresses with wide, flat tops flanked a tall staircase that ran up to two great wooden doors, braced by a more conventional-sized portcullis.

The white walls that climbed the slope of the mountain also climbed back down them, Eduardas realized, looking to the right and left. He couldn't tell with the black fortress blocking his view, but he figured they met again to close the gap behind the keep, sealing off the pass in the rear.

"Why is the outer wall a different color than the keep?" Olivia asked Captain Toraf.

Eduardas gave a nervous smile. His daughter's curiosity was a fine gift, but he had no way of judging the limits of this man's patience. So far, the captain didn't seem to mind. "The outer wall is all that is left of the first fortress the Raelians built over five thousand years ago," he answered. "Once they settled here, they coveted the rich black soil and abundant crops the land yielded and built this place to keep out any who'd want to get their hands on it. That ended up being a grave mistake."

"Why's that?"

"When our people finally drove them out, the Avaari gained

control and this fortress kept them from getting back in. Naron's Keep is relatively new in comparison."

"Naron's Keep? You mean that monstrous black thing?"

"You could say that," Captain Toraf said. "It was built just over one thousand years ago by Karrok-Masylian to honor Karrok-Naronei—King Naron, second King of Astymere. He repelled more Raelian invasions than any other ruler in Astymerian history, all from this spot. It was built to instill fear in any army foolish enough to march on it. Needless to say, it has been quite effective over the years."

The party made their way around the right side of the keep to a large cluster of tents erected side by side to temporarily house visitors until they had either passed or failed inspections. The tents looked small from a distance, but as the Goldblades approached, it became clear each was more than large enough to house the entire company. As they passed through the flaps, held open by men-at-arms, they saw a long table facing them in the center of the room, with another opening far behind it. There had to be at least fifty blue-cloaked guards standing behind the table, spears held at attention.

Eduardas swore that a shadow sat at the only chair facing them. But as he continued forward, he saw it was no shadow at all, but a dark-skinned man dressed in the exact same armor as the men around him. The hair atop his head had been shaved down, the whites of his eyes contrasting sharply with the blackness of his face.

"A beast!" whispered Attia, clutching his arm.

"Step forward, please," the man said.

Attia gasped. "Heavenly King and Queen of Stars, it spoke."

"Yes, sir," Eduardas said, shaking off Attia's arm as all in his party stared back and forth between him and the officer. He realized none of them had likely ever heard a dark man speak before; it was forbidden for a slave to speak in the company of free men. Therefore, it had become a widely accepted misconception they were incapable of speech at all.

"How many in your party?" the officer asked in a deep, somber voice.

"Let me see. I'd say nineteen or so."

"Or so?"

"Nineteen, sir," Eduardas said, swallowing nervously.

"You call it *sir*? What in the world has come over you?" Attia muttered. Eduardas coughed to cover her rudeness.

"Reason of arrival and duration of stay?"

"We seek asylum in the Crescent…indefinitely."

"*Indefinitely?*" Attia and Olivia squealed. Eduardas turned to shush them with a reassuring gesture.

"Very well," said the officer. "You will wait in the holding area while word is sent to the Crown to ask permission to begin the process of naturalization. Your guards will surrender their weapons to these officers so they may be catalogued properly."

He gave a subtle gesture with his hand as he dabbed a pen in ink to draft forms of passage. A short man of tan skin and black hair and another dark-skinned guard moved in toward the Goldblade guards, who had all huddled together once they entered the tent.

"Your swords," the short guard said.

"Over my dead body," Lukas replied.

"You heard the man," said the other, much harsher. "Surrender your swords or we will confiscate them."

He moved to take the sword away from Balian, the most wide-eyed of the Goldblade men-at-arms, when Attia's shrill voice cried out. "*Don't let it touch you!*"

Balian struck the dark-skinned guard in the face, knocking him to the ground. Lukas followed suit, attempting to strike the short man who moved for his longsword hanging at his hip. The little man was worlds quicker than he and grabbed hold of his wrist, twisting it to push him to his knees before Lukas could blink. A wicked chop from a spear held by a third guard sent Balian sprawling to the ground on his stomach, as the guard he had struck rose to his feet and held the point not an inch from Balian's hairless face. Before Eduardas could utter a word of protest, the whole company found themselves surrounded by spears, all pointed straight at them. The official at the table rose, drawing a curved blade.

Seeing this, Mylas, Holto, Emanas, and Titas drew their swords, stepping between Eduardas and the approaching Shields of Kar Naron. The black-armored coast men formed two tight-knit lines, one behind the other, shields raised and spears pointed. Dozens of others had silently filed into the tent after hearing the commotion; now, the Goldblades found themselves surrounded.

"Tell your men to drop their weapons or they will die," the deep-voiced guard demanded of Eduardas.

"You dare give orders, you filthy animal?" Attia snapped back. "I will have you know that if we were back in the civilized world where we belong, you would be drawn and quartered for such a crime!"

"*Shut your damn mouth, woman!*" Eduardas barked. Even at her worst, he had never raised his voice to her, but the situation had pushed him past his wits' end. Gods only knew what terror gripped Olivia and Amy, who had managed to climb back inside the carriage.

"Do as he says. Drop your swords. Now!"

With a look to their master and to each other, the four remaining Goldblade guards grudgingly dropped their swords into the dust.

"I…apologize…for this," Eduardas continued shakily, attempting to dig them out of the hole they'd just leapt into. "It has been a long journey, and this lot is easily excitable. Please understand—we are accustomed to a different way of life, and my wife…we meant no wrong, I swear it." He shot Attia a seething look, to which she responded with one of disgust.

"Shield Elijah," the officer said from behind the table. The guard stepped forward, a small trail of blood trickling from his mouth. "Take this lot into custody. Confiscate their belongings and find cells for them in the keep. I will inform Commander Stone of what's happened here."

He casually walked toward Eduardas as swarms of blue-cloaked guards seized his men and wife and began dragging them kicking and screaming through the open tent flaps.

"By the authority granted to me by Karrok-Ahl, King of Astymere and Chieftain of the Avaari, I hereby charge you with assault on the king's men and do place you under arrest. Get him out of my sight."

Two sets of hands scooped Eduardas up beneath his arms from behind and hauled him out into the sharp mountain air. All hope drained from him as they put more and more distance between him and the rear gate that allowed access to the kingdom beyond. *So much for a royal welcome.*

Chapter 26

Kar Naron: Astymere
10th Day of the Eighth Month
5017 A.S.

"Don't. Let it. Touch you," Eduardas grumbled to himself as he lay upon his cot. The straw mattress felt thicker than it looked, so much so that the ends jabbed at him relentlessly. The detention cells were lit only by the sunlight that streamed in through the barred windows along the walls. The chill of the mountain air flowed freely through the tight hall, and the members of the Goldblade company were wrapped tightly in their cloaks. Some who were paired off, like Olivia and Amy, huddled together for warmth, while the others struggled to manage on their own. Attia had been given the cell across from Eduardas. She paced her tight quarters and bit her nails furiously, her face reddening in the dimness.

"I suppose you would have just let that animal lay hands on your sworn guards. You know our laws—the laws of the Testament! *He who would come to touch a beast shall be as a beast in the eyes of the gods. So say the heavenly!*"

She sounded so sure of herself, so righteous in her recitation of the High Testament, that Eduardas began to wonder when the last time was she had any free thought. She, like so many, unfortunately let the Testament do most of her thinking for her.

"*Our* laws?" Eduardas chided as he sprang from his bunk to meet his wife's accusatory glare across the corridor. "*Our* laws mean nothing here, woman! By preserving *our* laws, we have broken *theirs*! How are we supposed to cross the border now that we've assaulted our hosts?" He cast his gaze down the cell block.

"Balian," Eduardas shot his voice down the hall, where he knew his guard could hear him. "What in the name of the Heavenly were you thinking?"

"I don't know, Dominaen," Balian replied weakly.

Eduardas couldn't see his face but could easily hear shame in his voice. He was able to make out the guard's sniffle, deep and wet, as he wiped his nose on his sleeve. "I panicked. I've never been that close to a beast before, let alone one that was armed. When Dominaia Attia spoke, I lashed out. I beg your forgiveness, Dominaen. If I could take it back, I would."

"Well, you can't, Balian," Taimin snapped. "And our master's forgiveness is inconsequential now. It won't get us out of here. All we can do is pray your crime isn't punishable by death."

"You don't think they would kill us, do you?" Amy asked.

It was the first time she had spoken in the hours since they'd been taken into custody. The guards had been gentle enough with the girls, but she had cried hysterically nonetheless. Eduardas couldn't blame her. His heart broke to see his youngest in such distress, but he was comforted by Olivia's resolve.

She had been on the verge of breaking, just as Amy had, but to see her sister overwhelmed with fear seemed to stiffen Olivia's spine. The strength she had shown was not for herself, but for Amy. Attia, of course, fought, cursed, and spit from the moment she was taken from the tent to the moment the door closed behind the guards.

"When the guards come again, whenever that may be, I'll demand to send a message to the king," Eduardas responded confidently. "If he remembers me, then maybe we can all get out of here. So, keep your chin up, and your eyes dry. Have I ever failed you?"

"No, you haven't," Amy said through heavy breaths.

"That's right, I haven't. And I don't intend to. Not now, not ever. So, just sit back, and don't worry a wink."

"It is rather wondrous…" Olivia began.

"*Wondrous!*" Attia shrieked, shattering the calm Eduardas had just worked to create. "What is *wondrous* about this? We have been stuffed into a freezing rat hole by a bunch of black-armored savages! We may be executed any minute, and we are half a world away from home—where is the *wonder*?"

"Mother, those *savages* built *this*!" barked Olivia. "This building is one of the mightiest fortifications in the world. It is as old as the Republic itself, and these people consider it new! The memories of centuries linger in these halls. This place has seen countless battles, against the greatest empire the world has ever known, and it has never seen defeat. It *is* a wonder, if you can look at it objectively."

"By the Heavenly King, you never cease to amaze me, girl," Eduardas marveled. Olivia had learned many things about Astymere during her days of schooling, and from hours of listening to the tales Casan knew about the Endless War. Eduardas realized that after years with Casan, she had begun to romanticize the whole thing, associating knowledge of the war with her betrothed.

"You sound like an old university Prosora, Domina," Mylas commented in jest. He had been silent since his master commanded him to drop his sword. "Not to mention, it *is* an oddly positive way to look at your prison. Yes, it's old; yes, it has seen its share of bloodshed; but this is not a place where we are welcome. You aren't free to leave as though you were an invited guest. You are trapped here. We all are. We should hope your father can talk us out of this, or we may be left to rot."

"Don't be so grim, Mylas," Olivia snapped back. "Father *will* get us out of here. And when we leave, I will bring you back here to look around some more. I'm sure there are things in these halls that would interest even you."

"I wouldn't count on it…"

"I wonder how many people have died in these cells," Holto interjected.

Eduardas could just make him out in the cell next to Attia's, leaning his shoulder into the metal bars. Silence filled the corridor once his voice died out. Whatever light spirits the group had made for themselves over the last few minutes, Holto had undone it with a single sentence.

"Not half as many as have likely died at the gates, I'd wager," Titas said, his deep voice resonating low in his throat.

Eduardas lay back on his cot, willing to suffer the endless jabs into his back from the stiff hay. The only sound that could be heard now was the mountain wind blowing outside as he crossed his arms under his head and stared up at the blank stone ceiling, weighing Holto's words. *How many men have died in these cells?*

He couldn't afford to let such thoughts creep into his mind. The guards would return eventually, of that he was certain, and when they came, he would need his wits sharp and ready. Being bogged down by fear would do his family no good.

EDUARDAS HAD DRIFTED OFF to an uneasy sleep by the time the door of the detention block creaked open on its old hinges. He had been dreaming of the wolves that chased them on the Plains, their howls echoing perfectly in his ears as though right outside his window. Though he hadn't seen them that night, he envisioned their fur was nearly as black as the darkness that hid them, and from their eyes came the same haunting green light he had seen beneath Vasur's hood in Gildara. Those eyes, like lanterns in the vast darkness, surrounded him and his family when the guards woke him.

Eduardas couldn't tell how much time had passed, for his window faced only the next cell block on the other side of a ten-foot-wide alley, offering him no view of the sky. But the day was still bright, and by his best guess, he thought it to be at least past midday.

Three men walked in and stood side by side in the narrow corridor outside Eduardas' cell, facing him. The two on the flanks were tall, common men, both helmeted and black-armored with blue cloaks, holding shields at attention. Though the bottom and two sides of the shields were straight as an arrow, the top of each was rounded, and they were both curved, bearing the imprinted shape from the castle's white banners in their center. Having only seen rounded shields back in the Republic, such a design struck him as odd.

The officer who had conducted the interview stood between them, noticeably shorter in comparison. He looked upon Eduardas with contempt as he removed a set of keys from his pocket. Unlike the others, he was dressed in a black velvet suit with a high collar that hugged his neck snuggly; however, he wore the same bright blue cloak.

With a sharp *clang*, the lock of his cell was undone, and the cell door swung open. The dark man took two deliberate steps into the cell, his boots hitting hard on the stone floor. To Eduardas, still sitting on his cot, he seemed almost like a giant, not only in his physical stature but by the way he carried himself. He gave off an air that everything around him was beneath him—not unlike Attia.

"On your feet," the man said, in a tone no more warm or friendly than it had been in the tent.

Eduardas rose and was ushered into the corridor among the two larger sentries.

"I'll be back before you know it," he said. He had been looking at Olivia and Amy, but he seemed to be addressing the whole company. The dark man in fine clothes brushed his way past Eduardas to take lead of the group.

"This way," he said, with as much emotion as a polished stone. The four made their way out an old wooden door one by one to make a left turn down a long set of stairs. With a quick glance behind him, Eduardas could see a long hall lined with doors identical to the one they'd just come out of. *Nearly a dozen cell blocks. I can't imagine they would ever all be filled at once.*

At the bottom of the stairs sat a wide, doorless opening that led into a small courtyard within the southern side of the keep. It had to be no more than fifty paces long, for Eduardas soon found himself inside again, working his way through grand corridors with high, arched ceilings, all just as black as the outside. Countless torches filled the halls with light and warmth, and the chill that had seeped into his bones was beginning to melt away. He wondered why there should be so many torches lit this early in the day, until he realized the corridor bore no windows—only thin vents to let out smoke.

With one last left turn, he found himself face to face with another staircase, three times as wide as the first and twice as tall, leading up to two large wooden doors fitted with round, iron handles. The trip up the stairs, though quick, caused his legs to ache and burn. Over the last month he had done an alarmingly small amount of walking, and his legs suffered for it.

A corridor ran past the double doors, stretching on endlessly in either direction but for a tiny white light in the distance. The dark man in front lifted both iron rings and gave a firm push, parting the doors. The groan from the old hinges echoed into the large room before him.

Eduardas surmised that this room had to be the heart of Kar Naron, the Great Hall. He counted over fifty long, wooden tables fitted with wooden benches. The room was split down the middle by two rows of blazing hearths, twenty in total. It was flooded by sunlight as well as torchlight, for the walls on both sides were fitted with high, thin windows. Strung between each window was the same banner that flew over the gates, each bearing the same black symbol. At the end of the hall, a large stone platform stood four feet off the ground, accessed by a staircase at its center. Upon the platform stood one huge wooden table fitted with high-backed wooden chairs, each with armrests. It was there that a hard-faced, dark-haired man glared at him from across the room.

"Sergeant Torn! Bring the prisoner before me!" he ordered without moving from his seat. Eduardas could feel the bitterness in his voice; things suddenly looked bleak. *If I can't soften this man, we may be as good as dead.*

"Yes, sir!" the dark man replied, firm and resolute. With a sharp signal from Torn, the two large guards grabbed Eduardas by the arms and lifted him off his feet, dragging him along the stone floor. He felt as if his toes were being roasted from the friction by the time they stopped before the stairs and dropped him. So sudden was the drop that Eduardas fell to his knees, allowing a short cry of pain to escape. These coast men were a hard type, he knew, and he couldn't afford to look weak—not with his family's lives on the line.

"Come forward," the gruff, impatient voice said from above. Eduardas wasted no time getting to his feet and scrambling up the stairs while still trying to maintain his dignity. Torn and the other two kept their posts at the bottom of the steps.

At first glance, this man almost appeared to be King Henry himself, but his hair was far too short, and his hard face was clean-shaven. He, too, was rather pale, but his skin was not as white as the king's. The biggest difference, however, was the eyes. Henry's otherworldly blue eyes had been brilliant, warm, and kind. This man's eyes were blue, but icy, matching the disdainful look on his face.

"My Lord," Eduardas began, attempting to maintain his resolve. "I would like to apologize once again for what happened…"

"*Silence!* You will speak when you are instructed. Is that clear?"

"Yes, my Lord."

"Commander. You will address me as Commander Stone."

"Yes, Commander Stone." Eduardas' resolve was slowly beginning to fade as his gaze fell from the commander's eyes to the floor. He felt like a child being scolded over a broken vase; it was unbearably degrading.

"Now," Commander Stone went on, examining a piece of paper on the table before him. "It says here you came into this fortress with a sizable armed force and led an assault against the men-at-arms charged with guarding this border crossing."

"That is not true, Commander," Eduardas snapped, with a bit more fight.

"You mean to say someone has lied in this report? You accuse the Shields of Kar Naron of bearing false witness?"

"No, Commander, certainly not. I merely mean to suggest the details of the incident, between their happening and the recording of the event, seem to have been skewed."

"I'm listening," Stone said, seemingly amused. It was plain to see he would find no truth in whatever it was Eduardas had to say.

Give it to him straight, Goldblade. Give him no reason to spin your words into lies.

"I came to this castle seeking asylum in the Crescent. My party consisted of nineteen souls, myself included, six of which were armed. I am no military man, but that hardly seems like a sizable armed force."

"Go on," Stone replied, his face and voice growing impatient.

"It *is* true that one of my sworn guards assaulted a…Shield of Kar Naron. We hail from the Gildarian Republic, and as you must know, dark men are a rather uncommon sight in a…military setting. My guard was unnerved when a dark man attempted to disarm him, and my…excitable…wife cried out without thinking, spurring him to defend himself from some perceived danger. This caused a reaction from his fellow guard, resulting in his broken wrist. I assure you, we came with no foul intentions. I actually wanted to make a home for my family here, and was hoping to work for the Crown."

"*Ha*! A foreigner steps fresh onto this soil and expects to work for the Crown outright? That is rich, I must say. It's been a while since I had a good laugh."

"I received an offer of employment from King Henry some years ago. I was unable to accept at the time, but my circumstances have…*changed.* I am here to accept the king's invitation."

The smile faded slowly from the commander's face. He didn't want to believe Eduardas, but the look of worry on his face showed he was not entirely willing to dismiss his words.

"Send a message to King Henry if you wish, and ask him about me," said Eduardas. "He may demand my immediate release."

The commander sat silently for several moments, tapping his fingers together. His light, condescending demeanor was gone now. Eduardas' ears began to ring in the growing silence, until distant shouts came floating in through the windows. The words were unintelligible, but the harsh tone suggested they were orders. In fact, Eduardas could now hear many shouts. *A fortification this large must need a whole army to keep it working. It must never stop.*

"Sergeant Torn." The commander suddenly broke the silence with a hint of eagerness. "Do we have the king's schedule for today on hand?"

"No, sir, we do not, but I believe he may be meeting with the Avaari tribal elders. A meeting of the Elders is not to be disturbed."

"Excellent," Stone said with a grin that made Eduardas' skin crawl—like a cat toying with a wounded mouse.

"I'm sorry, schedule?" Eduardas chimed in, trying to shake his uneasiness. "You have the king's daily schedule? Why would you need it?"

"This fortress does not simply guard the Crescent. It is a sworn stronghold for the Karrok family," Sergeant Torn said, joining Eduardas on the stairs. "We know the king's whereabouts at all times to be prepared to receive him and his family at a moment's notice."

"Sergeant," Stone barked.

"My apologies, Commander," Torn replied with a deep bow.

"I want you to write a message to the king. Mark it as Level One priority to be sure it makes its way straight to his hands. Inform him that…what was your name again?"

"Eduardas Goldblade, Commander."

"Tell him Eduardas Goldblade has arrived at Kar Naron and has been detained for unruly behavior. Let us see what his reply will be."

"Aye, Commander," Torn replied. "It shall be done at once."

"Oh, and Sergeant," Stone added as Torn turned to go. "Do not put my name to this message. It must seem it has come straight from you."

"Sir?" Torn asked, fear growing in his eyes.

"That's correct, Sergeant. It comes from you. If this man

speaks false, the king will be furious with whomever sent a Level One priority message when its contents were not worthy of such urgency. He will demand your punishment, which will be left up to me. I will simply tell the king you received five lashes, and that will be that. Then we'll be able to put the two men responsible for the attack to death and imprison this man here for the rest of his days for lying to an agent of the Crown. So go, now. Send the message and inform me the moment there's a reply."

"Yes, Commander," Torn said uncertainly. "You—follow me," he said with more conviction as he turned to Eduardas. "You will remain in your cell until your identity is verified." He grabbed hold of Eduardas' arm and yanked him down the stairs. As they reached the doors, the last thing Eduardas could see of the Great Hall before they shut behind him was Commander Stone's wicked grin.

OLIVIA HAD DREAMT INCESSANTLY in the hours after her father was brought back. Despite her exhaustion, she couldn't manage to force her eyes closed until he returned. As soon as she had seen him safe and heard his story of what happened in the Great Hall, she felt at ease once again, and within minutes, drifted off to sleep.

She was back in Gildara, in the Chamber of Coin, surrounded by her father's associates and the kings of the coast, but all were cast in shadow. The fires of the Minister's office were all ablaze, but the room was dark, nonetheless. The light of the flames, though bright and powerful, hardly penetrated the center of the room.

Those present moved slowly from the onset, but as what she perceived as time drew on, all motion in the circular room ceased. All were silent. Still faces bore dead laughs and frozen smiles. One man began to move, breaking the stillness. He stood next to the fireplace directly across from her, completely swallowed by shadow. When he stepped in front of the flames, Olivia thought he was a shadow himself, but his eyes gave off a light stronger than the burning embers. They were glowing green, just as her father had said.

Olivia wanted desperately to run, but as she moved her foot backwards to flee, it struck a chair behind her, and she toppled onto it. She felt as though she was cemented to the spot, as though the seat were covered in sap. Struggle as she might, not an inch of her body would move as the shadow approached. Her heart felt as though it would wrench itself free of her chest, as her gaze remained locked on the green eyes that drew nearer.

"You run to the end of the world, girl, but his gaze shall fall upon you. Cross the Great Marranthyne Ocean, but his dark eyes shall see you. The eyes of the Beast see all." The voice was like ice in her veins and needles in her eyes. *"He awaits, child. His awakening is upon us. The Beast shall rise."* The shadow stood two feet from her now, his hand outstretched, reaching for her.

Before it could take another step, the shadow fell to its knees, clutching its chest. Olivia's ears burst at the shriek of agony pouring from the shadowy creature, and she cried out in pain. She could feel the scream within her throat, but it was drowned out by the wailing of the dark spirit before her. When it removed its hands, two glowing red eyes had been burned into its chest, bright and fierce as two coals freshly plucked from the forge. The cries died in less than a moment, choked by an unseen hand. Then another voice washed over Olivia, cradling her like a babe, deep and rumbling. It came from everywhere and nowhere, filling every inch of the room. As she bathed in its warmth, the shadow was gripped by it, pained and restricted.

"The eyes of the Beast do not fall here. The eyes of the Beast see naught but darkness. She has passed under the gaze of Rahm, and she shall not be touched. She is not yours, nor his, to take. Be gone, and to your master, bring this message."

With those words, the two red eyes upon the shadow's chest erupted in flame, consuming and devouring it, until it was nothing more than a pile of ash, its words and cries only a distant memory.

Firelight filled every inch of the room, but Olivia was alone now. There was not a soul to be found but her and the voice.

"Olivia," it said. *"Olivia…"*

"Olivia! Wake up!" Amy was frantically shaking her by the shoulders, inadvertently slamming her head into the prickly straw mattress. She became more aware of this with each jolt.

"Amy, *enough*! I'm up! What's wrong with you?"

"What's wrong with *me*? What's wrong with *you*? You've been thrashing about and shaking! I thought you were having a fit or something."

"It was nothing," Olivia said, the sound of those two voices ringing perfectly in her ears.

"Everything okay over there?" their father called from his cell.

"We're okay, Father," Olivia said. "Just a nightmare."

"This place is a breeding ground for such dreams..." He had barely finished his sentence before the rattling of keys could be heard beyond the door, followed by the clanking of the lock being undone. Sergeant Torn entered with five men, each of whom stopped at a cell, fumbling with the locks. Torn looked angry.

"You've been released," Torn said in a flat, curt tone.

"What?" Olivia asked as her door swung open.

As each guard unlocked a cell, they immediately moved on to the next, not looking any of the imprisoned in the eye.

"You heard me, girl," Torn said. "It seems your story checks out," he said, turning back to Eduardas. "The king has demanded your immediate release and sent a royal escort to bring you to Vita Astym. Commander Stone wants you gone—at once."

"A royal escort?" Attia asked, her attention now fully focused on the conversation instead of the dirt on her dress.

"Crown Prince Karrok-Aht and High Lord Diero Carovensa come as the king's personal emissaries."

"What of our personal effects?" Mylas asked as he exited his cellblock.

"All personal items will be sent to you when you've settled in the Capital."

"Why?" Holto asked, eager to get his sword back on his hip.

"No more questions—from anyone! Keep moving, and keep your mouths shut until you're gone."

There wasn't another sound but the pitter-patter of over twenty sets of feet marching down the stairs. The setting sun struck them each in the eyes as they entered the open air, though none complained, not even Attia, for all reveled in the sweet taste of freedom. *Real* freedom.

Chapter 27

The Royal Highway: Astymere
10th Day of the Eighth Month
5017 A.S.

THE MOUNTAINS GREW SLOWLY AS MAYSON and Diero led the way, heading east along the smooth stone highway. Hammund and Tobias, the Carovensa Head of House, rode behind them, as well as fifty armed guards. Half were the black-cloaked Shadow Knights, there to guard Mayson, while the other half bore the brilliant golden cloaks of House Carovensa retainers, sworn to protect High Lord Diero. The air, which had been warm when the party set out from the eastern gate of Vita Astym, was slowly becoming more biting as they approached the Range of Gol Rayna.

Mayson and Diero chatted intermittently throughout the two-hour ride, while Hammund and Tobias told old stories and spoke of fond memories. Diero was in better spirits these last two weeks, now that he was on the mend. Conversation and laughter could be heard in abundance from the Carovensa retainers, for the men of the Southern Tip had always been more jubilant and boisterous than most. The Shadow Knights, as always, remained silent as a snowy night. The men rode side by side, holding the royal standard of the Crescent aloft, while the Carovensa guards flew the golden star on a field of violet.

After a brief lull in their conversation, Diero looked to Mayson on his right and exhaled audibly, giving no effort to hide his annoyance.

"Why is it that *we* have to fetch these people? It's not as if it is a difficult ride from Kar Naron. They couldn't possibly get lost. You can *see* the city from the rear gate. We could just as easily have met them at the city gates and not wasted two hours of our time riding to the border."

"Because your King commands it, Lord Carovensa," Mayson said, keeping his eyes on the mountains and the small fortress that was beginning to grow larger by the step.

"But I can't help but wonder *why* my King commands it. What is so special about these strangers that they can't make the trip without chaperones?"

"The king didn't specify, Diero," Mayson said, finally taking his eyes off Gol Rayna to look his brother in the face. "All I know is that my father and this Goldblade man became rather friendly on his last trip to the Republic, and the man has fallen on hard times. Father wants them welcomed properly."

"If the king is so eager to give this man a royal welcome, why did he not come himself?"

"The king is conferring with the Avaari elders, Diero. That takes precedence over personal matters."

"The Avaari elders…all the time carrying on about *tribal rights*, and *tradition*, and *blood purity*. You'd think they were some kind of oppressed sub-people, one breath from dying out, with the way they go on."

"You don't even know the half of it. No one knows their obsessions better than I. Nonetheless, they help keep the tribe unified and self-aware, so when the time comes, they will be *my* headache."

"I don't envy you that." Diero leaned back in his saddle.

The two rode in silence for another couple of minutes. For as long as Mayson could remember, the Elders had questioned his legitimacy within the tribe because of his Dalani blood. They even went so far as to urge Henry to take an Avaari concubine to produce a pure heir. Henry had gone berserk at that, and Lord Salac, Master of the Elders, never formally challenged Mayson's standing as heir again, but the sentiment remained. Nearly half of them didn't want him as their king, Mayson knew, and he dreaded the challenge of bringing them into his graces once he took the crown.

Only moderate traffic streamed from the fortress, as the majority of travelers and traders returning home had all but disappeared since the gates opened that morning. One group didn't look much different from another, all wearing finely spun wool clothes, some with smooth cloth and even a few silk suits, but Mayson could pick out his countrymen from the foreigners quite easily.

The first and most obvious sign of an Astymerian was the sight of knee after knee bending to the prince as they traveled. With each one came the usual phrase: *"Cayrian Karrok."* Some did it purely out of custom, for there wasn't a soul within the Crescent who wanted to be outed as a disrespectful lout. Others could not help but show great pride to bow before him. The Karroks had the love of the people—they had since time immemorial—and it never failed to bring a smile to Mayson's face, for he loved them in return.

The riders were now drawing up on Kar Naron, looming tall. It wouldn't be long before they came before the rear gate. Though half as large as the great portcullis in the front, the rear gate could still allow fifty men to walk through it abreast, making it no less impressive.

Diero examined the fortress as though this were the first time he was seeing it. Kar Naron had that effect on most people. When he spoke, the whimsical humor had gone from his voice, replaced by pure curiosity.

"What exactly do we know about these people? I would hesitate to give a royal welcome to some of my own friends. Are we sure they are the type to deserve such treatment?"

"Father says Goldblade is quite the master of finances, and has a rich humor. A sharp mind and an honest tongue—those are traits the king admires."

"Fantastic," Diero said, rolling his eyes.

"The king also tells me he has daughters." Mayson didn't have to look at Diero to know he had his attention.

"I'm listening," he said, raising his eyebrows in anticipation. It was no secret the pair had become rather popular with the highborn girls at court, and even some of the common girls of the citizenry. Since their meteoric rise at the Academy three years prior, the two were never lacking for female companionship. For young men in their societal position, the game of love had become easy, yet they were always ready to play. Ever since Henry agreed to the match between Mayson and Sharra Ahl-Kalin a year ago, however, Mayson's playing was at an end. Sharra was not one to be put in a queue, and one by one she had driven each of his admirers off, with varying levels of venom and glee. For what it was worth, he respected how she held herself, the power she created out of thin air making other young ladies fear her. Then again, the thought of being bound to her was more than a little frightening. He thanked all ten Gods that Henry had insisted the wedding not take place until after he graduated from the Academy and went through his lording ceremony.

Countless women still threw themselves at the young High Lord Diero Carovensa, however, and there was hardly one who was turned away. With Lily gone for months at a time, his young, fiery heart grew restless, aching to fill the void she left behind. *If only she would stay*, he'd once admitted to Mayson. *I would never be hungry again.*

"Put your tongue back in your mouth, Diero," Mayson said.

"My apologies," Diero said dramatically, extending his arm as though he were bowing. "Please, continue."

"One is our age, and the other is several years younger."

"That is practically nothing to go on. Are they fair? Common? I will not stretch my standards any lower…not after Alyss Vurtrin. Gods, that snaggletooth will haunt my dreams to the grave."

"Father says they are both quite lovely," Mayson said with a wide smile. "They are both dark of hair with brown eyes, or so I recall. It has been so long since he told me about them, I'm not sure I'm telling it right."

"Damn," Diero said, shaking his head.

"What's the matter?"

"I was hoping they would have golden hair. There is nothing better than long, golden locks. Isn't that right, Tobias?"

Mayson looked back to see Hammund and Tobias pause their conversation just long enough for Tobias to answer his Lord. The look of exhausted amusement he gave suggested he'd heard similar questions many times before from his young charge.

"I've never cared much about hair, my Lord," Tobias said, keeping his eyes on the fortress ahead. "For me, it was always about the eyes. Appearances can change, hair can lose its color, and a smile, though sweet as honey, can deceive you. But there is no dishonesty to be found in the eyes. They remain constant and unchanging and are the true looking glass into one's soul."

Diero gave an exaggerated yawn to show his contempt for his attendant's opinion; Tobias could only smile back.

"Appearances change, yes, which is why we must get all use out of our parts while we can."

"Very good, my Lord," Tobias said, turning back to speak to Hammund. Hammund, however, had other ideas.

"What of your opinions, my Prince? Where do you place your value?" he asked.

"For the most part, I would have to agree with Diero," said Mayson. "I find the rest of a woman more fulfilling than her eyes."

"I see," Hammund said, sounding disappointed.

"However," Mayson continued, "I have never seen a pair of eyes that gripped me as Tobias describes. If I did, perhaps I would be swayed." Hammund sported a wide, relieved grin at that.

"Girls," Diero muttered to himself. "I'm surrounded by little girls."

"I'm rather looking forward to this," Tobias said, appearing giddy now that the castle was mere minutes away. "It's been ages since I met anyone from the Republic. It will be nice to get a little taste of home after all these years."

"I look forward to getting a taste of the Republic as well," Diero said with a wicked smile. "Shall we make a wager, Mayson? Best man gets the older girl? I can only imagine how red your face would get in defeat, if your Avaari skin were *capable* of blushing."

"You place too much confidence in yourself and not nearly enough in me."

"You're far too reserved and quiet. Girls don't like stoics."

"Girls don't like obnoxious loudmouths, either."

"Who says?" Diero laughed raucously at himself; Mayson couldn't help but laugh as well.

"I accept no wager," Mayson said, composing himself, "but I will say this, just to spite you—I will get the older one to swoon within a minute. Just you watch."

"You have to give me *something*, Mayson. It's far too boring if nothing is at stake."

The prince pondered for a minute. "I've got it. If I can't get her to fall for me within a minute, I will polish your armor for the rest of the year."

"And if *you* succeed, I shall work in your next two apple harvests."

"Done," the prince said, extending his hand to his brother. The two shook, and with that the bet was made. "I hope you like apples, because you're going to be buried up to your nose in them before you know it."

THE GOLDBLADES HAD FOUND THEIR CARRIAGE and horses corralled near the rear gate, none the worse for wear. Sergeant

Torn and the guards had ushered them along quickly, refusing to answer questions or allow them any food or water before they left, for all their supplies had been seized upon their arrest.

Once each rider had been saddled and the carriage loaded with what little they still had in their possession, the rear gate, with the same grating sound of metal against stone that had filled the Great Pass that morning, opened before them. Eduardas found it much more bearable this time.

After the last of the Goldblade party made their way into the open air, Sergeant Torn, along with twenty guards, followed them out to ensure they were passed on to the royal party. The blue-cloaked Shields of Kar Naron stood side by side behind Sergeant Torn. Eduardas couldn't say for certain, but it seemed as if they were blocking the Goldblades from getting back into the fortress. *As if we would want to.*

Eduardas turned his attention westward and took in the landscape for the first time. After having traversed endless, empty plains for the last month, the vibrant, sprawling Crescent seemed like a work of art painted by the gods themselves. As far as he could see to the north or south, there were thick forests of wild-looking, deep green trees. The road before them stretched on into the west, where the forests thinned out, revealing rolling green farmland and grassy fields, all lined with occasional thicket. Beautiful as it was, though, what truly grasped Eduardas' gaze—and that of the rest of his company—was the lone mountain that jutted from the flat, green land, a single behemoth standing guard over all that came under its shadow. He could just make out the fabled walls, one hundred feet high, that wrapped around the city limits.

"It's just like in the stories," Amy said, her mouth agape and her eyes wide. "Is that where we are going to live?"

"Indeed, it is, my dear," Eduardas said, a smile growing wide on his face. For the first time in recent memory, he felt true satisfaction and relief. He had been optimistic at the gates of Kar Naron, but the incident with the guards had robbed him of that. Now that he knew Henry remembered him, the weight of the world had slipped from his shoulders. "I believe our luck has turned."

"Actually, there is just one more matter that must be settled before we allow you to leave," Sergeant Torn said, joining the Goldblades. Eduardas could see the slightest hint of a smirk upon the man's usually hard face.

"What matter might that be, Sergeant?" he asked, wary of what misfortune might befall them just before they came under the king's protection.

"Your man there assaulted a Shield of Kar Naron. I don't know how the law works in the Republic, but here, assault on an agent of the king is a serious offense. A simple punishment can settle things—a way to even the scales, so to speak."

"What do you mean?" Eduardas asked, growing more uncomfortable by the second.

"Shield Elijah, step forward, please," Torn commanded, keeping his eyes on Eduardas. The man who had been struck that morning stepped forward from the line, his shield and spear held at attention. His lip was fat where Balian had hit him.

"Call your man over here," Torn instructed with a nasty smile.

"Balian," Eduardas said with hesitation. "Come here, lad." Balian stepped forward slowly, like a child in fear of a whipping. It made Eduardas realize just how young he really was. He had known that Balian was the youngest of his sworn guards, but he had never given much thought to it. The boy was only nineteen, and aside from the training he had received to become a personal guard, he had never seen true violence in his life back in Gildara. Here, surrounded by warriors, Balian seemed like nothing more than a boy in someone else's armor. "Don't hurt him," Eduardas pleaded.

Torn shot Eduardas a deathly glare before turning his attention to the Shield.

"Shield Elijah," he said again, "do you have something you would like to say to this young man?"

Elijah looked up at Balian, who was several inches taller, and took him in for several moments, sizing him up.

"Yes, sir, I believe I do," Shield Elijah replied. In a cool, calm manner, he handed his shield and spear to Sergeant Torn and turned back to Balian. After taking a moment to plant his feet and breathe deeply, Elijah hammered Balian square in the jaw with all the force he could muster. With a resounding *crack*, Balian dropped to the dirt like a stone, where he lay tangled in his crimson cloak, unconscious. "No hard feelings," Elijah said with a grin. He then took his shield and spear back from the sergeant and rejoined the line in front of the rear gate.

"Get that mess into your carriage and get out of my sight," Torn said, returning to his usual cold demeanor.

"We can't wait here for our escort?" Attia asked.

"No," Torn grunted. "The king demanded your release. He did not say we had to hold your hands and walk you to the city gates. It is a straight and true trip from here to the Capital, so you will come across your escort in due time. Leave, before we find something else to charge you with."

The sergeant turned to take his leave, passing under the large canopy of the rear gate, followed by the twenty men-at-arms that stood guard.

Mylas and Holto scrambled to pick up Balian and brush him off. His eyes were closed and his body was limp. He didn't even make a sound until they got him into the carriage and laid him down. Even then, it was only a half-conscious groan.

Eduardas led his horse by the reins on foot as they moved westward along the smooth road. Each stone seemed to be carefully shaped and fitted to make a perfectly flush surface. As he looked, he realized the entire road had been constructed this way, from the rear gate of Kar Naron all the way into the distance. The thick, green branches of the trees that flanked the road seemed to stretch toward them like so many arms. In days past, they would have looked foreboding—frightening even. The forests of Gildar had been full of ghosts and monsters, all living in Eduardas' mind, but in this place, those green arms seemed outstretched to embrace him warmly—as if to welcome him home.

"Unbelievable," Attia snipped from atop Eduardas' horse. With Balian and the girls inside, she had felt unbearably cramped and insisted on riding herself. The breeze, which was growing warmer as they left the mountains behind, tossed her pink gown about her. She swatted furiously to keep it under control. "Who do these savages think they are? Kicking us out like common beggars; it's enough to make my blood boil."

Eduardas attempted to focus on other things, but her voice drilled through him. "You'll be living large before the day is out, dear."

"Living large on a massive rock," Attia jabbed under her breath.

From that moment on, Eduardas would expend no further effort to bring her spirits around. She would either see the good in their situation, or she wouldn't.

The trees gave way to open country within an hour, as the road took a sharp turn to the west. As the view opened up around them, Eduardas could see fifty banners flapping in the warm breeze, coming to meet them. They were at least sixty yards off, but he could make out the royal sigil that had flown above the gates of Kar Naron. It seemed that, besides the fifty men carrying the sigils, there were four who went empty-handed.

"Olivia! Amy!" Eduardas called to the girls. "Look at this!" Olivia poked her head out the window nearest to him, while Amy used the opposite. "Hold! Everyone hold!" he ordered.

Eduardas scrambled, half-crazed, hoping to arrange everyone in a dignified tableau before the royal party reached the group. Balian, of course, was left in the carriage to sleep off his injury. Attia stood beside her husband, as did the girls, while Mylas, Holto, and the other guards took position behind, and Taimin organized the attendants in the rear.

"Here we go," Eduardas whispered to Olivia, who stood with all the grace her tired body could pull together as the royals approached.

"I BELIEVE THIS IS THEM, my Lord," Tobias said from behind Diero.

"Yes, that is them, or I'm a pauper's son," Mayson replied. Even at fifty yards out, he couldn't mistake the bright gold and sharp crimson draped about the foreigners. "Hammund, Tobias, take point."

"Aye, my Prince," they replied, breaking formation to take the lead ahead of Mayson and Diero.

"Tobias, I want you to make the introductions," Mayson commanded. "After being trapped with the likes of Stone and his ilk, I'm sure a familiar-sounding voice will make them feel more comfortable."

"As you command, my Prince."

"What are my instructions?" Diero asked as the golden

company drew nearer.

"Sit in your saddle, look pretty, magnanimous, and one very important thing," Mayson said.

"What's that?"

"Shut the hell up."

The royal party now stood face to face with the Goldblades, each man-at-arms spread out across the road, completely blocking any passage in either direction. The silent Shadow Knights stood to Mayson's right; the Carovensa men at arms to Diero's left. Once they had picked him out, Hammund and Tobias rode forward side by side to speak with Eduardas directly. He was a bit shorter and rounder than Mayson had expected, and had it not been for his standing dead center in the group, the prince never would have guessed he was in charge. Mayson kept his eyes on his emissaries and listened closely as discussions began.

"Dominaen and Dominaia Goldblade," Tobias began, inserting as much of his Republican upbringing into his voice as he could manage. "The Crown of Astymere is honored by your arrival. Welcome to the Crescent."

"All my thanks, my Lord," Eduardas said with a deep bow.

Tobias couldn't help but chuckle. "That is not necessary, Dominaen. I am not a lord, and you are not required to bow before me."

"My apologies," Eduardas said with another bow he seemed to catch midway.

Tobias smiled, clearly beginning to like this man already.

"I am sure you've had quite an eventful day," he said, "as well as a long and strenuous trip. You all must be exhausted, famished, and chilled to the bone, so I will dispense with the pleasantries and present your hosts, so that we may be on our way."

Mayson and Diero rode forward slowly, each accompanied by two representatives who carried their banners. A sudden and brief wind blew in from the north, tossing their cloaks into a dancing myriad of black and gold. They passed between Hammund and Tobias, dismounting to join Eduardas. Eduardas looked to Tobias, who quickly pressed his palm toward the ground. He seemed to understand the signal, and without hesitation, he knelt, as did the rest of his party. Diero stayed back with the horses as Mayson stepped forward.

"Master Goldblade, I am honored to finally meet you in person. My father has often spoken of you with fondness and respect. It is my pleasure to welcome you to our home."

"The honor is mine, my Prince," Eduardas said, training his eyes on the stone beneath him and keeping his knee bent, despite visible discomfort.

"You may all rise." And so they did, one by one, all in their own time. Eduardas rose to look Mayson in the eye, which, at first, was no easy task for the rotund little man. "My Prince, you say?" asked Mayson. "I suppose you intend to naturalize yourselves then?"

"Yes, my Prince, that had been my intention. I wish to make each and every one of these souls here an Astymerian, if your father, and they, are willing."

Mayson couldn't help but smile. Foreigners had been flocking to the Crescent for centuries, looking to become citizens and fall under the protection of the Crown. Just as many were accepted as were turned away.

"I don't think that should be a problem. But we will concern ourselves with that tomorrow, once you are properly fed and rested. Your residence in the Capital should nearly be ready by now, so we will get underway in just a few moments. But first, I should like to meet these new friends of the Crown."

"Ah, yes! Here is my darling wife, Attia." Eduardas took a pinch-faced woman by the shoulders and guided her forward, forcing her to curtsy deeply and offer her hand to the young Prince.

Mayson gladly accepted it, feeling her discomfort. It amused him. He kissed the back of her hand firmly to feel her grimace behind that painted smile. *Father will enjoy this one.*

"A pleasure to have you with us, my Lady."

"And here is my youngest, Amy." Eduardas guided her just as he had her mother. Though she was near Mayson's age, he couldn't see much more than a child as she stood before him, wide-eyed and red-cheeked. With the same manners, she offered her hand, bashful and reserved. Mayson was less inclined to toy with this one.

"A pleasure to have you with us, dear girl." The girl's cheeks went from a light flush to full-blown scarlet as she giggled and looked to the stones of the road.

"And my eldest, Olivia," Eduardas said as he led another young lady forward.

Her dark hair cascaded over her shoulders in waves, and her golden traveling cloak was not enough to hide her womanly shape around the hips. Her lips, full and pouting, lent an air of authority to her face, which was slender, fair, and strong all at once. All these delights of the flesh pleased Mayson, but her eyes were what froze him. They were of the lightest brown—like the moss of an old tree that had seen countless wonders in its day. Mixed in with that wondrous brown were radiant veins of gold, the likes of which he had never seen before.

Eyes of brown and blue, sunlight and starlight, were locked on each other, and all thought had gone from his mind. In the swirling madness that encompassed his brain, he was certain of only one thing: he had never seen anything, or anyone, so absolutely, infallibly beautiful in his life.

He couldn't tell how long he stood there, staring. He also couldn't tell how long she had been holding her hand out, awaiting his royal greeting. Mayson was suddenly aware that every pair of eyes was watching him and felt a hot flush of embarrassment warm his face. He fumbled for her hand and clumsily brought it to his lips. *Say something, you idiot. You're supposed to greet her!*

"It would be a pleasure to have you." *What? What in the hell was that?* Olivia's expression was both confused and slightly offended as she attempted to draw her hand back. "*No!* I mean…what I meant to say was…it *is* a pleasure to have you *here*…with us. My Lady." She almost seemed amused now, humiliation boiling in the pit of Mayson's stomach as she fought back a laugh. *Rahm's eyes. You're pathetic. Get out of here. Get out of here now.* "Well, I think there will be plenty of time to meet everyone else once you are all situated in the Capital. If you will all follow me, please!"

Mayson hurried away from the Goldblades as quickly as he could without making it seem as though he were running. Diero had his face buried in his saddle as he stood before his horse, directing his laughter straight into the meat of his arm. As Mayson mounted, he cast one look back at Olivia, who did the same to him as she stepped into her carriage. Once again his eyes locked on hers, but only for a moment, as he tore them away to avoid staring again.

Less than a minute into the ride back to the Mountain City, Diero began to laugh openly and audibly from his saddle. The prince kept his eyes on the road, refusing to look at his brother's smug face.

"It would be a pleasure to have you," Diero said between fits.

"Shut up."

"I have never heard such sweet poetry."

"Shut. Up."

"That was absolutely masterful. As a matter of fact, I think *I* may have fallen in love with you after that. Hold me." Diero led his horse in close to Mayson's so as to rest his head against his shoulder and look dreamily up at him, driving the insult home.

"By Rahm's eyes, Golron's hammer, Patreonar's bow, the High Gods, the Gifted, the Chosen, and the stars, shut up. Shut up, shut up, *shut up!*" Mayson spoke through clenched teeth, fighting the urge to scream at Diero at the top of his lungs. Not only had he humiliated himself in front of a divinely beautiful creature, but he had lost Diero's stupid bet and was now forced to polish his brother's armor.

Her eyes. Mayson shot a look back at Tobias, who seemed to already know what was going through the young Prince's mind.

"The eyes *are* the perfect snare of the heart, my Prince."

And what a sweet trap it is.

Chapter 28

Vita Astym: Astymere
20th Day of the Ninth Month
5017 A.S.

OLIVA STROLLED THROUGH THE WILD FIELDS of tall grass and blue flowers as she climbed the slope of Mount Karrok. She had spent a good portion of every day since she'd arrived in Vita Astym exploring her new home, starting with Eastslope and working her way around to north, west, now south. She had dragged Amy along with her every step of the way, until today. When the sun rose that morning, she had run into Amy's room to try to ready her for another day of sightseeing, but after several minutes of poking, prodding, and pleading, Olivia begrudgingly gave up and resolved to spend the day alone.

She walked to the east gate and followed the path of the inner edge of the wall for about an hour until she reached the southern gate, where she turned right to head back toward the mountain. The buildings were all cramped and grouped close together near the wall, but as Olivia moved further into the heart of the city, she found Southslope was the most spacious and green of any part of the Capital.

It was still rather early when she reached Astrogol's Green, and there was hardly a soul to be seen. She sat on the southern bank of the lake, looking north toward the mountain, listening to the birds that clustered in the willow trees growing along the shore. For her first few days in Vita Astym, she could scarcely take her eyes off Mount Karrok, whether she was looking out her own window or wandering about the streets. Until her family had reached the Range of Gol Rayna, she had never seen a mountain before. To have her first mountains be works of art would spoil any other.

I wonder what this place looked like before it was a city. How large was this giant rock before it was carved down? Mount Karrok seemed enormous and imposing enough as it was, even with streets and buildings carved into its ancient, colossal body. She couldn't fathom how it must have looked before men got their hands on it. *I shall have to ask the king when I see him next.*

Olivia stood, wiped away the few strands of grass that clung to her, and moved on. There was only so much Olivia could do in the sparsely populated Southslope, especially with most inhabitants of the area still abed. The only people stirring were the street sweepers and public gardeners, whose daily tasks were to maintain and preserve the countless flowers that brightened every public space. Men with ladders and watering cans clung to tall, black, iron poles lining both sides of every major street, each holding a hanging basket filled with dangling red, blue, yellow, and violet flowers, the likes of which Olivia had never seen before. Several shouts had come to her from the few bakers and innkeepers she passed, all promising the finest breads and roasted field hens in the city. Olivia, who was not even remotely hungry, passed them all with a polite smile and a firm shake of the head.

The road, wide and flat with perfectly fitting stones, cut hard to the right as it climbed the slope, and then back to the left. Olivia realized as she climbed that this was how the center of the city had been built. One road would wrap all the way around while other, smaller paths connected it to the levels above and below.

She abandoned her ascent once she reached the palace level. Her legs were beginning to burn and sweat began to bead on her forehead, making a level, easy walk quite enticing.

The road wrapped around the southern side of the palace, allowing her to examine it fully for the first time in the light of day. She had gone with her father several times when the king called on him, but it had always been at twilight, and the finer details were lost to her until now. Each of the four walls rose higher than the one that stood before it, the fourth being so tall that only the high steeples of the palace could be seen from outside. Olivia could make out pitch black figures standing upon the ramparts of each wall. She remembered she had seen them before, when King Henry came to Gildara, and had mistaken them for empty suits of armor.

Even disciplined men moved ever so slightly from time to time—but not these. These men stood absolutely still, without any visible faces. There was no indication they were even alive until ordered to move. The feeling of hundreds of black eyes watching her from the ramparts sent goose pimples spreading across her skin and added some extra kick to her step as she continued on her way.

She took a narrow road to the final level that seemed no more than a goat path, the air thinning as she reached flat ground. Aside from the road, there was no other sign of human interference at this height. Southslope was the closest to what the mountain would naturally have looked like, with jagged rocks and even hints of snow that blew from the summit high above. The street split off to climb up the slope, just as it had so many times before, but as she looked up, Olivia saw only a handful of buildings. The closer to the top of the city one climbed, the older the buildings got, and those that had long since been forgotten—stone huts and hovels collapsing and tipping—were now nothing more than overgrown foundations.

Olivia turned her attention to the world beneath her. At this height, she felt as though she were the Queen of Stars looking down on all of creation. *This must be how the High Gods see us.*

Before long there wasn't any sign of civilization whatsoever, aside from the road. To her left was a sheer drop down the rock face to the level below; to her right, the slope of the mountain shallowed out, offering her a large field of long grass, weeds, and blue flowers. The slope of the field rose easily for one hundred yards before jutting straight up into the rock face that led to the snow-capped summit high above.

She felt at peace down by the lake that morning, but a new feeling now crept up on her. *What is so different about this place?*

It took several moments for her to realize that, although wonderfully peaceful, Astrogol's Green had been filled with all sorts of sounds, from birds yammering away in the branches, to frogs on the banks of the lake, to bees that flitted from flower to flower. For the first time since she had passed the palace, Olivia realized there was hardly a noise aside from the wind and her own breath. She stood still, gazing out upon the green vastness stretched out before her, and began to ponder if she'd ever experienced a silence that absolute before.

She continued her stroll up the easy slope of the grassy field, picking the small blue flowers that grew around her in bunches. *I'll put them in a vase in Amy's room to show her what she missed.*

Her stomach began to rumble, and she began to wish she had taken up an offer or two this morning. Even now she could smell the smoke rising from the vendors' chimneys, carrying the scent of fresh bread and seared meat with it.

Olivia soon had enough flowers to make a rather lovely, single-colored bouquet to bring back to Amy.

"I wouldn't do that if I were you," came a calm, low voice from behind. Olivia let out a sharp screech and involuntarily tossed the flowers, spinning to look at her intruder. The prince was sitting with his legs crossed beneath him, facing the world to the south with his eyes closed, his black curls and cloak wafting about him in the mountain wind. Behind him, five Knights of Rahm stood guard, motionless as always.

Collecting her nerves and the scattered plants, Olivia realized that perhaps it was she who was the intruder.

"Why not?" she asked, attempting to salvage a bit of dignity.

"They may not look it, but they aren't in full bloom yet. If you pick them before they bloom, they won't grow back, and the Elders won't be very happy about that."

"What?" Her curiosity began to overpower her embarrassment.

"The Ilymar only grow in this little field. The Elders use them for a variety of elixirs and draughts, recipes they've perfected over millennia. There are no bees that can live this high, and the wind can only carry their pollen so far. You can keep those, but I wouldn't pick anymore." The prince hadn't turned to her since he began speaking; in fact, he hadn't even opened his eyes.

"I'm sorry, I didn't know." She waved at him to see if he would react, but the prince remained still. "How did you know I was here?"

"I could hear you panting. I imagine you are used to thinner air, living hundreds of feet off the ground. Then again, you don't strike me as one who hikes."

"You could hear me breathing?" she asked skeptically. Beneath those closed eyes she could see a smile forming. His teeth were as white as his skin; they only stood out due to the black of his beard.

"If that doesn't impress you, Lady Goldblade, I could also hear you tearing the Ilymar from their stalks. When you sit in silence long enough, the tiniest sounds become clear as day."

Lady Goldblade. What I wouldn't give for just one 'Domina.'

"But how did you know it was *me*?" Olivia said, frowning as the prince kept his eyes firmly shut. "You spoke to me as if you knew me."

Mayson opened his eyes slowly, and looked at her solemnly. He was trying to find the right words to say, or so she thought. Olivia couldn't help but notice how bright his eyes were. She stood with her arms crossed, her crimson dress catching a brisk northern wind blown off the top of the mountain.

She remembered the first time she had seen him. Olivia noticed Mayson and Diero first as they rode to meet them. Atop their tall destriers, clad in black armor with cloaks flowing in the wind, they hardly seemed real. Diero, the one in the gold cloak, seemed normal enough. She had seen plenty of men with tan skin and brown hair in Gildara. He was fair of face, almost like her beloved Casan, but his hair was short and light brown, whereas her betrothed had long, curly locks of deep, rich chestnut. It was the black-cloaked young man to his right who hardly seemed human at all.

From what she remembered of the pale king, he seemed to be his exact copy in every respect. His hair and beard were as black as his cloak and armor, and his skin was snow white, making him appear translucent in the overcast, late-day sun. His eyes, even from a distance, shot out at her, radiant as sapphires, mixed with the brilliant glow of starlight. Had it not been for the way he carried himself, as though he already ruled the world, she would have found him to be the most beautiful creature she'd ever seen. Even her Casan seemed homely and ordinary in comparison.

Mayson sighed. "It was your scent, my Lady," he finally replied.

Now she understood his hesitation; it *was* a rather inappropriate declaration. She would have thought twice about saying such a thing to someone she hardly knew.

Apparently the embarrassment of their first meeting had taken hold of him, and once the prince had escorted the Goldblades to their new home in Eastslope, he attempted to avoid her altogether. Whenever she joined her father to see the king, it always seemed she had *just* missed him; even when he was present, he never said a word or looked upon her. Here she had been worried he was going to be a pompous rooster, strutting about with his chest puffed out and his feathers ruffled. What she received was worse: a mute recluse.

Aside from the strange nature of his comment, she was more shocked to realize he was actually holding conversation with her. She tried to shake off the feeling, lest he should see her surprise.

"My *scent?* What are you, a dog?"

"No," he said, laughing and shaking his head. "I wish I could say you were the first to ask me such a question. I've always had powerful senses, for as long as I can remember. Sounds, sights, smell, even touch are more vivid and gripping to me than most. It used to be quite overwhelming before I learned to harness and control it all. As if the impending doom of a crown wasn't enough to worry about, to go through childhood fighting to hear the person next to me when I could make out a conversation from the other side of the room was practically maddening."

Olivia sat beside him, placing her Ilymar flowers in a neat pile beside her. The way he spoke of his crown with such foreboding confounded her. Most men she knew would kill to be placed in Mayson's shoes.

"Is there something wrong, my Lady?"

"No," she managed. "It's just that…every man I've ever met has looked on power as a great treasure to hunt for. It always seemed a hunger that could never be satisfied. Men in the Republic covet it, and most of the time, the power they think they have isn't even real. Rather, it doesn't last. Even my beloved Casan isn't immune to the draw of climbing the ladder. Then I come here, where absolute power falls onto the shoulders of one man, and I meet you, the one person who will inherit that power, and you talk about it as if it were a weight, while others see it as a pair of wings. It's…odd."

Mayson nodded sagely. "The only men who crave power are those who do not understand it. Fools see it as a pair of wings. The select few who support it on their shoulders know what a ponderous weight it is. I'm not even the king yet, and I can already feel it crushing me." He paused. "Can I trust you with something, my Lady?"

"Well…yes. Of course." She realized she sounded uncertain, but he must have heard truth in her voice, for he continued.

"I've never spoken of this with anyone. Walls have ears, even in the palace. I need to know you will take what I tell you to the grave."

"I swear. I will never tell a soul."

"I…I don't want to be king," he said, taking his eyes off her to stare at the ground, as though he were ashamed to even think such a thing, much less say it out loud. He closed his eyes and breathed deeply, as if some burden had been lifted after years of living within his chest. "If I had any choice, I would give up the crown without hesitation. I've seen what it does to my father; it is slowly killing him, I am certain of it. The life of a king is fraught with endless horror and countless dangers, and I have felt the effects of those dangers firsthand…"

His voice trailed off as he absentmindedly fondled the silver buttons of his black wool doublet. His eyes now looked to things hundreds of miles away, and his mind followed them. He almost seemed to be in a trance of some kind. Olivia reached out a cautious hand and gently touched his arm, bringing him back.

"What dangers? What have you felt?" she asked gently.

"It's nothing, my Lady," he said, rising and dusting himself off. He once again looked like something out of an old fairytale, and Olivia looked away to the south, reddening for succumbing to such childish sentiments. "It is a story for another time. For now, I could eat half a horse, and your breathing wasn't the only thing I heard. Your stomach's been rumbling since you sat down. Come dine with me; you must be famished."

The prince offered her his hand, and after a moment's hesitation, Olivia accepted. She'd expected his hand to be cold, but to her shock, he was delightfully warm, as though he had just slipped from a hot bath. His grasp felt rather comforting after her morning in the cold mountain gusts.

Olivia gathered her flowers and the pair walked in silence to the road, where they found Mayson's destrier, Taronax, tied to a stone post. Mayson slung himself into the saddle, taking the flowers and putting them in a small sack before reaching down to pull Olivia up. With one arm, he plucked her from the ground and helped her mount up behind him.

"I want to apologize for my behavior before today, my Lady. It is no excuse, but I quite effectively humiliated myself in front of your entire family and my own men. Every time I saw you after that, I was reminded of it. I will not be a stranger to you anymore."

Olivia thought she heard him mutter something about a bet

under his breath, but she could not tell for sure. She wrapped her arms around Mayson's waist and clasped her hands together as he took off at a run. The five Shadow Knights had mounted and taken chase after the pair. Being this close to him, she could smell jasmine and other perfumes that clung to his skin; she wondered if she, too, could hone her senses enough to smell him at a distance.

When they reached ground level again, they worked their way over to Westslope, where the streets were so crowded, travelling by horse seemed inconvenient. Everyone seemed to know everyone else, and Mayson had to navigate through groups that would form in the middle of the road when members of the throng ran into friends and associates. Making matters worse, everyone who saw the prince's black cloak and recognized his face stopped in their tracks to bend the knee and recite the same salute.

"What's that they're saying? *Carry on carro?*" Olivia asked. It sounded so alien to her. The words seemed to emanate more from the throat than the mouth.

"No, my Lady," Mayson said with an amused smile. "*Cayrian Karrok.* It's old Avaari. The second *K* hardly has any sound to it. It means Glory to the Mountain. But those in modern times use it to mean Glory to the House Karrok. It's a royal salute."

Soul after soul stopped in their tracks, as if what they had been doing meant nothing to them, and bent the knee to this young man. *Cayrian Goysanar,* he said in response to every declaration. "That means Glory to the People," he told her before she could ask.

Olivia thought the few merchants in Southslope had been persistent, but these vendors were all shouting at the top of their lungs, not letting up in the slightest. There were more vegetables than Olivia had ever seen, all fresh off the second harvest of the year, and fruits, both dried and fresh, that made her mouth water at the very sight of them. The smells on top of it were unbearable on an empty stomach. On they went, passing butchers and bakers and fishmongers alike, until she thought she might go mad if they didn't stop soon.

Mayson pulled Taronax off to the right through a wide iron gate that served as the only opening in a large fence wrapped around a square stone courtyard. Two attendants sitting by the front door of the blue-painted inn leapt up and bent the knee to

Mayson before taking Taronax off to the stables in the rear of the building. Mayson shook each of their hands, slipping three mira to each as he did so, prompting hurried bows and excited thanks.

They spent the better part of the day feasting at a large table out in the courtyard, where none disturbed them but the servers who continued to bring ice cold ale in painstakingly crafted pewter mugs. Along with the drinks came spits of roasted beef, potato soup loaded with chunks of bacon, fresh golden bread with large slabs of salted butter, and plums so ripe they practically burst in their mouths.

When they finally had their fill and wiped their mouths to look respectable once more, they began to talk of their lives before their paths crossed. Mayson told Olivia of Darian Carovensa and how Diero had become his brother at a very young age, and Olivia tried to teach Mayson what little she knew of Republican politics, or what little she remembered from Casan's stories and explanations. The prince soon grew quiet and began to look as though he were mourning a terrible death. Before Olivia could ask, he told her that he was arranged to be married to a noble's daughter as soon as he graduated from the Academy. There was not a hint of joy in the proclamation, and he stared into his nearly empty mug as he spoke.

The owner of the establishment, which Olivia learned was called the Sky's Fall Inn, personally brought Taronax around from the stables once they were ready to depart. Mayson clapped the tiny, mustachioed man on the back, nearly making him stumble. He expressed his deepest gratitude and slipped their host a small leather pouch. Olivia couldn't guess how much money was in it, but it looked fit to burst as he gingerly cradled it with both hands.

The pair then rode north, making their way around the city, just grazing by the outskirts of the Bazeira. When Olivia suggested they go in to see what it had to offer, Mayson deterred her, suggesting there was no longer enough time in the day for him to show her everything the Bazeira held; he promised to bring her back another day. On they went as he told her whatever tales he knew about his family, the War of Independence against the old Empire, and the slow, gradual building of the Capital. She wanted to ask him about his betrothed, but the way in which he spoke of it earlier suggested that might not be the best idea.

"I'm sure you've figured this out by now, since you've done a good deal of exploring by yourself, but every section of the city is defined by one bold feature. For example, Northslope is the religious heart of the city. There you will find dozens upon dozens of temples, both small and great, dedicated to the Low and High Gods."

"I thought you were all against the Heavenly," Olivia asked with uncertainty.

"There is no abundance of love for the High Gods here, but those who hold the High Faith are still under the protection of the Crown. Then there is Eastslope," he went on, "which serves as the heart of administration and lawmaking. It is defined by the Mouth of the Mountain, which holds my father's throne."

He continued to explain that Westslope was purely a place of business, trade, and industry, while Southslope was set aside for open space and the larger estates of the city gentry. After a while, Olivia could hardly hear a word as she gaped at the many smoke plumes rising into the sky from the armories and steel works that ran throughout the day, making and mending weapons and shields for the Black Army.

Mayson stopped at one such foundry and dismounted, tying Taronax to a fence in front of it.

"I will only be a few minutes. I have to discuss a price for an order of ore the Academy requested. Guard him, will you?" With a quick smile, he hurried off down the drive and into the wide-open front of a tall building, where countless fires and forges glowed from within.

Olivia hopped down from Taronax and gave him several ginger strokes on the muzzle, earning a satisfied grunt. She scanned the crowded streets and looked off to the west as the sun began to set, turning back to see the Mountain City. In the deep orange of the fading sun, the mountain seemed to breathe with a life of its own; for the first time, she began to feel at home in this strange place.

She decided to take a short walk, keeping Taronax and the foundry in her sight, but had hardly gone thirty paces when a strange alley opened up to her right. She had seen countless alleys in her exploration, but there had always been people within them, occupied with all sorts of business. The longer she stood before this thin path, the more she noticed passersby stepping up their pace to avoid it. Some even gave Olivia dirty looks as she stood in the mouth of the opening.

It was not so much an alley as it was a crudely cut goat path running through natural mountain rock. The path curved to the right, cutting toward the mountain. With one last look back at Taronax, Olivia went on, seeing that Mayson hadn't returned yet. *Just a few moments. What harm could come from just a few moments?*

The path began to slope down as she walked, and the rock walls on either side of her grew higher, more imposing, and even constricting as she moved deeper into the mountain. Soon the rock walls totally enveloped her, and the sky was hardly visible anymore.

The tight path opened into a large clearing filled with loose rocks that made for treacherous footing. The sun was quickly falling behind the cliffs she had passed through, until its light was lost in the mouth of a cavernous opening against the side of the mountain. Olivia could see torches lighting the way into the cave until they disappeared. *Go on. You'll be back in no time.* The voice in her head seemed not her own.

As she entered the cave, a whistling breeze rang in her ears, not from the outside, but from deep within. The rock on either side crept in on her until the broad cavern narrowed to a tunnel only wide enough for one person to walk at a time, with torches lining the path ahead. Traveling onward, she came to a winding staircase that shot straight down.

The air is chilled, even against the fire. Her feet continued to move despite the conflicting thoughts in her head, with the same ease as though they'd walked this path one hundred times before. The air became heavy, both damp and close, and her unease turned to fear. She was convinced her heartbeat would ring off the rocks and travel on ahead of her, deeper into the cave. She wasn't sure why she kept moving, but the light of the fires seemed to pull her along, guiding and beckoning her downward.

The staircase bottomed out in a large, empty room. Only five flames flickered on the walls on either side, but the room was far too large for them to dispel the darkness. Besides there being too few torches to light the chamber, the fires seemed stifled, stunted, as if darkness itself were strangling the life from them. Onward her feet took her, until the weak torchlight gleamed off something—two metallic objects.

Olivia lifted a torch from the wall and held it aloft, revealing two long, curved swords held by pitch black hands attached to pitch black arms. She jumped back with a start when the flame revealed what little of the Shadow Knights' heads it could. Even out and about during the day, these sentinels chilled her blood. But down here, it was all she could do not to cry out in terror at the very sight of them. As she backed away, she could see they were guarding an enormous steel vault door that served as the wall behind them.

"What's behind that door?" she asked. The Shadow Knights said nothing, nor did they move a muscle. "What is back there?" she persisted. Silence. "*Answer me!*" Her voice filled the room and echoed perfectly time and time again before fading away, up the stairs and out into the world beyond.

From behind the dusty steel vault came the sound of a roaring wind, growing louder and nearer by the moment, until it washed over her. In that moment, the sound of guttural, inhuman screaming carried through and stopped her heart in her chest. The screams filled the room, even more so than her own, yet the Shadow Knights remained still and silent.

Dropping her torch, Olivia turned to run as fast as her feet would let her. She could almost feel bony, ice-cold fingers clawing at her back, trying to pull her through the door.

She hadn't gone ten steps before running straight into what felt like a solid wall draped in wool. Strong arms wrapped around her, the smell of jasmine and perfume filling her nostrils over the thick smell of fires burning. She looked up to see snow-white skin reflecting what little light was left in the hellish hall. Tears burst from her eyes, her body relaxing just enough to let them flow. Mayson's steel arms cradled her as he stroked her hair, as though she were a child woken from a nightmare.

Mayson then led her up the winding staircase, through the tight tunnel, and out the cave until they reached the streets of Westslope. In front of the foundry, he tenderly placed her in Taronax's saddle and untied him, leading him by the reins as he head back toward the palace.

"I wouldn't go back there if I were you," the prince said at last. His tone was harsh, but not unkind. She had heard the same tone from her father countless times when she'd wandered off as a child.

"What was that place?" Olivia finally willed herself to say. "What was behind that door?"

"I'm not sure I would be able to properly explain it, my Lady. Just know it is an unholy place—the closest thing to Hell any living man could ever experience—and it is only for the truly damned."

"Why do those men guard it?"

"Shadow Knights are the only ones with the fortitude to guard that door. Once, Silver Shields were assigned to guard it, but each one went mad within a week. Next, they used soldiers. None of them lasted more than a month before their minds crumbled and fell to pieces. Shadow Knights fear absolutely nothing, making them the only choice for a place such as that."

"This place, it seemed so beautiful. So…good."

"Where there is beauty, there is ugliness, my Lady. Where there is great good, there is terrible evil. This is the way of things. There is no fighting or changing it, so it would be wise to accept it."

The rest of the trip was spent in silence. Mayson unclipped his black cloak from his shoulders and draped it around Olivia, wrapping it tightly to fight the chill that had worked its way into her nerves. As they reached the palace walls, Olivia could feel hundreds of black eyes watching her from the ramparts. There was something different about their gaze now. *Is that pity I feel? Judgment? Somehow, they all know.*

"I'll send word to your father that you'll spend the night here, my Lady. My personal attendants will see to you." Mayson carefully plucked Olivia from the saddle and led her by the hand across the main courtyard once they had passed through the fourth gate. "Try to get some rest. You will be safe here."

I'll find no rest. Not until those screams are silenced.

Chapter 29

Vita Astym: Astymere
22nd Day of the Ninth Month
5017 A.S.

"GEREMY BRISBAN HAS DEALT A MOST DEVASTATING BLOW to this country," Henry addressed the Council, all sitting as solemn as though they attended a funeral. As of late, any room in which the disgraced Elavahr's name was spoken soon fell silent. The throne room was no different today. "A crime like this has not been committed in centuries; I strongly feel just one punishment would be suitable—that he be sent Below."

If the pit within the heart of Mount Karrok ever had a true name, it had long since been forgotten. In the Days of the First Kings, all those who incurred the wrath of the king were sealed in the dark tomb beneath the mountain's roots to waste away. Legend had it the darkness was so absolute that even the eyes of Rahm could not pierce it. Some said even the eyes of Tyranion the Heavenly King had no sight in those depths, making the banished truly damned and forsaken in the eyes of gods and men. It was a fate worse than death.

Mayson sat at his temporary seat at the half-moon table with the other Council members, watching Henry intently. Diero sat in his High Lord's seat, one of the four that sat below the throne.

"The queen, however, in her infinite mercy, has discussed the matter at length with High Lord Carovensa, in hopes of convincing him to make a quicker end of the traitor by agreeing to execution by beheading."

The voices of the Council began to rise up in murmurs, both positive and negative in regard to the queen's desire. Nearly half of them wanted Brisban to rot in the shadows beneath the city; the others wanted his blood at once.

"Send him Below!" Evan Mikkel shouted from his seat, silencing the group as the back and forth descended into babble. "A crime so heinous has not been committed in living memory; this rat must be made an example of!"

"And then what?" Beatrice asked. Her voice was soft in comparison, but it sliced through the room with a force Mikkel could never manage. It *commanded* everyone's attention. "Do we start throwing all criminals and traitors Below? Do we rename ourselves in the image of the savage Kings of Old? Do we begin to rely on the people's fear rather than their love and respect? Fear will only serve for so long, then it will turn to hate, and hate will be our downfall. Those who toppled Raelia should know this better than most."

"Our King is *not* some star-worshipping degenerate," barked Phillip Mostyk, Chief Architect of Astymere. "The people could never hate one so noble."

"The people love him as long as he *acts* nobly," Lady Keddra Vilzak, Chief of Agriculture and Commerce, replied. "If I may, my King, my Queen, my Lord…" She nodded to Diero. "If noble mercy is what you suggest, then why not stay any action and spare the man's life? Let him rot in Canlon Prison until he is nothing more than a pile of bones. He would be out of sight and out of mind. Keep him bound in chains, never letting him breathe the free air. A long life of such treatment is a great punishment."

"Lady Vilzak," Diero responded. His voice had taken on a new, powerful, commanding quality, through much practice—and Henry's help. "I bear a scar upon my belly that is just now beginning to heal. I was sliced open like a gutted stag, ready to be flayed and butchered. It is easy to suggest such mercy from where you sit, but Brisban's every breath is an insult to me and my entire bloodline, which he attempted to snuff out. It is because of this that I have agreed to forgo the appropriate sentencing of him being sent Below. He *must* die."

Lady Vilzak looked away and cast her gaze to the floor, deep in thought. After many long moments of reflection, she nodded in agreement, and sat without another word.

"It is decided. Geremy Brisban shall rot in Canlon Prison for another year before we grant him the mercy of a quick death. Let's move on," Henry announced. He waved to the back of the room, to a figure standing against the wall near the great doors. Eduardas Goldblade had waited in silence for nearly a half an hour, and now walked slowly to the front, as though called before a jury to testify in his own defense. His robe, trailing behind him, was of the finest gold silk, and along every seam ran the thinnest crimson trim, still bright enough to catch the eye.

"This is Eduardas Goldblade, my good Councilors. He comes

with troubling tales from the Gildarian Republic, and has brought his wife and daughters to seek permanent asylum in the Crescent." The Council each gave polite nods, but Henry sensed confusion— perhaps even apprehension. "He is Astymere's new Royal Treasurer."

Jordyn Stone stood, outraged. "*My King!* Surely you must discuss the appointment of a position with the rest of the Council!"

"*Sit down!*" Henry barked, forcing Commander Stone sheepishly back into his chair. "This is the decision of the king, as it has always been, and always will be. I may ask for opinions, but the power to appoint or remove a soul from this Council lies with me, and me alone. You would do well to remember that."

Henry noticed Eduardas awkwardly standing in the middle of it all, fiddling with the ends of his sleeves as he tried to remain on the outskirts of the argument.

"This man was a premiere authority of coin in the Republic," the king continued, in an attempt to bolster Eduardas' spirits. "No account under his management ever slipped into red, and through no advantage but his own wit, he rose from the ranks of a lowly coin counter to the foremost authority for one of the largest economies in the civilized world. He has been silently working with me, tirelessly, to bring this rudderless ship safely into harbor. Together, we have rooted out the many agents that helped Brisban carry out his crimes, reclaimed lost and stolen funds, and have begun to weave a discernable pattern from the frayed threads of the treasury…"

Henry was interrupted by the thunderous sound of the massive doors swinging open with unnatural force. An informal entrance into the chamber was punishable by public lashing when a meeting of the Council was in session. As the intruder approached, though, the unmistakable face of Raymund Wallis, bearded and haggard, came into view, followed by a man who was unmistakably a Dalani Hoof, wearing a green cloak and bright copper-colored steel breastplate.

"*My King!*" His voice boomed and echoed, loud enough to silence a packed alehouse. Raymund drew closer; Henry gasped at the severity of his appearance. His face was caked with mud, his white shirt in tatters, some of which was covered with blood, and his once proud crimson cloak was reduced to pitiful shreds.

He was covered with scratches and cuts, and it appeared he was walking with a severe limp.

"We need to ready men!" Raymund cried with what little breath he had left. "They sprang from the trees, from the ground…All dead…We ran…"

He collapsed before he could reach the stairs to his seat. Henry rushed to his side, with Beatrice, the boys, and Urnest not far behind. He sat Raymund up and took firm hold of his face to get Lord Wallis's eyes to focus. Lord Galen took several cushions from the Council seats and propped them under Raymund's feet, taking his head away from Henry and laying him flat. He slid one cushion beneath his head.

"Take a breath," Henry said. "Breathe, nice and deep."

"If I may, your Majesty," stated the Hoof. His scruff ran halfway down his neck, and he, too, bore mud and scars earned on his bloody mission. "We were patrolling the southern side of the Acrontian River in search of the trespassers."

"He said they came out of the trees. There are no forests south of the Acrontian; what did he mean by that?" Henry demanded.

"With the help of local hunters, we were able to pinpoint the direction the marauders had come from, the trail taking us northeast for many days and nights," the Dalani warrior replied, standing as straight and strong as his battered, weary body would allow. "We crossed over the Flat Hills as snow began to fall. We thought nothing of it at first, but the farther we went, it began to come down in thick blankets. We began finding men in small pockets, slaying a dozen here, twenty there. It never seemed to stop. We had planned on rendezvousing with a contingent of Kana border guards after a fortnight, but they never showed. Our numbers and our supplies began to dwindle, and on the morning Lord Wallis decided to turn back…"

"They're dead," Raymund cut in, his fog of delirium somewhat dissipating. "All of them. But for us two, the whole scouting party is gone. Hundreds of them descended on us like wolves. They came from the trees, the rocks…everywhere. We have been slinking through the countryside ever since."

Henry could see pain in his friend's eyes as Raymund began to cough violently. He turned to the Council members, all of whom were looking to him for an answer, and so Henry thought for a moment.

"It seems our course is clear. First, Diero."

"Yes, my King?"

"I need you to go fetch a wind swallow and send word to King Robert immediately; tell him all that we have learned. We need him here within the week and not a day later."

"Aye, my King." Diero ran to the table, dipped a feather pen into one of many inkwells with the mad speed of a hare, and began furiously scribbling out a message. Once he was satisfied that the ink had dried, he bolted from the room.

"Lord Galen. Have your best men tend to Lord Wallis and his companion. Their recovery is paramount. Mayson—oversee and prepare chambers for Lord Wallis and our guest in the palace until King Robert arrives. Stone, send word to the Shadow Knights outside to disband the crowd. We will see no supplicants today. Assure it is done peacefully."

Stone nodded and made a rather hurried exit.

"Eduardas, I'm afraid your formal welcome must wait."

The meeting hadn't officially ended, though all in attendance, whether they had direction or not, parted ways silently with objectives in mind. Moments later, Henry could hear the roar of the citizens who had just been told they wouldn't be seen. Though the commotion was loud and dismayed, there was no violence that day—a small victory for Henry in the face of this horrid defeat.

It wasn't until seven days later, when the streets were packed with business, that the citizens of the capital saw Dalani banners navigating through the wide roads, approaching the Council chambers with Robert, Ronin, and Jordyn Stone in company.

The Council members had awakened well before the sun rose to beat the Dalani party to the Mouth. King Robert and his men looked as if they would fall from their saddles at any moment, after seven days of hard riding with little rest. It was a wonder their horses did not drop dead upon the cobblestones. The Council had taken their places before the king and queen. Standing off to the side was the Dalani man named Dalton, now looking both well-rested and in good spirits. Raymund, too, was looking himself again, sitting in his High Lord's seat. His clothes were fresh, his cloak was mended, and his face was cleanly shaven. His cuts and scrapes were healing, but his face remained gaunt, haunted—distant.

The doors creaked open. King Robert stormed in looking just as tired as the rest of them, his patience already thin. "Please tell me, wise Karrok-Ahl, why I just tore across my own country like a hunted fox, rather than have this meeting in my *own* throne room? Why was my Hoof not brought straight to me with this news?"

"Lord Wallis insisted on coming here first," the Hoof tried to explain. "If I had left him, he may not have made it back, and I feared the exertion of forcing him back to Roleigh might kill him."

"Robert, there is little time to waste. Please sit so Raymund and your man may speak of what happened." Henry pointed to his chair once more, and Robert begrudgingly took his seat, grumbling to himself. Raymund and Dalton paced around the room for the next few minutes, informing Robert of all he hadn't heard: how the marauders had been using the forests of Casaack as a staging ground for incursions further into the south; how the Kanan border guards had failed to meet them, as they had likely been wiped out; and how they had greatly underestimated the force that had been gathering.

"Men swarmed us as we moved through the trees," Raymund stated. "Hundreds of men dressed in thick iron, and well-armed. We fought them off for as long as we could. As our numbers dwindled, they drove us into a deep ravine hidden under the canopy of the trees. Arrows flew from every direction. Our horses were struck and fell into the chasm, along with three of our brothers. Dalton and I clung to the rock wall, out of sight. Our pursuers surely thought us dead—the only reason we are still alive."

"Gods, we must act," Robert stated. "An expedition will no longer do. We need a proper army to face this new danger."

"I agree," Henry said with a curt nod. "Lord Raymund, how many of them would you say there were?"

"Anywhere from two to four hundred, my King."

"We shall match them, then."

"Match them?" Robert shouted over Henry. "We need to ride in with full force and *crush* them! We've already paid the price of underestimating them time and time again. We can take no more risks."

"The report mentioned nothing of cavalry, Robert," Henry replied, rising from the Heart to take slow, deliberate steps down to meet the Dalani party. "With a force of only a few hundred well-armed riders, we could cut these brutes down like wheat in an open field. Any more would be a waste of resources that would be better spent elsewhere. Should I prove to be wrong, a small force on horseback will be mobile enough to fall back to safety and await reinforcements."

"I can lead such reinforcements, my King," Mayson said, rising from his seat to steal the attention of the room. "I can think of no greater honor than to join you on the field."

"I volunteer to join Prince Karrok-Aht in this endeavor, my King," Diero chimed in from his seat, one leg crossed over the other in a manner too relaxed to be tolerated from anyone other than a High Lord. "Give me two days and I can have a battalion assembled and ready to await instructions. Allow us to coordinate with Lords Wallis, Rahmos, and the War Council, and we can have ten thousand men at your disposal."

"Silence," Henry demanded. He shot both boys a look of stern reproach. It wouldn't do to discourage their eagerness to serve, but until they graduated, they were wards of the Academy, and nothing short of a full declaration of war could pull Academy trainees onto the battlefield. "You both will be returning to the Academy, and there will be no argument in that matter. Lords Wallis and Rahmos can handle things well enough in my stead."

Mayson looked down at the floor and slowly took his seat, his head slightly bowed, but his nostrils flared with anger. Diero uncrossed his legs and straightened his posture, nodding in agreement, though his eyes held back a thousand words. Both were so full of fire, Henry hoped it wouldn't consume them before they had their chance to use it.

"Robert," Henry continued, turning away from the boys. "Once you and your men are properly fed and rested, send word back to Roleigh and give the order for your Hooves to assemble. Together, we will crush these bastards once and for all."

Chapter 30

Canlon Prison: Astymere
32ⁿᵈ Day of the Ninth Month
5017 A.S.

BEATRICE WRAPPED HER FINE WOOL SCARF tightly around her neck as the prison walls came into view. In the shadow of the mountains of Gol Rayna, the air had become harsh and biting, with the wind blowing from the snow-capped peaks sending dagger after icy dagger into the queen's heart. *I hope his blankets are thin and his clothes ragged. Just one of many hardships he deserves before his death.*

The queen's heart suddenly warmed thinking of how it was her own son who had undone Brisban's wicked machinations. From the moment Galen told her she would have a son, she knew one day he would inevitably be King, a great man remembered by history. But for all his accomplishments, he had always been her boy. After Brisban's arrest, something changed—in both Mayson and herself. She now looked on him as if he were a king already. Her two boys had become men under her very nose.

The two Shadow Knights riding beside her held the royal sigil aloft, the white fabric shining like beacons in the afternoon sun, with another twenty riding behind. She'd considered not making such a fuss, but Beatrice knew arriving with banners would make their entrance into the maximum-security prison easier. Prison Master Norren would be hesitant to open the gates, so if Beatrice wanted to avoid conversation with the gatekeeper, she must pull out all the stops.

As expected, the portcullis was open and ready for her arrival. From the high guard towers within the thick, barb-covered stone walls, the sentries had seen them coming. The drawbridge, newly rebuilt with fresh timbers, lowered with a *bang* as it locked into place, connecting the prison to the world beyond. Beatrice took the reins firmly in both hands to ensure she had absolute control over her destrier, Aranqa—"Sure Traveler" in old Dalani.

Beatrice looked down into the deep, mirror-still moat that surrounded the prison on three sides; the clopping of Aranqa's hooves seeming to bounce and skip across the surface of the water. It had once been a river current that ran down from the mountains but had long since been dammed off to keep the body of water stationary. Alterations over the centuries had made the moat much wider and deeper than the original river had ever been, and it was widely considered impassable, for none had survived crossing it. The prisoners of Canlon were fed little, and movement was restricted in direct effort to weaken them. Any who miraculously made it over the prison walls to reach the moat on the other side would find river snakes waiting for them in the deep water. The thought of falling in made Beatrice's skin crawl; she tore her gaze away from the murky depths and turned her attention forward as she passed under the open gate.

Once inside the walls, Beatrice found only blank desolation. The jailhouse at the heart of the complex resembling a heap of stone cubes stacked randomly atop each other, and the eight massive guard towers positioned in a semi-circle around it, were the only structures to be found. No men on the ground, no fires—not even a blade of grass. Canlon's bleak appearance matched its purpose: to allow traitors and criminals to waste away in the cold. She pitied the guards who took turns on duty here.

"Not much of a welcome," Beatrice remarked to the Shadow Knight on her left. She knew none would ever answer her while wearing those lifeless helms, but being a natural conversationalist, she could never help but speak to them anyway.

Horns from the rounded towers broke the uneasy silence. The pitch was high and unsteady, as though the horns themselves were in need of repair or replacement. The barbed gate of the central structure screeched open as she approached, and fifty men dressed in black chain mail and half-helms filed out to meet her. Each held a large, rounded shield and a thick club carved of polished ebony. They all bent the knee as she drew near.

Beatrice came to a stop ten paces from them and addressed the men assembled before her.

"Where is Prison Master Norren?" she asked.

A tall, slender man with a large, hooked nose stepped forward, removing his helm to reveal thinning blonde hair. "He has taken ill, my Queen," the man said in a deep raspy voice while bowing. "I am Ryan Halbart, Round Shield and personal aid to the Prison Master. He has instructed me to receive you."

"Word travels quickly within these walls," she replied, undeniably impressed.

He attempted to hide the smile that fought its way through his professional manner all the same. "The sentries saw you coming for over a mile."

"Very well, Shield Halbart. I have come to see our…*special* guest."

"As you wish, my Queen. I believe we may be able to fit you into his busy schedule," Halbart said, no longer fighting his smile. "This way."

He led her up a wide set of stairs, flanked by blank, perfectly flat walls dotted with dozens of arrow slits, up to a wide, steel-braced gate covered with razor sharp barbs, and ushered her in. Nearly all light was lost when the gates shut behind them, aside from the sparse torches hung along the walls. There was no other source of light, or even heat for that matter, as Beatrice, Halbart, and her two Shadow Knight companions made their way through the labyrinthine halls of Canlon's heart. In the dim corridors, Beatrice could see icy clouds trail ahead of her each time she exhaled.

"How do you work in such conditions? Does my husband know about this?"

"Yes, he does, my Queen," Halbart replied. "Canlon was designed this way. There is to be no perceivable comfort for those locked away here. The guards live better than the prisoners, mind you, but we have grown accustomed to such hard living. Keeps us sharp, or at least that is what Norren says. Personally, I wouldn't mind some thicker blankets, or even an extra hearth or two, but being able to withstand it does offer its own small comfort and no small measure of pride."

"Gods bless you. I wouldn't have the fortitude for such work."

"I'm honored, my Queen, but I fear you insult yourself. Word has it your constitution is somewhat legendary."

She raised an amused eyebrow at this. "Someone must have been exaggerating."

"If you insist, my Queen, but we here will continue to believe." Halbart led them around a corner. "It isn't far now."

After taking what seemed like an endless series of left and right turns, up one set of stairs and down another, Beatrice and her company turned onto a long, straight corridor lined with rusted iron doors of varying sizes and collections of dust, the smallest of which easily weighed over a thousand pounds. Halbart removed a set of oversized keys from his belt that were so large and thick, Beatrice was surprised the belt had been able to support them at all. The group came to a stop as Halbart gestured for his Queen and her guards to step back.

He fit the key into the lock in the center of the thick door and used both hands to force it to turn. Beatrice had expected a loud clang, but the lock hardly made a sound. Once it had been undone, Halbart grasped the bar running from floor to ceiling on the door's right side and pulled it open with a great heave. Despite its rusted appearance and great size, the door gave way easily and silently.

"Shall I go in with you, my Queen?" Halbart asked, standing clear of the opening.

"No. The three of you are to remain out here. Understood?"

"As you command, my Queen," Halbart said with a bow. The Shadow Knights who had accompanied her also nodded their obedience, though Beatrice knew they would remain close. "When you enter, do not cross the red line painted on the floor. Stay behind that, and there is no way he can reach you. If anything happens, call out; we will be in there before you can blink. Isn't that right, gentlemen?" Halbart asked of the Shadow Knights. His enthusiasm slowly died as the sentinels simply looked at him with black, lifeless eyes.

"Thank you, Shield Halbart, but I will be all right. Men such as Brisban have never troubled me much. I won't be long." Without another word, Beatrice left her companions in the corridor and entered the stuffy stone cell. Two torches hung on the wall to her left and right, yet enough of a chill still gripped the room to prompt her to wrap the scarf closer around her neck. The smell of piss-stained hay made her eyes water, as the smell of feces nearly choked her.

"My Queen," came a flat voice at the far end of the cell. "I wish you had told me you were coming. I am not dressed to receive, and the room is a mess. If you would like, I could call my attendants to sweep up. Bring you some hot tea, perhaps? One could catch their death in here with this chill."

The contempt in Brisban's voice was thick and unbridled. Though she couldn't see him, she could tell he was no more than several feet away, slumped against the far wall. She grasped one of the torches mounted beside her and moved forward until a thick red line came into view on the stone floor before her. Now she could see him plainly, the light of the fire reflecting off his faded eyes. He was dressed in tattered rags, with no trousers or shoes. His famed coif had vanished, replaced by long, matted locks and a scraggly, unkempt beard. His eyes looked sunken and wild, weighed down by heavy bags.

"I'm glad to see you are still in good humor, Brisban," Beatrice replied coldly.

"No *Lord* Brisban? Not even Geremy? *Tsk tsk tsk.* I know I have been stripped of title, but you were always one to respect formalities, *Beatrice*."

The insolence burned her briefly before she quickly regained composure. From his shadowy seat, Brisban gave a bored snort of derision. He no longer feigned manners and when he spoke again, he kept his eyes on the wall. "Why have you come?"

"To find out why you needed those blade galleys."

"Why not ask me why I tried to kill your pet snake?"

"You wanted to be rid of him before he came of age so you could hold your *temporary* position. It wasn't hard to put together. I'm only surprised you admit it so openly."

"There is no denying what can't be denied. I wanted him dead. I wanted him dead from the moment I convinced your fool husband to name me Elavahr, but he was always under your watch. A small part of me hoped he would cross the wrong person once he entered the Academy, but I quickly realized there was no one on that pitiful island that could beat him to death. I had to see to things personally."

"You certainly helped things along—but not in your favor," Beatrice chided. "I always found it odd no one ever seemed to last in the Treasury after your appointment. Now it makes perfect sense. Those you kept long enough have told Mayson everything they know."

Brisban continued to stare at the wall, his nostrils flaring.

"Your raiding of the Public Relief Fund is where you made your last mistake. According to your subordinates, instructions were passed down to the lowest rungs of the Treasury to hold all requests for inclusion. This was, I'm sure, to bide you time to somewhat replenish the funds, but it seems there were quite a few staff replacements made *after* the instructions went out. The new clerks conducted business as usual, with word that the funds had been depleted quickly making their way out of those dark vaults. Does it bother you, Brisban, to know that despite your clever tricks, such patient planning, you still made such a fool's error?"

Still nothing from Brisban but a hard glare at the wall.

"What were you going to use the galleys for?"

"Take your questions and stuff them up your skirt. Your wretched brat tried to get it out of me, and he managed nothing. You will have no better luck, I assure you."

"*Prince* Mayson single-handedly exposed you for being a shifty, thieving shit pile, taking him little more than a week to do so. Barely a man by law, he is already three times the man you could ever be. This burns you, I'm sure of it. Being outsmarted by a boy will haunt you until your execution—perhaps even into the afterlife."

"Yes, yes, I am just seething that little whelp stuck his nose where it didn't belong. Tossing and turning on my feather mattress, it's simply all too much…spare me. This is so much bigger than you know, and nothing your brat bastard or Bruiser can do will stop it."

Beatrice stifled a shudder. "Believe it or not, there was a brief time when I fought to spare your life. It was a lapse in judgment, I am now certain: these icy walls are a paradise compared to what awaits you in the pits of hell."

"I will see you there, my dear." Brisban's words oozed out like putrid slime; she could almost hear him licking his lips. "I will give this to your boy—his timing couldn't have been better. I was finalizing preparations to do away with you next. Losing you would have driven the old man mad, so much so I daresay he would have killed himself, leaving your precious boy alone to pick up the pieces. He never would have been able to stop me at that point."

For a split moment, her breath caught in her chest—Beatrice was his. She'd bitten down on the hook; all he had to do was yank to send her spiraling down a dark hole from which she'd never emerge. Brisban wished to destroy her balance, to turn this interrogation into a plea. But Beatrice of the House Suryn, Wara

Ahiashte, Daughter of the Wind, was not so easily broken. She let his bile harmlessly crash over her like diving under a wave.

"You would have tried, and I would have had blood on my hands. It wouldn't have been the first time. You don't know the position you find yourself in, Brisban. Tell me why you needed those galleys."

"Either tell me something of interest or get out," he demanded.

"No single person has ever possessed that many blade galleys. If it were simply greed, you could have gone on stealing from the Crown, hiding your tracks by buying ships one at a time…but no. You needed many, and you needed them immediately. Why?"

"To sell all your soiled gowns and undergarments to needy islanders. I could have gotten a steep price for them from those seawater-drinking lechers."

"Speak to me that way one more time, and I will have your tongue ripped from your mouth," Beatrice said, the full force of her voice echoing off the stone walls. Brisban eyed her with a furrowed brow. "I will ask one more time. Why did you need a fleet of ships?"

Beatrice swore she saw a flicker of fear in his eyes.

"What would you be willing to do for such information? If you can convince your *darling* husband to stay my execution and exile me, I will tell you everything you want to know. That is my price. Pay it, or get nothing."

"That seems reasonable," Beatrice said, pretending to consider the proposal. "But I have a better idea—with this being the *only* offer you will receive. Tell me what I want to know, and I will have your execution date moved up. You won't have to suffer in this icebox much longer. Remain silent, and I will have you sent Below."

After the attempt on Diero's life, the proposed attempt on her own, and the chaos he'd caused in Henry's Council, Beatrice had enough.

Brisban's eyes showed a sudden flash of terror as every muscle in his frail body tensed. She had his attention now—he knew she was no longer playing games.

"You wouldn't," he stammered.

She knelt down to look him in the eye on his level.

"You couldn't!" he yelled, desperation beginning to take hold.

"If you had learned every facet of the law while sitting in Lord Darian's chair, and not just the laws that benefited *Lord Brisban*, you would know there are six people in all of Astymere with the power to send prisoners Below. The High Lords, the king…and the queen. If I demand it, it will be done."

Brisban began looking about the room as though he expected someone else to be there, but Beatrice saw not a soul besides the two of them and their shadows. She had never seen Brisban look so stricken in all the years she had known him. Finally, he summoned the will to speak.

"…I was going to sell the blade galleys to the Hauakan, ruler of the Malkaua Islands, in exchange for…sellswords."

"*Sellswords.* Mastery over the Crescent's economy wasn't enough? You had to make yourself king as well?"

"The army wasn't for me," he replied in desperation. He then grasped his right wrist as though in terrible pain, his jaw and neck clenching, choking the sound out of him.

"Who was the army for, if not for you?"

"*No! I will say no more. Out! Out with you, please!*" he shrieked, lunging forward.

His fit had been so terrible and sudden that Beatrice fell back onto her bottom behind the red line. The chains caught him just before he reached the paint and collapsed to the floor, writhing in pain.

Beatrice backed up slowly to the door, gradually leaving Brisban in shadow, groaning and muttering, begging for mercy against an unseen assailant. The sight made her breath catch in her chest.

In half a moment, Halbart and her Shadow Knights were at the door, their double-handed sabers drawn.

"Is everything all right, my Queen?" Halbart asked, taking his large keys from his belt and locking the door once they'd all left the cell.

"Yes, thank you. It seems the gravity of Brisban's situation has hit him harder than expected. Thank you for your service, Shield Halbart. If you would be so kind as to lead us out of here, we will not burden you anymore with our presence."

Beatrice had mostly gained control of her nerves now that they had put some distance between her and the filthy wretch trapped in the cell, but she still couldn't keep her voice from shaking. Halbart had to have noticed.

Back through the black, torchlit labyrinth they went, winding and turning, climbing and descending, until finally they came back to the barbed front gate of the prison house. The guards were still assembled at the bottom of the steps, their eyes uncomfortable and wary. With aid from her two companions, Beatrice climbed back into her saddle, thanked the men of Canlon for their service, and wished the gods would treat them well.

She felt rather embarrassed she had needed help getting atop her horse. To think, a Spear Maiden of the Dalani needing aid taking the saddle. If her father could see her, she would never hear the end of it. Still, the sight of a dignified Lord of Astymere being reduced to a wild animal had rattled her bones. Even the presence of her loyal bodyguards wasn't enough to rid the image from her mind.

The tall towers had faded into the distance and the air had warmed considerably by the time Beatrice began to feel calm once more, focusing on the steady rhythm of hoofbeats against the stone road. She turned to her right to look upon one of the Shadow Knights. He looked back at her through the lifeless slits of his crested helm. She knew there had to be questions in those eyes— a desire to know hidden behind black steel.

"I'm all right," she told him. "Though we should make haste. The king will need to hear of this—immediately."

Chapter 31

Vita Astym: Astymere
30th Day of the Ninth Month
5017 A.S.

Olivia removed her shoes and crept like a ghost through the empty halls of her house, past her parents' bedchamber, and down the stairs to her front door. The city had long since gone silent; not a soul could be seen in the streets. She undid the lock and cringed as it *clicked.* In the stillness, such an insignificant sound may as well have been a vase falling to the floor, shattering into a thousand pieces. She fought the urge to secure the lock, run back to her room, and forget this whole thing while she still could. But the thought of leaving Mayson high and dry without a word of explanation was too much.

First bell after midnight, he said. Olivia took a deep breath, flung open the door, and silently shut it behind her.

Olivia thanked the Heavenly King that Eduardas had given Mylas and Holto leave this past week to tour several military encampments outside the city. Balian and Lukas were on duty that evening, and as luck had it, they'd drunk themselves into a stupor at dinner, lacking the discipline of the older Goldblade guards. For the past three days, security around their house had been relaxed and loose, which made Olivia's outing possible.

There wasn't a sound on the streets of Eastslope except the harmonious ringing of wind chimes and a light breeze blowing in from the south. Though the night wasn't cold, she could still feel the heat of the oil lamps twenty feet above her head lining the street as far as she could see in any direction. The orange glow bathed the smooth stone road, and for a moment, Olivia could have sworn she was back home in Gildara—but when she looked up seeking branches and golden leaves, she found nothing but stars and the twin moons bathing a snowy mountaintop in crisp, bright light.

She put her shoes back on and laced them tighter before making her way toward the mountain at the heart of the city. Every shadow she saw made her heart jump. The area was well-lit and the number of gubernatorial buildings drew many Silver Shields to the area to guard them, setting every one of her nerves on edge that she might bump into one. She could feel sweat begin to bead on her forehead despite the cool breezes caressing her. As she turned onto the Circym Street that ran along the base of the mountain to head north, she could not shake the feeling she was somehow doing something wrong. Why else would she be sneaking about the streets of Vita Astym in the dead of night? She had a choice, however, and in the silence, Mayson's voice rang clear in her head as though he were standing next to her.

If you wish, I would be honored if you'd meet me in front of the Great Temple of Rahm at the first bell after midnight. There is something I've been meaning to show you, but it will only last a short while.

He had been timid as a child when he asked. She feared he might revert to his old ways of awkward silence and stolen looks, but his smile was confident. It could have been a royal command, or he could have worded it so that she felt trapped between a rock and a hard place, but Olivia knew it was her choice and hers alone, and had agreed.

The Circym Street was nearly as wide as the royal highway, divided down the center by a long strip of carefully tended grass and trees whose wild-looking branches were highlighted by pink flowers hanging like ripe fruit. Olivia's stomach began to rumble, as supper had been hours ago.

The road curved off to Olivia's left around the base of Mount Karrok. Every several hundred paces, a road would cut across her path and travel up the slope to reach the highest levels of the city, but her course remained straight and unchanged. She passed under the arch of a massive ramp, a road built to connect the ground directly to higher levels. Had it been made of wood in place of smooth stone, Olivia would have sworn it was one of the Great Ramps that led from the forest floor up to the city platform of Gildara. She thought such a sight would make her homesick, but to her surprise, it only made her feel more at home here.

She had dressed in something comfortable but durable for her nighttime rendezvous. The jade-green gown she'd picked was far from her best, for she did not know if they would be traveling or if the prince wanted her to see something within the city limits. The fabric was thicker than her other gowns and more resilient, but it was glossy and reflected light under the right conditions, which made it one of her favorites. She'd even brought the black leather riding gloves her father had bought her, on the off chance she would be put on her own horse.

She had gone through every possible scenario before selecting shoes for the outing, which were more concealing than what she usually wore—lace-up ankle boots, in case there was rough terrain where they were going. *You're going to look like a fool if you end up staying in the city. You already look like a fool, kicking up such a fuss for this boy.* The thought came and went in the blink of an eye. If she dwelt on it, she knew she would force herself back to the house. The road had just made its way into Northslope when the silence was broken by steady, rhythmic stomping of feet on the stone ahead. There were many of them— creating a sound too forceful for a handful of night dwellers—that soon came into view as Olivia rounded the bend.

There were forty, she surmised, dressed in the black armor she'd grown accustomed to seeing nearly everywhere in this country. Each man carried a large, rounded silver shield and a pike no less than two heads taller than the one who carried it. Each had the shadowy look of fatigue on his face, yet they marched on with energy and purpose.

The Silver Shields played no small part in these streets being as safe as they were. Olivia had seen many town watches in her travels after leaving home, but all of them were poorly trained and equipped to the point where they almost seemed comical. The Silver Shields, however, were trained and equipped as thoroughly as any soldier in the King's army. The fact they were comprised of volunteers made no difference in their effectiveness.

Olivia felt the sudden urge to hide, as though they were searching for her. She began to slip into a nearby alley until they passed, but then remembered what Mayson told her: there was no curfew in this city. It was no crime to simply wander the streets at night without mischief.

Just keep moving and they will ignore you.

Olivia could feel several pairs of eyes on her as the Shields marched by. Realizing her running would cause *many* more problems than it would solve, she strolled on, not bothering to look back. The steady beat of their footsteps soon trailed away to the south behind her.

For the first time since she left her house, Olivia began to feel very much alone in the slumbering city. The icy feeling in her stomach that came and went periodically since that day down in the crypt started to creep its way up into her torso and spine. It had taken her three days to find sleep after she wandered down there, yet the horrid wailing still haunted her dreams. Her only comfort was remembering Mayson's embrace, the warmth of his arms fighting away the chill, the sound of his heartbeat against her ear...it was pure serenity tainted by shame. *Casan is still waiting for you, and you are letting your heart be stolen right out from under you.*

Olivia was so wrapped in thought that she nearly walked right past the road she had been looking for once she crossed into Northslope. She perceived the sign hanging from the lamppost as an afterthought: *The Holy Way.*

With the way the moonlight mixed with the orange glow of the street lamps, Olivia felt as if she had stumbled into a dream, until the towering cathedral looming over her snapped her back to reality.

The Great Temple of Rahm sat in an empty square surrounded by torches mounted into the ground, each as tall as a man. Two square towers stood silhouetted against the night sky as they rose above the tall, flat roof. At this angle, she could see the edge of the great dome at the far end, sparkling in a way that mirrored the countless stars in the night sky. The black colossus reminded her of Kar Naron, but whereas the mountain fortress filled her with wonder and curiosity, this place made her skin crawl.

Olivia had been by the temple several times during the day, but always had the same eerie feeling that she'd rather be anywhere else. She couldn't remember why she felt so uneasy as she scanned the face of the cathedral, trying to find some missing detail—until it leapt out of the darkness and struck her heart.

In the light of day, the eyes of Rahm, painted large and proud over the front entrance, were easy to see. In fact, they were so large and brightly painted they were impossible to miss against the black stone. But in shadow, the eyes seemed to melt into the darkness, and it was only when Olivia trained her gaze hard over the entrance that they stared back at her through the night. Suddenly all desire to meet with Mayson faded; the only thing she wanted to do now was run home, burst through her front door, and bury herself in her blankets.

"There you are." Mayson appeared astride Taronax, riding up the Holy Way behind her. He wore a look of utter joy. When he got close enough to see the fear in her eyes, his brow furrowed with worry. "Is something wrong?"

"The eyes…the temple. They startled me, is all."

"When you don't grow up with them, I imagine they can be rather unnerving. But I promise, there is only blessing and protection to be found in those eyes. There is not a shred of malice."

"That's not what I learned at home," Olivia said, looking back on the temple with a shudder.

"Yes—the High Testament has much to say about Rahm and the rest of the Worldly—I've read it once or twice. Some interesting insights, but very little truth, I'm sorry to say. All aggrandizement for the Heavenly and preachy stories of their infallibility, while anyone who doesn't swallow it hook, line, and sinker is deemed a *heretic* or *blasphemer*. I will show you some other Holy texts someday, like the Book of Stone, or the Mother's Sermon, to broaden your perspectives. You will see. For now, we must go before it is too late. Here, take my hand."

It took Olivia aback to hear Mayson insult the High Testament, but she nonetheless took his hand as he leaned toward her and plucked her from the ground, planting her in the saddle behind him in one smooth motion. "And don't worry, I've brought some food," he said with a grin.

"Is it far, where we're going?" she asked as they took the Holy Way to the northern gate, passing houses, shops, and smaller temples. The street grew narrower as they went, and the windows of many of the tall buildings on either side had those same terrifying red eyes.

"It will take a few hours to get there if we set a good pace. If we make it in time, we should be able to enjoy it fully and get back before dawn. I hope you're well rested."

"Don't worry your curly head. It would be nice if I knew what we'd be enjoying, is all, after such a long trip."

"That would spoil the surprise, my Lady. Trust me. You won't be disappointed."

The sound of Taronax's hooves clopping along the pavement

rang off the faces of the buildings that flanked them. In the dead of night, they sounded like thunderclaps, exploding one after another. The deep timbre of the city bells broke her thoughts as they chimed, their ringing sailing out into the night beyond the walls. *You were right on time.*

The walls now blotted out the stars in the northern sky, replaced by rows and rows of torches along their inner face. *What it must take to light all those.* The shouts of several drunks echoed down the street to their right as they approached the gatehouse. She could almost make out their red faces as they staggered along, yelling about nothing and laughing just as much.

The northern gate was open as always, for there were no threats to the Capital within these borders. That being said, the king was no fool, for the gatehouse and the towers above were always manned, ready to seal the gate at a moment's notice if the need ever arose.

Each guard and man-at-arms bent the knee for Mayson as Taronax passed through, offering their salutes and well-wishes. The gate, like its three brothers, was the size of the great portcullis at Kar Naron, allowing a hundred men to walk through it abreast. But in place of a portcullis, there was a swinging gate that surely had to be pushed and pulled by just as many men to open and close it.

Once clear of the gate, Mayson gave Taronax a light kick to get him up to speed, and Olivia clung to his shirt at the sudden lurch. She could feel his warmth through the thin cloth and, despite her best efforts, her fingers occasionally ran against the stone-solid muscle of his abdomen, causing a sudden, reflexive flush to her cheeks. Her hair streamed in the wind as they picked up speed, and when she looked down to spare her eyes from the wind, she was suddenly distracted by Mayson's sword.

From what she had learned during her time in Astymere, she could tell it was of standard military make with a simple leather grip, only longer and more carefully put together than a typical saber. Mayson had often mentioned he was in the end stages of the long process of learning how to make his own blade—the one he would carry with him after he graduated from the Royal Marshal Academy. She asked once what he intended it to look like, but he danced around the question, claiming it would reveal itself to him when the time was right. He had one more year at school to narrow it down.

What surprised Olivia was the fact she had found it on his right side instead of his left. All her life she had seen Mylas, Holto, and countless other men-at-arms with their swords on their left hips. It was as jarring as walking into a familiar room where all the furniture had been rearranged.

"Why do you wear your sword on your right hip?"

"What?" Mayson asked over his shoulder, fighting the roar of the wind.

"*Why do you wear your sword on your right hip?*"

"Well," he said, "it's because I'm left-handed."

"No one uses their left hand."

"Is that a fact?"

"Where I come from, yes."

"It's rare, my Lady, I'll grant you that. But I assure you, left-handed people like me are scattered across the globe—even in the Republic."

"Why choose to use your wrong hand, though? It seems you would be bound to do everything backwards your entire life."

"Tell me, my Lady. When did you *choose* to do things with your right hand?" he asked. It took her several moments to realize she couldn't answer. She *never* made a choice as far as she could remember; he seemed to take her silence as reassurance of that fact.

Mayson went on. "Everything you do, whether it is writing, eating, sewing, what have you, you do with your right because it came naturally to you."

His tone softened now as he slowed Taronax to a trot, tiring of fighting the wind. "Ever since I can remember, my right hand always felt secondary in comparison. My father and Lord Wallis tried to force it out of me by training my right hand double, but it never worked. Sure, I can use my right as well as anyone, but it just doesn't *feel* the same. Does that make sense, my Lady?"

"Yes, it does. You can't fight what comes naturally to you. It is one of the tenets of the High Testament."

"Ah—if you are good, you are unable to fight the need to do good, and if you are evil, you are bound to darkness and foul deeds. I know what the testament says, and it is terribly inaccurate.

It likens men to gods, making their traits absolute, but that is not how men work. They aren't black and white, clearly divided into good and evil. Good men are capable of terrible things, and even a fiend isn't beyond redemption. Most of the time, anyway."

The pale prince continued to surprise her. Olivia hadn't expected Mayson to be versed in the High Testament—nor had she expected to be lectured on the nature of good and evil. "I was trying to agree with you," she said chidingly, "but if that is the way you see things, I suppose it's admirable. A bit idealistic, but admirable."

"I hear aging is a wonderful cure for idealism. It will slowly fade away," he said with a casual smile over his left shoulder.

The lights of towns twinkled on the dark horizon all around them. Tall chimneys and temple steeples rose in the heart of the nearest, no more than a mile off to their left, as dozens of misty white smoke plumes twisted into the moonlight. The land seemed so calm, and yet full of signs of life.

Their ride soon brought them out of open country and farmland into dense green forests. The Northrode was wide and flat, even in these wilder, more rural parts of Astymere. On they rode through a seemingly endless pattern of woods and farmland, passing an assortment of settlements—villages, towns, even walled cities. Trant, just ten miles north of the Krystal River, was the largest. It was the closest rival to Vita Astym in terms of size and population, but that wasn't saying much. Twenty-foot stone walls were a mere fence compared with the perimeter of the Mountain City, and the ten thousand souls within those walls a mere gaggle compared to over a million. Still, the lamps, torches, and candles made for a dazzling sight in the dark, as if stars had fallen from the sky and lay sprinkled over the green earth to the east.

They rode over the tall bridge that spanned the Marsiryn River as the lights of Trant faded away, the water churning and frothing below them. Olivia could faintly hear the water rolling and crashing against rocks, and for a moment, thought she could feel the spray of it gently kiss her cheeks before they left the bridge and the river behind.

"Has there ever been a left-handed king here? Or will you be the first?" she asked.

"No, my Lady." Though their speed had picked up again, the wind had subsided; he no longer needed to shout to be heard. "There have been several, but there hasn't been a left-handed king since the days of the First Kings. Astymir himself was left-handed, or so legend says. After five thousand years, fact and myth become so blurred it's difficult to tell them apart."

"So, you will be the first left-handed ruler in thousands of years? That's something to be proud of, I suppose."

"There's no arguing that."

The conversation carried on into the night, talking more of small things and fond memories. The more she heard his voice, the more Olivia began to grow accustomed to it; soon, she realized, she craved it. Despite herself, she began to wonder if he craved hers' as well.

The Northrode wound on and on through rolling green country that seemed to spread before them without end. The stars were now blotted out by thick clouds hanging heavily in the northern sky. Even the twin moons found themselves fighting to be seen through the wisps carried on the night wind.

Beyond the silhouetted hills in front of them, a large glow was bouncing off the clouds above, as though tens of thousands of torches and bonfires were burning with fierce light. She tried to lean out from behind Mayson to get a better look at the source, but after nearly slipping from the saddle twice, he suggested she remain still. She agreed with displeasure.

Had the saddle two pairs of stirrups, Olivia would have attempted to stand in order to see what lay on the other side of the hill they were climbing a fraction of a moment sooner. It reminded her of the feeling she had when the trees of Gildara broke open to the roaming land and beautiful skies above.

Taronax trudged over the summit, his breath heavy from the long ride, shaking his head in annoyance with Mayson for forcing him the way he did.

At the top of the hill, with the entire Northern Tip laid out before them, Olivia was dumbfounded yet again. She was beginning to lose track of how many times this had happened since she'd left home. It didn't matter if she saw a thousand things in this ancient, wild place that took her breath away; she would gladly accept them all.

Below them, no more than a mile off, the endless green landscape was replaced by white light that stretched on into the north for miles, even to the east and west. It was as if the land itself were emanating a heavenly glow taken straight from the moons themselves.

"What is this? This can't be real."

"It is very real," Mayson said softly. "I was hoping you would like it. This is a very Holy place for us, Olivia; I have been wanting so badly to share it with you."

It was the first time he'd called her Olivia since they met, and it made her pause a moment before her attention returned to the vast field of light that rivaled anything she'd ever seen before.

"What is it, though?" she asked, whispering in his ear. She could smell the sweat that had dampened his skin along the ride, her cheeks quickly flushing before she pulled away.

"In old Avaari, we call it Karna'Sharahm, Leaves of the Watcher, but most people today refer to it as the Dark Wood. It is the home of Rahm."

The very name made Olivia's heart freeze. It was bad enough to see those horrible eyes painted on a building, but to go into those trees, with that…thing, if it was really in there.

Whether Mayson had prepared the speech to follow, or if he could feel fear replacing her wonder, Olivia could not tell. Regardless, he spoke with confident, soothing tones.

"My Lady—Rahm is kind and just. As long as you enter the Dark Wood without malice or ill intent, it serves as a sanctuary— a place of peace and serenity."

"We're going *in* there?"

"Yes, we are," he said with a chuckle as he gave Taronax a light kick in the sides. "I figured the best chance I had to get you to agree to go in was when it looked like this. Though it is always beautiful, it doesn't look as awe-inspiring during the day. Or even every night. Only in the days around full moons do the white leaves drink in their light and glow, so much so that we won't need torches. Our way will be well lit."

They were near enough now that Olivia could make out the dark shapes of the trees. As they grew closer, she could see the leaves giving off the mesmerizing glow, like countless, brilliant white lanterns welcoming them in.

"There is just one rule once we pass under the branches, and you *must* obey it."

"Of course," she said with trepidation. He wasn't usually this serious, his voice so stern. His look was hard as he stopped Taronax twenty yards from the edge of the forest. This was no joke.

"This is the last time we will speak until we leave," he said. "Under this white canopy is pure silence. Rahm has willed it. It must not be broken, or Heavens help you. Do you understand?"

Olivia nodded gravely. "I do. I swear, I won't make a sound."

"Good. On we go then." The road took them straight into the wild mess that was Karna'Sharahm. At first Olivia believed Mayson knew where he was going, dipping and turning to avoid the trunks and roots, but it soon became clear the hands of man had very little to do with this place. The branches weaved whichever way they pleased and, on more than one occasion, came close to striking the pair in their heads. The road wound to and fro, climbing short hills and taking unexpected dips.

Her wonder returned, her fear nearly forgotten, for all around her rained light as white leaves fell by the thousands, still emitting their haunting, nearly blue glow long after hitting the ground. She reached out and cupped her hands to catch as many as she could with a wide smile. She wanted to laugh and ask how they grew back so fast, but remembered her oath.

Each leaf slowly faded to darkness in her palms, like the last dying embers of a fire that had burned for hundreds of years. The disappointment never lasted long, for not a moment after one leaf's brilliance died out, another would fall into her hand to take its place.

She had been so enamored by the foliage that she didn't see the water sitting before them until Taronax came to stop on its southern bank. The lake was calm and flat as a millpond, mirroring the Twin Moons and stars above. With hardly a sound, Mayson hopped down from the saddle and lifted his hands to Olivia, suggesting he would catch her. She leaned down and allowed him to scoop her up under her arms to set her lightly on soft ground.

Taronax started drinking from the lake, and Mayson didn't move a muscle to stop him. Olivia felt the poor thing had earned a good drink; she could only imagine the prince felt the same.

They both shook their sore, stiff legs, and after they felt sufficiently loosened up, Mayson turned from her to remove his shirt, boots, and breeches. His snow-white skin seemed to glow under the full moons as he waded into the lake, further and further until nothing but the shadow of his head against the white light from above was visible. Olivia hadn't much experience swimming, but she found no harm in wading out to where she could stand comfortably. She unlaced her boots and slipped them off before pulling her riding dress over her wind-tossed hair, revealing her white silk underdress.

Even in the dark, she could see those ancient, brilliant eyes taking her in from the water. Mayson's looks were never covetous. Even Casan stared at her carnally more than once. She thought it was because he found her beautiful, desirable—all things her mother had taught her when Casan first sought her hand.

The way Mayson looked at her, though, was exhilaratingly different. He looked at Olivia the way he looked at his country— with absolute admiration. As her waist sank beneath the pristine surface, her foot slipped on a smooth stone. She would have gone completely under with a splash had he not gently grabbed both her wrists. She could feel immeasurable strength in his hands, but also unlimited tenderness.

His torso was now halfway out of the water, and for the first time, Olivia found an imperfection on his porcelain skin. She had noticed he would clutch and rub at his chest in times of stress, but he always shrugged off her questions whenever she'd ask why. A large, thick scar ran from the center of his chest and curved up into his left shoulder.

Olivia went to run her finger along the rough, silvery flesh that managed to stand out against his light complexion, but Mayson stopped her short. She simply gazed into his eyes, her look telling him everything he needed to know. After a moment, he closed his eyes and let her run her fingers along the rigid flesh. Even in the cool water, he was still warm, filled with the fire of ancient blood.

He let out a long, mournful breath, and as he turned his head, Olivia could see tears rolling from his closed eyes. She felt he had never let anyone see his scar before, let alone put hands to it. This seemed unbearably difficult for him. With all the care she could muster, she turned his head toward hers, his brilliant blue eyes suddenly opening at her silent command.

Comforted by her touch, he drew her in close with one hand, pressing the silk of her underdress between them and stroking the dark locks that hung low upon her back with the other. He then took his hand, closed it over hers, and moved it to his chest for what seemed like eternity, letting her feel his heartbeat grow more powerful. Without taking his eyes from hers, he moved his hand under her chin and pulled her in slowly.

She was barely an inch from his face, eyes closed, lips open. She could smell the salt of his tears when suddenly, she heard Casan's voice in her head. *From this day, until the end of time, I shall love you and no other.*

With a heavy heart, Olivia took the young prince's hands to give them a tender, forlorn kiss. She looked on him again, shaking her head as tears filled her eyes. She then quickly turned and swam back to Taronax as fast as she could without making too much noise. *He's not yours to keep. He is promised to another—just like you.*

They dried without looking at each other, at least in the eye. Olivia looked on him several times as she slipped her dress back over her shoulders.

The ride out seemed short in comparison to the ride in and, once the sky above was visible and the light of Karna'Sharahm far behind, Mayson spoke again.

"I'm sorry, my Lady." A frustrated sigh flushed through his lips, and he said no more.

Chapter 32

The Dark Wood: Astymere
20th Day of the Third Month
5018 A.S.

LILY SLEPT IN A HAMMOCK DURING her visits to Vytria, held up by hooks that had been slipped through tree roots emerged from earthy walls. She had her own secluded pocket of a room in a hallway lined with many others, long since empty. Years ago, many seers had inhabited these halls, but none now lived that could remember such times.

In the cool room, deep below the surface, Lily gazed up at the insects crawling along the ceiling. They didn't bother her as they had when she first ventured down into these tunnels; instead, she begun to develop a strange sort of affection for them. She would lend a hand by helping stragglers who fell to the floor, lifting them back to the ceiling with the others. Spiders, beetles, crickets—all had been cradled in her palms, and she no longer felt the need to wash her hands afterwards. They had become another part of her life here.

Every morning back in the Capital she had been waited on hand and foot: people dressing her, fetching water for her bath, laying food before her as if she were royalty. Here, Lily was a cook, a maid, a seamstress, anything she needed to be, just like everyone else who had stayed there—just like old times with her aunt Susa. She hadn't spoken to the king in weeks, or Diero for that matter.

Leaving Diero had been the hardest part of her isolation, but whenever she closed her eyes, she saw him there. She even found herself missing the queen. It took a few months, but once Queen Beatrice moved past her distrust of a Layda Arani, she took Lily riding through the streets and countryside. The young seer had finally begun to feel as though she truly belonged.

In the Whispering Delves, there was just one binding rule: no messages. Not a single exception could be made, lest someone track a wind swallow to their front door. Total isolation seemed to wear at Lily's mind at first, but she soon understood it was the only way Vytria had kept this place safe and untouched for so long. If there were ever the slightest break in custom, the delves likely would have been burned years ago by angry zealots.

Lily swung her feet over the side of the hammock and landed steadily—a vast improvement from her first days in the hanging nest, when she fell flat on her face more times than she'd care to admit to Vytria. She wore a thick, gray, wool dress, laced across her chest with a wide leather cord, and had given up shoes altogether whenever she was underground. Her feet sank into the dark soil as it squished between her toes with every step. She now relished in the once unpleasant feeling, like a child playing in the mud.

She followed the candle-lined hall to the kitchen. Though the walls were barer than the kitchens at the palace, the cutlery more rustic, Lily found it perfectly adequate. It was a simple room not meant for more than a few people at a time. A circular table and four chairs sat opposite a corner with a small stove resting above an open pit. This kitchen was homey and warming; it was if her aunt would walk in any moment carrying a fresh loaf of bread.

She walked to the pit and brushed off the iron stove. She then reached into a small pile of sticks and twigs, scooped a few handfuls into the pit, and used a candle from the wall to light the tinder.

"Good morning," came a voice from behind her. Vytria entered silently, her night robes dragging along the ground behind her. Lily could easily see the bones of her chest in the dim light. Lily nodded back with a sleepy smile as she reached for a black iron pan on the lower shelves.

A single bell rang and echoed down the silent halls. Four tan eggs rolled down a small wooden chute carved from the tree branches and plopped into a bowl of water sitting beneath it.

"Care for an egg?" Lily asked, taking a small dab of lard and dropping it in the center of the pan. She watched it melt slowly as the heat grew. Vytria nodded slowly and sat at the small table, keeping her piercing eyes on Lily. It had been a long night of meditating for the two, as they often lost track of time down in the Delves. "How does it work? I've always been curious."

Outside of lessons and mantras, Vytria was never one for stimulating conversation. The elder seer covered her mouth, blocking a yawn.

"Peculiar it's taken you nearly four years to ask," Vytria said with a hint of annoyance.

"I hoped I would find the answer on my own, but for the life of me, I still can't figure it out." Lily had spent much of her days inspecting the nearby woods and tunnels. Once, Lily had almost been lost again to the vastness of Karna'Sharahm, but Vytria luckily found her before she'd gone too far astray.

"A simple, rather ingenious network of chutes," Vytria said, with the satisfied smile of one with fascinating secrets. "Certain trees are riddled with them, with neat little perches perfect for building nests. Once eggs are laid, air is sucked through these chutes with such force that the eggs, and sometimes part of the nest, are pulled inside to end up here."

Crack! Lily split the shell of an egg and watched it sizzle as she dropped the golden yolk into the pan. She opened the other three and discarded the shells into the stove.

"Not many of these man-made nests are able to keep birds in them long enough to yield eggs. Most fly off after a night or two," Vytria added.

"Yet somehow there are enough to provide at least one serving per person," Lily observed.

"On a typical day, yes," Vytria replied, but offered no explanation.

Lily thought for a moment of what little hope she had of meeting another seer in the Delves. She and Vytria had been alone every time she'd come.

"How many seers are here when it's crowded?"

"It is rare for any to make their way here anymore. The old wisdom has died out, and many seers simply believe they've gone mad. Most live out their days in solitude until death takes them, or they take their own lives."

"Are there others in Astymere, besides us?" Lily used a wooden spoon to mix the eggs around, flipping them while narrowly avoiding getting sprayed with hot lard.

"Likely not, child. If any have been born during my stay here, I've not been made aware of them. We may very well be the only seers alive on this side of the continent. Even the Ara'Sa don't journey any further west than Colembria. Men of the Eastern world are far less hostile to our kind. Living beyond Raelia's influence has spared them the fear of the mystical ways that grip most Western men."

"The Are-wha?" She served Vytria, and they began to eat as they talked.

"The Ara'Sa are an Order of the most powerful of our kind—old, wise, and gifted with the sight of multiple visions. They have total mastery of their foresight, harboring great and terrible secrets of days yet to come, which they've used to garner great influence over many kings in the East. Some say they know how the world shall end. Some say they predict a spectacular union between the Worldly and Heavenly Gods. But none outside the Ara'Sa know for sure…it is not my business to speak any more of them. Go, dress and prepare yourself."

Lily wanted to ask more questions, but Vytria was unyielding in these matters. She retreated to her quarters and dressed in the clothes that had been provided for her upon her arrival—black flowing robes, practically light as air, that followed her when she moved. *Shadow silk*, Vytria had called it, rare and precious. Despite having little love for Astymere, it seemed to Lily her teacher had quite the affinity for the national color palette.

She hurried back to the shallow blue pond among the caves and sat upon the pool's edge. Vytria did the same, softly and elegantly. The young seer waited there, silently thinking about the last few nights.

She had been reliving the same dream that plagued her slumber since her days in Susa's hut. It had come and gone since, but hadn't been as frequent until the past week. She thought of her vision and how the object falling endlessly had become much clearer—a long, slithering outline of a moving figure, shining in brilliant flashes as it fell. She couldn't tell for sure, but it almost seemed like a snake the way it wound and twisted through the air.

The figure fell through an unclear, complicated tangle of arms, skinny and fat, straight and curvy. Now, after her years of work, she could see another beyond the shining object, a larger mass falling with it some distance away—but this was as unclear as the first had been in the beginning. It was as if she'd started all over again, taking one step forward and two steps back.

"Breathe, slow and deep, until you feel yourself traveling beyond this place." Vytria's instructions brought her back into focus. "Just as we practiced—cling to your vision for as long as it will allow. Don't try to force it; the more you force it, the quicker it will reject you."

She handed Lily a wooden cup filled with Afina and watched her gulp the whole thing. Soon, Lily found herself staring down into the same void that presented itself in her daily exercises. She leaned in closer, trying to get nearer to the falling shapes, but quickly slipped from whatever perch allowed her point of view.

Lily cried out as she reached upward for reprieve, but found nothing within arm's reach. She, too, fell into the dark abyss swallowing the faded shapes night after night. All sense of place and time left her, with half an eternity slipping by. The nothingness slowly peeled away, piece by piece, until she felt tiny, icy jabs of snow hitting her cheeks.

She felt no landing, but hard, cold ground was beneath her feet as though it'd always been there. Sound slowly crept its way into her ears. Only a faint hum at first, it soon became thundering, ringing clashes of steel upon steel.

Lily opened her eyes to behold something unnervingly familiar: men, as far as the eye could see, killing each other in the most gruesome of ways. Men armored in gold, stone, silver, leather, black steel, iron. Men of many nations soaking the ground with blood. Every moment felt repeated from a distant memory, yet she could not figure why. Some voice at the edge of consciousness told her she had been here before.

The sea of swords stretched on endlessly as she strolled through the carnage. The land crawled with commotion, the blood reaching up to Lily's ankles and soaking the hem of her dress, before she came upon a sight that stopped her in her tracks.

In a small clearing stood a giant, decked from head to toe in deep gray armor seemingly washed out from the dull, overcast light above. The snow clung to his shoulders, mixing with the filth and carnage sprayed across his breastplate. The horns of a great bull protruded from his monstrous, fanged helm as he swung the largest sword Lily had ever seen above his head.

Standing toe-to-toe with the iron monster was a warrior clad in black, helmeted and masked, a cloak of precious shadow silk clasped to his wide shoulders. With practiced skill, yet reckless abandon, the warrior wielded Rahmirion, expertly whirling it between himself and the giant. Lily forced herself closer to the melee—so close she could nearly touch the black steel upon the warrior's back.

Thump! Something fell directly atop her head, stunning her. She lifted her hand to rub the throbbing spot, but instead felt something wrapping around her legs. Lily looked down to see a black snake writhing between her ankles, its tongue rapidly piercing the air. Hundreds of snakes sprang from the snow and blood, drinking in the spillage of death. She tried to run, the world now shaking as snow fell in blankets. With the howl of the wind, it seemed the ground beneath her would tear itself open and swallow her whole in her mad dash for escape.

"Lily!" a voice shouted. "Lily! Come back, Lily!" The words rang over the roaring winds and the clanging of metal until the battle grew distant. The cries of struggling and wounded men waned until she felt warm, soft soil once again.

She had fallen out of thought to find herself back in the tunnels beneath the Dark Wood. Vytria was standing over her when she opened her eyes. Her sharp features seemed even more pronounced as her forehead and brows wrinkled in worry.

"Tell me what happened." Vytria sounded frightened, but very curious. Lily's skin was covered with a thin layer of cold sweat, with dirt marks covering portions of her dress and running up her arms.

"I saw the falling objects again. I can't be sure, but I think one of them may be a snake. And there was something else…" She hesitated, but Vytria drew close. "Something I've seen once before, I thought…"

"You saw something else?" Vytria demanded, taking hold of Lily's wrists and burning into the girl with eyes so wide Lily thought they might pop from her head.

"It was a battle. A terrible battle."

"You saw *something else*?" Vytria repeated in disbelief.

Lily nodded. "Only once before today, when I'd hit my head."

"Gods damn you, child! How could you not tell me you had seen another vision?" Vytria exploded, now pacing on her feet, disregarding Lily in her fury.

"I didn't know it was a vision!" Lily shouted, losing her patience. It echoed through the nearby tunnels.

"You must leave at once," Vytria stated as she rushed past Lily. She circled around with her hands behind her back. "They must know of this—they must make preparations…"

"Where am I going?" Lily asked, confused.

"Back to the Capital and then to the East. Beyond the Republic to the heart of Teranthion. There, in the mountains of Oremanse, you will find the Ara'Sa. Only they can help you now. Gods, two visions. You have gone beyond my aid, child. There is no more I can teach you."

"I must return to Vita Astym before I leave?"

"Yes. You must tell them exactly where you go and what you do. If you simply left from here, the king would surely suspect foul play, and people would tear this place apart looking for me. You must go back, now, and begin preparing."

Vytria practically pushed her from the room, mumbling that she would learn more when she reached Colembria. There were many there who could show her the way to the mountains of Oremanse.

Lily quickly gathered her few belongings, excited to feel fresh air after not seeing the sun for days. She soon found herself outside in the circle clearing marking the entrance of the Delves.

Guardian was there waiting for her, contently chewing a mouthful of grass. She never had the need to hobble him in the Delves; it was as though he knew his place was here. Lily couldn't help but stroke his nose after she saddled him. The horse responded with a grunt and affectionately nibbled the top of her head.

"They will try to stop you," Vytria said. "The serpent boy most of all. But you must fight. You *must* get to Oremanse. There is no telling what the strain of two visions can do to your mind if you don't get to the Ara'Sa soon. Some falling object is hardly anything to lose sleep over, but this battle you saw, that is something the Order must know at once. All our lives could be in danger. May the Watcher bless you, child."

Lily climbed atop her saddle and secured the reins in her hand. Vytria gave one last look at both Guardian and her pupil as they turned away from the entrance to the Delves and began their journey back to Vita Astym. Lily didn't know if she would see Vytria again, but like an aimless dandelion seed, she found herself once again caught up in the breath of another great wind, carrying her off, just as she'd begun to take root.

Chapter 33

Vita Astym: Astymere
1ˢᵗ Day of the Fifth Month
5018 A.S.

HENRY KEPT HIS GAZE ON THE CIRCYM STREET, allowing his mind to drift while hardly bothering to hold Thuro's reins. Beatrice followed close behind, attended by two hundred Shadow Knights flying the white and black banner of the Crescent. All kept formation as though a battle drum governed their timing. The streets of the Mountain City, usually bustling, were practically deserted; not even a stray dog wandered across their path. The only sound other than hooves striking the paving stoves was the occasional leaf scraping by, caught by the light breeze. Every shop was closed, the gates to every inn barred shut. It seemed the city was holding its breath, preparing for a deep, impending plunge.

"You are certain of what he said, my dear?" Henry asked Beatrice, snapping himself back to the present. He now saw nothing but the task laid out before him.

He had killed Brisban every night in his dreams since his sentencing. He would have liked to add Qirk, Perry, and practically every other incompetent fool in charge of running the Academy besides Addam. Each night they all lost their heads in Henry's dreams because they had allowed his boys to come to harm—*real* harm. The Royal Marshal Academy was not a battlefield. The training was meant to be dangerous and challenging, to push its students toward mental and physical excellence, but this—he didn't even know where to begin. "The Malkauans?"

"Yes, my King," Beatrice replied. She rode in close enough to reach out and touch his arm; part of him wished she would. But now was not the time for private comforts. The king needed the aid of his steady queen, not that of his loving wife. "Sail Master Colbia seems to think Brisban could have amassed an army of ten thousand Malkauan raiders for the price of the blade galleys," she continued.

"Rahm's eyes. To think, ten thousand Malkauans smuggled onto our shores; it chills my blood." Henry was furious with himself. The great Karrok-Ahl, the man who finally destroyed the Raelian Empire, the commander who'd won countless battles and steered his kingdom through the most uncertain times in living memory—coming within a breath of dismantlement from within. How could he have come so close to allowing a foreign army to *sneak* onto Astymerian soil? The idea was maddening. "And you say he wouldn't command this army?" he asked.

"From what little I could gather, no," Beatrice replied. "The army was for someone else, but a fit took Brisban before I could get him to tell me who."

"If this army was to infiltrate our defenses and slip onto our shores, someone within our borders was meant to command it." Henry frowned. "I used to be able to know whom I could trust. Gods, it seems every smile these days is hiding a dagger."

"If I may speak, my King," Eduardas said as he rode in beside Henry and Beatrice with his daughters in tow. Lady Goldblade rode in on the opposite side, slowly nudging her way toward the queen. Eduardas gave an apologetic bow in his saddle for interrupting the royal conversation. Henry gave him a quick nod, keeping his eyes on the road.

"Forgive my intrusion," Eduardas said, "but I couldn't help overhear—I could have sworn you said Malkaua. As in the island kingdom? It lies on the edge of every known map, practically in the Untraveled Waters. What trouble could island dwelling savages be to you?"

Henry regarded him with icy rebuke. He was not quite as harsh as others in his attitude toward *uncivilized* nations, but very few were spared the elitism of those who hold power in the Republic.

"Malkaua is one of the strongest nations in the Great Marranthyne, Eduardas," Henry explained. "It is comprised of nearly one hundred islands that for centuries have ravaged their neighbors with thirst for blood and gold. When I was a boy, an envoy from the Malkauan King, Oahn, came to Vita Astym, seeking to open trade with us. We had made such attempts ourselves in centuries past, but our envoys were always turned away, some less civilly than others. Imagine our surprise when *they* came to *us*. My father nearly foamed at the mouth when he heard the proposal, but what they sought to trade made his stomach churn."

Eduardas raised an eyebrow. "You mean—"

"Astymere does *not* tolerate slavery, Eduardas," Henry interrupted, looking back to the road. "Oahn sought to sell captives they'd taken in their war with the Pilaean Empire. For twenty years the two island nations fought each other; Malkaua finally won after sacking the Pilaean capital of Makra Toli. They took thousands as slaves, hoping to fetch a handsome price in Astymerian markets. Little did they know that my father, King Harruld, would quite literally spit on their offer and send them running back to their ships."

"Something tells me that is not the end of the story," Olivia said, boldly joining the conversation. "My King," she added with a bow. Both Henry and her father glared at her. *Like father, like daughter.* She held his gaze, not fearlessly, but certainly with more resolve than he would have expected from a girl her age. Henry allowed a slight smile to curl his lips.

Henry nodded and continued. "Hardly a month passed before my father received word our trade fleets were being raided along the Marain Archipelago, which borders the waters controlled by Malkaua. The few who made it back told horrid tales of men being skinned alive before having their bodies thrown to sea; of men forced to swallow whole scorpions; of others being raped. All the while Astymerian ships burned and sank beneath the waves.

"My father wasted no time in striking back. He raised the royal fleet and set sail with twenty thousand men. Malkauans are fierce warriors, but they are not soldiers. No armor, no unity—no discipline. Outnumbering them two to one, my father cut through their canoes and longboats, struck the Malkauan capital of Mana'Lak, and razed it to the ground. We haven't had any dealings with them since, but it is no secret they hold no love for us. I feel it wouldn't be expensive to convince Oahn to strike up war once again for a chance at revenge."

"Security has been doubled in the last months, my love," Beatrice said reassuringly. "Nothing afoul has been reported in any of the port cities."

"For now," Henry replied. His eyes locked once again on the stone before him as shade of trees passed by overhead.

Southslope was absolutely still as Astrogol's Green rolled by to their left. Bees made a light, almost musical hum through the countless scarlet tulips that filled the grassy median dividing the

Circym Street, as a breeze rustled the thick green leaves overhead. Henry took notice of a light dusting of snow that sprinkled down, each tiny flake melting before it could land. Even on warm days, the winds that blew from Mount Karrok's summit brought some form of ice down with it—sometimes a subtle dusting like today, other times, a legitimate snow. Every few minutes a flake or two would reach Henry's hair, adding white to his graying mane.

In the days of old, an Avaari was thought weakened and drained of vitality if the jet black of his hair began to fail. Even his own father had gone to the grave without a single gray strand. But these were different times, with his hair the least of his worries. The Old Bruiser was truly living up to the name long ago given to him in jest.

OLIVIA HELD OUT HER HANDS to try to catch one tiny flake, but most melted before they could reach her; the rest were blown away. Her father and Henry began to talk low amongst themselves so as to keep their exchange private. She fell in beside Amy, who remained as much in the center of the formation as she could to keep her distance from the Shadow Knights. They still made Olivia uncomfortable, too, but before Mayson left for the Academy, he tried to acquaint her with some.

What she found most peculiar was that Mayson seemed to know exactly who each one was, even while they were wearing those ungodly helms. He introduced several, but the Knights never even seemed to acknowledge their own names. She found it difficult to fathom there were men living under those helmets— flesh under that coal black armor.

The protection they offered should have comforted her, but to this day, she still associated them with the mysterious door beneath the mountain. Every time she looked at one of them, she could hear the wailing echoing perfectly in her ears.

"They aren't really that bad, once you get used to them," Olivia said to Amy, who was trying to look anywhere but their direction. "They only *look* frightening."

"Mother says they are the mating of men and demons from the darkest, coldest pits of hell." It was nonsense to hear from a girl of sixteen, but Amy was terribly impressionable, especially where their mother was concerned. Olivia glanced forward to see

Attia was still out of earshot, practically next to the queen, throwing her head back as she laughed and lightly touched her hand to her chest.

"Mother is a fool," she said in a voice only Amy could hear. "They are men; that is all. Not ordinary men, but men all the same. *Try* to relax." Amy nodded sheepishly, keeping her eyes on the road.

"How are you holding up, ladies?"

The voice from behind gave Olivia a bit of a start, but Amy nearly jumped from her saddle. To Olivia's left rode a young man, perhaps a bit aged beyond his years. His light brown hair was thinning and puffy skin clouded his eyes, but his face was wrinkle-free. He wore a finely crafted black velvet suit and deep brown leather boots.

Clasped to his shoulders was a brilliant crimson silk cloak, and upon his chest, sewn in the same, crimson-colored thread, were two small, red eyes. *The eyes of Rahm.* For so long those eyes had haunted Olivia and made her skin crawl, but ever since her visit to Karna'Sharahm, she felt a soothing peace when she saw them.

The memory of a dream she had when she first reached Astymere came back to her. For so long she had forgotten it, but it all returned as clear as day: the shadowy figure, those horrible eyes, the piercing voice. Then came the deep voice that cradled her and covered her- those same red eyes had kept her safe.

Mayson's words on the matter were reassuring, if not shocking. He wrote to her that Rahm had shown her his favor, and that she must truly be pure of spirit if he had thrown his protective gaze upon her in the dream. She blushed when he added he'd always known there was something remarkable about her. *Casan never said anything so tender that wasn't about my beauty.*

Thoughts of Mayson and the eyes of Rahm drifted away as Olivia realized she had yet to reply to this new visitor; Amy was far too shy to speak herself.

"We are just fine, thank you, sir," she said at long last, embarrassed that she had remained silent. "I'm sorry, but have we met?"

"My apologies to *you*, my Lady. We met once before, but we were never formally introduced. My name is Addam Wallis, son of High Lord Raymund.”

“Of course. We met at the Academy some months ago when Mayson returned. Tell me, how is his final year treating him?”

“He is a true leader among the students,” Addam said with a smile. “Even among some of the staff. He will take to command as a bird takes to the sky.” Addam paused. “He talks often about you, my Lady. He wishes he could make himself write more, but he fears he might bore you. Though he takes great pride in it, he fears the work he does would appear tedious to an outsider. But he did ask me to stay by your side today—an execution is never an easy thing to witness. He says he wishes for nothing more than to be with you when it happens.”

“I don’t understand why this man can’t just sit in prison for the rest of his life,” Amy finally said. “Why must he be killed?”

A new speaker joined them on Amy’s right. “Because his crime has warranted such punishment, my Lady. He should thank whatever Gods that haven’t forsaken him our King has given him such mercy.”

Though a man grown, this one appeared younger than his companion, but both had the same sharp nose and slim face. While Addam had weary brown eyes, this newcomer had gray-blue ones filled with fire, and a thick, short beard highlighting his pointed chin.

“Ladies,” Addam said, “I introduce my brother, Droyan.”

“Couldn’t they give the man a chance to repent?” Amy cut in.

“There is no remorse nor plea that could save his life now,” said Addam. He seemed to grow even older in that moment, his shoulders slumping as a great deal of light left his eyes. “But if he *has* repented, perhaps his soul may be saved.”

“His soul is useless to me,” Droyan said defiantly. “His life is all I want. All anyone wants, really. It is the only punishment suitable for spilling the blood of a High Lord—even more so than being sent Below.”

Olivia shifted in her saddle, dreading what the near future held. She brushed a loose strand of hair from her face and tightened her grip on the reins.

On they went, unobstructed and undisturbed by anything more than the occasional cat wandering in front of the party’s path. Henry continued his conversation with Eduardas for a time before openly sending for Lords Rahmos and Wallis. Once Brisban's sentence had been carried out, Henry would depart with two hundred riders for the Great Plains, and there was much to discuss.

From what Olivia gathered, it was decided that, as always, Urnest would sit upon the throne as the Guardian in Henry's absence, given Mayson was still bound to his service at the Academy. Raymund, by whatever means he was capable, was charged with rooting out the rest of Brisban's supporters who eluded capture after he was taken into custody.

The Circym Street soon wound its way past Almyn's Quarter and into the Westward Boroughs, the unofficial divide between South and Westslope. They hadn't gone more than several blocks before the plentiful room around them suddenly closed in. The streets of Westslope were not as wide as South, forcing the formation to ride more tightly than Amy would've preferred.

Small crowds meandered across the pavement here, each face bearing frustration and disappointment. Olivia could hear grumbling of how unfair it was, with others chastising their companions, for they would have been able to find room in the Bazeira to watch the execution if they had gotten there earlier.

Despite their arguing, not one among them failed to make way for the royal company. As each pair of eyes fell on the king, every person bent the knee, proudly reciting the ancient words of love for the Crown: *Cayrian Karrok.*

Henry raised his hand in respect and even saluted some who were veterans of the Black Army, recognizable by their swords and the dignified posture with which they carried themselves, despite their age. The crowds grew thicker as Henry led his small contingent west along the Baz'Styr, the main artery leading from Mount Karrok to the Bazeira, the largest market in the Western world after the destruction of the White City. Nearly one-hundred thousand people already gathered there, each of them itching to see a traitor lose his head. Many of them had likely been wronged by him directly. There would not be a single voice begging for mercy on his behalf; Olivia was sure of it.

The Bazeira was a wide-open square that ran nearly half a mile in each direction, usually filled with tents, stands, and pavilions of all sizes and colors, bearing every kind of wares imaginable. Mayson told Olivia that at its birth, it was little more than a handful of farmers that gathered from the surrounding countryside. As Astymere's trading prowess grew, so did the Bazeira, tent by tent, shop by shop, until it became a sea of shouts, smells, and coins.

But today the great market stood empty, aside from the crowd that had amassed around a large, round dais at its center. One thousand Silver Shields assembled there to keep order among the observers. The citizens of Vita Astym were not a particularly rowdy bunch, but in numbers like these, very many things could go wrong. If just one person lost control, mayhem might spread.

The Shields formed two lines leading from the eastern side of the Bazeira straight to the dais, splitting the crowd to allow a path for Henry and his party. As they began their passage through the throng to the rounded, two-leveled dais, each group separated into their proper order. First went King Henry and Queen Beatrice, followed closely by High Lord Urnest Rahmos and Lady Gloria, accompanied by their sons Tyrel and Jalen.

Next were High Lord Raymund Wallis and Lady Dawn, accompanied by their sons Addam and Droyan, then finally the Goldblades, mixed with the rest of the Royal Council and their families. Evan Mikkel required a thunder stallion to support his frame, and High Priest Rhivor, holding his head high and keeping his face solemn, rode a garron that was just as lean as he was. Like a sea of tipping tiles, the crowd all fell before Henry, knees bent and voices raised. *Cayrian Karrok*! Thousands upon thousands of voices cascaded in sequence, making it nearly impossible to distinguish one salute from another.

Henry dismounted first and, while handing Thuro's reins to an attendant appearing from the sea of faces, offered his hand to Beatrice as she slid nimbly from Aranqa. The queen scanned the crowd as she took her place upon the lower level of the dais. Henry kissed her hand and continued upward to take his place at the center.

The Shadow Knights took position around the base of the dais, their ranks four men deep, while the rest of the group took their respective places upon the raised platform.

"Olivia," Beatrice said. "Stand with me, and take my hand." Olivia squeezed through the group as politely and gracefully as she could to grasp the queen's outstretched hand. "The waiting is the worst of it."

Olivia surveyed the onlookers. Their utter lack of fear or even discomfort unsettled her. Executions were uncommon in Gildara, and public executions were even rarer. In those instances, the crime of the guilty was considered so severe that they were forced to pay their penance through pain. Her father said on more than one occasion that the screams of the victim could be heard anywhere in the city up to a quarter mile from the square. Her stomach began to churn at that thought.

"How will it happen?" she asked.

"The king will take his head, dear," Beatrice replied, rather matter-of-factly. She wrapped her right arm around Olivia's shoulders and drew her close. "It will take mere moments."

"I don't know if I can watch," Olivia said, her voice beginning to shake. Her heart hadn't pounded this hard since she had gone Below, and her breath was beginning to escape her.

"Fear not. I imagine this will be easier for you than you think." Beatrice gave her an amused smile, and lightly squeezed her arm.

Trumpets began to sound from the east, somewhere near the base of the mountain. The Bazeira had gone as quiet as Karna'Sharahm, and the only movement that could be seen was the rustling of cloaks and skirts in the light mountain breeze.

As the trumpets approached, the sound of drums came with them. Louder and louder they grew until the music filled every tiny space between bodies, flowing and crashing between onlookers like an all-consuming tidal wave. Then she saw it. A lone Knight of Rahm passed into the boundary of the Bazeira, his arms held aloft, holding a fine, black silk bundle. Ten warriors of the Black Army followed behind him, sabers held at attention across their chests, shields swinging in their left arms as they marched.

Next came four men carrying a large boulder that had been perfectly flattened on the bottom, with two large golden handles bolted into its sides. The top sported a shallow groove with a deep, dark stain running straight to the bottom. Last to cross into the Bazeira were two score trumpeters and drummers, like lightning and thunder incarnate. *Stars, shine on me this day. Shield me with your light.*

As the Knight carrying the bundle passed through the throng, the crowd not only bent the knee, but fell to both knees, holding their hands out on the ground before them in utter supplication. Olivia noticed even the Silver Shields—and to her shock, the previously frozen Shadow Nights—dropped arms and fell in the same manner before the lone traveler as he made his way to the dais.

Queen Beatrice and the High families did the same, prompting Olivia to drop with an uncomfortable *thud*. From the corner of her eye, she saw the only man left standing among the revelers was King Henry himself.

He stood silhouetted against the afternoon sky, his black cloak flying effortlessly about him with hardly more than a light breeze. It reminded Olivia of the first time she ever saw Mayson on the Royal Highway. Her lip quivered and her breath quickened at the thought. *Mayson will look like that one day. One man amongst millions who kneel. He will* be *that man one day, and* you *will be far from here.*

Henry unwrapped the bundle slowly, revealing inch by inch the black smooth steel within. Rahmirion looked flawless, and the king appeared to smile at her as he would an old friend. Taking her firmly in his right hand, he raised her high above his head, the dazzling reflectiveness of her black steel shining with godly brilliance. Moving as one entity, the crowd rose to its feet, as did the Shields, Shadow Knights, and honored viewers on the dais below him.

Olivia had half-missed it before she realized what she was hearing. When the king passed through the crowd earlier, the salutes to House Karrok were shouted in many voices, each cry piling atop the voice before it. This salute, however, was in unison, as if the crowd's voice was that of the green land itself. *Cayrian Karrok! Cayrian Rahma!*

With a flick of his wrist, Rahmirion sprang to life, and with a sharp, downward thrust, Henry planted her diamond shaped counterweight blade into the center of the dais. He gestured to the crew carrying the Kutshadahl, the Stone of the King's Justice, to bring it before him. Their trip up the stairs was slow and deliberate; Olivia could hear the grunting, huffing, and puffing of each man lugging the weighty boulder to the top. When they finally set it down, Olivia thought the whole dais might crash beneath it, but to her relief, it stood strong and true.

"Bring forth the condemned!" Henry declared to the crowd, earning an approving roar. Olivia thought the trumpets and drums had been loud, but now, Olivia felt the crowd might deafen her.

As the din died down, new sounds could be heard: hoofbeats and creaking of wheels. They crossed into the Bazeira, nothing more than distant shapes. Olivia could make out two riders, and behind them, a great wagon filled with straw, pulled by two bulls, black and white. A post stood in the middle of the wagon, supporting what looked like a scarecrow held in place by chains. The cart soon halted before the dais.

Olivia was trying so hard to get a look at Brisban that she barely noticed the wave of bows that preceded the newcomers. She did not register the snow-white skin of one rider and the impossibly bright golden sword hilt of the other. It wasn't until she could see his starlit eyes and curly black locks that Olivia finally knew who he was.

Mayson didn't seem to see her; he and Diero didn't seem to see anyone but Henry. Mayson held himself as though he were a king already, the sight of it making Olivia's loins burn with shame. She shot a heated glance at Droyan and Addam, who each returned a smile.

Mayson and Diero dismounted as one and sent their horses off. Side by side, the two climbed the stairs to meet Henry at the crown of the dais. Both fell to their knees and placed their hands and heads against the ground.

"Cayrian Karrok. Cayrian Rahma," they said in unison.

"Rise, my sons," said Henry. The two moved like liquid and, with a nod from Henry, Mayson took his place with the others while Diero remained still. He spoke as if he had rehearsed the words for this solemn ceremony for weeks.

"Great Karrok-Ahl," Diero began with a bow. It wasn't the voice Olivia knew; it was that of his lordly mask. "I present to you the condemned. He stands before you, proven guilty of high treason and grand theft. What is your will, my King?"

"The Crown declares he shall die this day."

"Your will be done, my King," Diero said with a final, deep bow.

With official business concluded, Mayson moved straight to Olivia's side, as though he had seen her from the moment he entered the Bazeira. He didn't embrace her, but he did take her arm, wrapping it in his. Henry began his speech as the two whispered discreetly.

"I thought you couldn't be here today?" she scolded. Keeping his eyes on the crowd, Mayson smiled with pride and gave her hand a tender squeeze.

"Brisban is *our* prisoner. It was our responsibility to present him before the King. Besides, this is more ugliness than you should face alone."

A bashful smile spread across his face, the same one he always gave when overstepping his bounds. He stroked her hand lightly as she clutched his tighter and leaned in closer to his body. She wondered if he could feel her trembling.

"Bring him before me!" Henry cried, his speech now finished. The calm veil that had fallen over the crowd lifted; angry and hateful shouts filled the air, some with language that made Olivia blush. Bits of rotten food, refuse, and countless pieces of unimaginable filth were hurled through the air, all aimed at the traitor's head.

Brisban, his arms bound behind his back, was already moving, led by a chain around his neck. Olivia figured they'd unfastened him during Henry's speech, of which she did not hear a word. Brisban was covered in grime, dressed in little more than a burlap sack, with dusty, matted hair falling to his shoulders and a beard down to his chest. This wasn't the man Mayson described, but it was the man he truly was.

The Shadow Knights who had taken hold of him placed him behind the Kutshadahl, facing the crowd. His face was indignant; he acted as if today was only a minor inconvenience. Henry raised his hand and the crowd fell silent once again, waiting for the inevitable.

"Geremy Brisban," Henry said without looking at him. "For your crimes against the Crown and the people of Astymere, you have hereby been sentenced to death. Do you have any words before the sentence is carried out?"

The voice that crept out of the haggard man sounded as though it hadn't been used in months, but it wasn't the sound of his voice that chilled Olivia's blood: it was the words he spoke.

"And so comes the Great Awakening. The eyes of the Beast, long held shut, shall open once again. In his dark gaze shall this world be remade, and the light of the stars be extinguished. In his black flame shall the world of man be consumed, and the last will of the gods be blown to the winds of time, scattered as dust. Woe to the world of the living, for the power of the Beast is eternal. Woe to the Heavenly, who shall be cast down. Woe to the Worldly, whose flesh shall feed new life into the cold fires of Hell. And so comes the Great Awakening; leave all memory of light behind."

He was reciting the Second Flame, a passage from the Book of the Beast, the unholy doctrine of the damned. It was often recited in the Temples of the Heavenly, to warn against the Beast's power and prepare man for the doom his Awakening would bring.

The throng stood aghast. Hardly any of them had ever read a word of the High Testament, Olivia knew, but it appeared all knew the words of the Second Flame. Every breath was stolen away.

"The black eyes of Vasurahn see you all, yet they remain closed," Brisban shouted. "What more shall they see when they finally open? The Second Coming is at hand! Weep for your gods! Weep for your stars! Weep as the Dominion is reborn and the Spirit undone!"

"Enough!" Henry ordered, easily overpowering Brisban's feeble voice. "Put him down."

Quick as snakes, the Shadow Knights forced Brisban's neck down onto the stone, but even their steel grip could not stop his last words, which seemed directed at Henry alone.

"May Rahm weep for you, old man, as your progeny will weep for Rahm."

With a snarl and a ferocious cry, Henry swung Rahmirion to silence the man's poison. His neatly severed head landed with a wet *splat* on the waiting stone. His blood seemed more black than red as it oozed and poured down the Kutshadahl, causing any who were near it to shy away.

Mayson drew Olivia into his chest to shield her from the sight as Diero moved to retrieve the head, still bearing the same dirty grin Brisban wore throughout his days of service to the Crown. He held it aloft for the roaring crowd to revile.

"It is done," Henry said, tired and troubled. "Get this pile of shit out of my sight."

Brisban's lifeless hands were unbound and his arms hung loose, with the exception of an occasional twitch.

Eduardas, along with the others, had moved to take leave down the stairs when Brisban's body was brought past him. Eduardas took one look at the headless corpse and suddenly went limp as a boned fish, dropping on the spot. Henry commanded two Knights of Rahm to take him from the dais and fetch a wagon, along with a cool cloth for his head.

Brisban's body was dumped into the hay-filled carriage to be brought back to Canlon for burning, his arms splayed out to his sides. And there, in the clear light of day, the sun shone down on the pronounced black *V* upon his wrist.

Chapter 34

The Royal Marshal Academy: Astymere
35th Day of the Sixth Month
5018 A.S.

MAYSON AND DIERO FINISHED SUPPER and walked back to the barracks to rest before their guard shift atop the perimeter wall. The Marshal had been stubbornly uncooperative regarding the boys' leave for Brisban's execution, demanding they be back at first light the next day, lest they liked the idea of shifts atop the wall each night until graduation. The last month had intensified their burning desire to move on and put as much distance between themselves and Qirk as possible.

They would be working through the dark hours, which were fit to be plagued with biting, harsh winds blowing from the north. When Addam saw the boys walking across campus, he advised they dress accordingly. It was predicted the entire Northern Tip would be gripped by chilling weather for the majority of the week, with frigid gusts coming off the bay turning any small breeze into a storm's tail end. The boys had packed their heavy fur cloaks by demand of the queen. Though they protested at the time, they were grateful now for the extra layer.

Mayson lay on his back, feeling the warm stew swish around in his belly, while Diero read a book on the art of sword forging. They hadn't spoken since their return from the mess hall, knowing they would have plenty of time to talk all night.

The younger students typically received night shifts, leaving the more experienced warriors to rest. Mayson and Diero couldn't fight it, though, for they had been late to their first class that morning only to lose their afternoon watch to Grayle Boreck.

Two years their junior, Grayle was among the strongest and tallest of warriors at the Academy. He had cultivated his own followers and was quickly becoming a nuisance to the pair. No matter how many times they bested him, he always came back for more, like a mindless rooster driven by blind instinct.

"Anyone is better than Blayk," Diero had said with a chuckle. It was true. Both boys enjoyed an easier existence with Brentin Kallyst and Blayk Mortryn already graduated. Kallyst had lashed out from embarrassment over the beating Mayson gave him during their first encounter, but Grayle, on the other hand, was truly hungry to strike the two down. He never seemed to learn his place.

Mayson had his eyes closed, thinking of Olivia as clearly as if she were standing over him. Her hair was alive, blowing in the wind, as wild as it was the day he first saw her. He thought of her scent and tried to force it from his memory, to no avail. Sharra Ahl-Kalin, the woman he was sworn to marry, was also beautiful, her knowing eyes—mirrors of his own—always analyzing his heart and mind, her pitch-black hair always done up in a complex braid. Visions of the two women rattled around in his head and made his stomach twist.

Diero broke the prince from his thoughts, muttering the same lines he had all day. "Five days before the Final Test, three before our Final Fights at the Kastigra, and Qirk insults us this way. Years of faithful service, and one strike of tardiness lands us grunt work. How are we supposed to rest if we are exhausted all week? If I were you, I'd be thinking of ways to repay his *kindness* once you come into your crown."

Mayson didn't react anymore; Diero merely shook his head and flipped to the next page. Ever since the attempt on Diero's life, the entire royal family had run out of its short supply of favor for the Royal Marshal. But Mayson knew from a lifetime of watching his father that an unjust king was a doomed king—which was why Henry allowed him to keep his post when all was said and done. The prince once again attempted to relax, closing his eyes and folding his hands over his chest, rising and dipping with each breath.

Minutes passed before he opened his eyes again, this time at the sound of the door creaking open on its old hinges. Grayle and his crew were returning from their afternoon watch and carried the thick smell of beef stew with them into the barracks. Grayle stopped between the foot of the brothers' beds, the rest of his crew forming a half-circle behind him.

"If this Kingdom is lucky enough, you'll freeze to death," he said coldly. "Or, the wind will blow our scrawny prince off the wall and into the water." His smug followers laughed and enthusiastically clapped his solid back. *Kiss asses.*

"Scrawny?" Mayson responded with a smile that hid his insult. Diero hadn't even removed his eyes from the pages in front of him. It was true: Grayle outweighed Mayson by nearly twenty-five pounds, but whatever muscle he had was wrapped in soft, lumpy flesh, despite the diet the Marshal had him on. Mayson's body looked like it had been carved from solid marble in comparison. His strength far surpassed the younger man's, as did his speed and experience. But he played along. "I prefer slim, but I hardly imagine *you* are the standard of what a *man's* body should look like." He put extra bite on the end. Bait for a beast too dumb to see the obvious trap. "I'd sooner see your dough baked and boiled than have you slowing my men down in the heat of battle. I doubt your heart would even get you through the first skirmish."

The laughing stopped as Grayle approached Mayson's bedside and leaned against it. "You're good with words, but that's easy. One day all you'll have to do is wave your hand and *real* men will march off to do your fighting for you."

Diero still looked upon his book and flipped a page. "Why send others when we can kill just about anyone ourselves? Or must we show you again?"

"I'm a slow learner," Grayle said, his eyes growing dark. He leaned down to speak in Diero's ear. "Thick skull, you know."

Mayson rose from his bed with the speed of a tightly wound bowstring, grabbing hold of Grayle's wrist and the back of his neck. His iron grip bent the boy to his will. Grayle's cronies all lurched toward Mayson, but one fiery look stopped them in their tracks. He yanked Grayle to the left, placing the boy between himself and his gang.

"One more step and he never uses this arm again," Mayson warned.

Once Grayle's whimpers were the only sound to be heard, Mayson whispered in his ear. "Enough effort, and even the thickest skull can crack," Mayson spat. "We're *done* playing with you, boy. Let it go."

Mayson released his grip on Grayle's neck and used his leverage on his wrist to push him to the ground, right at the feet of his followers. With a deathly glare, Grayle pushed his way through his crew and skulked off to his corner of the barracks. The rest sheepishly filed off one by one.

The brothers knew any moment a member of the Green Cloaks, the Academy guards, would come to retrieve them for their watch. Diero continued reading while Mayson lay back down and closed his eyes. He thought for a moment about the Final Test in a few days' time. Years after their admittance to the Academy, they still hadn't a clue as to what would come. Revealing the secret would only result in the immediate and permanent expulsion from the Black Army, regardless of rank.

The door creaked, and a weary looking sentry entered, followed by frigid wind. His long green cloak trailed on the ground, the tail end fluttering outside.

"Carovensa, Karrok, on your feet," he ordered in a deeply unkind voice. He scanned them and realized they hadn't yet prepared for their watch. "You have sixty seconds to dress properly and meet me outside that door. A second longer and you'll be atop the wall again tomorrow night."

The pair shot out of their beds and threw on their boots without lacing them. They grabbed their fur cloaks and draped them over their shoulders, covering their whole bodies in the only warmth they'd know for the rest of the night. Mayson tied a single knot to secure it around his broad shoulders and stepped outside, Diero still hobbling into a boot as they moved.

The stone barrier, five stories high, encompassed the very edge of the island, and despite its size, did little to shield Mayson and Diero from the relentless gusts. Diero clutched his cloak tight as the older sentry marched off, comfortable that the boys were well acquainted with their duties. Mayson closed his eyes and let the wind pull at his hair and cloak, allowing it to blow away his bubbling annoyance with Grayle. He took deep breaths to savor the salty air.

The boys trudged up the circular stairway that seemed more like a wind tunnel, their torch flames flickering in the gusts, and came to a narrow walkway atop the battlements that encircled the island. The cool mist from the breaking waves was now freezing and did not yield the entire first hour of their watch.

They walked together, side by side, occupying the full width of the path. The two other men they periodically encountered would have to pass one-by-one for the two groups to get by each other. Mayson faced out to the black ocean, watching the stars reflect off the water in the distant horizon. He thought of Olivia and hoped she was well in the Capital.

It had been over a month since they'd last seen each other.

Mayson, you are the Crown Prince. All you have to do is choose her, and it will be done. She is not of royal blood, but she is noble. Father would understand. Simply declare you won't marry Sharra, and there is no force in the world that will compel you.

Mayson was nearly resolved in his decision until he remembered. *She is promised to another. She is not yours to choose.* Then, another darker thought arose, raising goose pimples as it took root. *The Elders already say I'm not truly Avaari. What would they do if I were to wed one not of the tribe? What would they do to me, to* her*, if I spurned the daughter of one of the Council?* The thought made him shudder more deeply than the wind ever could. His spirits fell as he set his eyes against the dark stone, a single tear rolling down his cheek as his small hope was finally snuffed out.

The rest of the night was spent in relative silence, at least on Mayson's part. Diero was never one to shy away from one-sided conversations, but his efforts were now few and far between, for which Mayson was grateful. Behind his blustering and puffed out chest, Diero was exceptionally good at reading people; he seemed to realize pulling Mayson from his sullen introspection was a lost cause.

The sky remained clear throughout the night, making for quite a spectacular sunrise. Mayson could hardly believe how much time had passed when life and color slowly began to bleed into the sky above. But when he gave his legs a good shake, he realized how stiff and frozen his knees had become in the nightly chill.

"I am dying for a hot bath and stew," Diero said as they descended the circular staircase, stepping out onto the frostbitten grass. Mayson stepped slowly, savoring the small crunches he made as he moved. They walked past the Temple of Red Flame, heading toward the barracks. The Temple seemed to emanate its own glow in the early morning light.

"A bath sounds good. I'm not very hungry though," Mayson replied.

"Your appetite is usually the first thing to go when you get like this," Diero said knowingly. "Mayson, maybe you wouldn't feel so bad if you just talked about what was bothering you once in a while."

Mayson sighed weakly, looked up at the orange sunrise, then

turned to face Diero. He could look quite pensive when he wasn't sporting an insufferable grin.

"I'm just realizing more and more that I have *no* choices, Diero. Everything I do and will do has been pre-determined for me. I have long accepted that in regard to being king, but—I never fully considered what it meant to be forbidden to love freely."

Diero nodded, patting Mayson's shoulder. "I know, brother. I haven't slept right since Lily said she was leaving. If it makes you feel any better, I, too, have been fighting the urge to follow wherever she goes. There are times it comes boiling to the surface like magma…"

"Diero…"

"I know, I know. But you can't possibly blame me. As if *you* haven't been thinking of ways to make Olivia yours all night, without suffering the inevitable consequences. And believe me, there would be plenty."

Mayson lost the argument in his throat before it ever reached his mouth. Diero was right. More than one king had been struck down by enraged Elders throughout the ages. It was foolish to think he could escape such a fate. He sighed, nodded, and unclasped his cloak, letting it hang loose and free about his shoulders.

"I used to think our position meant freedom," Diero said after a few minutes. "That we could do whatever we wanted. Strange how you never see the other edge of the sword until it's already sliced you open."

For the first time in what seemed like days, Mayson chuckled, soft and low. Diero smiled so warmly at him that, for a moment, things didn't seem so grim. Mayson embraced him tightly.

"Thank you, brother. Now, let us boil away our sorrows."

"I hope they've replenished the coal stores for the baths. I want to *burn*," Diero replied as they continued on toward the barracks and Baths.

But then, Mayson stopped in his tracks, every muscle in his body rigid as stone. His eyes went wide, and his ears twitched. The air was calmer now, with hardly any wind to interfere with his sharp hearing.

"What…" Diero began.

"*Shhhhh*," Mayson hissed. The sound was coming from the

rear of the building, soft and hushed, but to Mayson, it was clear as a bell. "Follow me."

The two took off along the side of the barracks like a pair of deer, bounding along the grass with grace and speed. Mayson's cloak caught the air and flew off his shoulders, nearly hitting Diero, who unfastened and released his own when he began to fall behind.

"Mayson," he called. "This is the *last* thing I want to be doing right now!"

The sound grew stronger now, more urgent, more desperate. Mayson stretched his legs as far as they would tolerate, his heart pounding so hard within his chest he could hear it in his ears.

Mayson and Diero rounded the corner of the barracks and nearly charged right into the source of the sound. Grayle and his cronies had surrounded Brynden Ashford, a small first-year student who had barely stuck the last term out. He was a bright lad, big hearted and studious, but did not have much aptitude for physical combat. Despite Mayson's best efforts to tutor him, he simply lacked the warrior's spirit, and Mayson knew it would only be a matter of time before he was sent home.

Brynden was on his knees, his arms raised in a shield over his head. Blood dripped from his nose and mouth, and tears streamed from his eyes. Grayle stood over him, clenching a bloody fist tightly to his body, coiled to strike again. They were all still in their nightclothes. Grayle sported a large black stain on his shirt that spread onto his arm, neck, and shoulder.

"Please," Brynden pleaded, spitting out a mouthful of blood. "It was an accident! I didn't mean it, I *swear*!"

"Look what you did to my shirt and sheets, you little fuck!" Grayle raised his fist.

"*What do you think you're doing*?" Mayson bellowed with such force it strained his throat. His eyes were locked on Grayle, and for a moment, the whole world seemed to stop. The lot of them turned and nearly stumbled over themselves in shock, falling behind their leader to distance themselves from the newcomers. Only Grayle seemed unbothered by their presence.

"This little shit dumped a bottle of ink on me while I was sleeping—after I was *gracious* enough to let him borrow it." Grayle was fuming.

"By Rahm's eyes, I swear, it was an accident, my Prince. I'd run out…trying to write my father…and I spilled it…" It was all pouring out of the boy with such terror it nearly broke Mayson's heart. Mayson raised a gentle hand to stop the boy's blubbering.

"Diero," he said, "please take Brynden back inside and alert Master Wallis of what's happened." Mayson beckoned Brynden to join them. The boy scrambled on his hands and knees to cover the distance as quickly as possible until he was at Mayson's feet. Mayson scooped him up by his nightshirt and dusted him off. The poor boy barely stood up to the prince's chin, and Grayle had half a head on Mayson. *Disgraceful*, he thought as the boy wiped his nose and mouth.

"Thank you," Brynden said, fighting back fresh tears. "Thank you, my Prince."

"Think nothing of it," Mayson replied, with as warm a smile as he could manage despite his building rage.

"We've been in your shoes before," Diero said, placing a guiding hand on the boy's shoulder, "but we never had anyone come to our aid. Now, let's be quick. The prince may need *my* aid in a minute or two." Diero ushered the boy through the back door of the barracks, letting it slam shut behind him.

"You've got a lot of nerve…" Grayle began.

"Don't you *dare* lecture me," Mayson interrupted. "I tolerate your foolishness when you aim it at me, Grayle, but I will *not* stand for you terrorizing a child. I'll see the lot of you expelled for this."

"Like hell!" Grayle charged Mayson with every ounce of frustration he had, but he was as slow as he looked. Mayson had plenty of time to decide between sidestepping the attack or meeting it with his own.

He was running toward Grayle before he even realized what he was doing. Ducking a wild haymaker, Mayson put all his weight on his back heel and drove a straight shot into Grayle's solar plexus, forcing all the air out of him in a wet cough. The oafish boy tumbled like a freshly chopped tree. When he fell to his knees, Mayson gave him a straight kick to his chest to knock him onto his back. Before he could raise his fist to strike again, a firm hand gripped his right shoulder. With blind instinct, Mayson's left hand shot for the assailant's wrist and twisted with all his power, earning a satisfying *pop*. He continued to twist until his attacker was on the ground in front of him. Mayson knelt down on the boy's right arm and sent his right elbow crashing into the side of his head, putting him out.

Then, when a straight kick knocked him onto his back, Mayson rolled to his feet in the same instant, using the momentum to propel himself. Two of Grayle's cronies rushed him now. He didn't know them. He couldn't even tell if he had seen their faces before. They may as well have had no faces at all—they were targets, and Mayson wasted no time. The attacker on his right struck with a straight kick, but by the time it reached Mayson, he had already moved to strike the attacker on his left with a vicious head-butt square between the eyes, cracking his nose and spraying blood into the morning air. The other hadn't recovered from his missed kick before Mayson sent a spinning kick of his own into the side of his head.

Another in Grayle's group tried his luck, charging out of the cluster with manic energy and an uncertain look in his eyes. He swung wildly for Mayson's head, who ducked with ease to come up and grasp the boy's throat in his right hand. The boy's eyes went wide and his mouth fell open, giving him the look of a beached fish. Red began to flood the edges of Mayson's vision when the thought of picking the boy up and slamming him into the grass, smacking the back of his head into the ground, felt dull and weak. Instead, he released the boy, leaving him choking for air.

Grayle was just getting to his feet as Mayson locked in on him like a prairie wolf stalking its prey. No one else dared step in now. Grayle had barely raised his fists before Mayson launched a devastating shot into his jaw, shooting several molars into the air as he fell. Mayson was on top of him now, his vision growing blurrier. He could feel his arms rising and falling, his fists colliding with flesh. All sound was drowned out by Mayson's pounding heart, until…

"*MAYSON!*"

The voice stabbed Mayson in the back, the world suddenly crashing back in around him like a breaking wave. His hands hurt, his chest rose and fell in rapid succession, and his throat felt as if he'd swallowed a torch. He turned to see Diero, pale as a ghost, standing among Grayle's survivors. He looked at the bodies littered around the yard, most of them rolling and moaning. The others lay so still he couldn't tell if they were dead or alive.

"Mayson," Diero whispered as he stepped toward Mayson like he was a mad horse. "You don't want to do this."

Mayson looked down to find his forearm pressed tight against Grayle's throat, his near lifeless hands feebly gripping at him. His nose was shattered, as was one cheek, and both eyes were swollen shut with deep cuts over his eyebrows. Mayson removed his arm and rolled off his victim; Grayle desperately sucked in air and wretched in wet heaves.

Mayson stumbled to his feet and slowly approached Diero. "Are you alright?" he asked.

"I don't think so," Mayson croaked. "I think I need to lie down."

"Let's get out of here; Addam and the guards will be here any minute."

"No. It's best I stay here and await their questions." Every word felt like a piece of glass sliding around in his throat. Had he been screaming the whole time?

Mayson sat on the grass rather clumsily; Diero soon joined him. The rest of Grayle's group ran off as soon as Diero mentioned Addam Wallis, but Grayle still lay on his side, weeping. The sun shone on their backs as they sat in silence.

"Is Brynden all right?" Mayson asked.

"Yes. Nothing a little ice and bandages won't fix."

"Good," Mayson said as the alarm bells began to ring. It wouldn't be long now. In that moment, their harsh, monotonous clanging seemed sweeter than a birdsong. Mayson gingerly rubbed his hands and flexed his fingers to make sure he hadn't broken anything. They were sore, but they were whole, and Grayle's blood was beginning to dry, painting them a dirty brown in the morning light. "Good."

Chapter 35

The Dead Lands: The Great Plains
35th Day of the Sixth Month
5018 A.S.

Henry brushed ten layers of gray dust from his pants while his squire, Colt, applied his armor. His tent had done well to shut out the howling winds that plagued the blasted empty landscape, but somehow the ever-abundant dust still found its way inside in piles. He slipped his layer of black steel mail over his woolen undershirt, then held his arms out patiently as Colt fastened similar colored vambraces to his wrists. Colt then moved to fasten Henry's breastplate and clip his shadow-silk cloak upon his broad shoulders.

Henry insisted on dressing himself from the waist down, strapping his cuisses and poleyns to rest seamlessly with the tops of his boots. Grasping his crowned helm under his arm, the king then left his attendants to pack his tent, folding and tying it in such ways that the small pavilion appeared little more than a sleeping bundle.

Four hundred souls scurried through the ankle-thick dust, practically mindless of each other, all focused on their tasks to strike camp and move north. King Henry had brought two hundred riders with him to Roleigh, each of them seasoned warriors of the Black Army, with a select few trained by the sword and the lance. They had joined Prince Ronin's two hundred Sworn Hooves, and ever since the party left Dalan's capital, incursions with northern trespassers was nearly a daily occurrence.

Ronin and Henry found them in small pockets of no more than ten at first, but after a week into their hunt, the numbers grew. As they traveled further toward the Great Divide, they found themselves riding down clusters of fifteen, twenty, even thirty at a time, each man armed and armored as though already at war.

The party should have reached the forest of Casaack over a week ago, but each time one group was dealt with, Ronin's trackers picked up the trail of another, pulling them out of their way.

The most serious fighting occurred three days ago, when the riders repelled an attack on the small village of Ostetyn on the eastern border of Dalan. Henry lost five men that night; Ronin, seven. They were now driven by thirst for vengeance, each man swearing to either purge the land of every northern savage or die trying.

When both Henry and Ronin were satisfied that the men who had penetrated Dalan were dealt with, they steered their course hard east to the blasted shell of the Black City to take the Septaerine Road north, leaving smoking, crumbling walls in the distance behind them.

At the pace Henry set, they were now less than a day's ride from the Acrontian River, the former lifeblood of the northern Raelian Empire. Ronin was leading them northeast to the Turin Fords, where their passage would be easiest and the waters not as deathly cold to cross.

Henry found Ronin tying packs to the back of his saddle as he gave orders to Commander Haledon and Captain Eldric, his second-in-command.

"Onka and his scouts will remain behind until midday to cover our crossing," Ronin said. "Once we're across, I want riders scouting ahead. We've had no reports from north of the river since the last expedition, and I will *not* be caught unaware. Have Malyx take Corporal Caltrys, round up his lightest riders, and inform them they are to leave ahead of us."

"As you command, my Prince," Haledon said in his low, gruff voice. Time had done little to age the seasoned commander, and with hardly any effort, he was in the saddle and gone.

Ronin leaned in close to Eldric to speak in his ear, but upon seeing Henry, the prince's brilliant green eyes flashed, eager and energetic.

"Your Majesty! I've been meaning to speak with you," Ronin shouted. "There is no longer any use in avoiding your troubling words."

"I'm not sure I understand, Ronin," Henry said.

"I'd nearly forgotten what you told me back in Roleigh, but you said your Treasurer, Eduardas, had seen a black 'V' upon the traitor you executed, and that he had seen it before the attempt on his *own* life in the Republic, yes?"

Henry nodded with a growl. "When he told me about Brisban, I examined the man myself. It was upon his wrist, clear as day."

"What did Eduardas tell you about this man, Vasur?" Ronin

clasped his hands behind his back.

"He told me only what he knew—what anyone in the Republic knows. That he is some kind of conjurer. Eduardas had heard his name a handful of times, usually tied to some murder or theft, with most believing him to be a lowly gangster who dabbles in alchemy or some unsavory dark art."

"Is that what Eduardas thinks?"

"He…isn't sure. Those who are more superstitious think he marks the resurgence of the Vul Dakkar—and to walk out of an explosion unscathed *is* most unnatural."

The Vul Dakkar, the Tainted Ones, had been gone for nearly one-thousand years by the time the first stone of the White City was mortared in place. Once Te'Relecti, the great sorcerers of the ancient world who were granted the gift of wielding the power of the Gods, they were twisted and corrupted by the Beast's influence, binding their souls to him. For centuries, they wreaked havoc upon the world of man, even after the Beast was sealed into the depths of Hell. The possibility of just one roaming free in the world made the hair on the back of Henry's neck stand on end.

"Why do you mention this, Ronin? What trouble does Vasur cause you?" Henry asked wearily, having lost the warm feeling of a full night's sleep.

Ronin eyed Eldric, reluctant to answer. When he finally met Henry's sharp blue eyes, he gazed resolutely with the nerve and fortitude expected of a future king. "Your Majesty, Vasur does not trouble *me*, in particular, but may in fact trouble us *all*.

"Our scouts who took care of disposing the enemy slain returned from Ostetyn yesterday. They gave the usual report—body counts, costs of damage, time lost. They told me for the most part, the men we killed were no different from others: the same fur, the same iron, the same smell. But…some…were marked differently.

"It was difficult to spot at first, since so many were already covered in inks and scars. But out of thirty slain, at least twenty were branded with the black 'V.' They now believe there may have been more from our other incursions."

"Rahm's eyes," Henry murmured. "What could Vasur possibly have to do with Northmen?" *No. You will not let the seed of doubt grow. It matters not what these savages choose to cover themselves with. Hunt them down and be done with it.* Henry continued. "No—no more of this. I care nothing for these ink scratchings on unwashed barbarians. We are here to hunt them down and destroy them. We can worry about ghosts and shadows once this business is settled. Is that understood?"

"Yes, your Majesty," Ronin and Eldric said together.

"Good. Have my stallion brought to me at once."

"Yes, sir." Eldric jogged off to the far side of the ring of tents and torches, kicking up clouds of dust as he went. Every soul who moved made his own cloud, choking the camp with gray haze.

It wasn't long before Thuro was brought into view, led proudly by a young Dalani tribesman with hair nearly as black as Henry's had once been. It hung down to the center of his back in the ancient manner of the old Dalani, in the days before their subjugation under the White City. With a deep bow, he handed Thuro's reins over to Henry, almost relieved to be rid of the thunder stallion. Dalani riders were always around horses, but a thunder stallion was as alien to them as a jungle lion. Henry patted Thuro's broad nose as the beast lightly nibbled on his wrist.

"What is your name, young man?"

"Cryspyn, your Majesty," he replied.

Henry's eyes lit with recognition. "You stood before me with King Robert back in Vita Astym. You were one of the survivors of the attack."

"Yes, your Majesty, I was."

"Had you seen much combat before that day?"

"I hadn't, your Majesty, but I have been in service to King Robert for the last five years, almost six. I wasn't expecting it to be so…" Cryspyn struggled to look for the right word.

"Horrible?" Henry suggested.

"Yes, your Majesty."

"The first taste of battle usually is," Henry said. "Even if you survive, the person you were before dies. But the man you become is much better suited for fighting. I am only sorry you lost friends that day."

"Raloff, the first to fall, we trained together when we first joined the army and rode together for five years. Alyn Highrise— he taught me how to properly handle a spear, how to thrust without losing balance—and Commander Torz, well, I always thought him invincible. I've never seen such brutality, your Majesty."

"It's likely it won't be the last time you see it, either. I'm glad you're still with us, young man. It is because of *you* that your King was able to act before it was too late. Keep your mind clear and your arm strong, and you will have plenty of tales to tell when you return home."

"Thank you, your Majesty."

"Off with you now," Henry said with a smile. Cryspyn reminded him of Mayson in some ways: eager to prove himself, though still fearful. *He'll get his chance, sooner rather than later.*

With a groan and a hard push, Henry pulled himself into his saddle and rode to the northern end of camp to await Ronin and his commanders. Out of the bustle came ten dark figures, clinging to Henry like his own shadow. The Knights of Rahm had taken care of their own tents and now held their double-handed sabers atop their night-black horses. Without instruction, they formed two lines of five behind the king as he rode. Henry fingered the straps that bound Rahmirion to his saddle, ever wary of losing her out in the dust.

Henry had sought to leave the Knights behind altogether, but Beatrice would have none of it. "You will bring ten with you, or you won't go," she'd demanded.

Henry smiled to himself as he recalled the day he rode for Roleigh. Beatrice had been just as beautiful and spirited as the day he met her. *You'll see her soon, old man. Don't taint your sweet memory of her with bloody work.*

The riders of the Black Army followed suit with the Knights of Rahm once they were packed and squared away. Four lines of fifty fell in to await instruction, each as still as a statue, but unlike the Shadow Knights, they gave curious looks to check the progress of the Hooves. The Dalani Sworn Hooves were more than efficient, enough to put the armed forces of other Western nations to shame, yet they still lagged behind the Black Army. It took a minute longer for each green cloak and winged helm to form up as the Astymerians had.

When all men and supplies were finally gathered, Henry and Ronin ordered them to move north. The southern edge of the Dead Lands, which had been flat and blank, gave way to rolling hills of weeds as they approached the river. Younger Astymerian men, having only known the rich green land of the Crescent, looked upon the land with disgust and contempt. Even the Dalani sneered and spat in the dust. Only Henry and the older officers had ever known this place to look any different.

By midday the men could see the shimmering waters of the Acrontian River from atop the Hills of Borius. Far to the west, the river wound thin, deep, and treacherous; but, as it traveled several miles to the east, it widened dramatically and was no more than two feet deep in any spot for at least a mile. This small stretch of passage was the Turin Ford.

Before the fall of the Empire, there had been a small bridge built to aid in the transport of harvested wheat. A highway had led to the Septaerine Road, but the stones had long since been ripped up to try to maintain Raelia's high walls when the city fell into decline.

The men Corporal Caltrys sent ahead were already across the river by the time it came into view, and the ford was wide enough for all to cross at once, even with their ranks stretched thin. Once beyond, the white smoke of a signal fire led them further to the east than planned. *They've found something.* The leisurely pace they'd taken across the river broke as Henry and Ronin ordered double time, dashing through the thick dust to join the scouts.

Henry's mind raced as they rode, weighing the possibilities. The rolling land revealed two large stone outcroppings jutting from the gray waste. Henry recognized them from maps as the Shattered Sisters. Long ago, they may have been a single, minuscule plateau, but some force, either manmade or godly, had shattered the rock down the middle, creating a small canyon. Legend said it was here that Golron the Immovable first discovered his power over stone and earth.

As they drew nearer the ground became rockier than they had seen since entering the Dead Lands. The company's hoofbeats, which had been soft and dull for two days, suddenly rang out sharp and clear. The sound bounded off the small, narrow canyon, vibrating like bells. There, halfway between one end and the other, sat the scouts, carefully tending a small fire from which the white smoke slithered into the sky in thin wisps.

Their horses and armor were spattered with blood, and the corpses of six Northmen lay at their feet, blood pooling and trickling through the many cracks in the rocks. The men seemed no different from those they had already slain, yet the scouts all stared at the ground, pale as snow.

"Malyx," Ronin demanded. "I count six bodies here. There are ten of you. You were more than capable of handling this situation on your own. Why have you seen fit to waste our last signal kit? There is no wood to burn here—not for nearly a hundred leagues in any direction! The wood we have left is to keep warm at night. Explain yourselves!"

Malyx, a man of thirty with slightly stooped shoulders, a large nose, and light brown stubble, removed his helm and raised a shaking arm to point at the rock face to Ronin's left. The higher his arm raised, the more it spasmed and twitched. Malyx's head did not turn along with his arm. Henry noticed each of the ten scouts had their eyes locked on the ground, refusing to look their Prince in the eye. *Sworn Hooves are no cowards. What's gotten hold of them?*

Ronin followed Malyx's trembling arm, pivoting on the spot to look upon the cliff to his left. Henry looked as well. Halfway up the rise, etched into the rock with either ashes or soot, were two enormous black eyes. *The eyes of the Beast. Just when I thought things couldn't get any worse.*

"What of this, cousin?" Ronin asked after finally finding the will to speak. "Can this be dismissed? Or have we all been cursed by the mark of the Beast?"

Henry rode forward silently. Thuro tossed his head and whinnied.

"You forget yourself, Ronin," Henry said. "The wilder tribes of the north, as isolated as they can be, all know of the Beast. There isn't a soul alive who doesn't know his mark. It is not uncommon for them to mark their targets with black eyes to instill fear before an attack."

"Well, it has worked," Ronin said strongly, but Henry took it in stride. The black eyes were enough to unsettle even battle-hardened warriors. Ronin was not green by any means, but he was still very young, and his nerves were raw. "This is a terrible omen, cousin. I cannot simply brush it aside. I say we go back across the Acrontian River and set up patrols. We monitor all movement over the fords and allow them to come to us. We can cut them down like grass, as we always have."

"You would have us patrol over two thousand miles of river with this lot here? The Turin is not the only ford they can use to cross. What happens when these animals burn villages in Ilbaan and Lupfur? What happens when a larger, more heavily populated Dalani town is ravaged by these scum? Who will be to blame, Ronin? When the innocents of the West fall under these murderers' knives, who will be to blame? Surely not you," Henry swallowed hard. "We have come to this forsaken place for a purpose, and we do *not* leave until our task is done."

"Yes, your Majesty," Ronin said with a begrudging bow, all traces of confrontation slowly ebbing from him. That was exactly how Henry wanted it if his orders were to be obeyed out in the wild lands.

"Now, since you all find this *artwork* so unnerving, we won't waste any more time here," Henry said. "Rally the men and let us continue toward Casaack."

The mixed ranks of both Dalani and Astymerian men-at-arms traveled in neat, disciplined columns, with Henry and Ronin at the heart. So when panicked voices ahead shouted *"To arms! To arms!"* the sounds of battle reached the royals before they even came upon the sight.

Man by man, pair by pair, the riders charged forward, out of the pass and into the dusty open air beyond. Just beyond the rock formations, at the base of a low hill thirty yards off, soldiers in black and green found themselves mixed into a crowd of fur and iron. Henry hadn't the time to count as he urged Thuro to charging speed, but there had to be at least three hundred, their tracks still fresh in the thick dust that covered the hill.

Nearly half of his men were already tossed into the fray, horses side-stepping, leaping, and stamping at men on the ground, thrusting crude spears, axes, and swords. Several men had been knocked from their saddles and engaged the foes on foot.

"Riders of Rahm, on me!" Henry cried in a voice that sliced through the chaos. Those warriors who remained, including his Shadow Knights, formed a tight wedge around him, allowing Henry to take point in the center.

Henry ripped Rahmirion from her moorings in his saddle and unleashed her. With a shake of his wrist, she nearly doubled in size. In the moments before the collision, Henry looked to his left to see Ronin standing in his stirrups, spear pointed true and teeth bared in a horrific snarl, leading the remainder of his riders in a straight, tight line. Bodies flew to and fro upon impact, the sounds of iron scraping and snapping bones filling the air.

Henry struck down any who came too close, and before he knew it, ten had died by his hand. He looked to his left just in time to see a Shadow Knight knocked to the dust as his horse took a spear to the chest. Before his fall was even complete, the Knight was on his feet. With his long saber lost, he held his dagger forward against the foes who now closed in on him. With the speed of a greased viper, he slid from man to man, his high steel blade piercing each heart before they even had time to raise their weapons. Henry saw no more as the fighting led him deeper into the battle.

Ronin again came into view, now also knocked from his horse, but his steed, Ratako, ran about as one of Ronin's Hooves worked to rein the beast in. With a lifetime's worth of training and the reckless abandon of a young man, Ronin spun and swung his spear, spilling blood with each movement. All around him, Hooves and Astymerian riders fought to separate him from danger, as they did Henry. But Ronin was the last male heir of the House of Suryn. By all rights, Robert himself should have been there, but his age and injuries had ended his fighting days long ago. Henry pushed his wedge of black armor and high steel further into the heart of combat, hell bent on reaching his cousin.

Haledon and Eldric made it to him first, using themselves as shields as Cryspyn helped Ronin back into his saddle. It was then a piercing pain shot through Henry's right leg, as he looked down to see a dagger plunged into his thigh, slipped between his armor plating. Before he could bring Rahmirion to bare, a long saber burst through his foe's chest from behind, the handiwork of an ever-vigilant Shadow Knight.

The Knights formed a tight circle around the king, all but cutting him off from combat. Frustrating as it was, Henry accepted it. There was no greater slight to a Knight of Rahm's honor than to have his king's blood spilt. They would prevent it from happening again even if they had to throw themselves into the enemy's blade.

For several minutes, the clanging of steel against iron and cries of agony blanketed the area, allowing Henry's frustration to get the better of him. At the top of his lungs, he commanded his Knights to stand aside. Without argument, they obeyed.

Rahmirion flew as though she had a life of her own, hacking limb from body and opening throats by the handful, bathing both Henry and Thuro in the warm spray of blood. At long last the surviving Northmen turned to flee back over the hill from whence they came, leaving hundreds of their fallen comrades bleeding in the dust and stones.

Henry and Ronin stood face to face now, their breath coming nearly as hard and ragged as their steeds.' A quick survey of the carnage revealed fifty dead, split among Astymerian black and Dalani green.

"Nolan?" Henry called out. *"Captain Saldren!"*

"Aye, my King," the Captain of the Guard replied, riding forward from the stilled assembly.

"I want a full body count, and I want the tents of the dead repurposed for traveling bags. I want our fallen returned to the Crescent with dignity."

"Consider it done, my King," Nolan said, but before he could turn to carry out his task, Ronin spoke out.

"There *is* the matter of the survivors, your Majesty," he said, pointing his bloodied spear toward the hill, where the twenty stragglers were still attempting to reach the top. "You said it yourself—the job *must* be done. Surely you don't mean to let them get away."

"Right, Prince Ronin," Henry said with a heavy nod. "Leave one alive for questioning. Once we're done with him, do what you will." He took a bit of horse cloth from his belt and wiped Rahmirion clean. With another look to the hill, Henry raised her up, fresh as the day she was forged. "For your homes, for your wives, for King and Country! *Charge!"*

The battle cry seemed to last all the way up the hill. Three Northmen had reached the top, but the rest were not so lucky. Like so many training posts, they were cut down and trampled into the dirt, their cries silenced in a heartbeat.

"Just a few more, men!" Ronin cried as they neared the summit, spurring more speed from Hoof and warrior alike.

The company stopped dead at the top, all shouts and cheers quickly strangled. There at the summit, the Dead Lands stretched out endlessly before them, the mountains of Gol Garonath, the Great Divide, just ripples in the land far to the north. But the Dead Lands were now teeming with life—with thousands of wild tribesmen clad in fur and iron.

Battle horns blared from the bottom of the hill, as a chorus of howls and chants drowned out the cries of the Western party.

"Lord Wallis numbered them in the hundreds!" Ronin shouted, his eyes wide as saucers as he beheld the great army before him.

"He wasn't certain," Henry answered. "You could hide close to a million men in those trees and we would be none the wiser."

"What do we do, Henry? *Your Majesty?*"

Henry was now lost in thought. He had never been so careless in battle, yet here he stood, face to face with a small horde. Whatever there was to be done, it had to be done quickly, lest they all become food for the buzzards.

Henry turned to lead his men back down the hill. *The dead would have to wait.*

Chapter 36

The Black City: The Great Plains
38th Day of the Sixth Month
5018 A.S.

"Keep your voices down," Commander Haledon Swiftwynd growled under his breath. He and ten men had ridden out well after nightfall, creeping through the tall grass that surrounded the ruins of Raelia. They'd spent most of the night scouting the enemy camp, but now that dawn was peeling away the blackness, their discipline was waning from fatigue. Eleven of them had slipped past the Northern guards easily enough, but the danger was still great until they could get back behind what remained of the high walls of the Black City.

The moons were little more than thin, white smiles pressed against the night sky, mostly blocked by thick storm clouds that brought thunder and lightning, but no rain. The torches of the enemy camp had danced in anticipated victory as the Hooves watched from the thin, dry brambles, one-hundred and fifty yards off.

At last, out of the pitch, Haledon could make out the brindle coloring of his destrier, large spots of white glaring through the night. The horses had stayed put, despite not having been hobbled. The training and obedience of Dalani thoroughbreds never ceased to amaze him, even after over twenty years in the king's service. It was luckier still they could even see the beasts. If not for the white in their fur, they would have melted into the darkness along with everything else. This meant the city was only half a mile off now.

The dead grass crunched under their hooves as they carefully trot back to Harab'Shakor, the Black City. Despite himself, Haledon always referred to it as Raelia in his head, before realizing his error. That name had hardly been uttered since the city's destruction, and many of the young men he commanded had never even heard it spoken aloud. All they knew of these ruins was destruction and death. They had never navigated the endless throngs of people that mulled about; never tossed a wishing coin into one of the many fountains that lined the streets; there was no memory of a lighter time—only dark nightmares. The lot of them had stared, wide-eyed and shaking, the first time they passed into the labyrinth of smoking shadows.

The massive charred walls could be seen stark and clear against the faint light of the coming morning, as though night's darkness sought refuge from the light in its colossal form. The northern gate had long been crushed under stone, so they had to pass through one of the many jagged gaps along the wall resulting from abandonment.

Everywhere Haledon looked they were surrounded by blackened, twisted stone that appeared more like spent candle wax than the building blocks of the world. From the blasted doorways and caved-in roofs, smoke still seemed to leak and trickle with wispy breath. If they hadn't learned their route so well the day they arrived, the scouts would easily have lost themselves in the eternal black labyrinth of the city streets. But Haledon couldn't lose his way in Raelia's streets if he tried. Years of working every odd job the city had to offer instilled him with an unshakeable sense of direction.

Their way took them through grand avenues and narrow alleys that forced them to ride single file, squeezing past remnants of inns and Residae, broad and tall communes that once housed hundreds of Raelian commoners at a time.

It wasn't long before they passed through the five Mothering Hills, the northern section of the city where legend claimed the first stones of Raelia were set down thousands of years ago. Those alleys took them over the Valenine, the tallest of the five hills, where the blackened homes and shops had been spared the worst of the destruction, and brought them back down to pass through the vale. The four other hills—the Colasine, wide and flat; the Palanae, perfectly rounded with roads that spiraled up its sides; the Esquaeline, which now stood half crumbled on its eastern side; and the Quorinae, whose natural spire at its summit once served as the first Raelian watchtower—loomed on either side of them, imposing and menacing. Several men let out involuntary whimpers as they passed. Haledon himself gripped his reins so tight his knuckles turned white in the waning darkness; even he was not immune to the city's dark charms.

Once through the steep roads of the hills, the Vai Karrina, a wide boulevard that connected the northern Residae to the heart of the city, turned sharply to the south.

"This can't be real," Malyx said, breaking the silence. "What if we all died back at the Sisters and we're trapped in some nightmarish hell? The Beast has us all, I'm telling you."

"Shut. Your. Mouth," Haledon snapped. "You are a Sworn Hoof to the King of Dalan—start acting like one!"

Malyx dropped his gaze to the stone below. They wouldn't be able to take much more of this. A few more days trapped in here and discipline would completely fall apart; Haledon was sure of it. This was no longer a suitable place to hide.

"Let's pick up the pace, shall we?" Haledon said. "The prince will want our report before the sun rises above the walls."

The roads became wider the closer they drew to the heart of the city, until eventually they were all able to ride side by side with room to spare. The unholy fires that fell from the sky had been strongest here; nothing of what once stood remained.

To the left they passed a great stone plateau with a carved staircase running from base to summit. Apart from the many chips, cracks, and burn marks, it had been polished smooth from top to bottom. At the top of the crumbling stairs stood ten broken pillars with a mountainous pile of rubble behind them. The Great Temple of Tyranion had once stood here, dominating the city, looming over it with the god's all-seeing eye. The foundations of the Temple had been damaged and burnt away during the sack of Raelia, and the structure collapsed in on itself, crushing the golden statue of the King of the Heavenly beneath an avalanche of stone and tile.

Once past the Temple, the road ran straight for ten city blocks before winding southeast, finally entering the heart of the city to the blasted half-dome of the imperial palace that had sheltered them for three days now.

The sky was now a bright blue to the east, though the west still clung to night's dark veil. The square walls of Tiberian's palace, black and burnt as they were, were almost completely intact. There were cracks and chips along the façade, but not a single opening aside from the four gates, which had been busted down during the sack of the city. The eleven riders tightened formation.

"*Halt!*" came a familiar voice from the darkness. Haledon raised a closed fist and brought his party to a standstill. Haledon knew at that moment there were at least twenty arrows pointed at them from atop a wall, though he couldn't see where. The grunts of several horses filled the silence before the commander saw fit to speak.

"Cryspyn...*Cryspyn!*" Haledon choked. His patience grew thin. "Cryspyn, for the love of the Winged Father, let us in before I..."

"Yes, sir, right away, sir. *Stand to!*" the boy replied, practically stumbling over his own tongue in his rush to obey. The sound was just barely audible, but Haledon could hear the tension being relieved from the bows that stood ready to fire just moments before.

The single column resumed its march until each man was safely within the compound, dismounting and removing their winged helms. Cryspyn looked ready to soil himself.

"Honestly, Cryspyn," Haledon muttered as he moved about. "Did you think the Northmen had taken our clothes and suddenly learned Altung?"

"The day you think an enemy can't outsmart you is the day they do, sir," Cryspyn replied, composing himself and standing at attention with his hand resting on the pommel of his sword. "Prince Ronin said we cannot take *any* chances if we are to make it out of here alive. I serve him dutifully until my last breath, even if it means your displeasure."

Haledon stood silently, taking the young man in with his usual scowl. Against his better judgment, he was beginning to like the boy.

"Very well. Be about your business. We don't want those bastards sneaking up on us while we chatter like a couple of old women."

Cryspyn returned to man the wall while Haledon hobbled his horse. Malyx had been shocked the posts had been planted so easily when they first arrived, but the older warriors explained the southern yards of the complex had once been gardens, and were full of softer soil.

Those men who did not have watch duty were trying to distract themselves any way they could, telling stories and laughing. There was hardly a man among them that looked as though they knew they would never see home again. Haledon realized he preferred it that way. If they were to die here, it was best to die well, remembering life's simpler pleasures—not consumed with despair. A few more days and the last of the light would be drained from them.

Haledon broke off from the party, followed by Malyx, and entered the ruined palace at the center of the complex. The torches they had left were used to light the few passages that were used within the palace, the outer corridors of which wound around the hollowed center like a beehive.

The pair found Prince Ronin in what was left of the grand solar, the cavernous space around which the palace was built. It was circular, or at least it had been. The majority of the room was filled from floor to the half-remaining ceiling with stone and rubble, allowing the morning sky to shine through. The walls that stood undisturbed were covered in faded, chipped red paint, standing behind the remains of black granite pillars.

All around the room shattered pots created flows and piles of dirt and dust. Those that hadn't been broken bore shriveled, lifeless trees and shrubs, long dead and decayed. Larger trees had been cut for firewood, and the fruit of that labor lit the room in three different spots, all centered around a tattered half-circle bench deeply padded with cotton and sealed by ruined red linen.

Prince Ronin and King Henry sat together on the bench, musing over a pile of scrolls and letters. It seemed the royals had just dismissed a meeting, and there was great commotion as the officers broke to ready the defense. As Haledon approached, their conversation became clear.

"You're certain it made it through?" Henry asked .

"*Yes,* your Majesty. You saw the swallow take off. At the height it reached, there isn't a bow in existence that could have shot it down."

"It should not take three days to assemble an army of cavalry!"

"Cousin, we must be patient; the swallow made it through," the prince said, trying to soothe the anxious king.

Henry shot a quick glance at Haledon. "What do you want?" Henry was not himself; it was clear to see. He hadn't slept a minute since retreating from the Shattered Sisters three days ago.

"We have our report from last night, your Majesty," Haledon

replied, bending the knee, as Malyx quickly followed.

"Come on, then, let's hear it," Henry demanded, resting his chin on his fist.

"Our count of the northern camp reached nearly two thousand, mostly all on foot. No more than two hundred archers. From what we could tell, they seemed to be drinking and feasting as though they'd already won. A brief time before that, it seemed *some* were preparing for combat, dressing themselves in armor and taking whetstones to their blades, but I don't think they will wait much longer."

Henry dropped his hand from his face in disbelief. "That makes at least eighty-five hundred in total…we have just under two hundred men."

"My father *will* come, Henry," Ronin said, sounding as if he were trying to convince himself of this just as much as the king.

Henry rose in anger. "We should have gone south when we had the chance! We weren't supposed to be here longer than a night. This place was meant as a fallback position—*not* a tomb to seal ourselves in. We are surrounded! I let you talk me into waiting for your father. If he does not arrive, we are dead. If our sacrifice accomplished something, it wouldn't be for naught, but all we are now are men hurried to their grave, with an ancient, noble house snuffed out."

Both Haledon and Ronin stood stunned and speechless. The Old Bruiser had seemingly accepted his fate—the thought of the fight to come his only comfort. After a few moments of looking up at the brightening sky in silence, Henry continued.

"I will be the first Avaari king slain on the battlefield in centuries. Not such a terrible thing to be remembered for. I defined my reign with the destruction of this city; it is only fitting it should end here. It was in this very building that I took Tiberian's head. Wouldn't it be a great weaving of the gods if I were to lose mine in here, too?"

"It won't come to that, your Majesty," said Eldric, stepping into the light from the dim shadows. "This palace is easily defendable. They have no siege equipment. They can't climb the walls. All that is left for them to do is try to fight through the gates. That's where we have an advantage."

"An advantage, yes, but not a saving grace," Henry replied.

"We may hold them for a while, but we will inevitably be overwhelmed. When that happens, I am prepared to die on my feet. I pray you are the same."

Without another word, Henry took leave, as did the Shadow Knights who emerged from the darkness at the edges of the room. Haledon hadn't noticed Eldric at first, but the Knights of Rahm had been truly invisible. When they finally moved, Haledon felt as though his heart stopped. *Perhaps we're in Hell after all, and these are the demons meant to keep us company.*

"I've never seen him like this," Ronin said to Eldric, resuming his study of the papers before him. "He can't truly think I meant for this to happen. This was the most defensible position we had available to us, and they were closing in from every direction. I swear, I didn't think we would be here for more than a day."

"You did what you believed was right; the king is not himself…"

"But what if he is right, Captain? If my father doesn't arrive…"

"He will, my Prince. He will. If he doesn't, yes – then, we must prepare ourselves for the end. You are the blood of the oldest of the Dalani houses. Your ancestors were the first men to tame horses, and the first to ride them like the back of the wind. You will go charging into the afterlife as one worthy of such honor. And it will be my honor to ride alongside you."

"Thank you, Captain," the prince replied with a forlorn smile. "It has been my greatest honor serving with you."

Haledon suddenly felt as if he were intruding. The silence was deafening until Eldric changed the subject.

"Have you found anything in the sewer plans?" he asked, sitting beside the prince. "Could they be used against us?"

"It doesn't appear so." Ronin fingered through a pile of diagrams and blueprints. "We were lucky the vaults of the Hall of Records were undamaged, or we never would have found these designs. They show six waterways into this building, and just as many service tunnels. I've had each of them checked and am told everything is blocked off by debris. It would take a month to clear any of them out. Even so, I hardly think those savages out there would know the internal layout of a city as large as this. I would bet my wings the only way they come is through those four gates."

"That makes defending this place all the easier."

Haledon and Malyx hadn't yet been dismissed and remained at attention. Malyx gave a bit of a cough; Haledon couldn't tell if it was genuine or meant to draw the prince's attention. Regardless, it got a response.

"Thank you, gentlemen," Ronin said. "Commander Haledon, I give you command of the north gate. Take your pick of fifty men and begin preparations. The attack will come today, I am sure of it. May the gods be with you both."

HENRY LOOKED OUT THE LARGE, HALF-MOON WINDOW, long devoid of glass. The western sky was a deep violet as the sun slowly crept up in the east. The floor around him was cracked and splintered. Where once thousands of shining mosaics had depicted imperial glory and prosperity, there remained only wreckage, with only one or two burnt, faded tiles remaining. The hall, wrapping around the rounded outer edge of the palace, smelled of sulfur and oil; the dark power that washed over this city left a foul stench clinging to all it touched. Piles of blasted steel and remnants of torches were pooled against the walls every twenty feet, and at the end of the corridor, two mangled doors lay limp upon the ground. The emperor's bedchamber beckoned to the old king, and he found himself answering the call.

His footsteps echoed ahead of him and, for a moment, Henry saw this place for what it was nearly twenty years before. Tiles the color of sapphire and ivory flew back into place as the cracks and holes filled in. The faded color of the walls came alive, revealing brilliant red paint adorned with masterfully drafted gold and black designs. Torches hung from golden sconces, lighting the way toward the carved, golden double doors, shut tight.

Henry saw his companions clear as day: Robert and Urnest marching to his left, Raymund, William, and Darian to his right. Hundreds of footsteps resonated behind him as the men of the West flowed through the emperor's halls. The ringing of steel drilled into his ears as he relived his battle with the Pritaelian Guard, Tiberian's last line of defense. Nearly fifty of Henry's men fell before the battle was won; Darian had taken a grave wound to his belly while saving Henry from a sneak attack; and William was found beneath a pile of guards, the back of his helm dented and his skull cracked.

Henry reached out to touch the doors, and the more he fought it, the more the voice of the Raelian emperor mocked him. *Tell me, Karrok. Does the boy look like you? Does the proud blood of the Avaari flow within him, or has your whore given him too much of her mark?*

"Silence," Henry said, turning from the doors to break the illusion. He nearly stumbled upon a line of burnt skeletons strewn across the floor. "One more word and your death will be slow, I swear it. You will *curse* the day you first drew breath."

The illusion had been broken, but the voice remained. *I wish to know the face of my enemy, Karrok. When we come together at last, I wish to know it well.*

"You will *never* touch him! Do you hear? You will *never* lay your hands on him!" Henry swung about, striking at the source of the voice, but it came from within, as slippery and foul as pond scum. *The Beast will have his day, Karrok. You know it. One by one, those you hold dear will fall under his might. Your wife, your mongrel—even your precious Rahm shall be consumed by the Second Flame. But first, they shall all weep for* you. *You shall mark the beginning of the end.*

The voice dragged Henry back into his false vision, forcing him to once again see the devastation he could not prevent. The windows blew apart around him as fire rained from the sky, drenching the White City in blazing destruction that consumed flesh, stone, and steel. It seemed like minutes before Henry finally took control of himself and stood before the emperor on his balcony, overlooking the growing inferno, listening to the sounds of screams. Tiberian's hands were outstretched, his arms spread wide. His smile was filled with what Henry could only describe as pure, unhinged madness as he gazed upon the burning city and laughed. Even after Rahmirion took Tiberian's head from his shoulders, that smile remained—and the emperor's laugh could not be silenced.

"*Nooooo!*" Henry bellowed into the empty corridor. The vision was gone, and so was the voice. Those words stayed with him for nearly twenty years, but he had never heard them so clearly. He had tried to forget the look of glee on Tiberian's face as fire bled from an otherwise clear sky. He had tried to forget everything, and he nearly had. He had been too late to save the city. He had been too late to save thousands of his men. Those that did survive were lucky, himself included. He could think of nothing besides divine intervention that had allowed them to escape Tiberian's devastation. He never admitted it to himself, but a primal, fearful part of his mind was convinced Tiberian was Vul Dakkar, his voice long since buried—until this trouble with Vasur began. It all suggested the Beast's grip on this world was growing tighter.

Henry's head swam as he limped his way out into the morning air. Those who spent the early hours carousing were now fully armored, running from the palace to their respective gates, hauling rubble to block the openings as best they could. Those who had been asleep were beginning to stir, rubbing eyes and stifling yawns, forcing themselves to move at the pace expected of them.

Every banner that remained had been planted upon the ramparts of the square wall wherever there was enough strong stone to hold them. The black shape of Rahmirion upon the snow-white banner gave Henry strength as he looked upon it. The sun now peeked over the walls, the tiniest orange sliver along the blue silver of dawn.

Henry thought of the sketch of Rahmirion found in possession of one of the slain Northmen on the Plains years before. The savages had undoubtedly seen him with her; they would go to great lengths to take her from him. If it came down to it, he would have to hide her, bury her in the rocks of the city, and get a message to Mayson to tell him where he'd left her.

The sight of the white banner of the Crescent and the green of Dalan would make for a beautiful final sight—the colors of ancient nobility standing in defiance of certain death. The same morning breeze that caught them lifted his shadow-silk cloak, dancing like a wild flame.

He found Captain Saldren at the western gate, up to his elbows in rock and wooden planks, aiding in the effort to create sturdy barriers in their defense. Each gate had been burned to cinders during the sacking of the city, which left wide open entries into the palace grounds. Behind these piles of stone and wood, the Westerners could only buy more time.

"Captain," Henry called as he approached. As weakened as he was, his voice dominated the air. Nolan nearly dropped a large stone on the foot of the man next to him, for he bent the knee in answer to his King's call before he realized what he was doing. The captain kept his gaze on the ground until Henry ordered him to look upon him. The red-stained gauze over his right eye brought Henry back to the Sisters, where Nolan had lost it.

They had fallen back, back into the pass where they could not be outflanked. Henry had intended to stay there and allow the Northerners to funnel in, where their numbers would be useless. All that afternoon, the royal company held their ground, fighting from two directions, for the Northmen had circled to the other side of the rock formation to attack both ends. Henry couldn't count the dead, friend or foe, but by the end, the blood of the slain ran up to their ankles, unable to seep into the rocky ground.

Once the assault on the southern end of the pass had failed and their path had been cleared, Ronin gave the order to mount and fall back across the river. Henry tried to stop him, but too many men had followed the command to keep up the defense. Begrudgingly, Henry rode after Ronin, losing an extra fifty men who didn't have to die, all remaining behind to give him time to escape. *A king of Astymere running like a whipped dog—my father would be ashamed.*

Once they were back across the river, their luck did not change. Henry had been right about the possibility that the enemy could cross at other fords, and they found themselves cut off from the west and east, each force just as large as the other, with the enemy from the north still in hot pursuit. Ronin suggested they ride for the Black City, for they were sitting ducks out on the Plains. Henry hadn't liked it, but it was their best option.

He laid into Ronin that night once camp had been made within the palace. The pass between the Sisters could have easily been defended. It would have taken more time for reinforcements to arrive, but they could have held it. Once he let his rage burn out, he had instructed Ronin to write his father, imploring him to raise the Spears of Dalan to break the Northern host. They had one wind swallow left after the incursion at the Sisters, and it couldn't be wasted traveling all the way to Astymere. The winged animal disappeared into the clouds once the message was written, and they hadn't seen a trace of it since.

"My King?" Captain Saldren said.

Henry snapped his attention back to Nolan. It was still strange to hear those words from anyone but William Otter. Sometimes he thought he could see William's face in young Nolan, if he wasn't focusing. *My brother. I will see you soon enough.*

"I want you to hand-pick fifty men and take three Knights of Rahm to defend the southern gate. I will take the remainder of our men and hold them here at the western side. See if Haledon is able to spare any of his soldiers as well. You will need spears in the front."

"My King," he said, frowning. "With all due respect, my place is by your side."

"Your place is where I command you to be, Captain," Henry replied. "If I am to die this day, there is nothing you can do to change that. You can serve me best by protecting my flank. It will be much easier knowing I don't have to constantly watch my back." Henry clasped his captain's shoulder. "This may be the last time we speak, my friend. I wish to say that you have truly lived up to the task with which you were charged, and it has been an honor to know you."

Henry offered Nolan his hand, the first time he had ever given him such a gesture. Nolan took it slowly and uncertainly, but his grip quickly turned to iron.

"The honor has been mine, my King. But by Rahm's eyes, I will not fail you."

WAHHHHHH. Battle horns shattered the morning stillness and froze each man to his spot. They were close. Too close. There was no telling now how deeply the enemy had infiltrated the city.

Three of the four watchtowers that protected the palace in the days of old still stood, and from two came the answer to the Northern call—melodious, high-pitched trumpet blasts countering the deep, cumbersome sounds of the crude horns used by the Northmen. *If they didn't know where we were before, they do now.*

"Smoke! There's smoke!" *Voices at the northern gate.* Henry had a difficult time maneuvering through the chaos with his wounded leg. Everywhere he looked, men dressed in black and green scurried like roaches caught in torchlight, each making a mad dash to their assigned gate to ready the defense. Haledon was already there, shouting up to the sentries in his gravelly voice. He turned as Henry drew near.

"The sentries are reporting hundreds of smoke plumes rising alongside the Great Temple of Tyranion, your Majesty. Light smoke—not the pitch black wisps we are used to. The first wave isn't a half-mile off now!"

Yells now came from the eastern and southern gates as well—indiscernible racket mixed with the continuous blaring of trumpets.

"Those must be the rest of our *guests!*" Henry mused.

The remainder of the officers who had been conferring within the palace came rushing out in one heaping wave, with men crossing in front of each other, racing for their assigned gates. Ronin and Eldric were among them, and upon seeing Henry, rushed to the northern gate, drawing their swords.

"Gentlemen," Henry began, "your orders are simple. Haledon shall command the northern gate, Nolan the south, and you two shall take the east. The assault may be heavier on some sides, and the need for reinforcements may vary. If anyone receives a runner from one of the other gates, you will accommodate in any way you can that will *not* compromise your ability to defend your own position. Is that clear?"

"Yes, my King," they replied in unison.

"This is where I leave you," Henry said, with the smallest hint of a sad smile. "We shall meet on the other side. Attend to your men."

The group quickly disbanded. *"Ronin!"* Henry cried after him. The young prince wheeled around on the spot. "May the gods be with you, boy," Henry shouted with a woeful heart. It almost felt as if he were speaking to Mayson, though to see his son's face in this awful place, about to die alongside him, would have been too much to bear.

COMMANDER HALEDON SWIFTWYND straightened his winged helm on his head and plucked his high-steel bastard sword from the soft earth. He had never given his weapon a name, though many had urged him time and time again to do so.

Haledon always brushed it off as nonsense to name something that cannot answer when called, and even today, he did not regret his decision. He stood before the heap of stone erected to slow the incursion of the army beyond and turned to look on his men. Forty-six Sworn Hooves stood before him, standing at attention, spears planted firmly by their sides, swords ready to be drawn. If he were to fall, Haledon decided this would be the last beautiful sight he ever lay eyes on.

He looked to the ramparts above. Only fifteen archers would be able to rain hell down on their attackers. It would accomplish little, but every man killed before he reached the wall would matter a great deal to those within.

"My good men," Haledon called out. "I am not one for noble speeches. I am a man of action, and that is what I expect of each of you today. We will die here, Hooves—that is a certainty. Stand and fight, or drop your spears and run, it makes no difference. Your number has been called. Accept it, and the fight to come will be that much easier. For there is nothing more dangerous than a man with nothing left to lose. When you pass through to the other side of eternity, by the gods, Low and High, you shall go screaming with your hands around the enemy's throat!"

At this, Haledon received a resounding hero's cry. They were ready, at least many were. Haledon could only imagine that some of the younger Hooves only *thought* they were ready, but that would have to suffice for now.

"I want mixed ranks! First rank spears, second rank swords, then so on and so forth! We do not fight one at a time. Each line shall actively aid the line in front of it. Now, form up and take position!"

Haledon took his spot in the dead center among the first spears. If these savages were to try and reach the men behind him, he would make them pay.

There hadn't been enough stone to seal the gate completely— at least not enough that could be carried by hand. With no equipment and no masons, the larger pieces of debris were all but useless to them. The barricade rose just above Haledon's head and no further. The enemy would climb the pile to leap into the ranks, incapacitating men and quickly overwhelming the formation.

"First two ranks, on me!" Haledon began to climb, leaving the swords standing on the ground behind him.

From his new position, he could finally see. One hundred

yards off, in the emptiness that was the heart of the city, marched an unwashed mob, their distant voices, resounding perfectly in Haledon's trained ears: war cries and chants in strange, unnerving tongues; swords and axes slamming against shields; time kept with bearskin drums and hunting horns. Haledon counted fifty banners, if they could even be called so. They were a quick assembly of sticks tied with rough twine; hanging limply from each was the image of a horned skull.

Haledon crouched so that only his eyes and wings would show above the top of the barrier. He could almost smell them now. The sticky scent of their filth, carried on the smoke of their torches, nearly choked the grizzled soldier. With one last blow of a hunting horn, the vast host stopped and stood, staring at the blackened, blasted palace. Haledon couldn't say what was happening at the other gates around him, and he didn't want to. Until this business was done, those gates did not exist. There was only himself, the men behind him, and the men in front of him.

He sat on the unshapely stones beneath him to save the strength in his legs. To his left, he saw young Cryspyn, spear in hand, crouched against the slope of the barrier.

"Ready, Corporal?" Sweat dripped from the boy's nose, but his eyes were just as hardened as the commander's.

"As I'll ever be, sir," Cryspyn replied. The solid look in his eye did not match the uncertainty in his voice. He was no coward, but fear had sunk its claws in him.

"Nothing can make this easier, boy. But you *will* earn your wings after this day is over. That, I swear."

For a young man of the king's army looking to prove himself, the prospect of earning his wings was as good a motivator as any—even if he never got to wear them.

A long-winded, piercing blow of the hunting horns outside sent a shudder through the tense formation. Haledon rose just a bit to peek over the top of the stones; now, nearly two thousand Northern warriors barreled toward the gate at full speed, screaming at the top of their lungs. There were no more words— just shouts and screeches meant to strike fear into the defenders' hearts.

Commander Haledon looked to the ramparts above to give his final order before the enemy bore down upon them. "Archers! Fire at will!" The roar of the charging barbarians drowned out everything else. "Steady! *STEADY!*"

"Come on then! Send them to me!" Nolan succumbed to blood lust as the first of the attackers forced their way over the southern barrier. Even with one eye, his sword flew with deadly accuracy, slicing men under their arms to open their arteries, slashing throats, and as part of a personal vendetta, driving the point of his sword into every eye he could reach.

He stood in the center of the second rank, behind a line of ten Dalani spears. The three Shadow Knights beside him moved with fluidity and speed that seemed almost inhuman. Their long sabers, held forward like spears, seemed to know their targets before their masters did.

Over one hundred screaming Northmen had fallen when the influx of attackers suddenly doubled, forcing its way into the ranks of the defenders. It was then that Nolan and the Dalani in front of him found themselves fighting as individuals—not as a unit.

"Swords of Rahm! On me!" Twenty black shields rushed forward to rein in the chaos beginning to unfurl at the front of the formation, the black shields now bearing the brunt of the savage attacks. They rang out like great city bells with each blow.

Nolan ordered the Dalani spears to close rank and push forward. If they were shoved too far back, the attackers could slip past on either side. He ordered the rear rank to split and cover the left and right flanks to seal the Northmen in.

Something whizzed by Nolan's head. He thought he had imagined the sound at first, but he soon found the source was far from imaginary. Ten men were felled in an instant from arrows that rained down from over the wall. One came so close it pierced Nolan's black cloak on its way to the ground.

"*Shields up!*" he cried. As one, the warriors of the Black Army and those of Dalan raised their shields to create a canopy of steel. Each man fought this way for the next several minutes, with one arm raised against death from above, and the other thrusting forward in an attempt to find soft flesh beneath iron shells.

The bodies were beginning to pile; the earth of the southern palace yards had become thick, blood-drenched muck. The cries of the horses, which had been moved further into the heart of the grounds, added to the chaos. The defenders were already half what they had been at the start, and this time, when the enemy surged again, the formation broke entirely.

"Sir Orynar!" Nolan cried to the Shadow Knight fighting beside him. The black knight did not seem fatigued; his sword kept moving as those lifeless eyes met Captain Saldren's. "Make haste to the eastern gate! Bring back as many men as Prince Ronin will allow!"

With barely a nod, the Shadow Knight carved his way through the throng and took off sprinting once his body was free of human entanglement.

"Kastja!" came a cry from Nolan's left. A hulking man, bearing two axes and a helm crowned with ram's horns, tore out of the mob and rushed Nolan with mad desperation. Captain Saldren ducked a swing that would have lopped his head clean off, and with what energy he had left, sliced at the brute's exposed leg, dropping him to one knee. Nolan rose, using his blade as a crutch to help him stand, and raised it to the man's throat. Before he could thrust the point home, his foe's large, meaty hand grasped the blade in a vise grip. Taking the hilt in both hands, Nolan tried to wriggle his sword free, to no avail. As blood dripped from the warrior's hand, his left circled upward, bringing the second axe with it. The last thing Captain Nolan Saldren saw was the fine line of the curved blade before it struck true.

"HOLD THEM! HOLD THEM!" Ronin's voice was raspy and ragged. It seemed all he had done was scream since the assault began. His spear had long since broken, and now his two-handed, high steel broadsword did all the work.

The blinding sun was now beating down upon them with glorious morning light. The Hooves had pushed the rush of attackers back over the barricade and presented a solid wall of spears to those who tried to climb the pile. The prince broke himself from the fray, pushing a Sworn Hoof forward to take his place as he tended to Eldric.

The captain had been removed from combat and propped against the palace dome, a trickle of blood leaking from beneath his breastplate. He had been stabbed just above the hip, in his lower belly. The wound itself did not stop him at first, but before long, the loss of blood made him unsteady on his feet. Now he nursed the injury as best he could while watching his countrymen fight for their lives.

"Eldric, are you all right?" Ronin asked. The voice was that of a commander of men, but his gaze was that of a frightened child. His eyes had grown wide with panic the moment he saw blood dripping between his friend's fingers.

"The bleeding is slowing, my Prince. If I'm ever able to be stitched, I should be fine. Don't worry about me. Get back to the damn gate—if you leave it again, I swear I'll thump your skull. Go!"

Ronin had barely taken five steps toward the eastern gate when a crushing grip clutched his shoulder. It felt as though it would tear flesh and break bone through his armor. He spun, sword in hand, to find the black eyes of a Shadow Knight looking back at him.

"What is it, sir?" Ronin managed to ask through his surprise. The Knight pointed back the way he had come, and then to Ronin's men holding their position, firm and unwavering. Ronin understood the gesture and rushed back to Eldric to get him on his feet.

"What the hell are you doing?" the wounded man barked through gritted teeth.

"You cannot fight, but you can command. I want you to stay here and hold the gate while I reinforce Captain Saldren. Can you do that, Eldric?"

"Aye, my Prince. I believe I can," Eldric replied through heavy breaths, unsheathing his sword with his left arm to avoid opening his wound.

"Good," Ronin said as two Hooves led Eldric to the gate. "*I need twenty men!*" There were over thirty who wished to go, but not one willing to break formation. "I want the rear two ranks to follow me, now! Move!"

This time the order was followed without hesitation. Twenty spears ran alongside Ronin and Sir Orynar back to the southern gate. The madness came into full view as they passed under a supporting brace that connected the wall to the palace dome. The southern gate had been completely overwhelmed, and the fight was spreading to the western gate.

"Mal ta Eiruashte!" Ronin cried out in the ancient tribal tongue of the Dalani. *Glory to the Winged Father.*

With speed and power as though they were on horseback, the Dalani Hooves crashed into the sides of the unprepared Northmen, each Hoof knocking their large targets to the ground, sticking them like roast pigs before they could even wipe the dust from their eyes. From man to man Ronin flew, swinging his broadsword without care for whomever it came in contact with.

His countercharge seemed to be working to push the savages further and further back toward the southern gate. The young Prince thought for a moment that the honor was his and his alone, but to his shock, he found the snow-white skin and bright blue eyes of King Henry himself leading his own countercharge. His leg seemed to affect him little as he slid gracefully from foe to foe, a lifetime's worth of training and experience fueling every motion.

Henry's helm had been knocked away, a fresh gash bleeding on his cheek, but he didn't seem to notice. Henry, four Shadow Knights, and twenty of his own warriors overcame impossible strength with uncanny speed and agility. The sight of Rahmirion drew the enemy to him like moths to a flame and, like stalks of grain during the harvest, the foes fell in bunches, spraying their hot crimson blood into the cool morning air.

But the countercharge began to lose momentum, as one by one the soldiers of the West fell. Ronin, who could hardly still lift his great sword, was contemplating certain death when the horns blew again from beyond the walls. The Northmen retreated immediately, climbing over their dead and scrambling over the barricades. So spent were the defenders, they had nor the will or energy to press an attack as the enemy fled.

The trumpets from the high towers resounded one long, sustained note, followed by four short bursts.

"They are all fleeing south," Henry said through heavy breaths. "They will regroup and hit us again before midday; I'm sure of it."

"If they regroup," Ronin said, wiping blood from his face, "we should do the same." He looked to the weary faces of those around him. They were battered and beaten, but not yet broken. "Gather the dead!"

It took nearly an hour to pluck their fallen from the masses of enemy dead. One by one the valiant men of the West were laid side by side, arms crossed over their chests, looking as though they were in a deep, peaceful sleep. Henry, Ronin, and Eldric stood at the end of the line closest to the northern gate, stooped over the last to be found. Haledon had been practically cut to pieces. His face was slashed beyond recognition and four arrows protruded from his belly; a deep, wide-open gash ran across his throat.

"It wasn't until the fourth arrow dropped him to his knees that one of the bastards came up behind him and opened his throat," Cryspyn said as he approached. "He tried to make off with the commander's sword, but I broke my spear through his back and reclaimed it. I fought with it until the horns blew."

"Young man," Henry said, resting a hand on his shoulder, "your country will remember you for this day. This lot, here, will remember you, for as long as we live. You have earned your wings." Cryspyn could only nod, for this personal victory now seemed hollow. "Commander Haledon would agree that his sword belongs to you now. What will you name it?"

Cryspyn looked down on the bastard sword, so heavy in his spent arm, glistening with slowly drying blood. "Swiftwynd," he said softly, tears welling in his weary eyes.

Once everyone had their fill of the canteens and the surviving horses had been calmed and corralled, Henry and Ronin gathered the remainder of their men along the western gate. Barely one hundred were left, and there were still at least seven thousand screaming barbarians recuperating outside the city walls.

"We cannot hold them a second time," Henry said to open ears and searching eyes. "If we remain here, we will be overwhelmed. If we try to flee, we will be cut down like dogs. Our course is clear, gentlemen. Let us die hurling ourselves at our foes. Let them hear *our* battle cries now. Let them feel *our* fury!"

Henry was met by chants and cheers, accompanied by the rhythmic beating of swords and spears against shields.

"Everyone take a stone from the western gate and set it aside. We will never get the horses out through that pile. Once our way has been cleared, you will all mount up. Is that understood?"

"HOOAH!" answered the skeleton force.

The work was done so quickly and efficiently that by the time the hour died, the last men were riding out of the western gate, proudly flying the banners of their countries. Their path was straight and true once they passed the charred, unrecognizable remains of the Marble Palace, marching down the royal causeway that ran over the top of Baradir's Hill. The Marble Palace had been home to the Kings of the West on the Night of Knives, and Henry dared not look at it for long.

From this height, Henry could see the afternoon sun bathing the decayed, forsaken city that had once been the light of the civilized world. Before he turned away, he took in the sight of dozens of smoke plumes rising into the air—never-ending since the night Tiberian unleashed hell on his own people.

The way ahead was clear all the way to the southern wall. The wooden buildings of the Southern Residae had long since burned, ashes carried off by the winds, erasing any trace that anything had been built there at all. Behind the wall, enemy campfires released hundreds of smoke plumes, creeping like spider legs into the sky.

The southern gate on the outskirts of the city had been reduced to a pile of rubble, much too high and uneven for the horses to cross, so the party turned to the west. They followed the path of the wall until they came upon an opening wide enough for two men to ride abreast and flat enough for the horses to make way without risk.

Out in the open, Henry could see the dark clouds that had gathered in the southern horizon quickly rolling in toward the northwest. Though he barely felt a breath of wind, such heavy darkness was sure to mean rain, thunder, lightning—but the air remained dry and hot. Not a sound came from the Plains to the south besides the distant chatter of thousands. *Into darkness, we ride.*

There was no longer any cause for words—nothing more Henry could say that hadn't been said before. In one last act of defiance, Henry drew Sollyria, cleaned and sharpened for her final moments, having hid Rahmirion where, hopefully, she wouldn't be found.

The sound of trumpets sailed off across the vast southern plain. Careless of nation or rank, each rider stood side by side in one straight line. Within moments, the trumpets were met with the crude horns of the Northerners, every last warrior now gathered together just two hundred yards south of the wall.

"*Forth, riders of Rahm!*" Henry cried, the proud strength of five thousand years fueling his words. *"Cayrian Vazur'Ugrahma!"*

"*Mal ta Eiruashte!*" Ronin followed in the tongue of his people, that predated ancient Astymere—even the construction of the White City itself.

Time wound itself down to a crawl as the riders of the West galloped forward with all their horses had left to give. Henry looked past the long sabers of his Shadow Knights on either side of him to see spears and swords raised as one, but he no longer heard any sound. Sound was a luxury of the living—not for the condemned—not for dead men.

The enemy countercharge was slow and unorganized, and the paltry few who reached the riders first were quickly erased as though they hadn't been there at all. Dozen by dozen, the enemy fell, their blood soaking the withered grass and cracking soil. Henry and Ronin drove on, trampling and impaling whomever they could see. Those they could not ride down slipped behind them, and those in front were now dense enough to stop the momentum of the charge, forcing the riders to a slow walk. Henry turned in the melee to see they were completely surrounded by the enemy host, cut off from escape. *There will be no chance to run.*

Thuro suddenly collapsed from beneath the king, dumping him to the hard, dusty ground. His clear view of a spear thrust straight into the proud thunder stallion's chest broke Henry's heart completely.

Through bitter tears that stung his eyes, Henry hurled himself at every man he could see, desperate to take revenge against whoever had dealt the deadly blow to Thuro. It was then an unseen axe suddenly caught Henry in the side with such force, he was knocked off his feet. Though his armor absorbed the brunt of the blow, a rib cracked and his breath was gone.

Looking up from the ground, Henry saw Ronin not five paces away, his broadsword gone, shoving his dagger into a man's throat. Eldric had his hands around another's neck, his strength quickly draining. The eight Knights of Rahm who remained frantically cut through the throng of fur and iron in a mad dash to reach Henry. All around his brothers fell, cut down and tossed to the dirt. *May this field take my flesh and blood, and spring new life into this place—even if just one blade of grass.*

King Henry closed his eyes and waited.

SILENCE NEVER CAME. Instead, the muddled sounds of battle turned once more to trumpets…trumpets, both high and whistling, low and rich, followed by rumbling thunder that shook the ground.

Henry opened his eyes to see the Northmen running once more. Some raced into the west with weapons raised—some to the east with empty hands. He crawled to lean against his fallen stallion and steady himself.

Charging out of the west came a sea of heavily armored horses and spears, covered by a canopy of green banners bearing the white spears and crown of Dalan. Like an avalanche of steel, they flowed over the low hills, the full might of the Dalani engulfing both earth and stone as they barreled forward. The sun shone upon their backs as twenty thousand lances and spears pointed forward, like many steel fangs belonging to a single beast.

Henry could hear the crash of steel-covered stallions colliding with iron-clad forms. The fighting lasted mere moments as the Dalani cavalry washed over the battlefield like a cleansing wave, erasing imperfections in the sand upon a shore. Those who survived the charge now followed suit with their comrades, dropping their weapons in an attempt to flee south and east, while the slow, heavy horses contended with those who would still fight.

This, too, was a fruitless endeavor, for out of the southwest came another wave of black armor and colored cloaks. Above thousands of crested helms flew hundreds of white banners bearing the proud black shape of Rahmirion. As elated as Henry had been to see the riders of Dalan, the sight of his countrymen, with cloaks of black, gold, crimson, silver, and even the light blue of Kar Naron, brought King Henry to his knees. He held his head in his hands and wept for such beauty, such miraculous favor shown by Rahm.

The lighter, faster horses of Astymere circled to the south to cut short the escape of those fleeing combat. As they drew near, Henry counted at least three thousand. They all rode together, colors mixed, a veritable rainbow sprawling across the battlefield.

THE STRAGGLERS WERE CUT DOWN in short order. Of the force that laid siege to the palace, fewer than twenty now remained. Each was bound hand and foot, and most were gagged, save for the few who could be distinguished as the closest thing to officers the invaders had.

Henry sat with Ronin and Eldric against the city walls, impatiently allowing Healers of both the Crescent and Roleigh to tend to their wounds. Eldric lay on his back, barely conscious, as his medics stitched the wound in his belly. His breastplate and chainmail waited against the stone several feet away.

Henry winced in pain. "*Watch* what you're doing!" Henry bellowed as a young Healer clumsily disinfected his wounded knee.

"A thousand apologies, my King," the young man squeaked as his hands shook.

Ronin snickered and grabbed a full, fresh canteen from the Healer's pack to dump over his head, washing away the blood and grime of the last month.

"Well, look at this sorry excuse for a king," approached a voice Henry could pick out from a crowd of hundreds. Lord Raymund Wallis looked like his old self, sure of foot and bright of smile. He had removed his crimson cloak and stood before Henry appearing little more than a soldier, with Gods' Justice at his hip the only way to distinguish him. "I leave you alone for a month and you have the whole Great Plains in bloody chaos!"

"Raymund," Henry cried. With some difficulty, Henry rose to embrace his friend and brother as though he might vanish if he let go.

"Easy there, old man. I'd hate to have ridden all this way just to have to kill you myself."

Henry laughed exhaustingly and limped with Raymund toward Ronin and Eldric. "Were my instructions received? Were the dead checked?"

"They are being inspected now, my King," Ronin replied. "It is going to take some time. So far, we've found nearly a hundred 'Vs' printed in different—places—on their bodies." Ronin cleared his throat.

"I don't understand," Henry said, shaking his head. "What influence could this Vasur hold over the North? No one had even heard of him ten years ago. There are men from over a dozen tribes here. How could a man from the Republic get to them all? And get them to fight *together*, no less?"

"Your Majesty," Eldric coughed. "Our new…*friends* won't be keeping it to themselves for long."

Ronin applied a wet cloth to Eldric's forehead. "I know several men who would *love* a private audience with them."

"I'm sorry to disappoint you, young Prince," Raymund replied, "but they are your father's prisoners now. I'm told his orders are to have them brought immediately back to Roleigh, to be questioned by the Spear Lords. Several of them are well spoken in the Northern languages. They will get them to talk."

"All right. If my tent is ready, I will need a hot bath and fresh clothes," said Henry. "Raymund, if you would be so kind as to walk with me? I have a bit of a…cramp…in my leg." Raymund snorted, but dutifully offered his arm to the weary king. Henry turned back to Ronin and Eldric. "I shall see you tonight, gentlemen. We have gods damned earned ourselves a proper supper and feather beds."

Eldric sighed, his forearm resting over his eyes to block out the late afternoon sun. "*Real* food. It will take me a month to get the taste of trout out of my mouth. And I'd skin you alive for just a drop of wine…"

Henry raised an eyebrow at the remark, unsure how to react. The day's bloody business had drained both his mind and body. His silence, however, got Eldric's attention, for he removed his arm to reveal his mouth agape, unable to find the words.

"Your…Majesty…" he finally managed.

Henry laughed with a dismissive wave of the hand. "I shall let that one go. Next time, you won't be so lucky."

Eldric let his head fall back to the dirt as Ronin gave him a playful smack in the shoulder. Henry turned to limp with Raymund back toward the sea of green and black tents.

Henry eased himself into bed as gingerly as he could, taking care not to strain his freshly stitched leg. He lay atop fur blankets and let his body sink into the feather mattress laid out for him. It seemed like years since he'd had a proper bed—or a proper night's sleep. He began to doze off before snapping himself back to the waking world.

"Has Thuro's body been recovered?" he asked Raymund. Henry had hardly a moment to think on it.

"He has been found, my King, but we haven't yet been able to bring him to camp. As big a beast as he was, it will be difficult to get him on a sledge, but I have my men seeing to it."

"Thank you, my friend," Henry said, propping himself up on his elbows. "I want him treated with dignity and buried as such."

"Yes, my King," Raymund nodded.

"We must also send a battalion to the Shattered Sisters to collect the dead we were forced to leave there. I want the bodies identified and letters sent home to their families so they may receive proper honors. And we will need to collect our dead from inside the city. Spare no man for that job. I want it done quickly, and with order."

"We will begin tonight, my friend, once you have conferred with King Robert. He is most eager to speak with you after you've properly rested."

"I will see him in short order, he can be assured." Henry pushed himself up to sit up straight, his hamstrings singing as he stretched his legs out in front of him. "I am grateful to have you here, Raymund. For the life of me, I cannot fathom how you managed it."

"You were never one to give wind swallows their proper due, my King," Raymund replied with playful scorn. He pulled a stool from beneath the desk brought for the king and sat with a groan. "After Ronin sent his last wind swallow, Robert had the message in hand within the hour. He immediately mustered his banners and sent his own swallow to Urnest. We began gathering riders by nightfall and nearly killed our horses getting here. I don't think we stopped for more than an hour or two. It will be days before the horses are ready to ride again, but Rahm has smiled on us, Henry. I've never been so sure of it."

Henry's weary smile faded. "Not all of us," he said, his shoulders slumping. He closed his eyes, trying to shut out the horrors that now plagued him. It did no good. The face of every man he killed flew by like kites in a gale, but the faces of those he *lost* stuck with him. "Nolan fell today, Raymund. He is still in that forsaken place. Another friend, another captain, butchered by those beasts. How many more brothers must we lose before this madness ends?"

Raymund looked to the floor and rubbed his hands together, searching for the answer. "Only Rahm knows, Henry," he said. "But I pray the worst is behind us. These events will unfold as Rahm wills them. All we can do is sit back, allow ourselves to be taken by the current, and try to stay afloat."

Henry lay back again and ran his hands through his hair, sweat and blood now drying in his clumped locks. "That reminds me. Will you see to it that a tub is brought in here?"

"At once, my King," said Raymund, springing to his feet as quickly as his sore, aging legs would permit. He was already through the tent flaps before Henry shouted something else.

"Tell them I will strangle any man who wakes me before nightfall!" Henry bellowed out after him. He sat up for a moment, wondering if Raymund heard, then allowed himself to plop back down into the feathers. He closed his eyes, his racing mind beginning to rein itself to a crawl. He thought of Beatrice and Mayson; Nolan and William; all their names were on his lips as he drifted off. He hoped it wouldn't be too long before he could see them all again.

Chapter 37

The Royal Marshal Academy: Astymere
40th Day of the Sixth Month
5018 A.S.

MAYSON TOOK AN OIL CLOTH TO HIS freshly sharpened sword as Forge Master Varin Buchanan scanned his students, each putting the last details into their blades. Every day since the beginning of term, the room had rung with the sound of hammers against steel, shaping the swords that were now nearly completed after the students' years of training in the art. A thin haze caught the sunlight in sharp beams through the open, glassless windows of the sweltering room. Keeping his eyes on his work, Mayson trained his ears on his teacher's speech.

"I don't want to see anyone getting careless this close to end of term," Master Varin said. "This is a crucial time for you lot. You Final Years may get your blades to pass inspection tonight, but a lot of good it will do you if your hand is too busted to wield it."

Though they were growing stale, Mayson and Diero always took Master Varin's stern warnings to heart. There was no help the Baths could provide for a lost finger or hand. Master Varin clasped his wrists behind his back when lecturing, fidgeting his fingers nervously, never quite trusting his students enough to fully relax. Mayson had begun to think the man didn't know what to do with his hands if he wasn't hammering something. Grounding himself in the Forge Master's ticks helped solidify some normalcy that had finally returned to Astymere.

The school had been wracked with terrible worry ever since news of the king's plight reached the Academy. Once King Robert's wind swallows arrived at Kar Naron, it seemed the whole country knew in less than a day; the lonely island was no exception.

Mayson and Diero had hardly been able to focus on anything else for days, even leading up to the Final Fights—the very first Henry had not been there to witness. What should have been relatively easy victories for each turned into long, drawn out scraps. Mayson had two ribs broken by Cordarion Tyne, and Diero was nearly choked into submission by Phylip Hempher. Such sloppy performance had soured their moods as they stewed on their mistakes in the mineral baths, but that quickly changed when news of the king's victory reached them. They now had the luxury of going into the Temple of Red Flame with clear minds.

Taking a break from his labors, Mayson leaned against a nearby wall and stared hard into the stone floor, while Diero clamped down on the hard steel of a small blade that glowed bright orange. He had already finished drawing his final sword, and was now finalizing a counter-dagger. Stifling a yawn, Mayson reflected on just how lucky he'd been not to have been expelled, let alone allowed to participate in the Final Fights. With Mayson, Diero, Brynden, and even some of Grayle's weaker allies telling the same tale, Mayson was cleared of all formal charges after what happened behind the barracks. Though Grayle and his co-conspirators were expelled, Mayson merely pulled night watches atop the wall for the remainder of term. It was a small price to pay; he made up sleep whenever he could.

Mayson pulled off his thick leather gloves and rubbed at the callouses that had long since formed on his palms, musing over the name he would give his sword. He had had many fireside conversations with his father over this very subject the last few years, and aside from his time with Olivia, these memories were some of the sweetest he made at home in between school terms. Henry told him that naming a sword was not too dissimilar from naming a child. It wasn't just a name; it was an identity, a proper mark for an object that would become an extension of oneself. "Once you truly know the sword," he said, "the name will ring in your head clear as a bell. Once you hear it, it cannot be ignored."

After months of work, Mayson was beginning to feel like he knew the piece of steel in front of him; if he concentrated hard enough, he could even hear it whispering to him.

He had crafted the hilt into a black snake, its winding body offering a perfect, curved grip. The head of the snake served as the pommel, with four great fangs bared in a wide-open mouth. With the exception of the coloring and the quality of the steel, it was an exact mirror image of Morning Star, which Mayson took great care to get right. *Gelaya'Khash*, the voice called to him in Avaari, the power of the ancient language of his people giving him goose pimples. *Night Serpent*.

Diero, on the other hand, had fashioned his with a rose made of red steel to serve as his pommel, with green vines wrapping all the way up the hilt to a thin, straight blade.

"I'm going to call mine Rosethorn," Diero said.

"Why?" Mayson asked, slipping out from his deep thoughts.

"In honor of my father. Tobias always talks about how much he loved roses. They were my mother's favorite, too, and according to Tobias, my father planted them anywhere he could on our property in Southslope shortly after they were married. This will be perfect to hand down to a second son. If I can keep it in fighting condition, that is."

After designing their personal swords, the hardening process began. The blades were scorched to the hottest temperatures the students had used thus far, and thrown into a quenching tank. The water was cold, nearly freezing, where the blades would steam and cool, rapidly and evenly.

Tempering the blade was the final step. It was periodically heated to low temperatures and quenched, the repetitive process making it strong but not brittle.

"So—this is it," Mayson stated, walking closer to Diero, who had just finished hammering his dagger. He carefully brought it to the water tank to cool.

"Yes, it is. Amazing how fast five years go by." Diero removed his gloves and set them on a table against the wall. "Are you nervous?"

"I think so. I mean, I know I should be. But for some reason, I just feel indifferent to it all. Almost numb."

Diero chuckled and smirked. "You've been *trained* to be indifferent your entire life."

"It makes for a good ruler."

"And boring conversation," Diero jested. "I know beneath your stoic mask your nerves are jumping just as mine. But men like us feed off nerves. They propel us, give us focus, make us stronger. A racing heart can give you half a step ahead of an opponent—just enough to overcome them. Together, Mayson, we'll be unstoppable, whatever this test may be."

Diero was never willing to underestimate himself, but this was different. As Mayson regarded his brother, he saw the blaze of belief in his eyes. The two gave each other a nod at the sound of the bell.

"Okay, gentlemen, class dismissed—for some of you," Master Varin continued, "I will see you back here tomorrow. Final Years, retrieve your swords, go back to the barracks, and await your summons. I've been instructed to inform you that you are not to leave your quarters. Supper will be brought to you promptly at six. Spend your time wisely, and try to get some rest. The Final Test will begin at the stroke of nine."

Mayson and Diero sheathed their swords and wrapped them from end to end in thick, linen cloth to keep them hidden from prying eyes. The weight of his saber felt more natural than any sword Mayson ever held. He had tailored it just right; even under layers of linen, it felt as if it were an extension of his own hand. *Gelaya'Khash,* the voice now declared so loud in his mind Mayson flinched. The word drained from his ears and lodged itself in his chest, surrounding and encasing his heart. The final piece of the puzzle slid perfectly into place.

MAYSON LAY ON HIS BUNK with his hands crossed over his chest, feeling them rise and fall with each breath. For the last several hours, after the dinner trays had been cleared, he'd been in a state of seamless transition between heavy, dream-filled sleep, and disconnected meditation. He saw his father entering Vita Astym with a full military parade, streamers and flowers raining down upon him. He saw William Otter sparring in the palace yards with Knights of Rahm, unarmored and unarmed in a rare moment of comfort. He saw Olivia sprouting from the lake, the light of the twin moons making her glow as bright as the falling leaves around them. In that moment, he had known peace—a peace he would never come close to again in the waking world. Just as he began to wrap himself in it, his vision melted as his living senses returned. He saw Sharra Ahl-Kalin, her wicked smile, her blood red lips curling over pearly white teeth. Her beauty was more than beguiling, but those piercing eyes and her skilled courtly manners unsettled him to his core.

He blinked and shook his head as the soothing warmth of his dream slowly drained from him, leaving a pit in his stomach. The sun had long since set, and the ring of bunks arranged in the center of the empty barracks were illuminated by several hearths placed at the center. Mayson stood and stretched the weariness from his legs and back, walking over to the nearest fire. Diero and the rest of Mayson's classmates were all still, some lying on their backs as Mayson had, while some sat up, gazing into the fires.

They all bore the same look of fearful determination one would see in men readying to march onto a battlefield for the first time. This *would* be their true first battle, Mayson knew, and he could think of no finer army to march alongside than the seven people in the room with him.

The bell tower sounded from the other side of the island, filling every corner of the empty room with an echoing clatter, blowing the silence away like a pile of dead leaves. They all moved as one, grabbing their sheaths and strapping them to their belts. Mayson knew once the ninth bell tolled, Commandants Grein and Barton would come through that door to summon them. He straightened his black velvet doublet, making sure the line of silver buttons was centered over his torso, and crossed his arms behind his back, standing at attention.

The final bell still echoed off the bare stone walls when Grein and Barton flew through the door baring torches. The eight companions were instructed to unsheathe their blades and form a single file line at the door. Mayson took point, to which no one argued. Behind him went Diero and Kristian. After the sons of the High Families came Kip Kinder, still nearly a full head taller than the rest of them, followed by Teren Ashon, who was now only *little* by name; he now stood head-to-head with Mayson and nearly matched the prince in swordsmanship.

Cordarion of House Tyne and Foran of House Pleke came next. Both had fashioned bastard swords of high steel for themselves in the style of the Silver Knights of Kaladan, with ornate cross guards, and gilded grips and pommels. Phylip of House Hempher, who had fashioned a light, straight-bladed sword with a simple leather and steel grip, brought up the rear. Each held their blade in their right hand across their chest, except for Mayson, whose blade faced the opposite way. The bright silver hue of his high-steel saber leaped out against the black of his doublet.

The commandants led them outside, where packs of students lined their walk to the Temple of Red Flame, all shouting encouragement and well-wishes. The Great Eight, as their peers called them, did not regard the crowd. Mayson blocked everything from his peripheral vision to hone his focus on the Temple in front of him, even managing to drown out the din from his classmates.

When the group reached the Temple, they rearranged their single file line so they each stood side by side. Opposite them stood every one of the Masters, centered by Royal Marshal Qirk, encircled by the remaining student body.

"Graduates," the Marshal stated, approaching the Final Year students. "Behind these doors lies a secret that has remained carefully guarded for centuries. Countless souls before you have confronted it, and countless souls have fallen before it. There is not much I can say that can prepare you for what you are about to face, only that I hope the skills you have learned here will be enough to carry you through. If not, the strength of your brothers beside you will be your only hope. May the gods be kind to you. Now, present your weapons for inspection."

Mayson swallowed hard and took a deep breath as the Great Eight held out their weapons for inspection. Qirk scanned each of them silently, calming the rest of the crowd with a raised hand.

He started at the far end of the line, asking for the name of each blade.

"Razor's Edge," said Cordarion. Qirk nodded and moved on.

"Trinity," Foran said.

"Eccalasar," Teren said with steadfast seriousness.

"Ballatest," Kip answered with a sense of pride.

"Dragon Fang," announced Phylip, louder than the others.

"Honor's Call," Kristian spoke out proudly.

"In honor of my father: Rosethorn," Diero said.

"He would be proud," Qirk responded. His crotchety demeanor had softened this night; he truly seemed a proud mentor. He moved to Mayson and gave the slightest of bows, almost too subtle to register. "And yours?"

"Gelaya'Khash," Mayson replied. "Night Serpent."

The crowd roared as Qirk retreated to the line of professors.

"Boys, you will become men in this kingdom's eyes if you emerge from that door tonight," Qirk said, pointing to the Temple's entrance. "You will be entrusted by the king himself with the privilege of leading the brave men of the Black Army into battle."

The cheers and whistles of the crowd nearly deafened Mayson as he stood motionless. Qirk walked back to the beginning of the line, shook each man's hand, and wished him luck. "Your time has come. Follow Master Varin into the temple, and may Rahm cast his gaze on you."

The crowd chanted for their fellow students as they made their way inside. The torchlight from outside, along with the slivered light of the twin moons, cast long shadows into the small chamber. Mayson felt his body begin to shake despite the warmth of nine bodies crammed into the tight space. *You are the Blood of the Mountain. You shall feel no fear.* He took deep breaths, repeating the mantra in his head until his hands were still and his heart at peace—though his nerves still fired with mad energy. The door closed behind them as the exuberant crowd slowly went mute. It was just the eight students and Master Varin now, on a stairway that spiraled downward, lit by torches ablaze with rich, red flame on either side.

Cobwebs adorned the corners of each faded, white stone step, some of which had cracked off and crumbled to powder. Mayson, now at the back of the group, examined each torch, red as polished rubies and dancing wildly. The hallway had a thick scent of smoke that made him miss the cool, salty, island breeze.

"How long *is* this staircase?" Diero asked when no end could be seen.

"I have no idea," Kristian said. "But if this is part of the test, I'll consider it an easy final!" As tempting a thought as it was, Mayson knew the nightmare hadn't even begun. They carried on further until Mayson guessed they were ten stories beneath the surface.

The group fanned out in front of him as they finally reached the bottom. The room almost seemed like a library in the dim red light. Rows of marble bookshelves stretched from the floor to the ceiling nearly two stories above them, split down the middle by a wide walkway. The end of each case was illuminated by a scarlet torch.

Mayson trained his eyes in the deep red light to see what sat upon those shelves. In place of books, there were countless marble busts of human heads all staring ahead into the darkness, all covered in dust and cobwebs. The students dispersed into rows, as directed by Master Varin. Mayson and Diero stayed near one another, as did most of the boys who paired off, though Kristian held a separate row of his own. Master Varin glided to the end of the long walkway in the middle of the room.

More marble busts and faded relics lined their paths, and the further they moved, the more the features on the stone faces seemed to fade and recede until the last of them was practically smooth. Only a few empty spaces remained, each statue labeled with a name upon a gold plate. Mayson began to feel like he was sealed in a tomb.

"Who do you think they are?" Diero murmured.

"It's hard to tell," Mayson whispered. "I don't recognize any of the faces, or even the names. I have a feeling these are the ones who didn't make it out." Mayson heard Diero gulp, though outwardly, he showed no other signs of discomfort.

Nearly an hour passed as the Final Years examined each row closely, until they all found themselves standing before Master Varin without fully realizing how they'd gotten there. Behind him was a much narrower walkway upon which he'd lead the group single file.

A wide, dark room with an arched ceiling opened into a much taller space on the far side, where the blood light of the torches bathed a great dark figure towering above Master Varin's tall head—the figure of a man with long, flowing robes, carved from pure, shining obsidian. Mayson and the rest could only wonder how any stonemason could get the fragile, glasslike substance to behave in such a malleable way. Behind the figure, two staircases curved toward each other and met at a landing one story above, decorated with a thick, rough-hewn railing.

Two dazzling ruby eyes inset into the statue's face caught the light of the flames and reflected them into hundreds of pinpoints imprinted on the walls. Atop his smooth, shining head emerged two great horns, each as long as a man's arm, curving outward from the sides of the head and bending back inwards to meet in the center.

Master Varin knelt on both knees and lowered his head to the ground in supplication before the likeness of Rahm. The Great Eight followed suit without instruction.

Rahm's outstretched hands held a great stone chalice; on its circular edge, around the circumference, sat eight cups no bigger than thimbles. Master Varin rose, all traces of humanity replaced with the Holiness of the ceremony, and instructed the graduates to make a ring, taking his place in the center.

"You will each take a cup and fill it from the basin. Then you will drink as one. *As one*."

"Yes, Master," they replied in unison. His insistence they all drink at the same time perturbed Mayson. He didn't ignore the instinct, but he didn't follow it either.

"Gentlemen," Master Varin continued, "I can attest to the trial you shall all be forced through this evening. Truth be told, I thank my lucky stars it is far behind me. I do not envy you for what you will experience down here, but there is no doubt in my mind, you will emerge into the light of the stars with glorious victory. There has hardly been a group of graduates like you in recent memory. With that vote of confidence, this is where I leave you. When I have gone, you will fill your cups with the Elixir of Rahm, drink them *together*, and climb the stairs. At the top, there will be a single door. On the other side of it, you will find your destiny. May Rahm cast his gaze upon you, gentlemen."

With a foreboding sense of urgency, Master Varin took his leave of the Great Eight.

FOR SEVERAL MOMENTS AFTER, they all stood in a circle, looking at one another with eagerness and uncertainty.

"Well, this is it," Diero stated. "I'll be damned if any man here isn't worthy or capable of passing this test. I trust you all with my life." He paused a moment. "We heard the man." He walked forward. "Everyone take a cup."

One by one, with the lightest tinge of trepidation, the Great Eight took their tiny cups, so smooth and delicate Mayson feared he would drop and shatter his.

It was difficult to tell the true color of the liquid within the basin. The light of the torches made it seem as black as the statue that held it. Before long, each miniscule cup was filled, and the Eight looked on each other once more.

Mayson held his cup aloft in salute to his classmates; the rest followed suit. He began to recite the Soldier's Prayer, which had been uttered by Astymerian warriors since the War of

Independence.

"The blood of the Wise be my strength; may his all-seeing eyes be my guide." One by one the entire group joined in. "Show me light in darkness, bring me certainty in doubt, and let the strength of the Mountain flow through me. May I be as hard and unfeeling as stone. May I be as relentless as the tide, and like the great oak, may I never fall. Cayrian Karrok. Cayrian Rahma."

With one last nod to each other, they emptied their cups to the last drop as one, as Master Varin ordered. The sweet liquid seemed thin as water when Mayson scooped it from the basin, but it ran down his throat like sap. The edges of his sight immediately began to blur. They all seemed affected so, blinking hard and shaking their heads as if to clear their vision. Mayson closed his eyes and took a deep, centering breath. With a tap to Diero's shoulder, he then led the way up the right staircase, as Kip led three of their companions up the left. The door that waited for them at the top of the stairs looked like nothing more than a broom closet, with old, dusty planks nailed together and a rusted iron hoop for a handle; it was only wide enough for one man to pass through.

Mayson wiped a solid dark line through the thick dust with his finger and tentatively reached for the handle. He took firm grip of the flaking, rusty iron, and turned to the others. "Follow me." The boys all nodded at their Prince and formed behind him, allowing him to take point into the unknown.

Mayson's heart began to race. He had a million thoughts as to what the Final Test might be, each more unpleasant than the one before. Now, after long waiting, he was a few steps from finding out.

They all drew their swords to signal to Mayson they were ready to start. Mayson gave the iron loop a hard twist and pushed the door open, the rest of the group filing in behind him. Once they'd all passed through, the door swung shut on its own, echoing through what sounded like a deep, empty cavern.

"What do we have to do?" asked Diero. The boys, utterly confused, stood on a staircase that led straight down, a central railing ablaze with red flame. The only other light in the room came from a lone torch on a far wall. "Do we have to find something?"

"I have no idea," Phylip replied.

They spread out in two groups of four, each heading to a different side in search of anything that might offer some clue in the sparse light. When Cordarion stepped on a small stone that crumbled beneath his foot, the crackling stirred a shadow in the darkness on the far side of the room. A low, growling noise filled the empty void. The red torch along the back wall began to move, swaying slightly back and forth. Mayson felt his nerves catch fire as the ground began to shake, and the room grew warm.

Suddenly, the flame spread, crawling along dark, scaly skin to further illuminate a hulking black shape lay crouched against the far wall. Its eyes, like flaming coals, burned through the waning darkness. The red flames spread along its torso and under its belly, crawling up the creature's back to atop its horned head, illuminating the square room around them.

Mayson and the others stood rooted to their spots, staring with eldritch horror at the living nightmare they had now been locked in with. Mayson drew Gelaya'Khash with blind instinct, his mind momentarily paralyzed by fear.

The creature slowly dipped to the ground, its body now encased in rich veins of crimson fire. It hissed at the boys and crept slowly toward Mayson and Diero, who stood in front of Kristian and Phylip. The four scuttled behind a boulder protruding from the wall and stared at the others across the way, still gaping at the monster. Mayson tightened his grip around the dark hilt of his blade and breathed deep, feeling just a sliver of peace return to his mind. Just enough to form a plan.

"This is what we do," he said, immediately silenced by a most horrific roar. It pierced each of their hearts, robbing them of their wits.

"This isn't happening! *This isn't happening!*" Diero shouted over continuous growling.

Mayson peeked over the boulder to study the animal as it took in another breath and let out another stone-wrenching roar. It was even louder as it sprinted toward the group at the other side of the room. The walls and ground shook, as cascades of dust fell on the boys' heads. The swinging, serpentine tail brought the total size of it to over fifty paces front to back, Mayson figured with shaky judgment. The body was as wide as two carriages abreast, and the scaly ankles of its four legs were ringed in reflective flame.

The boys on the other side began to scream and run around the back side of a boulder, reappearing only to sprint toward Mayson and Diero's group. The beast turned and ran after them, spewing a line of scarlet fire from its steaming jaws. The back of Foran's tunic became alight as he scrambled to take his place within the group. In a heartbeat, Kip and Teren ripped it from him and stomped out the flames, with great difficulty. It was as though the flames themselves fought for self-preservation. Foran soldiered on despite the blistering burns that formed on his back.

Diero fought to be heard. "We need to separate quickly—give it too many targets to track!"

Everyone nodded as the beast turned the corner behind the rock, causing the boys to sprint from yet another jet of flames. The monster let out a screech and whipped its tail against the rock, splitting it in two. Mayson and Diero ran and ducked together. The boys dispersed around the room, each looking for a chance to attack, but the tail was long and moved unpredictably, making it nearly impossible to sneak up on it.

A flame hit the wall next to Kip as he dove out of its path, leaving his sword on the ground behind him. He attempted to go back for it, but the great beast quickly closed in, forcing him to head for the nearest cover next to Kristian. The creature's long neck presented a distinct disadvantage; it could easily peek over and around the large boulders.

The monster quietly crept up the stone behind Kristian and Kip. Mayson watched as the boys stood unaware of the slithering tongue flickering right behind their heads.

"Run!" Mayson shouted. Both sprinted to barely avoid being snagged by the beast's fearsome jaws. It gave an angry screech and fully spread its wings.

They were large and very dark at first, but fiery veins soon spread from its shoulders to its wingtips. The beast shot fire straight up and delivered an enraged roar before jumping into midair to crash to the ground. When its feet hit, it sent a shockwave of flames across the floor to fill the room. Kristian managed to hurl himself over the ring of fire, but Phylip didn't get airborne in time. The bottom of his pants caught fire as he fell to the ground. He attempted to douse it, but the red flames quickly consumed him, his agonized cries strangled before they even had a chance to form.

The beast closed in on Foran, who had tried to run to Phylip's aid, but ended up pinned by one of its long talons. Mayson and the rest struck their steel against the ground and boulders, in an attempt to distract the behemoth, but its eyes were focused on the helpless prey before it. Foran struggled to rip his pant leg free but was quickly cast to the ground by a whip of the monster's tail.

"*No*! Over here!" Mayson shouted.

The beast moved on top of Foran, who stared into its red eyes. Steam billowed from its mouth as it opened wider, flames stirring deep inside to illuminate the back of its throat. Before anyone could help, red flame erupted from its mouth and consumed. Foran's screams were unbearable to hear, but didn't last long. He was gone in moments.

Mayson ran to Diero behind a boulder while the monster dragged the blackened body of their brother to a corner of the room. Both of them stood silent, speechless, immobile. Diero looked pale and wasted, his arms trembling; his eyes seemed to scan the room without seeing a thing.

"Diero," Mayson said. "I need you to distract him." Diero didn't respond, forcing Mayson to take him by the shoulders and shake him. "Focus, Diero! While there is still breath in your lungs, I need you to *fight* with me, as I fight with *you*. Do you hear?"

Diero's eyes snapped back to reality with just a spark of recognition, and he finally responded with a nod. He grabbed Rosethorn firmly by the handle and ran to the others to spread the word.

A minute of dipping and dodging helped the six boys take cover behind a rock as the beast charged its way around the room, cracking and splitting every boulder it touched into crumbling pieces. Mayson hid behind one of the few boulders still intact, several spaces away from the others, darting from one pile of rock to the next to keep the beast angered and confused.

Whenever it seemed to hone in on one brother, another would pelt it with one of the now plentiful stones scattered around the room, diverting its attention to earn enough time for the others to slip away. This strategy kept the beast pinned to the center of the room as Mayson slowly climbed atop a boulder and locked eyes on his prey. There was a spot on its back where there were no veins of fire—just large enough for someone to stand if they landed right.

Mayson looked to his right and saw Diero stumble on a pile of loose stones, twisting his ankle. He began a mad scramble to crawl away from the beast, but with his back to it, he could not see how close it was getting, despite the others' best efforts. Mayson drew Gelaya'Khash and held her steady, channeling all his energy into his legs and arms. There was no more time to waste.

He could see light emanating from the edges of the monster's mouth, steam pouring from its nostrils as Diero struggled to regain his feet.

"*Nooooo!*" Mayson cried, launching himself from his perch. He soared through the air like an arrow, bringing his blade straight down into the back of the beast's neck like a stake into rocky ground. He was nearly deafened by the shriek the beast unleashed, as a spray of black, steaming blood nearly blinded him. As it pooled around his hands and feet and dripped to the floor, Diero led the others to press the assault.

In its death thralls, the beast was more dangerous than ever. However, its flames were now useless, giving the attackers a chance to approach. Six masterfully crafted pieces of high steel slashed, stabbed, and cut at the beast, each spouting a new fountain of hissing black ooze. Teren was sent sailing into the stone walls with a flick of the beast's tail, but the onslaught continued. Mayson couldn't tell how long he hacked before its legs gave out. None could tell who struck the killing blow, but the beast suddenly fell silent and still.

When the flames went out, the room grew dark once more, the red flames of the staircase casting long shadows across the wreckage. The boys stood, taking in deep breaths of the sweetest air they'd ever tasted. They gathered around the defeated demon, nodding and embracing each other.

"Well, I imagined it would be much worse," Diero said to Kristian, wrapping an arm around his shoulder and leaning on him to support his ankle.

The door swung open and Royal Marshal Qirk entered, joined by the other Masters of the Academy. Even in the dim room, the bright smile on his face said it all.

"Gentlemen! I must say, you did better than even *I* expected.

Hardly a loss of life, and such a forceful show of it. I expected at least half of you might fall. Several previous classes danced around for hours before ending the challenge." He paused, rubbing the stubble of his chin and eyeing the burnt husks that were once Foran and Phylip. "Barton!" he cried, turning over his shoulder. "Fill some buckets with water and come rouse these two!"

Mayson began to feel his blood boil. "Rouse them? Is that some kind of joke? There's hardly anything left of them!"

"Isn't there? Take another look, boy." The Marshal didn't seem the least bit angered by the prince's biting words.

Mayson tore his eyes from Qirk to cast them down at the piles of charred meat that had once been his friends. The blur around the edges of his vision was beginning to fade, and as it did, the burns upon the fallen gradually melted away to reveal two perfectly unharmed young men.

"What is this devilry?"

"Mayson, look!" Kristian cried. The stones were all of one piece; there was no blood upon the floor, and the great beast was gone, as though it had never existed.

"What have you done to us?" the prince demanded of a smiling Qirk.

"We imbibed you with the Elixir of Rahm and pitted you against a fragment of his spiritual power. What you saw was not a falsehood, but only a battle of the spirits, and not so much the body. Those of you who lived have been deemed worthy by Rahm to carry the banners of the Crescent to face our enemies. The two who died will unfortunately have a tougher go of things when they come to. They will be allowed in the armed services, but their place as leaders must be earned once more. Now, return to your barracks, boys. You've earned some rest."

Mayson and Diero, followed by Kristian and Addam, trudged up the stairs, through the room of statues, and up ten flights to the outside.

The moons, which hovered just above the ocean as they entered, were now high in the night sky. The group crossed the grounds toward the barracks and settled in for the night.

"Rest easy tonight, boys," Addam told the group of graduates as they settled into their beds. "We will gather your items. Tomorrow you will dine on the Feast of Champions in the

Marshal's private solar. You will then spend the day in the Baths, to ensure you are well enough for the graduation ceremony tomorrow evening." He turned to go but stopped as he reached the door. "You've made us all proud today, boys. You've made *me* very proud." With a warm, weary smile, he let himself out into the silent night.

The sweet softness of the pillow against Mayson's head was bliss beyond description. The Elixir of Rahm left his mouth feeling dry and his eyes heavy, but he didn't care. He lifted his head as far as he could to try to confer with his classmates, but each of their heads were buried in their pillows. There would be time to talk about their triumph later; time to talk about how they could help Phylip and Foran once they graduated; time to try to make sense of even a small piece of what had happened; but not tonight. Tonight, the only thoughts swimming through the young prince's head were of glory and victory. For the first time he could remember, Mayson Karrok slipped off to a warm, peaceful slumber with a smile.

Chapter 38

Vita Astym: Astymere
10th Day of the Seventh Month
5018 A.S.

MAYSON STOOD ON THE LANDING of the grand staircase, looking down at the open double doors that led onto the palace grounds, the last of a long procession that had been making its way to the feast for several minutes. The whole city was bursting with celebration for the graduation of the latest Academy class, and the cream of all Astymerian society had gathered at the palace to celebrate his lording. His parents led the way of course, with King Henry aided both by Queen Beatrice and a sturdy cane Hammund had crafted for him. Next came the Wallis and Rahmos families, complete with fully armed retainers and essential members of the household. After came the Royal Marshal Academy's graduating class, honored with their own grand entrance.

Diero had waited with Mayson while the others filed out the door. His ankle had healed quickly in the Baths, and he hopped about with boyish excitement for his first major public appearance as a High Lord, Morning Star bobbing and swaying at his hip. He even threw a few playful punches at Tobias as the befuddled Head of House did his best to swat them away.

"Don't enjoy yourself too much out there," Mayson said, taking Diero by the shoulders to straighten his golden cloak. "Remember, we're not supposed to have fun anymore."

"Indeed, I'll try," Diero replied with feigned seriousness. "As long as I stay away from the wine, I think I can be as stoic as…well…you."

"First of all, no, you can't—you don't have it in you. Secondly, you most *definitely* will not be staying away from the wine. Nevertheless, let us *try* to remain somewhat respectable tonight. Every eye in the place is going to be on *us* for a change, and if we're not careful, we could really trip ourselves up before we even get running."

"Will you just relax for five minutes?" Diero pleaded, cupping Mayson's cheeks in his hands. "This may be your last opportunity before your life is utterly consumed with Princely duties. Besides, most of them out there are drunk as sin already; the rest will soon follow. No one will have any moral high ground to stand on after tonight, so let yourself go for a few hours. Hell with every eye in the place; there's only one pair out there that ought to concern you." Diero gave him a light pat on the cheek and made his way down the stairs with his retainers. "Well, maybe two," he shot over his shoulder with a knowing grin.

Mayson stood lost in a myriad of thoughts as the crowd gathered in the yards cheered for Diero. He knew he would find no peace tonight, no matter how much wine he drank or how many courtly ladies he danced with. *The mountain stands tall against the wind and rain. It shall not falter.* He slipped on his princely mask and made his way down the stairs, flanked by six Knights of Rahm. He stopped to straighten his doublet of steel-gray velvet, and ran a nervous hand over the serpent head of Gelaya'Khash's hilt at his right hip before stepping out into the evening light.

Several hundred voices rang out in salute as Mayson crossed from out the doorway's shadow, bathed in the light of the dying evening and dozens of torches mounted on tall, steel poles. Music began to play from the heart of the yard, loud enough to be heard over the sounds of screaming admirers, officials, friends, and even some soldiers of the Black Army. The dark outlines of hundreds of Knights of Rahm stood stark against the evening sky as they stood watch atop the four palace walls.

Mayson made his way down the steps onto the gravel and toward the grass, where so many years ago he had first learned to hold a sword. First to greet him was his father, followed by a loving embrace from his mother, silent tears rolling down her cheeks. The rest of the crowd then threw their love and well wishes upon him. Ladies of the court curtsied deeply before him, and lords and nobles alike bent the knee as he passed.

Chefs stood over open flames; roasted pigs and spits of beef filled the air with the intoxicating scent of smoke and charred meat. Fresh fruit and vegetables had been wheeled in from the surrounding farmlands earlier in the day and sat in bowls along long tables, allowing guests to help themselves. Jugs of fresh wine sat in abundance upon each table, loud, drunken laughter already overpowering the jubilant music in the background.

The main table looked down upon the open dance floor, with the band in a nearby corner. The smooth, wooden floor was enough to hold nearly a hundred people and was packed to the edges with dozens of happy couples reveling in both the melody and each other's company. The sight was a myriad of colors that delighted the eye, as the music delighted the ear. Mayson saw Hammund and Tobias standing near the cooks, chatting away while still looking diligent as ever. *Perhaps Diero should lecture them about relaxing.*

He spied Mylas and Holto standing on the outskirts of the party, both men clean shaven and wearing their full Gildarian armor. The sight of them reminded him Olivia was somewhere in the crowd, and while that thought should have made his heart sing, tonight it soured his stomach and made him sweat.

Mayson realized from a distance that Holto was keeping eyes on the Goldblades, and throughout the crowd, no member of the Goldblade guards were more than twenty feet from Eduardas. Mylas had his eyes on a small gaggle of ladies congregating near the edge of the dance floor.

Mayson joined the Rahmos table, where Kristian and Tyrel sat tearing into plates piled high with meat, cheese, and bread. Both had foaming mugs of ale beside them that made Mayson's mouth water. Jalen sat across from them, silently sipping from his mug. From his pained expression, it was something a *bit* stronger than spiced wine.

"Care to share some of that, brother?" Kristian asked in between chomps of roasted mutton, a small trail of juice trailing down his chin. Jalen held his gaze mid-sip.

"Not on your life," he said, downing what was left. "I'll need all of this I can get in order to make it through this circus with what's left of my sanity." Tyrel rose from his seat as he spotted Mayson, raising his mug in an over-exaggerated toast.

"It's about damn time you came down from your room! We thought you might have gotten lost, or run into a busty serving wench eager to earn the new Lord's favor," Tyrel joked as he wrapped Mayson in a tight hug around the neck.

"Gotten a bit of an early start, have we?" Mayson heard Diero ask as he placed his hand behind Mayson's shoulder.

"And it won't be an early finish, I can assure you," Tyrel responded, leaving the group to fetch another drink.

Mayson grabbed a crystal glass from the passing tray of a nearby server and took a long draught of wine. Peering through the crowd at the hundreds of smiles and laughs, he could almost feel the warm revelry seep into his tightly wound shoulders. His eyes stopped short as they scanned over his parents' dining table, where Olivia was speaking with his mother and Lily. Her crimson gown fell in a silk so light it looked like it was made of wisps of cloud. Golden embroidery crawled down her sleeves to her wrists and spiraled around her body all the way down to her ankles, while her hair hung in loose curls flowing over her shoulders.

Mayson turned to Diero, hoping he would have some sort of sarcastic comment to distract him, but his brother was frozen solid, staring at Lily in her silver gown adorned with pearls across her upper chest and shoulders, her hair falling straight from two small braids running along each side of her head. She, too, was a vision, and came quite close to offering the distraction Mayson sought.

The three of them looked to be as thick as thieves as they laughed together, sipping from their wine glasses. Mayson tried to mark every detail of that picture, everyone finally happy and at peace. Between Lily leaving within the fortnight, and the conversation he would be forced to have with Olivia, it would not last.

"Well," Diero said, placing his glass down on the table. "They didn't get all dressed up for nothing. Let's go ask them to dance before someone else does."

The boys made their way over, stopping for a few more words with other guests along the way. Even Commander Stone had made his way from Kar Naron for the occasion, though his humorless face seemed to scowl at every man or woman enjoying the party.

Mayson drew near enough to smell Olivia's perfume when he was cut off by a pair of Avaari blue eyes, piercing and knowing. A young lady curtsied before him, two loose ringlets of hair falling about either side of her face while the rest of her long, black locks were bound to her head in a dazzling spiderweb of braids. Her smile was sweet as honey with a slight aftertaste of venom, her lips blood red against the snow-white of her face.

"My Prince," she said in a melodic voice trained for public speaking. Mayson had prayed he wouldn't run into his betrothed until after he had the chance to speak to Olivia, but maintained his princely mask as he internally cursed his luck. "I apologize I haven't been able to offer you my congratulations sooner, but you are a rather difficult man to track down. I'm hoping you won't be making a habit of this once we're married." She took a sip from the slender, silver cup she held, but kept her eyes trained on him.

"My dear Sharra," Mayson said as magnanimously as he could manage in his frustration and discomfort. "I assure you, once the madness of all the pomp and circumstance dies down, I will give you, and our wedding plans, my full attention."

"You have a reputation as a man of your word, among other things," she said with a grin, taking another sip to lightly bite the rim of her cup. "I look forward to this *attention* with great anticipation." Mayson took a sip from his own glass and held her in silent regard. Everything about her seemed *designed* to be intoxicating, from the light smell of honeysuckle to the sweet song of her voice; even her piercing gaze seemed to reel him in like a snagged fish. Worse yet, her father, Lord Haamin, was likely watching from some unseen vantage, gauging and calculating whether Mayson had enough genuine interest in his daughter to feel comfortable with their arrangement. If he was to be bound to this woman for life, he would have to steel himself against these powers, lest he end up enslaved by her charms. Of all he knew about her, one fact shone clear as day: she was dangerous. For now, he decided, it was best to play the game.

"As do I," he said with as much honey as he could muster. "Now, if you will excuse me, my Lady, there are many people to attend to this evening; I must play the dutiful host. Perhaps I could call on you tomorrow afternoon for a private lunch?"

He thought he saw a glint of frustration, but Sharra quickly recovered before it could be plainly read. *She's good. She's very good.* She smiled and simply offered him her hand. "It would be my pleasure, my Prince." Mayson kissed her hand and felt a burst of heat nearly burn his lips. The look she gave him as they parted made him feel like a rabbit caught in a snare, unsettling his already deteriorating nerves as he wove through the crowd toward Olivia.

Olivia saw him coming, giving him a smile that nearly broke his heart into a thousand pieces. *Be strong. You can't falter now.* She reached out her hand for him to kiss and began to curtsey, but he wrapped her in an iron tight hug, taking in the smell of her— all of her. Her hair, her skin—the very air she moved around in.

He soaked in her essence, wanting to draw in every last ounce of it.

After recovering from her shock, she returned his embrace so tightly that he could feel her heartbeat quicken against his chest. When Mayson finally released her, the queen, Diero, and Lily were all staring coldly at him; Diero and Lily as though he were soft in the head, and the queen as though he had just taken a piss in front of the entire Astymerian nobility.

"My Lady," Diero said, breaking the silence that grew around them like a dark bubble. "Might I have this dance?"

Lily broke her gaze from Mayson and Olivia and turned to Diero with a loving smile. "Yes, you may."

Diero led Lily out onto the dance floor while Beatrice's eyes remained locked on Mayson. "My Lady," Mayson whispered to Olivia. "May I have a word in private?"

Olivia cast a nervous look at Beatrice before giving Mayson a slight nod. Mayson gave his mother a loving pat on her shoulder before leading Olivia away through the crowd. *You don't have to worry, dear Mother. I worry enough for myself.*

The voices and music had faded by the time Mayson let go of Olivia's hand. They were now on the western side of the palace, yards behind several tall shrubs, the last blue light of day casting deep shadows all around them. The mountain wind made Mayson's shadow silk cloak dance wildly about him and Olivia tremble. She seemed to be caught between confusion and amusement, but Mayson thanked his lucky stars she did not seem the least bit concerned or afraid.

"Mayson," she finally said with an exasperated laugh. "What in the world are we…"

"If I don't get this out now, I may lose my will, and I couldn't bear to live with that regret, not for a single day." Her amusement quickly drained from her face. "I need you to know something. Two things, actually. One I have been dying to say to you since I first laid eyes on you; the other, I wish with every beat of my heart I didn't need to say."

Mayson expected another question but got only deafening silence, broken by the crackling of torches and the blowing of the wind. Olivia stood silently, sadly, waiting for him to continue.

"I love you," Mayson forced out in a cracking voice. "But I

don't *only* love you. You are every bit of love I've ever felt, every bit of pure joy I've ever known, and in my darkest times, you have been the light I cling to. Before Rahm's all-seeing eyes, under Estrelda's blazing stars, I declare I would choose you every day for all eternity, if you would have me."

Burning tears blinded him as his knees grew weak; his chest felt as though it would burst open like a broken dam. Olivia took his face in her hands and wiped his tears away, the gentle touch of her skin against his the sweetest agony he had ever known. He took a firm hold of her hands in his and brought them to his chest.

"But I can't choose you, and you can't choose me. We've both known this from the start, and I have been a fool to think it could be any other way." Olivia's eyes now began to well, a few silent tears rolling down her cheeks, but unlike Mayson, she did not weep. She stood resolute in her pain. "I've imagined a thousand times how I might say to hell with the Elders, the Avaari, my gods damned crown, and declare to the world that I choose you. If I were anyone else, I would have done it already, if you would have had me. But if I did, it would be the end of the both of us—the end of Astymere, and everything my family has built. It all rests on my shoulders; every day I feel as though my legs will buckle under the weight of it. This is such a disgracefully unfair thing to do to you—and I have never hated myself more."

He looked into Olivia's deep brown eyes, mirroring the dancing flames all around them, and tried to burn every detail into his mind to hold onto forever. She stared up at him, unblinking, before slamming her lips into his and wrapping her arms around his neck. The world around them vanished as the flowing mountain wind wrapped them together in a wild embrace. Mayson's heart leapt into his throat. He lost himself to the softness of her lips, wrapping his arms even tighter around her. In that moment, he could have been speared through the heart, shot with a thousand arrows, and lit aflame—and he wouldn't feel a thing. In those sweet moments, there was only the two of them, the last wild flames of a love doomed to die.

She finally released him and pressed her forehead into his chest as he ran his fingers through her hair. "I choose you, now and forever," she whispered. "Wherever I go, I carry you with me. Every face I see will be yours. I will love you for a thousand years and beyond."

Mayson swallowed the new tears that fought to come. He wiped his eyes on his sleeve and sniffled his nose clear, pulling out a satin kerchief to offer to Olivia. She graciously accepted it and dried her eyes before offering it back to him with all the fine manners expected of a high-born lady.

"Keep it," he said. "Carry it with you, wherever you go."

She offered him only a sad smile back that nearly tore his heart in two.

"Shall we return, my Lady?" he asked, offering her his arm. She swallowed hard and closed her eyes tight.

"Nothing would please me more," she replied in a wavering voice.

The walk back seemed to take weeks as time slowly crawled by. Every sound seemed muted, every color illuminated in the firelight faded; Mayson felt as though he were four inches shorter, his very life blood drained. Once they entered the outskirts of the feast, he attempted to straighten himself to full height and placed a hand over his chest as though to cover the gaping hole newly ripped in it. The world slowly sprang back to life as he slipped on his princely mask and wrapped himself in his resentful duty. Tonight, it would be his only source of strength.

"I think I will rejoin my family, my Prince, if you don't mind," Olivia said, looking out toward the crowd of revelers. Mayson released her arm without a word and stared at the ground, listening to her footsteps fade away. If he looked at her, if he watched her go, he knew he would chase after her. He dared not.

Instead, Mayson found Diero sitting at the end of one of the long tables adjacent to the dance floor. His hair clung to his forehead in a sweaty mat and he was breathing heavily, downing the last of a mug of ale. A small group of well-wishers had just turned their backs on him, and Lily was nowhere to be found. Mayson slumped into an empty chair beside him, resting his elbows on his knees.

Diero placed an unusually tender hand on Mayson's back.

"I want to die, Diero," Mayson croaked. "I want to die and be reborn as *anyone* else."

"I know, brother, I know. But here you are: Mayson Karrok, Prince Karrok-Aht, High Lord of Astymere, and the blood of the

First Men. If it were meant to be, it would be. We can't change our fate, no matter how hard we wish." Mayson tore his thoughts from his own misery.

"Where is Lily?" he asked.

"The wine and dancing went to her head a bit quicker than expected. She went off to bed a short while ago. I hate saying goodbye to her, Mayson, even for just a few hours. How the hell will I survive when she leaves—probably for good?"

Mayson looked out through the crowd at Olivia, who now sat with Amy, trying to seem cheerful. "We will find out, together."

Mayson grabbed a mug from a passing server and downed it in several forceful chugs that ran out the corners of his mouth and soaked into his velvet doublet. He slammed the mug down on the table and let out an uncharacteristic belch everyone around him could surely hear.

"I think I'll go to bed too, brother. Things will be different in the morning, if the gods are good." Diero rose to embrace Mayson, who squeezed his brother tightly to fight the chill growing in his bones.

When he finally parted from Diero, Mayson was forced to weave through a sea of lower lords and courtly gentlemen showering him with praise and invitations to dinners, dances, and hunts. Now that he was officially a man of power, they were all dying for a small token of favor—to just be seen with him. As king he would be far too busy to answer such frivolous calls, but for now, he must learn to tolerate them.

He did note, however, that not one of the Avaari Elders approached him. The few that showed up supported him and his father, but he guessed they weren't brave enough to risk the wrath of Henry's detractors. *I'll make note of it all.*

Mayson had nearly reached his parents on the edge of the dance floor when a voice called out, cutting through the crowd to silence the feast.

"*Toast!*" the voice cried. "I wish to propose a toast!"

An Avaari man had climbed the musicians' dais and began waving his wine glass about with the unbridled enthusiasm of one who'd crossed the line of 'drunk' hours ago. Several guards moved to get him down, but Henry raised his hand in objection, amused by his antics. The man wasn't dressed fine enough to be one of the lower lords, but he might've been a landowner or some kind of well-off merchant. Invited, of course, but at the bottom of the barrel.

"My fine lords and ladies, my friends, my King and Queen, my Prince: I would just like to say what an honor it is to be among such *fine* people on this glorious night!" This earned a cheer from the crowd, including Henry, whose knee hardly seemed to bother him anymore.

"Yes, all the finest people Astymere has to offer, here to revel in the company of divine royalty—though I'd say the real divinity was poured into these glasses." The crowd laughed at this, many raising their own glasses in agreement. Then the man's smile faded. "*Divine* royalty. Beyond reproach; beyond correcting; beyond consequence."

The crowd now grew silent, with the exception of a few confused murmurs scattered about the yard. The man's voice grew hard and clear, his drunken fogginess burning away. "*Consequences*! Were there any when our *great* king forsook his own tribe and brought a foreigner into his bed? When they sired an *illegitimate,* half-blooded mongrel, and called it Prince?"

Mayson could hardly believe his ears at first. As the crowd began to shout him off the stage, Henry simply stood there, silently fuming. The man continued his rant. "Were there *consequences* when that mongrel inherited his father's decadence, and took a foreign whore into his *own* bed?"

"*Enough!*" Mayson shouted, stepping forward to confront the man. "You disgrace yourself, you drunken fool!"

"*You* are the disgrace!" the man roared. "Every day for over twenty years, I've had to sit by and endure this slight to Avaari honor. No more! I come here tonight bearing you the fruit of your family's sinful garden!" The man gave a flourish with his right arm and produced a long, thin knife from out of his sleeve before Mayson could take another step. He flipped the point into his grasp and hurled it at the prince before Mayson could pick a direction to dodge, the blade growing nearer with each passing heartbeat.

Something slammed into Mayson's side and knocked him to the ground, the knife sailing harmlessly by him. His shock and confusion lasted only a moment before he got his bearings and locked eyes on his assailant. People were still shrieking from the sudden viciousness of the attack, several soldiers already in pursuit.

Mayson scrambled to his feet and took chase, sliding Gelaya'Khash out her sheath. When he locked upon his target in the dim light, he let the sword fly with boiling fury, losing sight of it as it sailed through the darkness; a wet hiss and an accompanying shriek told him the shot wasn't wasted. He came upon the dark outline of the man crumpled on the ground, writhing in pain. The soldiers and dozens of Knights of Rahm caught up a moment later, the light from their torches revealing the sword had struck the assailant in his lower back.

Mayson yanked the sword out and turned the rat over, grabbing him by the collar to hold the high steel blade to his throat. The wretch was smiling, his eyes closed as if entranced by a sweet dream. Mayson grit his teeth and tightened his grip on the black serpent fitting perfectly in his grasp, ready to plunge it into his throat.

The crowd yelled and scrambled in the confusion behind him, but one panicked howl pierced through the din and grabbed hold of Mayson's mind. He turned back to the feast to see the crowd congregating in one large clump near the edge of the dance floor. "Keep him here and make sure he doesn't bleed out—yet," Mayson instructed the soldiers, as he rose and dusted himself off.

Mayson marched back toward the crowd, and as he approached, he saw Knights of Rahm huddled together as others tried to keep the crowd at bay. Dozens more sprang up from out the night and surrounded him in a tight cluster as he moved. Lords Urnest and Raymund fell to their knees, hovering over someone lying on the ground. Mayson quickened his pace to a sprint, unclasping his cloak as it held him back. The terrible wailing that had grabbed his attention grew louder and clearer now, with pure panic pulling him faster than his legs would allow.

His heart was pounding out of his chest by the time he reached the dance floor, with several Knights of Rahm still in his way. "Let me through!" he cried. "*Let me through!*"

He cleared the swarm of black-clad knights to find his mother cradling his father in her arms, wailing and sobbing as Galen tended to the King. The assailant's knife was lodged just under his left pectoral, buried in flesh up to the hilt. In his black ceremonial robes, it was hard to tell how bad the bleeding was until one looked upon the growing pool of it in the grass beneath him.

By the Gods' mercy, Mayson saw his father's blue eyes light up as he approached. He reached out, beckoning him with what little strength he had. Mayson fell to his knees, dropped his sword, and crawled to his father's side. Beatrice lay him flat so he could wrap his arm around his son's shoulder. The king's hand was still reaching, and Mayson took it, desperately squeezing. Henry feebly squeezed back.

"I wasn't going to lose you," he whispered.

Mayson's voice caught in his throat. "Galen is here; he can fix you—lie still."

"I'm sorry, Mayson." Henry's voice grew weaker as he began to cough small dribbles of blood out of the corner of his mouth.

"Stop," Mayson demanded, fighting back tears. "Focus and stay with me. You can tell me you're sorry tomorrow, when the sun rises. Do you hear me? Tell me *tomorrow*."

"Rahm…calls me home."

"*No*," Mayson demanded. "If Rahm wants you, he'll have to take me, too." Henry let go of Mayson's hand to touch his cheek.

"The blood of a king is always bound to spill, Mayson—but Rahm's not finished with you yet," Henry whispered. "You are the blood of the mountain; you shall feel no fear."

"Father, please," Mayson begged, now openly weeping.

"*You* are the blood of the mountain," King Henry repeated, his voice beginning to falter as the light in his eyes dimmed.

Mayson stared down at his father through the burning sting of tears and fell sidelong into his mother's embrace. He lowered himself over the king's body, taking his face in his hands and pressing his forehead against his. He sat there for what felt like hours, bellowing his pain into his father's lifeless chest while the rest of the crowd remained silent and still. Mayson had nearly cried himself into a stupor when a soft voice rang out through his sobs.

"Long live the King," cried Lord Urnest.

"Long live the King," Raymund managed to choke out.

"Long live the King," Diero repeated through his own gasps.

One by one the chant spread through the crowd until it became a somber chorus overcoming the once-joyous celebration.

Mayson stood to look upon the face of each speaker as the bleak reality of the moment crashed down on him.

All now stared at their new King, waiting. What decree or word of hope could they want? *What more did they want from him?*

Mayson did his best to sever his heart from his mind. There would be a proper time to mourn—but it wasn't now. Now, there was work to be done, and no one else to do it.

"Sound the palace bells. I want the palace locked down and the city gates sealed. *No one* leaves the Capital," Mayson declared in a worn, raspy voice devoid of all feeling. "I want *every* man and woman here questioned; every spy in the Heartlands on full alert, every port and dock closed until further notice.

"The assassin shall be bound and thrown in a cell. See to it he gets a Healer's attention. I will *not* have him die before justice is properly served." Mayson paused to take a solemn breath.

"My…father's body needs to be taken to the Hall of Healers to be cleaned and prepared for funeral rites." He scanned the crowd of stunned faces, none moving except the Knights of Rahm and the High Lords to carry out his orders. The others stood dumbfounded. "*Now!*" he bellowed.

The soldiers began ushering people into groups, separating and seating them at the long dining tables. "Lord Urnest," Mayson called, fighting through the pain in his throat. Urnest turned to face him, sweat beading on the top of his head—drops of blood spattered across his silver petticoat. "I'll need you to send a swallow to the Silver Shields. The city watch will need to know what's happened. Once word spreads beyond the palace, there will be havoc in the streets." Urnest gave Mayson a shallow, weary bow, and took leave.

Mayson couldn't tell how long he had stood there before Hammund plucked Gelaya'Khash from the grass and handed her to him. He seemed twenty years older than he had an hour ago, his once sharp eyes now sunken and blank, his sure step replaced by unsteadiness. Mayson couldn't bear to look at him another second; he slipped Gelaya'Khash back into her sheath and kept moving.

Party-goers clutched each other in fits of grief, crying into each other's shoulders. Mayson saw several members of the Council split off from the soldiers organizing the crowd into groups. Keddra Vilzak took several children by the hand in an attempt to find their parents, while Evan Mikkel worked with Galen and his Healers to conceal Henry from the public as they prepared to move him.

Lady Dawn Wallis sat Beatrice down on a stool and fed her sips of water from her goblet as the queen violently sobbed. Beatrice hunched over, one hand gripping tufts of her own hair as her body shook. Her white gown was drenched in Henry's blood—her once mighty disposition reduced to rubble.

"Mayson!" cried a voice from behind. Addam and Droyan came bustling through the crowd. They had surrendered their crimson cloaks to drape over Henry and looked unusually plain in the blazing torchlight. "How can we help, my King? Whatever you will, it will be done," Addam said.

Mayson stood silent and unsteady. *My King…My King…*

"I don't know," Mayson managed to say before a rush of realization washed over him. "Do *not* leave this palace—don't let anyone from the High Families leave either until otherwise instructed."

The bells in the palace steeples began to ring, their ominous tones falling over one another to create a dark, familiar call. Mayson hadn't noticed the city celebrating, but the silence that filled the empty air when the bells stopped was unmistakable. Crowds of revelers stopped their singing and dancing; street vendors stopped peddling; and curious tavern patrons filed out into the streets.

Hours went by in a daze. An endless gauntlet of sullen faces and muffled voices flit past Mayson as the night wore on. After Mayson gave his last instructions, he didn't speak to anyone, and few dared come near, for he was now surrounded by no less than thirty Knights of Rahm, never more than five paces away.

The wailing from beyond the palace walls had died down by the time the attendants cleared the yards, the eastern sky changing from black to deep purple, signifying a red dawn. The Commander of the Silver Shields had delivered his report that the city was pacified, and every one of his men were out marching the streets. Mayson left instructions with Hammund that those who had already been questioned were free to go, with his deepest apologies and most humble thanks. He then took his Knights and stepped out into the deserted streets, allowing his weary mind to soak in the silence.

In a city of over a million souls, Mayson felt perfectly alone. Aside from a few candles burning in the windows, the capital seemed nearly abandoned. Fear and dread took hold of the people's hearts as soon as those bells began to toll, and Rahm only knew how long it would be before they'd find courage again. Rahm only knew how long it would take for the new King to find courage in *himself.*

Mayson found himself standing at the base of the stairs leading up to the Mouth of the Mountain. He hadn't meant to come here; he hadn't meant to go anywhere in particular. All he wished for was solitude—to break free of the sea of miserable faces that now looked upon him with pity and fear. Somehow, his feet decided this was where he needed to be, and the next thing he knew, he was climbing the stairs, his Knights close in tow. The Silver Shields had left the gates open, but the torches along either side of the staircase and at the top landing were still lit. The ebony doors gave way much easier than usual as he pushed his weight against them, though still sounded like thunder as they echoed through the empty throne room.

The young king commanded his bodyguards to leave the door open and let the air in as he strolled through the chamber. Mayson ran his fingers along the Council table as he moved toward the Heart of the Mountain, the great stone throne that now belonged to him. The very thought made him ill. *This is my father's throne— not mine. It is His crown—not mine.*

He climbed past the chairs of the High Lords to stand face to face with the Heart. If he closed his eyes, he could picture his father sitting there, a weary smile on his face. Mayson grazed his fingertips along one of the armrests, turned to face the coming dawn, and sat.

After years of imagining what it would be like, the reality of it was disappointing, to say the least. It was cold and hard against his sore body, making him painfully aware of just how much he'd gone through in mere hours. The seat retained none of his father's old warmth; it shared none of the secrets he still had inside when the knife pierced him. *It was your knife—not his. It should have been you.*

Mayson rested his chin on his fist and let the last of his tears silently pour down his cheeks. There he sat, feeling as though the cold stone seat would suck the heat and life right out of him—a prospect he almost welcomed. He sat so long that the red light of dawn crept over the peaks of Gol Rayna and shot directly into the throne room, exposing a king who silently prayed for death.

Shadows moved in the wide-open doorway as several figures hurried across the stone floor toward the king. Mayson couldn't quite make out their faces, but Urnest's voice was unmistakable. "Gods, here you are!" he proclaimed. "You nearly scared us into our graves, boy."

"Boy?" Mayson asked, giving no effort to hide the bitterness in his voice. "Boy, you say? May I ask, Lord Rahmos, to whom, exactly, do you believe you are speaking?" The two shadows stopped in their tracks, the red dawn behind them beginning to rage in the eastern sky, and fell to their knees. When Urnest spoke again, his tone had made the desired change.

"Forgive me, my King," Urnest said. "We feared for your safety."

"I had my Knights of Rahm with me, Lord Rahmos," Mayson replied, closing his eyes against the fury of the rising sun. *My Knights of Rahm* tasted like sour milk in his mouth. Their silence made his skin crawl. *Let them know you're still in there somewhere.* The voice came from within, but it was foreign and unfamiliar. "I couldn't be there anymore, Urnest. I couldn't see my mother's face or smell my father's blood in the air for another second. I needed to be alone, and what better place than this chamber, where I shall be alone for the rest of my life."

It was a few moments before the ever-calming voice of Raymund cut the tension. "The Council will be relieved to know you are safe, my King. If you wish to be alone, we will take our leave."

"No," Mayson replied. One more idle hour would rob him of what was left of his sanity. Now was the time to occupy his mind. "Inform the Council I wish for them to meet me here. Gather Lord Carovensa as well. We have much work to do, I'm afraid."

The sound of frantic footsteps rang against the stone pillars as another shadow burst through the open doors. Mayson stood and raised a hand to block the morning sun. Diero hurled himself toward the throne, his eyes wide with panic. Sweat completely soaked his doublet as his gold cloak flapped heavily at his sides. Mayson stepped down from the throne as Diero rest his hands on his knees. Lords Wallis and Rahmos stepped forward to put supportive hands on his back.

After several moments of heavy breathing, Diero finally straightened and looked his King in the eye, grim as a grave digger. When he spoke, it sounded as though his blood had been drained and replaced with icy river water—his soul ripped from him in a thousand pieces.

"Lily is gone," he cried.

Epilogue

Lily's head was spinning when she finally fell into bed, wrapping herself in fine satin sheets and a thick over blanket. After drinking nothing but Afina and water with Vytria in the Dark Wood, the wine she'd consumed sent her reeling. Diero understood when she said she wished to lie down, and the queen offered her own handmaidens to guide her back to her room.

She dreamed of Diero. Though her visions were foggy and full of turmoil, her dream was as modest and easy as a babbling brook. They strolled together through the palace gardens; she picked flowers with one hand while clasping Diero firmly with the other.

"I wish you didn't have to go," he said hopelessly. The sound seemed disconnected from the sweet scene she'd constructed.

"I wouldn't if I had any choice," she replied.

"What if I forbade you to go?" he asked with a wicked grin. "What if I declared you could never leave the Crescent again?"

"You don't have that kind of power," she replied, laughing at his silly posturing. "Even if you did, it wouldn't stop me. This is something I must do, for my sake, and yours. There is no telling what my vision could mean. I owe it to all of us to try to make sense of it." Diero cracked a smile known only to lovers who understand their time, no matter how sweet, is up.

"That is why I love you." He pulled her in close and kissed her softly, taking her face in his hands. Lily's heart pounded in her chest as her breath quickened. When she pulled away from him, sharp, impossibly blue eyes looked back at her, filled with hundreds of shining pinpoints like stars in the night sky. The skin around them was snow white, and curly black bangs dangled low in front of them. Mayson's face stared back at her, digging straight into her very soul in a way she'd never felt in the waking world. Her hands fell cold as her chest began to ache.

Lily, he said, his voice ringing like bells in her head. The bells continued long after his voice faded. They repeated, low and ominous, shaking the foundations of her dream until they cracked.

Lily sprang up in bed, sweat soaking her nightgown. The palace bells rang relentlessly through the air, echoing across the mountain slope. She went to her wardrobe to slip on a fresh robe when she began to hear shouts and cries of despair floating in through her open window.

She walked to the windowsill and looked down on the grounds to see what was happening. The music had still been playing when she dismissed her handmaidens and put away the maps King Henry had given her to study for her trip to Oremanse. Now, there was not a single lute or pipe left. Everyone had gathered near the edge of the dance floor, some wailing, others shouting. What it was they were staring at, she couldn't quite see. She leaned out her window a few inches farther, hoping to find a better angle.

A hand wrapped her waist from behind as another pressed a damp cloth into her face. Its grip was iron-tight and in moments, she felt her legs go weak and a fog devour the world around her. The last thing she heard was the incessant ringing of the bells. All sight and sound faded away as the world around her disappeared into another deep, powerful sleep, where no dreams, either sweet or vile, could reach her.

The Dark Crown: Book Two of the Rahmirion Chronicles will be published in 2023. Follow Wells and Bruzzi at www.wellsandbruzzi.com and on Instagram at @wellsandbruzzi to learn more.

Acknowledgements

We would like to acknowledge everyone who has supported us in publishing our first book, particularly our teammates who helped us put it all together, and our wonderful Kickstarter backers:
Lindsay Adkins, Maria Alessi, Patrice 'Dede' Barletta, Joseph Bonici, Jessica Bruzzi, Lisa Bruzzi, James Cipriano, Frank Cresencia, Franklin Cresencia, Brandon Cresencia, Anthony Crouchelli, Jeff Cruz, Michael Curcuru, Margaret DeProspero, Amanda Dilonardo, Ioannis Dokouslis, Robert Dugan, Christina Eliades, Justin Fishman, Meg Fry, Louise Fry, Pamela Fry, Carol Gaskin, Mert Genccinar, Frank Godino, Becca Grek, Sally Glick, Corey Kirschner, Eric Kirstein, Josh Krattenstein, Ashley Leone, Wally Marzano-Lesnevich, Holly Logue, Kyle Manning, Edwin Menzo, Karen Hodges Miller, Morgan, Dani Morris, Christina Moxley, Erica Nadera, Richard Novak, Cassandra Otten, Robin Parker, Daniel Pellicano, Justin Powers, Jason Rader, Abigail Roberts, David Roberts, Emily Roberts, Lynn Roberts, Mike Russell, Greg Scalera, Steve Sharkey, Peter Skolnik, Nicole Stanziale, Victoria Steinberg, Michael J. Sullivan, Wendy Temple, Samantha Tilney, Charlie Trilivas, Khalid Uddin, Claudio Venancio, Heather Wells, Matt Wells, Zach Wisniewski, Igor Yegorov, Mark Zebro Jr.

About the Authors

Jonathan Wells

JONATHAN WELLS, lifelong fantasy and sci-fi lover, has been making up stories for as long as he can remember. Some have been scribbled on scraps of printer paper, others were left to just rattle around in his head. And that is exactly how this novel came to be.

The seeds for this epic fantasy were first planted in his 12-year-old brain, a day-dream world where he could wander off when school became too boring. After ten years, the daydream had taken on such a clear shape, with a linear plot and fully fleshed out characters, that he decided it was time to give it a proper "birth."

Dennis Bruzzi

After showing a rough sketch of one of his characters to college roommate, DENNIS BRUZZI, his friend "wanted in," and the rest is history. Dennis, a proven storyteller through his work in journalism and producing videos, is for the first-time taking pen to paper in the fantasy realm. An avid reader and a fantasy enthusiast, he is ecstatic to have worked with his longtime friend to bring this unique and expansive story to life.

"And *The Blood of a King* is only the tip of the iceberg," promise Jonathan and Dennis. There are eight more books planned in this epic fantasy series.

The Dark Crown: Book Two of the Rahmirion Chronicles will be published in 2023. Follow Wells and Bruzzi at www.wellsandbruzzi.com and on Instagram at @wellsandbruzzi to learn more.